ROWAN'S LADY

BOOK ONE OF THE CLAN GRAHAM SERIES

SUZAN TISDALE

SUZAN TISDALE NOVELS

SUZAN TISDALE NOVELS

For my mom, the original lady Arline, my aunts, Marilyn and Jerry. Always the faces of grace and dignity, even in the darkest of times. Thank you all for teaching me how to laugh.

ALSO BY SUZAN TISDALE

The Clan MacDougall Series

Laiden's Daughter

Findley's Lass

Wee William's Woman

McKenna's Honor

The Clan Graham Series

Rowan's Lady

Frederick's Queen

The Mackintoshes and McLarens Series

Ian's Rose

The Bowie Bride

Rodrick the Bold

Brogan's Promise

The Clan McDunnah Series

A Murmur of Providence

A Whisper of Fate

A Breath of Promise

Moirra's Heart Series

Stealing Moirra's Heart

Saving Moirra's Heart

Stand Alone Novels

Isle of the Blessed

Forever Her Champion

The Edge of Forever

Arriving in 2018:

Black Richard's Heart

The Brides of the Clan MacDougall

(A Sweet Series)

Aishlinn

Maggy (arriving 2018)

Nora (arriving 2018)

Coming Soon:

The MacAllens and Randalls

PROLOGUE

SCOTLAND 1350

The Black Death did not discriminate.

Like fire from hell, it spread across England, Wales, Italy and France. Untethered, unstoppable.

It cared not if the lives it took were of the noble and wealthy or the lowly born and poor. It showed no preference for age or gender. It took the wicked and the innocent. It took the blasphemers and the righteous.

The Black Death took whomever it damned well pleased.

It took Rowan Graham's wife.

Rowan would not allow his sweet wife to die alone, cold, afraid, and in agony, no matter how much she begged otherwise. He would not allow anyone else to administer the herbs, to apply the poultices, or to even wipe her brow. He was her husband and she, his entire world.

Knowing that the Black Death had finally reached Scotland, Rowan's clan had prepared as best they could. The moment anyone began to show signs of illness, they were immediately taken to the barracks. Seclusion was their only hope at keeping the illness from spreading.

Within a week, the barracks could hold no more of the sick and dying. In the end, the quarantine was all for naught.

By the time Kate showed the first signs of the illness, the Black Death had taken more than thirty of their people. Before it was over, Clan Graham's numbers dwindled to less than seventy members.

At Kate's insistence, their three-month-old daughter was kept in seclusion. It was the last act of motherly love that she could show her child. In the hours just before her death, Kate begged for Rowan's promise on two matters.

"Ye shall never be afraid to speak of me to our daughter. It is important that she know how much I loved her, and how much *we* loved her together." 'Twas an easy promise for Rowan to make, for how could he ever forget Kate?

'Twas the second promise she asked that threatened to tear him apart.

"And ye must promise ye'll let another woman into yer heart. Do not save it long fer me, husband. Yer too good a man to keep yerself to a dead woman."

He swore to her that yes, someday he would allow his heart to love another. Silently however, he knew that day would be in the very distant future, mayhap thirty or forty years. For there could never be a woman who could take Kate's place in his life or his heart.

"I love ye, Kate, more than me next breath," Rowan whispered into her ear just before her chest rose and fell for the last time.

Fires were built to burn the dead. When Rowan's first lieutenant came to remove Kate's body to add it to the funeral pyres, he refused to allow Frederick anywhere near her. Rowan's face turned purple with rage, his chest heaved from the weight of his unconstrained anguish. He unsheathed his sword and pinned Frederick to the wall.

"If ye so much as think of laying a finger to Kate, I shall take yer life," Rowan seethed. Frederick knew it was a promise Rowan meant to keep.

Later, with his vision blurred from tears he could not suppress, Rowan bathed his wife's once beautiful body now ravaged with large black boils. He washed her long, strawberry blonde locks and combed them until they glistened once again. When he was done, he placed a bit of Graham plaid into the palm of her hand before wrapping her cold body in long linen strips.

Alone in the quiet hours before dawn he carried Kate her to final resting place under the tall Wych Elm tree. He stayed next to her grave for three full days.

Frederick finally came to see him late in the afternoon of the third day.

"I ken yer grievin', fer Kate was a fine woman," Frederick said. "Ye've a wee bairn that needs ye, Rowan. She needs ye now, more than Kate does."

Rowan was resting against the elm tree, with his head resting on his knees. In his heart he knew Frederick was right, but that did nothing the help fill the dark void that Kate's death left in his heart.

For a brief moment, Rowan could have sworn he heard his wife's voice agreeing with Frederick. Deciding it best not to argue the point with either of them, Rowan took a deep breath and pulled himself to his feet.

For now, he would focus on the first promise he had made to Kate.

"Ye be right, Frederick," Rowan said as he slapped one hand on his friend's back while wiping away tears with the other. "I need to go tell me daughter all about her beautiful mum."

ONE

SCOTLAND, AUTUMN, 1354

"**D**o ye love me?"

Lady Arline felt weak in the knees. Her stomach fluttered with unease when she looked into the dark blue eyes that belonged to her husband of three days, Laird Garrick Blackthorn of Ayrshire. She wasn't at all certain if it was the *question* that gnawed, or the cold, stony glare his face held when he asked it. She swallowed hard, willed her legs and stomach to settle, and decided honesty was at all times the best policy.

"I am sure I could learn to love ye, m'laird." She prayed she didn't sound as foolish as she felt.

Laird Blackthorn of Ayrshire was a very handsome man. Tall, lean, and well-muscled, he stood a head taller than Lady Arline. Short cropped blonde hair framed a more than handsome face. Lady Arline imagined most women would swoon if he chose to grace them with a glance from those dark blue eyes of his. And if the eyes didn't lead to swooning, then perhaps the muscles that rippled under his snug tunic would do the trick.

Truth be told, Lady Arline nearly swooned herself when she met him for the first time three days ago. They had been introduced just moments before exchanging their wedding vows. It had been all she could do not to jump with glee that *this* husband was not only closer in age to her own, but he was handsome as well. He exuded power, virility. Mayhap, finally, there would be children in her future.

After the death of her first husband, Lady Arline had sworn she'd never be duped into another arranged marriage. But her father, bless him, had been quite insistent that she give marriage another chance. She had resisted her father right up until the moment she saw Garrick Blackthorn for the very first time.

There was something, something she could not quite put a name to, something in Garrick's blue eyes…they held *something*. But what? A secret perhaps? She was as yet uncertain and that made her all the more nervous. Whatever it was, she found it difficult to keep her legs and fingers from trembling. She clasped her hands tightly in front of her and tried to at least *appear* as if she were not completely terrified.

Perhaps it was the anticipation of what lay ahead, on this their first night in her new home as his wife. Her husband had yet to lay a hand on her, save for the chaste kiss at the altar three days past. He had barely spoken a word to her during the journey from Lochbraene to Ayrshire.

She wondered, if by chance, he too, was just as nervous as she.

It was doubtful. A man as handsome as Garrick Blackthorn must certainly have a significant amount of experience with women and loving. Nay, it could not be nervousness she saw in the depths of those dark eyes. It was something else.

Lady Arline reckoned that perhaps it was her own widespread nervousness that made her mouth go dry and her legs weak. Undoubtedly he would want to consummate their marriage and perhaps before doing so, he wanted to know what her feelings toward him might be.

The thought of consummation brought back the quivering sensation in her legs. She cursed at her own silliness. Her thoughts suddenly turned to Minnie, her auld maid who had died two years ago. *Just close yer eyes and do yer duty on yer weddin' night. It will hurt like bloody hell, but it does not take long.*

It was early evening and they stood in Lady Arline's appointed chamber. She wore a heavy silk robe over her thick linen nightdress. Her wavy and oft unruly auburn hair tumbled down her back and stopped just above her knees. She hoped that he had a fondness for redheaded women. She shivered and cursed inwardly for what must have been the hundredth time that day.

It was those cursed eyes of his that left her with such a sense of discomfit.

She studied him more closely as he paced in front of the tall window. He did not look pleased with her honest answer. He had raised an eyebrow ever so slightly when she had given it.

After several long moments, Laird Blackthorn stopped pacing and turned back to face her.

"Ye see, lass, therein lies the problem."

There was no mistaking his disdain. It was quite evident in the tightening of his jaw and the hard, icy glower he sent her way. She was no longer worried over pleasing her husband this night. Instead, she worried over *surviving* it. The room suddenly felt cold, mayhap from those cold, dark eyes and the freezing tone of his voice.

"I do no' want ye to get any notions of fallin' in love with me. Fer 'tis a certainty that I will *never* love ye."

There was no mistaking his meaning. It stung like an arrow through her heart.

Controlled anger, contempt and derision dripped from his tongue. Arline knew instinctively that this was a man who said what he meant and meant what he said.

Any hope that she may have had at someday forging a bond with her new husband, one made of mutual admiration and respect, fell as rapidly as a rock from a cliff, landing at her feet with a thud. *Why am I so cursed when it comes to husbands?*

"This marriage," he told her as he turned away to look out the window, "is but a farce."

She forced herself to remain steady. Fear wrapped itself around her like a cold, wet blanket, sending shivers down her spine.

"Are ye aware of what was in the marriage agreement?" he asked. "Of all it entails?"

Words were lodged in her throat. She cleared it once, then again, and managed to utter a choked "aye". She had not been given the opportunity to read it with her own eyes. Her father had given her a brief summation of its contents. But, knowing her father as she did, he had probably left out some very important details.

"Tell me what ye ken." His voice was low, steady, commanding.

"I am to be yer wife, in exchange for the troth of three wagons of food and ten horses, as well as land." Her mouth had suddenly turned quite dry, her tongue sticking to the roof of her mouth. What she would not give for a tipple of whisky.

"And?" he asked.

That was all she knew. Dread thrummed in her heart. Silently she damned her father to the devil. What on earth had the man done to her now? "That is all that I ken of it, me laird."

He came to stand before her, just a step away.

"After one year, one month and one day, if there be no heir born or conceived, the marriage will be annulled." He crossed his arms over his broad chest and stood, glaring. "There will be no heir."

The only way she could have concealed her surprise was if she had been hiding under a blanket.

There was no mistaking his ire and no way to misinterpret his words. There were no "ifs" in his explanation of the marriage agreement. No wiggle room, no hope. Plain and simple. She'd gone from thinking him quite a handsome fellow to knowing that behind those good looks lay a cold, hard man.

He continued to glare with one eyebrow arched as if he was waiting for her to say something. He shook his head and snorted at her continued dumbfounded silence.

"There will be no heir," he repeated.

It was a statement of fact. A point that would not be argued further or open for any discussion at a future time.

"I'll not bed ye," he said bluntly, looking at her as if he found the mere thought of sharing a bed with her repulsive.

"I do not love ye Arline. And I never, ever will." He turned away from her again. "Do ye understand?"

Aye, she thought to herself. *I understand far more than ye ken.* She took a deep breath and muttered her affirmation at his back.

"I think ye need to understand more fully what be at stake here." He took a deep breath. "Ye see, I *am* capable of lovin' a woman."

Lady Arline's stomach plunged to her toes.

"I simply will no', under any circumstance love ye. Me heart, ye see, belongs to another," he tossed his remark over his shoulder.

Her surprise was quickly replaced with a sense of numbness. "If yer heart belongs to another, then why did ye agree to marry me?"

He turned around slowly, the derision he felt toward her plainly written in the hard lines of his face. "Have ye met me father yet?"

Lady Arline shook her head. "Nay, I haven't."

"Ye be no' missin' much. He's a whoreson if ever there was one. He does no' like the woman who *does* own me heart. I had to marry *ye* in order to get the fool off me back." Crossing his arms over his broad chest, the lines of his face hardened further, deeper. "In a year's time, this marriage *will* be annulled. Make no mistake of that."

Arline lifted her chin showing him that she did not care. 'Twas in fact, the opposite of what she truly felt. She *did* care.

Not for him precisely, but for all that could have been.

"So we will pretend then, m'laird, to be married fer the next year, only to satisfy the marriage agreement?" she asked him through gritted teeth.

For the first time she saw him smile. The curve of his lips did nothing to ease her fears or worry.

"Yer no' nearly as daft as I've been told," he said. "I'm glad ye see it then, lass. One year, one month and one day and this marriage *will* be annulled."

Arline wondered what her father would think of this and immediately decided that she did not care. In a year's time she would be of an age where she would no longer be forced to marry *any* man. Ever.

If Laird Blackthorn did not want her, then so be it. She would play along with this farce in order to gain the freedom she had been denied her entire life. She could travel the world, come and go as she pleased and she'd never be forced to answer to anyone or anything but her own heart.

Although the thought of freedom brought a tingling sensation that spread throughout her body, her heart felt empty. Void. And she felt severely *lacking*.

It was enough to break a weaker woman's heart. But Lady Arline refused to be weak. There wasn't a man in all this world worthy of her heart, let alone one worthy of breaking it.

He turned to face her again. "I'll no hear any complainin' from ye. Ye'll do as I say, when I say it. Ye'll stay in yer room unless I give ye permission to leave," he began listing his rules, ticking them off one by one. "Do no' ever question me or any decision I make fer ye'll suffer fer it, that I promise."

He came to stand before her again. This time, he lowered his face only inches from hers. It took every ounce of courage she had to look him in the eye.

"Lady Arline, ye will heed me warnin'. Ye do as I say, and ye may just get out of this marriage alive."

He quit her chamber then, without so much as a by your leave. His warning hung in the air, long after he left, like damp, heavy fog. Though a fire burned in the fireplace, the air still felt chilled, cold, filled with his inescapable warning.

Now she knew the secret that lay hidden in his dark eyes: sheer unadulterated hatred. And all of it reserved for her.

With her arms and hands still trembling, she walked to her closet, found the trunk that held her writing materials, her embroidery, and art supplies. On shaking knees, she rummaged through until she found a piece of charcoal she used for sketching.

Quietly, she closed the lid and scooted across the wood floor to the back of the closet. She drew a short line on the wall. *One day down.* With a heavy sense of dread, she slid the trunk across the floor to hide the mark that had begun her countdown to freedom.

Taking in steady breaths she hoped would calm her nerves, she left the closet and climbed into her bed, drawing the covers up to her chin. A hundred blankets would not be enough to quell the chill she felt.

Earlier, before speaking with her husband, she had been worried over things that now seemed mundane by comparison. Less than an hour ago, she had been nervously pacing her room, hopeful that she would be able to please her husband and begin to build a future with him.

She cursed under her breath; angry with her heart for allowing even a glimmer of hope for the life she so desperately wanted. A husband who would care about her feelings, a husband she could admire and respect. She wanted children. Lots of children. Arline longed for a home filled with love, laughter, bairns …peace.

She would survive the next year. She would *not* let Laird Blackthorn of Ayrshire win.

TWO

The cursed dreams were always the same, varying only in intensity and their ability to completely unsettle Lady Arline's nerves. She hated these dreams filled with a faceless man on horseback who was coming to rescue her, to whisk her away from Laird Blackthorn.

Though she could never see his face, something in her heart told her he was a fine looking man. The dream would not allow her to see him clearly. It was like trying to hold fog in the palm of your hand. You mayhap could *feel* the damp, wet air, but you could not hold on to it.

The faceless hero of her dreams would soothe away her fears with tender kisses and the touch of his gentle hands. He would mend her, put her back to rights, and give her a life filled with love, laughter, and hope.

That was how she felt in the deep, dark of night, in those traitorous dreams.

During the day, however, when she had better control of her faculties, she thought differently. She knew that in reality, no such man existed.

Four and twenty years of age, her hopes of a happy life had been repeatedly quashed, with the multiple failed marriages her father had arranged. No longer did she yearn for that happy life, filled with a husband's love and too many bairns to count. Concluding that such dreams led to nothing but heartache, she decided that once her marriage to Blackthorn was annulled, *she* would be in charge of her own destiny. No longer would she be subjected to her father's consistently bad matchmaking choices. World travel seemed to be the smartest way to keep her heart safe.

Once she was away from Blackthorn, she would demand that her father hand over her funds -- money that was rightfully hers, left to her by her first husband -- money her father had been waiting to get his fat greedy fingers on for years. With it, she would take her sisters, Morralyn and Geraldine away. They would book safe passage and travel the world. They would meet all sorts of new and interesting people and live out the rest of their days in blissful solitude. Most importantly, she would live it without the aid of a husband. She would protect her heart from any further disappointment. She would do her best to keep her sisters from the miserable existence that came with ill-suited husbands.

Arline had constructed an invisible shield around her heart with a promise that soon she would be in charge of her own life and future. She would allow no one access to it. Hopes, dreams, those things led to nothing but heartache and regret. She would live the rest of her life without any expectations. She would simply *live*.

This night, as she dreamt again of the faceless hero, somewhere in the recesses of the dream, was the sound of a child crying. As the crying grew louder the foggy image of her faceless hero faded.

Half asleep, her thoughts muddled, lingering somewhere between a sweet dream and reality, she pulled her blanket more tightly around her chin and tried to fall back to sleep. In the daylight hours, she would never admit to anyone, not even herself, that she *did* have a strong desire for a tall, handsome husband who would woo her with a bright smile and tender kisses. She fought to pull the image of the man back into the forefront of her mind and to shoo the crying child away. But the stubborn child continued to cry, the sound of it growing louder and sounding quite close.

The plaintive wail floated into her room again. Shaking away the fog, she sat up in her bed and rubbed away the sleep with her fingertips. She sat still and strained her ears to listen. Mayhap it was the wind she heard and not a child's cry.

An ominous sensation prickled across her skin as the sound again floated in on the dark night air. The cries grew louder and sounded as though they were coming from the fireplace.

Flinging her legs over the edge of her bed, she tucked her bare feet into her slippers as she pulled her robe from the end of her bed. Slipping her arms into the sleeves, she tip-toed across the floor to stand beside the fireplace.

As the low embers burned and crackled, the sound floated in once again.

She had not been dreaming. It *was* a child's cry that she heard. But whose? There were no children living inside the walls of the keep. Anyone with children lived in little cottages scattered here and there.

Whoever this child was or belonged to, he or she was *not* at all happy. The wailing continued to float into her room, along with the low grumbling of male voices.

Arline had lived in the keep for a little over a year. She knew the sounds were coming from the grand gathering room just one floor below her bedchamber. Night after night she had lain awake listening to the raucous, drunken revelry that took place in that room. A room she was no longer allowed to enter due to her husband's severe dislike of her.

Instinct told her the child was terrified. Curiosity grew and swelled along with the child's cries. The men's grumbling grew worse, angrier.

Good sense dictated she should stay put, stay out of her husband's line of vision as well as his wrath. It cautioned her that whatever was going on below stairs was none of her business. She had but two weeks left to survive the farce called her marriage. Two weeks. Fourteen days. *Survive fourteen more days and ye'll be free.*

SUZAN TISDALE

But the child's shrieks grew louder. The grumbles were turning into shouts and bellowing. The angrier the child grew, the angrier the men grew.

Something was very much wrong below stairs. As the moments ticked by, caution and the desire to survive fell to the wayside. Though Lady Arline had never been blessed with a child of her own, something instinctively maternal kicked in. It tugged at her conscience, her heart, urging her forward.

Before she realized it, she had left her room and was quietly stepping down the stairs toward the grand gathering room.

Her heart nearly stopped at the scene before her.

A great commotion was taking place. Garrick and at least ten of his men were standing in the middle of the gathering room. One of them, whose name she didn't know for they'd never been formally introduced, stood near the fireplace holding a red-faced cherub of a child!

Long auburn ringlets tumbled over the child's shoulders. The poor thing wore nothing but a nightdress. No shoes, no robe, no cloak. Lady Arline's earlier assessment that the child sounded angry had been correct. Her little face was red with fury, her hands balled into fists as she wailed and screamed at her captor.

"Stop that screamin'!" Garrick shouted toward the child. "I swear, I'll beat ye senseless if ye do no' stop!"

Arline knew it was not a threat, but a promise. Her husband was nothing if not honest.

Without thinking, Arline flew down the last few steps, raced into the gathering room and grabbed the child from the man's arms. He responded with mouth agape before his expression changed to one of relief.

Arline bounced the child in her arms as she whispered soothing words into her ears.

"Wheesht, babe, wheesht," Arline said as she pressed the child close to her breast.

Some time had passed as Arline became oblivious to the men surrounding her. She continued to offer soft, soothing words. It wasn't until the child began to calm that Arline became aware that all eyes in the room were on her.

When her eyes fell to Laird Blackthorn, she knew she had made a terrible mistake. He was beyond angry. He looked positively livid.

It was no longer a matter of surviving the next two weeks. It was now a matter of surviving what remained of the night.

"I'm sorry, me laird," she whispered as she continued to pat the child's back. "She sounded so distressed. I wanted nothing but to help calm her before she drove any of you to madness."

As soon as the last words left her mouth, she realized she may have not phrased them correctly. Her husband's jaw worked back and forth, and she could see the vein in his neck throb. Two weeks had turned to two hours, but now, she wondered if it weren't but a matter of moments she had left to walk the earth alive.

The babe thrust her thumb into her mouth and hiccuped. Arline felt the child begin to relax in her arms and decided that she had made the right decision. Even if it meant angering her husband to the point of murder, she could not allow an innocent child to be harmed.

When Laird Blackthorn next spoke, his words were clipped and teeming with fury. "Give the child to Torren. *Now.*"

Every fiber of her being screamed for her to do as her husband demanded. Her heart, however, begged to comfort and calm the bairn. She hesitated a moment too long.

Laird Blackthorn was before her in three fast strides. Without a word, he yanked the child from Arline's arms and thrust her into Torren's. The child began to cry out again, her little arms outstretched toward Arline.

"I warned ye before, do no' defy me. *Ever.*" Blackthorn spoke through gritted teeth as he grabbed Lady Arline by her forearms.

She gasped with surprise the moment he took hold of her arms. His fingers dug into her flesh, squeezing tightly before giving her a good shake and tossing her to the floor.

"I'm sorry, me laird!" Arline squeaked out. "I meant only to comfort the babe."

"I do no' give a damn what ye meant to do. Ye go back to yer room and ye stay there!" he ground out as he angrily threw her to the floor.

The child cried louder, inconsolable, and afraid. Her cries were too much for Arline's heart to bear.

"Please, me laird," Arline begged. "Let me help, let me help ye with the bairn!"

Laird Blackthorn loomed over Arline. In one swift motion, he bent at the waist and gave her a harsh, heavy slap to her face with the back of his hand.

Arline fell backward as blood filled her mouth. The shock of being hit overwhelmed her. She was stunned, too stunned to cry. No one had ever hit her before. Not even her father, cruel as he was, had ever laid an angry hand on her.

Blackthorn hauled her to her feet by her arms. "That was the last time ye beg me fer anythin', including yer life."

As Garrick angrily shoved her away, two of his men caught her, each grabbing an arm. With a quick nod from Blackthorn, the two men dragged Arline away. As they hauled her up the stairs to her room, she didn't know which hurt worse; her broken and bleeding mouth, her arms where the men grabbed her, or her heart as she listened to the wailing babe she was forced to leave with her furious husband.

Arline had been unceremoniously and quite rudely tossed into her room. As much as she wanted to cry out and curse the ground her husband and his men walked on, she did not possess such boldness or bravery. Instead, she poured cold water from a pitcher into her wash-basin. Her hands trembled so much that she had a difficult time holding the washcloth. After several attempts, she took a few deep breaths and somehow managed to clean the blood from her face.

A little more than a year had passed since she'd arrived at Black-thorn Castle. Her hatred for her husband had grown with each day that had gone by. But these last four months had been the worst of her life. After the events that took place below stairs, Arline doubted a word had been created yet that would describe the absolute and intense hatred she now felt for Garrick Blackthorn.

After washing her face she started to pace in front of her fireplace. Tiny beads of sweat clung to her upper lip, her stomach felt as hard as stone, her nerves a jumbled mess as she waited for her husband's punishment to be meted out. Without a doubt, she knew she had signed her own death warrant the moment she took the babe into her arms. Garrick would kill her for her transgression, for defying him in front of his men.

While she knew her death was imminent, she worried more over the babe than for her own wellbeing.

Garrick would not be swift in killing Arline. Nay, he would make sure that she suffered first. Horrible. Painful. Brutal. Laird Blackthorn had made that promise on more than one occasion over the past year. There was nothing in their history together that would prove otherwise.

The image of the terrified little girl pulled and twisted Arline's stomach into knots. Such a beautiful little cherub with auburn curls and big blue eyes, or she could have been had she not been crying and frightened.

She knew not to whom the babe belonged and decided it didn't matter. Chances were the child had been taken from her parents to be held for ransom. Garrick Blackthorn was just that kind of man. One who would take a child from the loving bosom of its family for a bag of coins.

Prior to her father-in-law's death four months ago, Arline's stay had been comfortable albeit boring. She had been allowed to visit the chapel every morning and to take walks around the keep. At night, she would sit next to her husband at the evening meal, pretending to enjoy herself and married life.

Phillip Blackthorn's death had changed all of that.

Now, she was kept secluded in her room, with the door oftentimes barred from the outside. She was no longer allowed her daily visit to the chapel, nor could she walk freely about the keep. Her meals, if one could call them that, were brought to her room. Her lady's maid, Margaret, had been reassigned to work elsewhere in the keep.

Arline was fully alone every hour of the day save for when her meals were brought to her or when maids came with clean linens. They rarely spoke to her save for a *yes m'lady* or *no m'lady*. Arline supposed they were as terrified of Garrick Blackthorn as she was.

To help stave off insanity from her solitude, she read the books she had brought with her from Ireland. When she wasn't reading, she worked on her embroidery, her sewing or her painting, though she was far better with her stitches than her brush strokes.

She wrote letters to her two sisters, Morralyn and Geraldine. Letters that she could not send per Garrick's decree that she have no contact with anyone outside the keep.

It mattered not to Arline that her sisters were the illegitimate castoffs of her father, she loved them all the same. Each had a different mother but they all had one thing in common: a father who cared very little for any of them.

Her mind wandered hither and yon as she paced and chewed on her thumbnail. She could hear her father's voice in the back of her mind, chastising her for her own stupidity. *Ye couldn't keep yer mouth shut, lass. Ye just had to step in. Ye only had two weeks left!*

A cold shiver fell over her skin as she thought of her father. Arline didn't believe it was his actual intention to be mean or cruel. It was simply how he was. The man was blunt, to the point, and always went straight to the heart of any matter. Arline supposed that if her mother still lived, she would have had her to go to in times of trouble and doubt. As it was, her mother had died when Arline was seven, left to be raised by a man who made no qualms about how easier *his* life would have been had Arline been born a lad instead of a lass.

Now here she was, consigned to her rooms and for the briefest of moments she found herself wishing her father *was* here. She didn't necessarily miss the man, but she knew that her father would keep her from being killed by her husband. Aye, she may have to agree to another arranged marriage, but even that was better than death.

At the moment, she was more than tempted to bargain with the devil himself in order to ensure the safety of the little girl below stairs and to live through the next two weeks. What she needed was a plan, a way out of this mess and a way to keep the child out of harm's way.

Mayhap she should throw herself at her husband's mercy and beg. Begging wouldn't be such a bad thing, if it meant she would have the chance to live through the next fortnight. And it would be worth it in the end, if she knew she had saved the child.

Bribery was another option. Arline's father had been holding onto a substantial sum of coin for her. It was a large amount, left to her by her first husband. She had hoped to use the funds to travel the world, once this farce of a marriage was annulled.

Strictly speaking, she couldn't actually get her hands on the funds until she reached the age of five and twenty, just a few months away. Under her current circumstances however, she felt certain her father would part with it if it meant securing her life and future.

Arline was jostled out of her thoughts by a commotion that was taking place in the hallway outside her chambers. Sounds of heavy feet and grumbling, agitated men's voices grew louder as they neared her rooms.

Arline stopped pacing and pulled the heavy, iron poker from its stand next to her fireplace and hid it behind her. She was uncertain at the moment, just what made her decide she'd not go down without a fight. Insanity perhaps, or the maternal instincts she'd not known she possessed until less than an hour ago. Or it could be something altogether different. Whatever it was, it did not matter. She was determined to keep breathing for at least a few moments more.

Arline nearly jumped from her skin when the bar on her door was thrust upward. The scraping sound made her skin prickle with fear. She could feel her blood rush from her face when five large, angry-looking men hurried into her room without so much as a knock or polite request to enter. Rude beasts, every last one of them.

Her husband led the pack of men into her room, but left them near her door as his heavy feet pounded across the floor. Garrick towered over her, his face red with anger, his blue eyes nearly black with rage. He made no attempt to hide his displeasure, his anger. Arline's head began to swim with fear.

She tried to look him in the eye but could not. The courage she had mustered only moments ago fell away the instant he stood before her. Arline felt very much like a fool as she tightened her grip on the iron she hid at her back. *Courage, ye foolish woman!* She cursed silently. *Ye had it a moment ago. Do no' let the bastard win.*

"Ye will never, *ever* defy me again," Garrick seethed as he grabbed Arline's forearms. "Do ye understand that?"

Garrick had grabbed her so suddenly and with such force that she let loose her grasp on the iron. Thankfully, it did not tumble to the floor but instead it fell toward her and rested against her bottom.

"Aye, m'laird," she scratched out, nodding her head rapidly.

"I will give ye no more chances," he said as he dug his fingers into her arms and shook her. "Do ye hear me words, woman?"

Her arms burned where he dug into them. Biting her lip to keep from crying out -- which was no easy feat for it stung considerably -- Arline nodded her head again and held her breath. He had given her a reprieve. For what reason she could not at the moment understand nor did she care. She would simply be thankful for it.

As if to make certain she did in fact understand him completely, without question, he dug at her arms even harder and gave her another good shake before letting her loose. He spun on his heels to look at his men.

Arline could feel the iron begin to roll from where it rested. Rubbing one hand along her arm, she reached around with the other in time to keep the poker from falling over. Blood rushed in her ears as her heart pounded against her breast bone. If he saw the iron poker he might realize what her intent had been. She knew he would immediately withdraw his earlier reprieve and order her put to death.

She took a deep breath, turned around slowly and very carefully put the iron back in the stand. Once it was back in its place, she began to rub her forearms. There would be bruises tomorrow, reminders of just how powerful her husband was. Reminders of how he held her life in the palm of his hands.

"Ye'll take care of the brat." Garrick tossed his comment over his shoulder. "Me men have no time to waste on wiping noses or arses."

Arline spun around uncertain she had heard him correctly. Her doubt was put to rest when the same man from below stairs carried the little girl into the room. He stood near the doorway, looking perturbed and disgusted, as if he were holding a bag filled with manure instead of a sweet little babe.

Her little cheeks were blotchy, her tiny nose as red as a beet, and her eyes bloodshot from crying. Hiccupping, her thumb in her mouth, rattled sighs, the poor babe looked a frightful sight. But Arline was beyond pleased to see her and to hear that she would be allowed to care for her.

"Thank ye, me laird," Arline whispered, frozen in place, afraid to dash to the child and pull her from the man's arms.

"Do no' *thank* me, woman," Garrick bit out as he turned once again to look at Arline. "'Tis only temporary, until her da pays the ransom."

Arline choked back a retort. She thought it odd that her courage had returned now that he was not within arms reach of her person.

"Ye've no' much time left here, Arline," Garrick reminded her. "I recommend that ye do no' question me again. And do nothing to make me question me decision."

Garrick gave a quick nod of his head toward the man holding the babe before he quit the room almost as abruptly as he had entered. His man stomped toward Arline and without saying a word, he thrust the babe into her arms. A moment later the men left the room and pulled the door shut behind them.

A rline was, to say the least, stunned at this turn of events. She would not die this night, and neither would the babe. There had been no need to beg for mercy, no need to argue or to fight. For whatever reason, Garrick had decided to let her live, if only to take care of the frightened little girl who was now resting her head against Arline's shoulder.

Between hiccups and tear-induced heavy sighs, the babe finally spoke. "I do no' wike the mean man." Arline stifled a giggle at the babe's inability to say her *l's* and kept her own opinion of Garrick to herself. There was no point in upsetting the child further.

"I want me da," she said with her thumb still tucked in her mouth.

Arline choked back her own tears, kissed the top of the child's head and gave her a hug.

"I'm sure ye do, child," Arline whispered into the auburn ringlets. She took a deep breath before stepping to the washbasin. "We'll wash yer face, get under the blankets and get some sleep. In the morn, ye can tell me all about yer da," Arline told her, trying to sound far more confident and hopeful than she truly felt.

The child winced when Arline sat her down on the stool next to the basin. "Me bum hurts," she said, unwilling to relinquish her thumb.

It was not a huge leap to reason out why the little girl's bottom was sore. Arline clenched her jaw and began counting to ten.

"That mean man spanked me fer cryin'," the little girl said as she struggled to stand. "I want me da. Me da never spanks me." Her eyes began to fill with tears again.

Arline decided ten was not nearly a large enough number to count to in order to settle her anger toward her husband. She grabbed a clean cloth, poured fresh water over it and wrung it out while the little girl stood clutching at her skirts. "When can I go home?"

Deciding it was far too late and the child far too young to consider all the factors in answering that question, Arline began to wash the little girl's face and hands. "What is your name, sweeting?"

With her thumb still planted firmly between her teeth, the little girl answered. "Wiwee."

Knowing the child struggled with her *l*'s Arline took a good guess. "Willie? Do they call you Willie?" Even as she said it, she thought it an odd name for such a sweet little girl.

Willie nodded her head yes, still sucking her thumb. With her free hand, the child absentmindedly grabbed at a length of her auburn hair and twisted it around her finger. Arline thought she was the most adorable child she'd ever seen. Though in truth, she'd not been around many babes or children. It was a solitary life she had led.

"Willie," Arline said the name again. Mayhap it was short for Wilhelmina. The child was far too precious to have such an old sounding name. Named after a grand mum? It was possible.

24

"When can I go home?" Willie asked again before she yawned and shuddered. "Where is me da?"

There were many questions the child could ask. Arline knew she'd not possess the answers for many of them. "Soon, I imagine," Arline whispered softly, trying to disguise her own doubt. Arline rinsed out the cloth and folded it over the drying rack below the basin.

With no idea as to whom the child belonged, Arline had no way of knowing if her father could pay the ransom. Garrick, though he may be cruel and selfish, was not a foolish man. Certainly he would not have taken a child from someone who couldn't pay the ransom. Hopefully the child's family was not far away nor without the means to pay.

Arline took her comb from the table beside the basin and carefully ran it through Willie's auburn locks. The child's night dress was dirty and tattered. Led to the conclusion that the child had been taken from her home in the middle of the night, Arline shuddered at the mental images that flashed through her mind. Images of a nighttime raid, women and children screaming, men shouting and fighting. Willie, terrified and crying, wrenched from her mother's bosom, stolen away to be held for ransom.

What horrors must her mother be going through right now? If this were *her* child, Arline knew she would be sick with worry if not already mounted, armed to the teeth, and on her way to retrieve her daughter from the clutches of a most cowardly, brutal man.

Arline shook the dreadful thoughts from her mind and took a closer look at the nightdress. It was a simple gown but made of a fine muslin fabric with tiny silk bows at the ends of her sleeves and the hem. The dirt and tears on the nightdress suggested mayhap a long journey or perhaps it had been torn during the raid. Another thought entered her mind, one she did not like to think. Perhaps the child was not properly cared for. Perhaps she was sorely neglected, her parents not interested or capable of caring for her.

Gently, Arline guided the child to the bed. "Up ye go, sweeting. We'll get ye warm and in the morn, we shall break our fast and talk then." Arline lifted the child into the middle of the bed and wrapped the blankets snugly around her.

There was no doubt the child was exhausted. Red rimmed eyes, blotchy cheeks, heavy eyelids stared up at Arline. "What if the mean man comes back?"

Arline's stomach tightened at that thought. Certainly it would be a day or two, mayhap more, before the ransom was paid. She tried to convince herself that Garrick would not return until Willie's parents had paid the ransom.

Arline added another log to the fire, grabbed the poker and prodded at the coals until the log caught. "Ye needn't worry about him coming back," Arline told Willie. *At least not until tomorrow.*

Garrick was probably above stairs, in his quarters, with his leman, Ona. Aye, Arline knew all about the woman, or at least of her existence. Though she had never met her, she knew that Ona was the woman to whom Garrick had given his heart. And as far as Arline was concerned, Ona could have it. Arline wanted no part of her husband's heart or, for that matter, anything else he had to offer.

From what she had learned from the servants, Ona was breathtakingly beautiful, with dark hair and eyes the color of the ocean. Nothing at all like Arline with her unruly auburn locks and green eyes. Where Ona was petite yet buxom, Arline was tall, slender and lacking the curves her husband apparently admired.

'Twas all the better, Arline supposed. Let Ona keep the fool happy and satisfied. *I'd gladly take me freedom over a husband.*

With the fire adequately banked, Arline stood, slipped off her robe and laid it on the chair next to her bed. She blew out the candle and paused beside the bed as the light from the fire washed the room in warm light.

Willie had finally succumbed and was fast asleep. Her little thumb was still between her lips and she had a lock of hair twisted around her finger.

Arline slipped into the bed and snuggled next to the sleeping babe. She took great care not to disturb the sweet cherub. Arline rested her head in the crook of her arm and watched the child sleep.

Try as she might, she could not keep her heart from feeling sympathy for this child. The invisible shield she had constructed months ago, the one meant to protect her from disappointment and heartache, was being chipped away, one sweet baby breath at a time. Arline tried to convince herself that there was no harm in feeling something for this innocent babe. But her heart warned no good would or could come of it. As soon as the child's father paid the ransom the babe would be gone. And Arline would be left alone again, with a gaping hole in her heart.

Curses! What had she done to deserve such agony? Had she not always done her best to be a good and dutiful daughter? A quiet and acquiescent wife? Never a day passed that she did not say her prayers. She did her best to always put others' feelings ahead of her own. She had sacrificed so that her sisters could eat and have a decent roof over their heads.

Her sisters were one of the main reasons she had agreed to marry Garrick. Her father had threatened to take them away, never to be seen or heard from again. There was no doubt in her mind that he would have done just that. So she had acquiesced and married Garrick Blackthorn.

If the Good Lord had ever seen fit to give her children, Arline thought they would have looked like the innocent babe sleeping next to her. Auburn ringlets, thick lashes and alabaster skin. If a stranger were to see the two of them together, they would probably assume the babe was hers. No one would be the wiser.

Arline began to worry again over what would happen if Willie's father could not pay the ransom. What then? Garrick had proven time and again that he was not a man to be toyed with. There was no doubt in Arline's mind that he would have no compunction about killing the child. If not for the sheer amusement of it, then simply to punish the little girl's father.

Guarded heart be damned. Arline could not let that happen.

She was guarding her heart against loving a *man*. A child was an altogether different story. A child, *this* child, was an innocent. It wasn't her fault that men were fools.

Mayhap, this was God's way of making up for the fact that Arline would never have children of her own. He had put the child in Arline's life for a reason. Arline was meant to keep the child safe.

Her mind began to race with different possibilities and scenarios for stealing the child away from Garrick. Disguise herself as a servant and tuck the child into a sack, slinging it over her shoulder? Or mayhap hide in one of the many wagons that came and went from the keep? Nay, a bold, daytime escape was far too risky.

There had to be a way out of this castle.

It was treacherous ground she trod upon. If she failed, Garrick would probably kill them both.

THREE

Rowan Graham lounged peacefully on the ground propped up on one elbow, his long legs spread out and crossed at the ankles. He gazed into the campfire, only half listening to his men. His mind, as well as his heart, was back at his keep with his four-year-old daughter, Lily.

Rowan and ten of his men had been gone for more than a sennight, hunting red deer to add to the winter stores. He did not enjoy being gone from his daughter for more than an hour, let alone a week's long hunt. The hunt and being away from his daughter had played hell with his nerves. Tomorrow could not come soon enough. He missed Lily. She was all he had left of Kate.

He could not help but think of Kate whenever he thought of Lily. Lily was like her mother in many ways. Stubborn, adorable, beautiful, adventurous. She had successfully wrapped Rowan around her wee finger the moment she was born. As the days and years progressed, the hold grew tighter.

If he had his druthers, his life would be decidedly different.

He would not be chief of his clan, Clan Graham. His wife, Kate, would still be alive. He would not have lost his mother, father, and youngest sister, and countless others, to the Black Death. He would not feel so insufferably alone. And Lily would not be an only child.

The Black Death had destroyed so many lives, his own included. It seemed that no one or no clan had been left unaffected by it. Not a day went by that he did not curse that damned disease.

While Rowan reflected on his life and what he *wished* he had, his men were proudly discussing the number of deer they'd killed and how glad they would be to return home on the morrow. Many of the men were married and talked anxiously about needing the company and warmth their wives offered. Rowan envied them.

If Kate had lived.... If Kate had lived, then he imagined that he would be joining in the conversation regarding warm, loving wives, whispers and giggles in the dark, and the joys a man could find in his wife's open arms.

As it was, there was no such talk for him. He hadn't been with a woman since Kate died more than four years ago. There had been plenty of women over the years, who had happily offered to warm his bed, but he would have none of them. His heart, he supposed, would always belong to Kate. He couldn't imagine inviting another woman into his bed, let alone his heart.

Guilt, to be honest, was what kept him in solitude and away from women. Why should he be allowed to enjoy his life while his wife lay in the cold, dark earth? There was no fairness to it. It should have been he who died, not his beautiful sweet wife.

Although he had promised Kate -- just hours before she succumbed to the Black Death -- that he would *someday* open his heart to another woman, he hadn't. He couldn't.

To his bones he believed that if he did by chance, open his heart to another woman, he would be saying goodbye to Kate permanently. He didn't have the strength, nor the desire, to do that. She had been his whole world. He was not ready yet to say goodbye to her.

Rowan knew that were it not for Lily, he would have died from a broken heart long ago.

Lily.

Rowan's lips curved into a warm smile when he thought of his little girl. Lily was the only reason he took one breath after another. She was his sole reason for living.

His beautiful daughter, with her curly auburn hair and big blue eyes, was his entire life now. Lily was the light of his life. Spoiled, but not so much that people did not want to be near her. Nay, he spoiled her in other ways.

She was the only four-year-old girl he knew who owned a sword made specifically for her size, along with a quiver and bow. She loved to be out of doors, riding with her father, traipsing across the countryside. He was allowing her to do all the things her mother had wanted to do as a child, but was prohibited from doing. Rowan was fully determined to give Lily the kind of care-free life her mother never had but had longed for, allowing her to do things that would have driven his mother mad.

He chuckled slightly at the thought of his mother. Enndolynn would have been a good grandmother for Lily. She would have taught her how to be a prim and proper young lass. Rowan would concede that point. Oh, how he wished his mum had lived, just to see the look on her face the first time Lily rode astride or pulled the string on a bow! An all-out brawl between he and his mum would have quickly ensued, but it was a fight he would have loved to have fought. As much as he hated to admit it, he missed his mother.

Rowan's thoughts were disturbed by the sound of horses heading toward their camp. He and his men quickly pulled themselves to their feet as Frederick, Rowan's second in command, came pounding into the camp followed by five other clansmen.

Frederick was off his horse and walking toward Rowan before the horse had even come to a complete halt. From the look of dread on Frederick's face, Rowan could tell it was not good news he brought with him.

"Rowan!" Frederick exclaimed as he raced forward. His clothes, as well as his ginger-colored hair, clung to him, soaked with sweat. Out of breath, his chest heaved in and out.

A thousand thoughts raced through Rowan's mind, and Frederick had yet to utter a word as to why he was here.

Lily. She would be the only reason why Frederick would be here, looking as though the world was about to come to an end. Frederick's next words would confirm Rowan's thoughts.

"'Tis Lily!" he blurted out.

Oh, God, do no' let her be dead! Rowan thought as he braced himself for the worst possible news. He tried to still his nerves, to push the images of an injured, ill or worse yet, dead, daughter from his frantic mind.

"Is she ill?" Rowan somehow managed to speak the question. His mouth and throat felt horribly dry.

Frederick shook his head and took a deep breath before answering. "Nay," he said before swallowing hard. "She's been taken."

Rowan felt the world around him begin to spin. It was all he could do to take his next breath as his heart fell to his feet.

Taken? His mind raced with possibilities and outcomes. How had anyone gotten to her? Had their keep been attacked? He could only assume that she had been taken to be held for ransom. The why was not nearly as important as the who. He needed to know whose throat he'd soon be cutting.

Several long moments passed before he found his voice. "How in the hell was she taken? Were we attacked? Who has taken her?" His words tumbled out as quickly as he thought them.

Frederick had finally managed to get his breathing under control. "We were no' attacked, at least no' from outside," he answered.

Rowan's brow drew into a knot of confusion.

Frederick did not relish the thought of explaining what had happened. He was consumed with guilt for Rowan had left him in charge. The clan had been experiencing some semblance of peace for the past year. In hindsight, it had been too much to hope for that peace would be everlasting.

The keep had been fortified. Every precaution taken to keep the clan safe in the event of an attack from outside sources. Mayhap they should have spent a little more time on shoring up defenses on the *inside* of the keep.

"We were attacked from *within*," Frederick told him. "We do no' ken who, yet, but someone slipped a sleeping draught into the ale last night. By the time we realized what was happening, Lily had already been taken."

Rowan had never before worried about traitors among his clansmen. Many of his people he had known since the day he was born. There were many new clan members, people who had sought refuge with clan Graham after the Black Death. How could anyone betray him like this?

Frederick pulled a folded piece of parchment from within his tunic and handed it to Rowan. Rowan unfolded it and scanned the contents with angry eyes. His blood boiled with anger and he could feel his skin heat with it.

"Garrick Blackthorn," he seethed. His fingers shook, not with fear but with unadulterated rage. If it was the last thing he did, he would see Garrick Blackthorn dead.

I t seemed to Lady Arline that the past sennight had flown by. Willie was as energetic and curious as she was adorable and precious. The child was also very intelligent. It had taken very little time for Willie to figure out that Garrick Blackthorn, or *the mean man* as Willie had come to call him, was not a man to be trifled with. Neither were any of his men.

When Arline had asked for the opportunity to take Willie out for fresh air, she was met with a resounding "no". She tried to explain that it would be in his best interest to insure the child was healthy when the ransom was paid and the child returned to her father. Garrick answered with a swift backhand across her cheek that left her reeling for several hours.

So they were kept in seclusion inside Arline's private quarters. Although secluded, they were not without hope. Arline had to hold on to the belief that Willie's father would soon pay the ransom and have his child back in the loving arms of her family. To think otherwise was a useless waste of time and energy. Worry solved nothing.

Not wanting to risk more retribution from Garrick, Arline refused to ask for anything further. She took three of her own dresses and in a matter of days had constructed two suitable dresses for the little girl, along with a cloak. Out of the remnants, Arline sewed stockings for the child's bare feet as well as mittens. She also made tiny chemises and nightdresses from one of her older undergarments.

Arline taught the child how to sew, something she was surprised to learn the child hadn't already been taught. It wasn't much of a surprise to learn that the little girl had been treated more like a son than a daughter, once Arline learned that child's mother was dead. Her poor father was, Arline had to assume, doing the best that he could under the circumstances.

Apparently Willie was being raised by a group of men. There were very few women left in their clan, Willie had informed her. Aside from the clanswomen who worked in the kitchen and the keep, there didn't seem to be any who could take her under their wing.

It was quite evident that the child adored her father and, from what Willie said, her father adored her in return. Arline had heard of such things as father's adoring their children, spoiling them and doting on them. She had no first hand experience for her own father was a cold, distant man.

"Da says I be the angel God sent to take care of him after me mum died," Willie explained as she practiced her stitches. "He says God didna wan' him to be alone. He says me mum was pretty, like me. And she was verra smart too."

Arline listened intently as she finished the hem on the night dress she was making for the child. She envied the little girl. Aye, she'd been pulled from her home, was a pawn in a ruthless game made up by foolish men. That wasn't what she envied. What Arline coveted was the way the child loved her father, and if what the child said was true -- and she had no reason to believe otherwise -- the way *he* loved her. What she would not give to have her own father treasure her thusly.

"Me da will come fer me," Willie told her as she carefully pulled the bone needle through the cloth. "He will run the mean man through with his sword."

Arline looked up from her own sewing and eyed the child. She wasn't bragging. It was a statement of fact in her eyes. How wonderful it must be to have such faith in another individual. Especially one's own father.

A thought suddenly occurred to Arline. *What if her father doesn't come for her? What if he cannot pay the ransom?* She shuddered at the prospect. What if what Willie was telling her was only the fanciful notions -- or worse yet, wishful thinking -- of a very young child? There was a very strong possibility that Willie's father might not have the funds necessary to procure her freedom. What then? What would Garrick do?

Arline had witnessed his ruthlessness on many occasions this past year. There was nothing in their history together that would lead her to believe he would show the slightest bit of compassion toward the child.

Panic welled. Her mind screamed what her heart already knew. *Garrick will kill this child.*

There was no doubt of it. He would kill her if he did not get what he wanted. He certainly wouldn't keep the child around until her father could come up with the ransom. Arline's mind raced with worry. How long had Garrick given Willie's father to pay the ransom? A fortnight? A month? She had no definitive answer and could not begin to guess.

Willing her nerves to settle, she went back to her sewing. She needed a plan of escape, a way out of this castle. Guards patrolled the corridors virtually around the clock. No doubt Garrick had doubled the men outside as well, on the off chance that Willie's father would be more inclined to attack than pay.

Walking through the front door and out of the gate was out of the question. Arline chewed on her bottom lip as she tried to focus on the stitches. The last thing she wanted was for Willie to pick up on the fact that she was worried. Nay, not worried. *Terrified.*

As she tried to think through the situation, she poked her finger with the bone needle and cursed out loud.

Willie giggled. "Ye said damn!"

35

Arline cast her a disapproving look as she sucked on her finger. "Young lasses should no' use such words, Willie."

"Ye did," Willie challenged.

"Aye, and 'twas wrong of me to do so. I'll have to say extra penance tonight fer it. Ye'll do the same fer repeatin' me words."

"Da lets me say damn," Willie told her.

As if her father had anything to say on the matter. "Yer prayers have just been doubled, Willie. And if ye dare say it again, ye'll go to bed early."

Willie stared back at Arline. Arline had to fight the urge to laugh. She could tell the child was thinking hard on her threat. Mayhap the child was used to having her own way with her father or mayhap she was simply testing her boundaries. Either way, it mattered not to Arline. She would not have the child go back to her father using foul language.

Willie turned her attention back to the scrap of cloth. "I do no' like sewin'. I'd rather be out of doors playin'."

Arline couldn't argue with her. She too would have preferred to be out of doors, taking in fresh air, walking through the autumn leaves, anywhere but in this room or this old, damp castle.

Arline went back to her project. There had to be a way out. Mayhap she could bribe one of the guards? But with what? The promise that as soon as she turned five and twenty she would send him money from the funds her father held for her? Even she wouldn't be inclined to help someone on that promise.

Nay, there had to be a way out. Over the past year, she had discovered a few passages hidden behind walls and tapestries. But they had led to nowhere other than the gathering room below stairs and the kitchens. She had supposed they had at one time been used by servants. Over the decades rooms and additional stories had been added onto the original castle. Endless stairs that led to nowhere could be found quite easily.

But, could there also be stairs that led to freedom? Arline had to believe there were. Even the home she grew up in had hidden escape routes. And it was by no means a castle.

Arline looked out the window at the bright autumn day. The trees were just beginning to turn. Arline knew that very soon the autumn rains would begin and likely not cease for quite some time. All too soon rain would turn to snow.

But she wouldn't be here to see another winter. In less than two weeks her marriage to Garrick would end. He would have it annulled and she would be sent back to her father.

If Willie's father did not pay the ransom before she was sent back to Ireland, then who would care for her? Her heart went heavy with the thought of this sweet, innocent child left alone in the care of servants or, worse yet, Garrick's men.

Arline could not allow that to happen. She had to find a way out and had to find it quickly. No matter what the consequences if she were caught, she had to do what she could for Willie's sake.

As soon as night fell and Willie was lost in peaceful slumber, Arline would begin what she could only pray would be the first step toward freedom. She would find a way out.

FOUR

I t had taken Arline five nights of prowling through black corridors and hidden passages before she finally found a way out. Blessed Mary, she had done it!

She had found a small hidden door in the small chamber she used as a dressing room, and she had found it quite by accident. She'd been rummaging through her trunk looking for buttons to use as eyes for a doll she had made for Willie. The buttons were mismatched, but Arline was certain that Willie wouldn't mind.

She had dropped one of the buttons behind the trunk when she shut the lid. In her search for the errant button, she had felt a draft coming in from the wall behind the tapestry where the trunk had sat all these many months.

It had not been an easy feat, after three nights of scraping her hands and knees from crawling around on rough stones, bumping her head, running into dead ends, she had finally found the way out.

Tonight would be the night. Her marriage would undoubtedly be annulled in three days. More likely than not, Garrick would send her away as soon as the priest granted him his request.

There was no time to lose and there was too much at stake if she waited.

Arline breathed a sigh of relief when she finally crawled through the hidden doorway and back into her room. Willie slept soundly, curled into a little ball in the big bed, her little thumb thrust into her mouth. The child slept like that each night, one thumb in her mouth whilst the index finger of her other hand was wrapped around a curl.

As quietly as she could, Arline scrubbed away the grime she had accumulated during her sojourn through the dark passages. Dawn had yet to break over the horizon and she had no desire to have Willie wake just yet. For the past several nights, Arline had forgone sleep in order to find a way out of the castle.

If they were to escape tonight, Arline would need more than just a few minutes rest. She did not enjoy the thought of running through the countryside with a small child in tow on very little sleep. She needed to keep her wits about her.

After stripping off her stockings, rinsing them and hanging them by the fire to dry, Arline slipped quietly into the bed. She soon found that she was too excited and nervous to sleep. Mentally she ran through her list of supplies, limited and sparse as they were.

Since she had made the decision to find a means of escape, she had been preparing. She hoarded away small slices of bread and cheese, sewed extra stockings and added a lining to Willie's cloak. She had even taken a blanket, cut holes in it and affixed straps so that she might be able to carry Willie on her back when the child grew weary.

Arline hadn't the foggiest idea how close the nearest town might be for she had not left the castle since her arrival last year. She had remembered passing through several small villages and towns when Garrick had brought her here. From her recollection, she felt certain they were all to the South. With little else to go on she had to be comfortable in that decision.

Once she and Willie -- she refused to think of "ifs" -- reached a village, she would make the ultimate sacrifice. She would send word to her father.

That was the only part of her plan that made her apprehensive.

Until Willie had arrived, her only goal once her marriage was annulled, was to travel as far away from her father as she could manage. She only had to survive until her birthday, which fell around Christmastime. Once she reached the age of five and twenty, she would no longer be forced to heed her father's bidding. She would be free to go wherever she wished. And never again, would she be subjected to an arranged marriage and the humility such unions brought.

But that was before Willie.

She was afraid that if she let it be known that the child she traveled with belonged to Rowan Graham, then word would quickly spread and Garrick would find them. She could not allow that to happen.

It was worth the sacrifice of her own freedom to see to it that Willie was reunited with her father. Mayhap she could put her father off a few months, feign an illness, or simply run away once Willie was returned safely to the loving arms of her father.

As tired and exhausted as she was, sleep continued to evade her. She wondered about Willie's father. What kind of man was he? He had to be a good man and a kind father, Arline supposed, else Willie wouldn't idolize him as she did.

Although she had sworn off men and hopes of a happy marriage and babes of her own, there were times, like this, when sleep was elusive and the cold air enveloped her, that she did wish to have a set of warm, strong arms wrapped around her. The thought of warm arms left her with a huge sense of longing.

Silently, she cursed her heart and mind for allowing the images and thoughts through the barrier she had built. *It does no good to want for somethin' ye'll never have,* she admonished. *There will be no man and no home filled to the rafters with babes.*

FIVE

T he Blackthorn Keep stood black against the indigo sky. Torches that lined the large curtain wall cast eerie shadows against the massive four-story keep. Rowan was thankful there was no moon this night for they needed the complete cover of darkness to gain entry.

Had the kidnapping taken place five years ago or even a few more years into the future, Rowan would have had hundreds of men to help him lay siege to Blackthorn Castle. But the Black Death of 1350 had decimated not only his own clan, but countless others across Scotland. It would be years before the Graham Clan could ever reach the number of able-bodied fighting men they had prior to that awful, dark time.

Two of Rowan's best men had been watching the keep for days, hidden in the forests that surrounded it. Rowan had requested help from clans MacDougall, McKee and McDunnah the very day he had received the news that his daughter had been taken. The chief from each of these clans had brought with them as many men as they could, which was not many. The numbers of these clans had been significantly reduced by the same cursed epidemic that had come close to wiping out Rowan's clan.

Though their numbers had dwindled and their resources were just as scarce, not one had turned down Rowan's request for help. Rowan had never been more thankful for the alliance and friendship that had been forged amongst himself and these clans as he was this night.

Nial McKee and twenty-five of his men, along with the thirty that Duncan McEwan brought from clan MacDougall, were encamped and well hidden some two miles south of Blackthorn Keep. To the North and east, Caelen McDunnah and fifty of his men waited for word as well. Rowan had brought nearly every able-bodied man in his clan, a sad number at twenty. He had left behind barely enough to defend his keep.

As Rowan waited in the dark forest, he quietly tallied the number of men at his disposal. It was, to say the least, a dismal number. He sorely wished he could simply lay siege to the damned keep, rush in, find his daughter, and then leave nothing but burning embers in his wake. Instead of a full out invasion, Rowan and his men would have to rely on cunning, stealth, and a heavy dose of divine intervention.

His men had reported that the best way into the keep was at the weakest point on the North side. That part of the keep was not well guarded. Rowan could only suppose it was because the entire north side was nothing but flat land and it would be quite easy to see someone approaching.

They would have to make their way in from the West and work their way around to the North side. It would by no means be an easy expedition, but it would be worth it.

They decided that Rowan, Frederick and Daniel would be the three men who made their way into the keep. Frederick had tried, quite unsuccessfully, to talk Rowan out of actually entering the keep. Rowan, however, was unmovable on the point. It was *his* daughter who had been kidnapped. Rowan was fully intent on getting her back. And if God saw to it and allowed him the opportunity, he would be the one who cut Garrick Blackthorn's throat.

The three men were covered from head to toe in black clothing. They had also painted their faces and hands with black paint. Every weapon, even the rope they carried, was painted black. Ginger-haired

Frederick and blonde-headed Daniel had black hoods draped over their heads. They were taking enough chances as it was without the light from a torch or candle somewhere within the keep glinting off anything.

With quiet, stealthy precision, they made their way across the western portion of Blackthorn lands, toward the keep by crawling on their bellies. It took some time, but after more than half an hour, they reached the outer wall.

With no more sound than a cat walking across the grass, they made their way along the outer wall to the North side. With practiced skill, they maintained steady breathing, as well as steady steps until they were able to find a good place to climb over the wall.

With great care and silence, Frederick removed the rope draped across his shoulder. Taking the looped end in one hand, he twirled it about his head before tossing it high into the air. He missed his first attempt at securing it around the parapet of the walk wall. Gritting his teeth and cursing under his breath, he tried again, this time with success.

Moments later, the three men were over the walk wall and working their way into the castle.

Arline had spent the better part of the day and evening, quietly making preparations for their impending escape. Wanting to make certain they had at least two days' worth of food for their journey, Arline had skipped eating lunch and instead, tucked the meat, bread, and cheese into her satchel.

It had taken Arline some time to finally fall asleep that night, her nerves a tangled mess of fear induced excitement. Thankfully, Willie had fallen asleep with little trouble, clinging to the little doll Arline had made for her.

Arline had not been asleep long when Garrick pulled her from her bed. Her mind was muddled and for a moment, she could not fathom why he was dragging her from her bed and into the hallway, without saying a word.

The light from the burning torches stung her eyes. It did not take much time for the cobwebs of sleep to be replaced with abject fear.

He's found out! He knows I planned to escape and now he's come to kill me. Arline swallowed the knot that had formed in her throat and looked fearfully up at Garrick.

He looked positively livid. His face was red and she could see his heart beating furiously in the vein of his neck. His large hand dug into her arm painfully. Arline knew better than to complain that he was hurting her. Complaints would do nothing more than to further incite his anger.

Garrick had taken several steps away from her bedchamber door before tossing her against the wall. Her breath was momentarily taken from her from the force as much as the welling fear. Somehow she managed to remain standing and mute.

Garrick came and stood inches away from her. "Do ye ken what day this be?" he asked gruffly.

Arline quickly shook her head, unable to speak at the moment. Inwardly, she thought mayhap this would be the day she died.

"It is just past the midnight hour. 'Tis a special day, to be sure." His smile was evil, sinister. Cold fingers of fear shot down her spine.

"It has been exactly one year, one month and one day since we were forced to marry."

Arline's brow knitted into a fine line of confusion. She had been diligently keeping track, using marks on the wall of her closet, to mark the passing time. "Today?" she asked breathlessly. "I thought there were three more days," she said, more to herself than to Garrick.

Garrick's laughter was clearly maniacal. "I can assure ye that it *is* today."

She wracked her brain trying to figure out where she had gone wrong. *Three days. I had three days! I've kept track since....* 'Twas then that realization hit her like a wall of cold water. She had been counting down the days since her *arrival*, not their actual wedding date. She had neglected to take into account the three days it took to arrive at Blackthorn Castle.

How could I be so stupid! She cursed herself.

Garrick took a step closer. "The priest has just granted me the annulment. Ye are no longer me concern. I want ye out of this castle. *Now.*"

Her only thought at the moment was of the innocent child sleeping a few steps away. She could not help herself. "But what of the babe?"

Garrick was on her in an instant, grabbing her arms with both hands. "The brat is no' yer concern," he seethed as he gave her a shake.

Arline was beside herself with worry and fear for Willie. Her mind raced for a way to persuade him to allow her to stay. At least long enough for her to flee with Willie. Certainly, he did not mean for her to leave immediately.

"Me laird, perhaps ye would allow me to stay, at least until Willie's father pays the ransom. I promise, I will ask nothin' else of ye--"

She saw the fury flash in his eyes and had no time or way to respond. A large hand landed across her cheek. He grabbed her arms again and slammed her against the wall, pinning her there. Her teeth cut her cheek and her mouth filled with blood. Tiny flecks of white flashed in her eyes and she felt instantly woozy.

Her hatred toward Garrick grew.

"Have ye learned *nothin'* this past year? Are ye truly *that* stupid that ye would question me decision?" He was yelling at her now, but she could barely hear him over the blood that rushed in her ears.

"I'm sorry," she whispered frantically.

He pushed her against the wall again. "Ye will leave this castle this night. I give ye half an hour to pack and leave. If ye argue further, I will think nothing of squeezing the life out of ye and sending yer corpse back to yer da. Do ye understand?"

Arline nodded her head yes, but her heart pounded *no, no, no! I do no' understand how any one man can be so cruel!* She made a solemn vow that if she were to survive this night, she'd never allow herself to be hit by a man again. From this point forward, she would carry a dirk with her at all times.

"Who will care fer the child?" It was, mayhap, the most stupid question she had ever asked for it did nothing but inflame his anger further.

Before she realized what was happening, Garrick had thrown her to the cold stone floor. "Why do ye test me?" he growled as he stood over her before one foot landed hard into her thigh. "Do ye wish to die this night?" he asked before kicking her again.

She curled herself into a ball, covering her head with her hands. She had indeed pushed him too far, she knew that. She'd only been thinking of Willie. Soon it wouldn't matter who would take care of the child for Arline was as good as dead.

Another swift, hard kick was delivered to her ribs and knocked what little breath she had left completely from her lungs. She'd never known such fear before. She could not beg for mercy, could not crawl away for she was trapped in the corner.

"M'laird!" came a muffled voice. "M'laird!"

Arline barely recognized the voice. It belonged to Archie, Garrick's second in command.

Archie had placed a hand on Garrick's shoulder and was gently leading him away from Arline. "M'laird," Archie repeated. "Ona waits fer ye in the kirk. She wishes to be married this night."

Arline had never had any kind feelings toward any of Garrick's men. But had she been able to move, she would have kissed Archie for pulling Garrick away from her. She lay in a heap, trying to catch her breath and willing her stomach to settle. One more kick and she would certainly wretch and that would not help her case with Garrick.

"Go to Ona, m'laird. I'll take care of Lady Arline," Archie spoke quietly and in even tones. Arline didn't care *why* he was helping, but she would be eternally grateful to him.

Garrick finally turned his glaring eyes away from Arline and focused on Archie.

"Go to Ona," Archie told him again.

It was as if the name alone was enough to calm his anger. Slowly, Garrick's angry face softened before he smiled at Archie.

"I'll take the lady back to her da, m'laird," Archie said. "Ye needn't worry. I'll have her gone before yer done speakin' yer vows." He offered a reassuring smile.

Garrick shook his head. "Nay, she gets no escort. No horse. Nothin', do ye understand? Cast her out. She can fend fer herself. She is no longer my responsibility."

Archie looked appalled at the thought of just turning Arline out. "But, Garrick!" he argued. "Ye canna be serious. We canna just turn her out in the middle of the night!"

Garrick shoved Archie away. His voice was filled with disdain. "Ye heard me orders. Cast her out. Now. Do no' argue it further. I care no' what happens to her. I didn't want her to begin with!"

"But, Garrick, if we do this, and anythin' happens to her, her father will be sorely disappointed in ye!"

Garrick would not listen to reason. "I do no' care what her father thinks. Turn her out, turn her out now." He said nothing else as he stomped away leaving a disgusted Archie and a terrified and confused Arline in his wake.

Archie went to Arline and knelt down. "Are ye all right, m'lady?"

Arline wanted to laugh at the absurdity of his question. *All right? Nay, I am no' all right. I hurt, I am afraid, and I ashamed. I have failed an innocent little girl.*

Instead, she lied. "I will be fine soon. I thank ye for helpin' me, Archie." It was a struggle but she managed to pull herself to sit, with her back leaning near the door that led to the chamber next to her own. "Please, let me at least get my breath and wash before ye cast me out."

"Take yer time, m'lady. He'll be quite busy with Ona for the next few hours."

Arline drew her knees up and placed her palms on the floor. She could see the concern written in the lines of his face and in his hazel eyes. Why he was concerned did not matter much to her at the moment, she was simply grateful for it.

Droplets of blood trailed down the front of her night dress. She could feel her cheek begin to swell as it throbbed painfully. Her thighs and ribs throbbed along with it. *Damn, ye are a fool!*

49

She closed her eyes and moments later heard footsteps coming toward her. *Please do no' let it be Garrick back to kill me,* she prayed silently.

"Archie," a young man called as he approached. "Garrick wants ye in the kirk."

Archie muttered a curse under his breath and stood upright. He stood with his fingertips on his hips and looked as though he were trying to assess the situation thoughtfully.

"He says fer me to throw the trash out," the young man said proudly as he leered down at Arline.

Archie grabbed the young man by the collar of his shirt and shoved him against the wall. "Do no' show her further disrespect young Gunther, elst I'll show ye the end of me blade." Arline stared up in utter surprise at Archie's threat. When on earth had the man come to be her champion? She found his sudden change of attitude toward her quite confusing.

"Back off, Archie!" Gunther threatened. "Since when do ye care what happens to her? Garrick certainly does no' hold her in any high regard. Why should ye?"

Archie took a deep breath and let it out slowly before releasing his hold on Gunther. "No matter what *yer laird's* opinion of her is, she is still a lady and deserving of yer respect. Ye treat her with compassion, Gunther, or, I swear I will gut ye through."

Gunther sneered at him but remained silent as Archie went back to Arline. "Me lady, I fear I must leave to see to Garrick. Please, go to yer room and pack. I shall return as soon as possible to escort ye out."

Arline stared up at him, dumbfounded at his kind tone and offer of assistance. "Thank ye," she murmured softly.

Archie offered her his hand, which she politely refused. "I do no' think I can stand just yet. I will be fine in a few moments. Please, now, go see to yer laird."

Archie gave a curt nod before turning to leave. He warned Gunther one last time to leave the lady alone and show her no ill treatment.

Gunter waited until Archie was out of sight before he said anything to Arline.

"Our laird wants ye out of his castle this night. I would strongly suggest ye hurry and do as he says." He crossed his arms over his chest and looked at her as if she were covered in manure.

She'd learned her lesson with Garrick and dared not do or say anything that would give the young man reason to act rashly. Inwardly however, she was cursing him to the devil.

The door to her chamber seemed too far away at the moment and she would have to pass by the young man in order to get to it. She chose instead to slip into the empty chamber that sat next to hers. The empty room was part of her chamber but it had never been furnished for her.

She took a deep breath and rolled to her knees, embarrassed and humiliated. Using the latch to the door for balance, she slowly and carefully pulled herself up to stand. She nearly tumbled into the room for the latch hadn't been fully engaged.

Pain irradiated from her ribs to her toes but she wasn't about to let anyone see it. She especially would not give Gunther the satisfaction.

Carefully she pushed the door open and stepped into the dark room. There was no moonlight or lit candle to help her find her way. It was nearly as black as pitch. She slowly closed the door behind her and took a deep breath.

She hadn't taken three steps into the room when a hand came around and clamped across her mouth while another held her about her waist. She nearly jumped from her skin as the room spun around her.

Good lord, what now?

F rederick and Daniel had witnessed a good portion of the attack on Lady Arline. They were hidden in the dark room with the door slightly ajar. Frederick had to restrain Daniel to keep him from bursting through the door and running Garrick Blackthorn through.

As much as Frederick wanted to assist the lady, his first priority was Lily.

His mind raced for a way to do both. Just as he had decided to damn the consequences and go to the lady's aid, the man appeared and pulled Garrick from her. Frederick was thankful for the man's assistance and prayed God's forgiveness for not intervening sooner.

He and Daniel had been quite relieved for the man's assistance. They were forced to wait in silence, praying that the occupants would soon clear the corridor. They were trapped and could not do much until everyone left. The only other option was to leave the way they'd come in, via the balcony.

They were surprised when the lady entered the room they were in. It was a small room with nowhere to hide. And if the lady lit a candle they would certainly be seen.

So they did the only thing they could think of.

Frederick now held the battered, trembling woman against his chest with one hand firmly over her mouth. "Me lady, please do no' make a sound. We mean ye no harm," he whispered into her ear.

His assurance that they meant her no harm did nothing to quell the fear or ease her pounding heart. Had she not just had the hell nearly beaten out of her, she would have fought and struggled. She wished for no more.

"Lady, I swear it to ye, we truly mean ye no harm," he tried to reassure her. "We ken ye hurt. And were we able, we would have gutted Blackthorn for ye. If I let ye go, do ye promise no' to call out?"

Arline nodded her head realizing that had they meant her any harm, they would have done away with her by now. She breathed a sigh of relief when he carefully lowered his hand from her mouth. Had he not still been holding her about the waist, she would have fallen to the floor.

"I ken ye hurt, m'lady and fer that, I be truly sorry. I am Frederick of Clan Graham and this is Daniel," he said, still holding her closely. "Are ye well, m'lady? Can ye stand?"

Arline nodded her head again, her voice frozen in her throat. Slowly, the arm around her waist loosened. Suddenly a memory of Carlich flashed in her mind. Her first husband, a sweet old man who had died seven years past. He told her that a man's heart could be seen in his eyes. She wished she could see his face so she could better judge his sincerity.

She felt woozy and lightheaded but managed to push it aside by taking a few deep breaths. Finally, she was able to speak. "I do no' ken why ye be here, and frankly, I do no' care." She was wasting valuable time and needed to get to her chamber next door, to Willie and somehow come up with a plan to get the child out.

"If ye've come here to kill Blackthorn, ye have me blessin', now please, I must leave."

Frederick stopped her with a light touch to her arm. "M'lady, we are here to find our laird's daughter."

It took a moment for his words to sink in. Hope rose again, washing her body in warm relief. *Praise God!* "Ye've come for Willie?" she whispered excitedly.

"Willie?" Frederick chuckled. "Her name be Lily, m'lady. But she canna say her l's verra well, so it comes out *Willie.*"

Arline rolled her eyes, feeling dumb that she had not figured it out sooner. "Lily!" she repeated, much relieved to learn the child had been given such a beautiful name. It made perfectly good sense, now that she could think on it. *Lily.*

"I've been takin' care of her," Arline told him. "She is a most precious little girl."

"We thank ye kindly, m'lady," Daniel finally spoke from the shadows. "Her da will be verra grateful to ye."

"Och, 'twas the only right thing to do," she told him.

Arline was about to take the men through to her room when a knock came at the door. Fear rippled up and down her spine. She whispered to Frederick and Daniel to remain quiet as she stepped to the door and slowly opened it.

"Ye best hurry if ye wish to leave the castle alive." Gunther had returned. "The laird sent me to check on yer progress."

Arline stepped into the hallway and closed the door behind her.

The presence of the two men behind her gave her hope as well as energy to press forward.

"I will only need a few moments," she told Gunther. "Ye may assure yer laird I shall be gone from this place verra soon."

Gunther smiled down at her, but it was anything but pleasant. "I hope ye be no' afraid of the dark, lass." He took a step forward and reached out to touch her hair. "Pray tell. How do ye plan on gettin' back to Ireland?"

Arline did not like what she saw in his eyes. He looked at her as if she were a succulent leg of mutton or a slice of sweet cake. Her stomach recoiled.

"I ken the laird has no' warmed yer bed. Ye must be longin' fer a man's touch. I'd be willin' to see ye to Ireland if the price were right."

The thought of this young man with the crooked teeth and dirty hair touching her was revolting. For a moment, she considered inviting him into the room behind her and asking Frederick and Daniel to cut his throat on her behalf. Although the thought was a tempting one she could not risk it, no matter how appealing it might be.

"Go tell yer laird I'll be gone shortly. And do no' ever touch me again." Her words were clipped and to the point. Her tone warned him that she would not be fooled into thinking he would help her with anything. She spun and slipped back into the room, shutting the door and locking it behind her.

She took a few steps into the room and was about to whisper to Frederick and Daniel to follow her when once again, she was grabbed around her waist and a hand covered her mouth.

She was utterly confused as she was dragged away from the door and slammed hard against the wall. In the next moment, a hand covered her mouth and she could feel the cold sharp edge of a dirk as it pressed against her throat. Had Frederick and Daniel suddenly changed their minds? Did they think she had somehow betrayed them?

"Do no' utter a sound," a harsh and unfamiliar voice growled at her. "I have no' problems with cuttin' a woman's throat."

"Rowan!" Daniel and Frederick whispered harshly at their laird.

"Rowan! Do no' harm the lass!" Frederick said as he grabbed Rowan's arm. "She has been takin' care of Lily!"

Daniel stood on the other side of Rowan now and tried to grab his laird's arm. "Rowan, she is injured! Hold care with the lady."

Rowan paused for a moment. He had come into the room from the balcony at the same time the woman had come through the door. He hadn't known the situation or that Frederick and Daniel were within. He moved his dirk away from her throat and loosened the pressure on her chest.

"Where is me daughter?"

Arline began to wonder if she would ever survive this night, let alone make it safely out of this castle. Strange men seemed to be lurking everywhere. Her heart pounded against her sternum, blood rushed in her ears as the pain in her ribs increased with every heartbeat.

When she didn't answer immediately, Rowan pressed his arm against her chest again. "I will no' ask ye again," he warned. His voice was low and menacing.

"Rowan!" Frederick admonished him. "I tell ye the lass is injured! If ye do no' show her some kindness, I'll have to kill ye."

The seriousness of Frederick's tone caught Rowan by surprise. Either Frederick had said it only to gain his attention or he meant every word.

"Me laird," Arline managed to find her voice. "I mean ye no ill will. I have been takin' care of yer wee one. She is asleep in the next room. I swear, I have let no one harm her." Arline hoped he was not too overcome with anger to hear the sincerity in her shaky voice.

"Take me to her then," Rowan seethed. "But if this is some kind of trick," his words trailed off, heavy with warning.

Frederick stopped him again by placing a hand on his shoulder. "Rowan, the lass speaks the truth. We will explain it to ye later, but fer now, ye must have faith that no' all those within these castle walls mean us or Lily any harm."

Rowan shrugged Frederick's arm from his shoulder. He knew he was too angry to act rationally. His primary concern was getting to his daughter and leaving this place without any further obstacles or problems.

He let go of Arline and returned his dirk to the leather sheath on his belt. "Take me to her," he ordered.

Arline was not about to waste any more time or take the chance of angering this man further. She took a few steps along the wall with her arms outstretched to feel for the door. She found the iron latch and carefully opened the door and quickly led the men into her sleeping chamber.

Thankfully, Lily still slept, curled into a little ball. Arline stepped out of the way to allow the men to enter. She watched as they reluctantly stepped through the door and scanned the room.

The light from the low fire and the candle Arline kept lit during the night cast the room in a soft white light. When she turned her gaze from Lily to the three men in her room, she nearly collapsed from the shock.

"Daniel!" Arline whispered loudly. "Is it truly ye?"

Daniel and Frederick turned to look at her, but Rowan's gaze remained transfixed on his sleeping daughter.

Arline could see the recognition as it grew in Daniel's eyes. After a moment, a warm smile grew and he came to her. Taking her hand in his, he knelt on one knee. "Lady Arline," he said before giving a slight kiss to the back of her hand.

"Och! Stand ye foolish man!" Arline tried to return the smile, but it made her cheek hurt.

Daniel smiled and stood before her. "I canna believe me eyes, m'lady. Is it truly ye?"

Arline nodded her head and gave his hand a tight squeeze. It had been seven years since last she'd seen him. She had been married to Carlich Lindsay at that time.

It seemed a lifetime had passed. She had been a naïve young woman, married to a man three times her own age. Arline had been instrumental in helping to stop the unjust deaths of two men.

"Ye are a sight fer sore eyes, m'lady," Daniel said. "How on earth did ye come to be here?"

"'Tis a verra long story, Daniel. I'm afraid there be no time to tell it. We must get ye out of here and quickly."

Daniel nodded and turned back to Rowan and Frederick. "Rowan, do ye ken who this be?"

Rowan was too focused on his daughter. The relief he felt at seeing her was immeasurable. She was alive and she looked quite well, even in her sleep. He knelt beside the bed, one hand tenderly caressing the back of her head. He could not help it, but tears of relief and joy filled his eyes.

"Rowan," Daniel repeated. "I asked if ye ken the lady."

Rowan finally turned to look at the woman. Anger swelled when he saw the blood on her night dress, her cut lip and red, swollen face. Unruly auburn hair framed her face and cascaded down her shoulders. Guilt enveloped him for having treated her so harshly before.

He thought she looked vaguely familiar but he was having a difficult time placing her face with a memory.

Arline however, knew *him. Good lord!* she thought to herself. *'Tis him.*

She had never known his name but his face had been permanently burned into her memory. Theirs had been a very brief encounter in a dark hallway seven years past. He had come to thank her for helping save the lives of his friends, Angus McKenna and Duncan McEwan. Nothing else had happened other than the stranger thanking her for what she had done.

It had been his beautiful face and dark brown eyes that taken her breath away back then. Time had done nothing to lessen the affect he had on her.

He still wore his dark brown hair long, past his shoulders. His face, though seven years older now, was still beyond handsome. If anything, time had only added to his good looks. Arline felt her legs grow weak as his dark brown eyes stared up at her.

"This be Lady Arline Lindsay," Daniel explained.

"It be Lindsay no more, Daniel," Arline corrected him.

Daniel gave her a thoughtful nod. "Aye, I heard what Blackthorn said in the hallway, m'lady. But ye no longer be married to the whoreson, so I think we can call ye a Lindsay again."

Arline supposed it was better than being referred to as the former Lady Blackthorn and decided now was not the time to argue it further.

Daniel turned back to Rowan who continued to stare at Arline. "She be the one that helped Angus and Duncan back in '47," Daniel explained. "She was married to Carlich Lindsay. Do ye remember now?"

Rowan's eyes grew wide with surprise. He remembered. She had been younger then and not quite as skinny as she was now. She had saved Angus and Duncan from hanging. Angus was the chief of the clan that Rowan had fostered in, the Clan MacDougall. Duncan was married to Aishlinn, Angus' eldest daughter. To this day, he and Duncan remained as close as brothers.

Had it not been for Lady Arline Lindsay, Angus and Duncan would be dead. Rowan had told her seven years ago that he would be forever in her debt. Now, it seemed, he was beholden to her again.

His face suddenly turned ashen with embarrassment. "Me lady, please, fergive me," he began.

She stopped him with a wave of her hand. "Do no' worry it, me laird. There is no time now. Ye must get away from this place now!"

Rowan stood, looking perplexed and torn. Frederick stepped forward to speak. "Rowan, there be no time fer explanation. But we *must* take Lady Arline with us. Blackthorn has annulled their marriage and is casting her out this night. Without escort or even a horse."

Rowan blinked in disbelief. "Ye canna be serious," he exclaimed. Although he had known Garrick Blackthorn for many years and knew him to be a selfish bastard, this bit of news shook him.

"Aye, I am," Frederick said.

"Nay," Arline interjected, finally pulling her eyes away from Rowan. Had circumstances been different, she wouldn't have minded staring at him for, say, a few short decades. "I canna go with ye! Garrick is sending a man back at any moment, to escort me from the keep. If he returns and finds us both missin', we'll no' be able to survive this night!"

Arline made her way to the closet and pulled out the dress, cloak and stockings she had made for Lily. She had no time to think about the pain shooting down her side or her legs. Quickly, she made her way around the wall of men and to the bed. "I was plannin' on taking Willie--" she corrected herself quickly, "Lily, away this night. I found a way out just last night!" She explained her plan to the men as she carefully drew back the blankets and began to dress Lily.

"There is a secret corridor that leads to a set of hidden stairs. Ye'll take those to the bowels of the castle. There is a metal gate at the end. The water spills out into the stream. Ye can follow that east, to the forest."

Lily fussed and slowly opened her eyes as Arline pulled the dress over her head. "Will -- I mean, Lily, please lass, do no' make a sound. Yer da is here to take ye away," Arline explained as she wrapped the cloak around the child's shoulders.

With sleepy eyes, Lily began to look for her father. Before she could squeal with delight, Arline held a finger to her lips. "Wheesht, child. If ye make a sound, the mean man will hear. I need ye to promise no' to utter a word or a sound until yer da gives ye permission. If we're found out, Garrick will be verra, *verra* angry."

Tears welled in Lily's eyes as she listened carefully to Arline. "I do no' want him to hurt ye again," Lily whispered, looking quite fearful.

"Wheesht, sweeting!" Arline told her, forcing a smile. She tied the cloak and gave Lily a kiss on her forehead. "There is no time to waste, lass. Ye must go with yer da, now."

Lily held out her arms and Rowan lifted her to his chest. He hugged her, kissing the top of her head. "Och, child, how I've missed ye!"

"I missed ye too, da! The mean man took me. But Lady Arline took care of me."

"I ken, Lily. I be ferever in Lady Arline's debt. Now, no more talking. We have to hurry."

Arline made her way around the men again and went to the small closet. She pushed the trunk away and lifted the tapestry. "In here," she directed the group. "Ye will turn right here. Ye will turn left in about twenty-five paces, then left again when ye come to the T. Not long after ye will find a door on the right. There is a staircase that winds all the way down. Once ye reach the bottom, ye'll be in water to yer ankles. Turn right and follow the water until ye reach the gate. 'Tisn't locked, but it is old and squeaks a bit. Remember, it leads to the stream that runs through the forest to the east."

She pushed Frederick through first and then Daniel. Rowan paused briefly. "Me lady, what of ye?"

"Do no' worry over me! Ye must get Lily away from this place and quickly. Hurry, before they come fer me."

She gave Lily a kiss on her cheek and pulled the hood up. "Please, child, remember to be quiet, no matter what happens, aye?"

Lily looked positively forlorn. "Yer no' comin' with us?" she asked.

"Nay, I canna come with ye, babe. But we'll see each other some-day." Arline felt her heart shattering like fragile glass slammed against an anvil. She would miss the precocious and sweet babe.

"But," Lily began to protest. Arline held her finger to her lips once again.

"Wheesht, sweeting. I shall write to ye soon, I promise. Now, be a good lass and listen to yer da!" She turned her eyes to Rowan's. "Please, hurry me laird," she told him as she pressed down on his shoulders. Rowan bent to his knees and handed Lily through the opening.

Turning back one last time, he said, "If ye ever need anything, me lady, anything at all, ye need only ask it."

And with that, he turned, crawled through the opening and disap-peared into blackness.

SIX

Originally, Rowan and his men had planned to escape with Lily by the same route as they entered. But with most of the castle unexpectedly awake, they decided not to take the risk and use the means Arline had given them. After losing themselves within the walls more than once, they began to question their choice.

But once they found the correct staircase and made their way to the dark recesses of the castle, it took very little time to make their way out and into the frigid stream. The water was quite cold, stinging their feet and ankles.

It had been an unexpected change of plans. Thankfully, Rowan had allies waiting on all sides of Blackthorn lands. They waited until they were well within the forest before climbing out of the icy water.

Rowan was quite proud of his daughter for she had remained quiet throughout the entire ordeal. Even when he had stumbled on slippery rocks and fell to his knees. Lily had gasped when the cold water hit her feet and legs, but she did not cry out. Instead, she tightened her hold around his neck and buried her face against him.

By the time they met with Caelen McDunnah and his men, Lily's teeth were chattering and she was trembling from head to toe. Rowan removed her wet stockings, overdress and cloak before handing her up to Caelen.

Caelen was not accustomed to small children, but he was not completely inept. He pulled a fur from the pack of his saddle and wrapped the trembling child in it and pulled her into his chest.

"Och!" Caelen whispered to Lily. "We'll have ye warm soon enough, lassie."

"Caelen," Rowan began. "I leave me daughter in yer care. We'll no' be far behind. Our men are expecting us on the other side of the keep. We shall retrieve our horses and meet you at dawn, at the forests west of *Tulach Cultraidh.*

Lily chose that moment to find her voice. "Nay, da! I want ye!" she exclaimed, trying to free herself from Caelen's grip.

Rowan shushed her with a caress on her cheek. "Lily, this be me verra good friend, Caelen. He'll no' let anythin' happen to ye, I promise."

While he could not see his daughter's face clearly, he could hear the tears in her voice. "Are ye goin' to get Lady Arline?"

Rowan swallowed down the guilt he felt over leaving Arline behind. At the time, he felt he had no choice in the matter. If they had come for her and discovered both she and Lily missing then all hell would have broken loose. Chances were good that he would either be heading to Blackthorn's dungeons or dead.

"Nay, lass," he told her. "Lady Arline will be fine though."

"But da, she's me angel! Just like I'm yer angel."

Rowan knew exactly what his daughter meant. He had told her time and time again that God had given her to him to watch over him after Kate's death. Lily apparently thought the same of Lady Arline.

"Da, ye must help her! If the mean man finds her, he'll hurt her again. He doesna like her, but I do. She would no' let them hit me again, da. Ye must get her!" Her words tumbled out, making it even more difficult for Rowan to understand her. She was upset, crying, and begging for him to help *her* angel, Lady Arline.

His guilt blended with his anger over the harsh treatment of both the lady and his daughter. There was no time now to question her.

The hour was growing late and every moment they stayed here arguing, the greater their risk of being caught.

Caelen thankfully interjected. "Little one, if ye are quiet and good, I will come back fer yer lady meself."

Rowan could have hugged him.

"Ye promise?" Lily asked.

"I do so promise," Caelen said. He gave her no time to question him further. He pulled rein and tapped the flanks of his horse, quietly leading his men away from Rowan.

B efore Garrick entered the chapel to exchange vows with the woman he loved, his beautiful Ona, he pulled Gunther aside. They spoke in hushed tones. To the untrained eye it would have appeared nothing more than a harmless conversation between a laird and one of his men. The unsuspecting observer might believe the laird was speaking about his soon-to-be bride, or the upcoming winter.

But the shadow man knew better.

Years of training had taught him that things are not always what they appear to be.

And spending the past three years inside Blackthorn Keep, earning his way up through Blackthorn's army, had taught him much. Garrick Blackthorn was cunning and devious. He was far more intelligent than he led others to believe. And he had a mean streak as long as the River Tay.

The shadow man hid in plain sight. No one would suspect him to be anything other than a devoted follower of Garrick Blackthorn. He had made sure of that, even going so far as to show a strong dislike of the laird's wife; behavior that was strongly encouraged by the laird himself.

Garrick's attitude and his mistreatment of Lady Arline sickened the shadow man. There were many times when he had to stop himself from running a sword through Garrick's gut. Far too much was at stake to allow his honor and his vow to protect the innocent, to get in the way of the mission at hand.

The shadow man had felt confident that Lady Arline would be safely away from Blackthorn Keep before the rest of his mission was put in place. But Garrick had surprised him by taking Rowan Graham's daughter. And Lady Arline's actions the night they had returned with the child had changed everything.

He should have known that Lady Arline would not stand by and allow an innocent child to suffer. He should not have expected anything less from her. Time and again the woman had proven she possessed a sense of honor as strong as his own.

Were circumstances different, had he not made a pledge and taken a vow ten years ago, he would have been sorely tempted to take Lady Arline as a wife.

As far as he was concerned, Garrick Blackthorn was nothing more than a spoiled brat in a man's body. The fool did not know what a good woman he had in Lady Arline.

He stood not far from Garrick now. Though he could not hear the conversation he *could* read the man's lips. A wave of anger scraped across his skin when he saw Garrick's intent.

If he did not move now, Lady Arline would not leave the keep alive.

B eing cast out of the castle in the middle of the night, without escort or even the use of a horse, was not the most ideal situation. However, Arline was grateful that she now had the freedom she had been longing for this past year.

As soon as Lily and her rescuers were in the hidden corridor, Arline scooted the trunk back against the wall and began packing. There was no sense in trying to pack everything for she had no means of transporting it. Once she settled somewhere, she could send for the things she was leaving behind. Granted, her worldly possession only filled two trunks, but still, they were hers.

Gunther's words kept jumping to the forefront of her thoughts. If she spent too much time thinking of highwaymen or other men of that ilk, she would not be able to focus on the tasks at hand.

She grabbed a satchel and stuffed it with extra woolens, a clean chemise and a spare dress. It would hold little else.

Each time she bent to retrieve something from her trunk, it was a new adventure in pain. As she packed, she cursed Garrick Blackthorn to the devil and wished him a very painful and agonizing death. Arline knew it wasn't very Christian-like, but she didn't care. The man did not deserve her respect let alone any wishes of good fortune or health.

She took a pillow and tucked it under the blankets to make it appear that Lily was asleep. She could only pray that if someone entered the room, they would think the child was still abed. Arline also prayed that they would not look for Lily until long after dawn.

Grabbing a cloth she took care in scrubbing the dried blood from her chin. The cold water felt good against her swollen and throbbing cheek. The pain when she raised her arms to lift off her bloody nightdress nearly sent her to her knees. She swallowed hard and took deep breaths in hopes of quelling the overwhelming sense of nausea.

She struggled, but managed to don a clean chemise, heavy skirt and over dress. She had just slipped on her boots when her heart leapt to her throat as the door to her room opened suddenly and without warning.

Archie quickly closed the door behind him and strode across the room. "Me lady," he said with some urgency.

Arline shot to her feet, her fingers shaking, quite fearful.

"We've no' much time."

Arline understood all too well that her life hung precariously by a very thin thread. Archie didn't need to explain that to her.

"Me lady, I need ye to listen verra carefully," Archie said as he grabbed the cloak from the end of her bed. "I've no' much time to explain, but ye have to trust me that I do mean to help ye."

Arline stood quietly, curious as to what Archie meant *and* why he felt this sudden urge to help her. Instinct warned her not to trust this man. She took the cloak from him and wrapped it around her shoulders.

"When ye leave the gates of the keep, I need ye to take the road east. About a mile down, ye'll come to a fork in the road. I need ye to go right, me lady. I shall meet ye there before the sun rises."

She could not resist the urge to ask him why he was helping.

"Me lady, there be no time to explain it, but I do need ye to trust me. I mean ye no harm."

Arline had serious doubts as to his sincerity. Not once in the year she had been here had Archie acted in any type of friendly manner. If anything, he had been completely indifferent.

Archie grabbed her satchel and ushered her to the door. "Pray tell, why should I trust ye?" she asked indignantly.

He stopped and turned to look at her. The candlelight flickered in his hazel eyes as he appeared to do battle with some inner dilemma.

"Do ye have Carlich's box with ye?" he asked quietly.

Arline's eyes grew wide, stunned by his question. Her mind raced as she tried to figure out how he knew of Carlich or his box. She could think of only one other person who might know that she had kept that box all of these years.

"Do ye, me lady?" His voice held an urgent tone to it.

Arline nodded her head as a thousand questions ran through her mind. The box was tucked safely into the pocket of her dress. In it, a letter from Robert Stewart, a letter she would not use unless her life was in danger from forces other than Garrick Blackthorn. That letter could not protect her from Garrick, but it might, in the future, be a very useful tool.

Archie studied her for a moment before giving a quick nod. "Good," he said, sounding quite relieved as he guided her out of the room. Her voice was lost as he led her down the quiet corridors, torch lit stairs, and out of the keep.

How could he know? Who is this man and why does he wish to help me? She had no answers. Very few people knew about Carlich's box. She searched her memory hoping to find Archie's face somewhere among the men who had been at Stirling Castle all those many years ago. Had he been there? Had he been one of the witnesses?

It had been so long ago that, try as she might, she could not place his face among those in the crowd. Arline doubted she would recognize anyone, save for the brave MacDougall men who had helped her and Robert Stewart.

Mutely, she decided to trust Archie, at least for now. She allowed him to escort her from her room, down the stairs and out of the keep.

She saw no one, save for the men who stood guard along the walk wall, as Archie took her to the gates. She shivered, not so much from the crisp night air, but from the fear that had wrapped itself around her.

"I shall meet ye before dawn, I swear it. I'll have the child with me."

Panic welled. Archie did not know yet that Lily was long gone and she did not think she could tell him. She would feign ignorance for now, allowing Rowan and his men the time they needed to get as far away from Blackthorn Keep as they could.

There was no moon, but the courtyard was bright enough, lit from the dozens of torches flickering in the late night breeze. Archie whistled twice and a moment later, the heavy wooden gate began to open.

"Remember, me lady," Archie whispered into her ear. "the men in the shadows are always there fer ye."

There was no way for her to hide the tremendous shock she felt. The slightest bit of wind would have knocked her over. Archie gave her arm a reassuring squeeze. "Wheesht, me lady," he whispered. "I'll meet ye in the woods before the sun rises."

And with that, he gently pushed her through the gates, turned and walked away. There was no time to explain that Lily was already safely away from the keep and no time to ask him any questions. Was he one of the men, the silent and invisible protectors that Robert Stewart had promised so long ago would always be there, watching over her? Or, did he simply know of their existence? She had not thought of the Stewart or his silent army in many years. Why hadn't Archie made his presence known sooner? She supposed there had been no need until this night.

F or a year now, she had dreamt about the day she would leave Blackthorn Castle. But traipsing down a rutted dirt road in the middle of the night was not how she had imagined leaving. Cast out or not, she was finally *free*. Arline knew she had to focus on that fact and that fact alone, otherwise she would not make it to the fork in the road before turning into a heap of babbling and fear-filled insanity.

Although the night air was cold and damp, tiny beads of sweat covered her brow, the back of her neck and the palms of her hands. It was the combination of tripping in the deep ruts and fear that made her heart pound so ferociously and her skin feel so clammy. Still, she pushed on. She had to. Freedom lay at the fork in road.

The men in the shadows are always there fer ye. She ran Archie's words over and over in her mind as she trudged onward. Could he truly be one of the shadow men?

It had been years since she had thought of the men in the shadows or of Robert Stewart, the great Steward of Scotland. She had supposed Robert Stewart had forgotten all about her and his promise of protection should she need it. Honestly, she could not remember the last time she had looked into the darkness and wondered if one of Robert Stewart's men were there watching over her.

Why now? Why after all these years had one suddenly unveiled himself to her? She had nearly been killed seven years ago when she had helped prove the innocence of two men, men she had never met. She could not in good conscience allow the two men to hang for crimes she *knew* they had not committed. She had helped because Carlich had asked her and because she knew she could not have lived with herself if she didn't.

And now here she was seven years later, walking down a road in the pitch black of night, cast out, alone, cold and terrified. Arline wondered if Garrick would have acted differently had she not begged and pleaded to stay to take care of Lily. Would he have given her an escort back to Ireland? She supposed it did not matter for she could not change what had happened.

She stumbled again for the fourth time and fell forward into a large puddle of mud. It soaked through her skirt and chemise. Cursing Garrick to the bowels of hell as she pulled herself to her feet, she wiped mud from her hands as best she could on her cloak. She imagined she'd be covered head to toe in mud before she reached the fork in the road.

Taking a deep breath, she grabbed her satchel and moved forward.

So focused on not tripping and falling again, Lady Arline did not hear the men on horseback approaching until they were but a few feet away from her.

She spun around in time to see three men on three large horses heading right for her. Caught unaware and completely by surprise, she had very little time to react. She dropped her satchel, picked up her skirts and ran as fast as she could, heading toward the forest.

She was at the edge, just steps away from jumping into the dense line of trees when one of the men jumped from his horse and gave a quick pursuit. Before she could run and hide in the forest, he had an arm wrapped about her waist and had lifted her off her feet.

Surprised and terrified, Arline let out a scream as she kicked her feet, struggling to get out of the man's tight hold. He tightened his grip around her waist and laughed at her.

"Settle down ye wench!" a familiar voice spoke in her ear before he clamped his hand over her mouth. He pulled her deeper into the woods before calling out to his partners.

"I have her, lads!" he shouted and laughed again, dragging her further away from the road.

Arline knew that voice. Gunther.

She knew his intent.

Arline continued to kick and pound at his arms with her fists. Her actions seemed to urge him on more than they did to convince him to let her go. Her heart pounded against her breastbone and blood rushed in her ears.

Gunther laughed in her ear again. "Ye be a fighter, aye? I like that in a woman," he told her. "But I canna figure out why ye be fightin'. Ye've no' had a man betwixt yer legs the whole time ye were married to me laird. One would think ye'd be ready fer it."

The thought of Gunther having his way with her was revolting. Had he not had a hand over her mouth, he would have received an earful. *Over me dead body!* She screamed in her mind.

He would have to kill her first.

R owan saw the men approaching Lady Arline before she did. His first thought was to call out to her, to not only warn her but to draw the men away from her. In the end, the bastards had moved so quickly there was no time to do either.

They had retrieved their horses and were making their way silently along the edge of the forest when they first caught a glimpse of Lady Arline walking -- stumbling was more like it -- in the same direction they were heading. Rowan and his men were about to make their presence known when they heard the pounding of hoof beats heading their way.

Rowan jumped from his horse, followed quickly by Daniel and Frederick. Dirks were drawn as they silently, yet quickly, made their way toward Lady Arline and the men who surrounded her.

I n the span of a heartbeat, Arline had decided she hadn't gone through all she had gone through in her life only to end up raped and dying in the cold dirt of a forest floor. She'd fight these men tooth and nail before she would allow them to do her any harm.

She went limp in Gunther's arms, pretending she had fainted. She slumped toward the ground. Gunther laughed as he bent slightly at the waist, adjusted his grip around her and started to haul her back up. It was just what Arline needed.

As soon as he bent, she planted her feet firmly on the ground and lunged backward. The back of her skull landed hard against Gunther's lips and nose, catching him completely off guard. He groaned and let loose his grip enough that Arline could fall away.

She landed on her hands and knees. She took one fast breath, pushed herself up and ran.

Gunther was momentarily dazed. He covered his face with his hand and felt the blood oozing from his nose. His nose throbbed painfully, his eyes watered, making it quite difficult for them to focus. He cursed out loud at the darkness, scanning the woods for a glimpse of her.

A murderous rage coursed over him as he let out a low, deep growl. He'd find her and kill her if it was the last thing he did.

It was too dark to see exactly where she was going. Her heart pounded and her chest heaved as she raced through the trees. She could hear Gunther yelling and cursing as he crashed through the brush. Fear of dying kept her moving forward no matter how badly her ribs screamed in protest.

Running as fast as the uneven terrain would allow, with her arms out before her, she pushed through low lying branches. Soon, the brush and trees were so thick she could barely make her way through them. She veered to her right, trying to find her way through the darkness, hoping for an opening that would allow her to run faster.

Gunther continued to yell and holler, making threats to cut her throat once he found her. She did not doubt that he would make good on his threats. His voice echoed off the trees and made it difficult for her to tell exactly where he was. One moment he sounded as if her were just steps away and in the next, he sounded as if he were on the other side of the forest. It rattled her nerves not knowing where he was.

Soon she was covered in sweat and the pain in her ribs intensified. Still, she ran and stumbled and fought her way through the thick brambles and bushes. Arline came upon some very thick, dense bushes. Mayhap she could crawl inside and hide until dawn. Fully believing Archie would wait for her at the fork in the road, she decided hiding made the most sense. Mayhap Gunther would give up his pursuit of her in the interim.

On her hands and knees, she began to make her way through the bushes. Branches pulled at her skirts and cloak as if they too were trying to capture her. A thick branch scratched along her forehead as she fought her way through.

Sweat dripped into her eyes and stung at the cut along her forehead. She wiped her face on her shoulder, fighting back tears of frustration and fear. She wanted only to get far enough into the thicket that she could hide and wait out Gunther's search. *Just a little further,* she tried to encourage her fearful heart. *Just a little further and ye can rest.*

Just a little further ended up being a dreadful mistake.

R owan had seen what Arline had done to Gunther's nose. He couldn't help but feeling a bit of pride toward the woman. She was certainly proving to be a woman of strength and heart. He could admire that.

He and his men had been just a few feet away when Arline rammed the fool's head with her own. Rowan sent his men off to take care of Gunther and his friends while he went in search of Arline.

Several times he stopped in order to listen. The rustle of leaves and skirts were barely discernible, but discernible nonetheless. He had jumped the row of bushes that Arline was crawling through. The bushes stood along a gulley. At its bottom lay the stream that wound its way through the forest.

He stopped once to listen and could hear her panting and cursing under her breath as she made her way through the bramble. If she were not careful, Gunther would hear her. Worse yet, she'd tumble into the gulley and likely break her neck before she rolled down into the stream.

He crouched low and waited for her to finish making her way through the bushes and prayed for her to move more quietly.

A rline felt the rush of cool night air hit her skin, realizing a moment too late that she had climbed out of the bushes. Her intent had been to make her way to the middle and hide. She cursed under her breath and was about to turn around and go back when a hand clamped over her mouth and a large arm wound its way around her waist. Her back landed against the hard wall of a man's torso.

In the next moment, she felt her body being pulled to the ground. *Mother Mary, no!* Her mind shouted. She struggled against his hold and began to kick her legs.

"Wheesht, lass!" A voice whispered in her ear. "'Tis me, Rowan, Lily's da! I beg ye to be still!"

Relief washed over her. She ceased to struggle but her heart continued to pound. It was quite difficult to breathe with his hand over her mouth and the pain shooting in her ribs.

As soon as Rowan felt her relax a bit, he slowly removed his hand from her mouth. In a very low whisper he warned her that Gunther was not far. "Gunther," he whispered against her ear, "be close."

Arline took slow deep breaths and prayed no one could hear them. Moments later, she heard a great rustling of leaves. Gunther. He was making no attempts to be quiet. "I ken ye be here ye whore!" he shouted. "Ye can run, but ye can no' hide! When I find ye, I'm going to strip ye naked and have my way with ye!"

Had Rowan not been holding her she would have run. But he was there and she knew, instinctively or hopefully, that he would not let anyone, least of all Gunther, bring her harm.

Gunther was not far. Arline could hear him just on the other side of the bush row. She thought she heard him give pause, and she could imagine him looking about, listening.

"Ye ken ye want it as bad as me, ye wench! Och! I ken ye canna wait to feel me crawl betwixt yer thighs and--"

His words were suddenly cut short. A moment later, Arline heard a distinct thud reminiscent of something or some*one* falling to the ground. Confusion settled over her before being replaced with fear. Had he somehow seen her and Rowan lying on the ground? Was he preparing to climb through or over the row of bushes?

A moment or two passed as she strained her ears to listen. All she could hear over her racing heart was the sound of tree frogs and crickets. Rowan kept a gentle yet protective grasp around Arline as he imitated the tree frogs.

Arline was afraid to move, to breathe, to make a sound. They lay there on the cold, damp forest floor, waiting, but for what, she was not certain. As the moments passed, Arline began to wonder if Rowan hadn't taken a hit to his noggin. She prayed her assumption was incorrect as he continued his conversation with the tree frogs.

She was about to inquire if he was well when two large men approached. It was all she could do to remain calm for she could not make out their faces.

"We got them, Rowan," Daniel said in a hushed tone.

"The whoresons be dead," Frederick added.

Arline could feel the tension leave Rowan's body at the same time it left her own. Rowan sighed, relieved, before he loosened his hold on her waist. "Thank God," Rowan said as he pushed himself to his feet. He extended a hand to Arline and helped her to her own. "How fare ye lass?" he asked, sounding quite concerned for her.

Arline wasn't sure how to answer that question. *How am I? I've been beaten, kicked, thrown out of me home, chased down the road and then through the forest by three despicable men. Me ribs ache, me legs hurt, I've got bruises on top of bruises and scratches. I'm covered with mud, sweat, tears and blood. How the bloody hell do ye think I am?*

Instead of voicing her honest answer, she lied. "I'm well, thank ye." 'Twould do no good to tell the truth, for there was nothing to be done about it.

She felt Rowan's hand reach out and take a gentle hold of her arm. "We must hurry, lass. There may be more men about."

Arline stood still, refusing to follow. "Hurry? To where?" She had to get to the fork in the road. She had to get to Archie.

"With us, of course," Rowan said. "We canna leave ye here alone."

While she could certainly appreciate the fact that he had no desire to leave her alone, in the middle of heaven only knew where, she was torn. Seven years ago, she had been sworn to secrecy. On her life and her honor, she had sworn never to mention the men in the shadows. It was vitally important that those men's existence remain undisclosed.

How on earth could she explain it to Rowan without divulging the truth of the matter?

"Lass, we *must* go, now," Rowan urged her to follow.

Blindly, numbly she allowed him to lead her away. Perhaps a partial truth would work. "Me laird," she whispered to him as he led the way through the darkness. "If ye could take me east, to where the fork begins, I would be most appreciative."

Rowan paused, but only for the briefest moment. "Nay, we'll no' abandon ye, lass. Ye can go with us, to Castle *Áit na Síochána*," Rowan explained. His pride was wounded. How could she think he'd just leave her on the road, especially after what had just happened? Did she think him no better than the Blackthorn men?

"Castle *Áit na Síochána*?" Arline murmured. "Ye mean to take me to yer home?" This was not going as planned. Of course, nothing this night had gone as she had planned, why should getting to the fork in the road be any different?

"Aye, we do."

"But I only need to get to the end of the road, me laird. Ye needn't take me to yer home."

Rowan stopped and turned to look at her. "I'll no leave ye alone, lass. I offer ye our protection. Ye kept me daughter safe and well cared for." For that alone, he owed her more than he could ever repay. "Now, do no' worry it. We'll be safe on Graham lands in a few days. We can make plans fer ye then."

She had to think of something and fast. "But there is no need fer that, me laird," Arline told him as he began leading her away again.

"No need?" Rowan said, sounding perplexed. "Have ye somewhere else to go this night? Do ye have someone else to take ye home?"

Arline swallowed hard. "Well, actually, I do me laird," she told him.

"Ye do?" Rowan asked, sounding as though he did not believe her. "And who, pray tell, is that?"

Arline cleared her throat and pushed her shoulders back. "One of Blackthorn's men has offered to help me." Until she said it aloud, she hadn't realized just how absurd it sounded.

Rowan was silent for a short time. "Is he yer lover?"

Arline was suddenly quite thankful for the darkness for in it, he could not see her burn red from head to toe. She was stunned by his frankness. "Nay!" she said, astonished. "I have no lover." How dare he accuse her of such a thing.

"Then why do ye trust him?"

There was no way to answer that honestly. She stammered, searching for the right words. "He seems to be an honest man. He stopped Garrick from killin' me this night."

"So, this man, he's been yer protector this past year?" Rowan asked. "He's defended ye against yer husband?"

Well, not exactly, but she couldn't admit that to Rowan. Until tonight, she had believed she was completely alone, without a soul to call friend. But tonight, for whatever reason, Archie had finally stepped forward. Though he hadn't actually admitted to being one of the shadow men, she had to assume he was, at the very least, one of their allies.

Rowan waited for her to answer. Even in the darkness he could tell that she was mulling over an appropriate answer. He had no time to spend arguing. She may not have been lying outright, but something told him that she was holding back. Mayhap she lied simply because she did not trust him any more than she trusted any other man.

"Lass, I give ye me word that I and me men will protect ye. I'll no' let anyone harm ye. I swear it."

Arline soon realized he was not going to give in. His honor would prevent him from leaving her here alone. She decided it would make more sense to trust Rowan and his men. Though she had not seen Daniel and Frederick in many years, she did know them to be men of high moral character and honor. She could not say the same for Archie.

"We must hurry lass. Someone might soon realize that three of their men are missin', and if that be the case, then these woods will be filled with Blackthorn men."

Fear jumped into her belly and danced around. She hadn't thought of that. It had been difficult enough to hide from Gunther. Had

Rowan not been there to help...she found the thought as terrifying as she did repulsive.

Aye, Rowan could very well take her to the spot that she and Archie had agreed upon earlier. But what if he could not get to her in time? What if the woods were suddenly filled with men that *did* wish her harm?

"Verra well, me laird," she whispered. "I thank ye kindly fer yer offer."

Rowan felt some measure of satisfaction in her answer. He believed he'd been correct that she was simply afraid of him and his men. And who could blame her?

"Good, now, mind yer step," he said as he took her hand and began to lead her away. "Our horses be no' far from here."

Arline remained silent and followed close behind Rowan. If Archie were in fact one of the shadow men, it would not take long for him to find her. A new sense of dread settled in her stomach. Much had happened these many years. There was nothing to say that the shadow men still worked to protect her or Scotland, as had been their sworn duty those many years ago. She didn't even have proof that the shadow men still existed.

The further she walked away from the Blackthorn Keep and Archie, the better she felt about her decision. There was just something about Archie that did not sit well in her stomach, something she could not explain. Her instincts did not warn her against following Rowan, Daniel or Frederick. Nay, instead, she felt an overwhelming sense of peace. She would follow that peace and see where it led her.

Archie cursed under his breath, doing his best not to panic. Garrick had refused to let Archie out of his sight for a good hour after he and Ona had exchanged their vows. He could only surmise Garrick had done it because he was still angry that Archie had come to Lady Arline's aid earlier, had kept him from killing her.

As soon as Garrick left to enjoy what remained of his wedding night, Archie slipped away. His plan was simple: he would hide the child in one of Arline's trunks. He would lie to anyone who asked, telling them the trunk was filled with gifts for a nonexistent lass who lived nearby.

Archie had endeared himself to most of Blackthorn's men. None would question him. He would be able to leave, with the child, and as promised, he would meet Lady Arline before dawn.

He hadn't arrived in time.

The child was gone. The pillow was the only clue left that someone had taken her. But whom? He knew it hadn't been Lady Arline, for the only thing she had on her person when he escorted her out of the keep was her satchel. The child was far too big to fit inside that.

Had Garrick ordered someone to take her? Nay, he doubted that. None of Garrick's men would have tucked a pillow under the blankets. If not them, then who?

He couldn't very well ask about the castle. To raise the alarm now would be the same as issuing a death warrant for Lady Arline. Garrick would call all his men to arms to search for her. There would be no way to protect her from all of Garrick's men.

So he left the keep on horseback not long after discovering the child was missing. He had to get to Lady Arline. Her safety was his main priority.

Soon afterward he had come upon three rider-less horses that had been left along the side of the road. Bloody hell! Those were Blackthorn horses, no doubt left by Gunther and whoever else the man had enticed to help him carry out Garrick's orders.

Anger rose as he left his own horse beside the road and entered the forest. Mayhap they hadn't killed the lady yet. Either way, he'd kill any and all who had touched her.

It was the sound of tree frogs speaking to each other that first drew his attention. Anyone else may have thought nothing of the sounds the forest made at night, but Archie could recognize that those weren't real tree frogs talking to one another.

Carefully, he made his way through the dense woods, listening, praying, hoping he was not too late. Not far from the road, he found one man dead. A quick inspection told him it was one of Blackthorn's men. Had Lady Arline managed to kill him? The man's throat was sliced so deeply it nearly decapitated him. Nay, Archie doubted Lady Arline had the strength to do such a thing. But who?

He trekked further into the woods, listening to the tree frogs. They seemed to be coming from the East. Silently, he headed in that direction, doing his best not to give away his own position. Who knew who else might be in the woods?

Very soon, he came upon another dead body, slumped against a tree. Another of Garrick's men, stabbed through the gut and his throat cut. It made the hairs on the back of Archie's head stand at full attention. Whoever else was in these woods knew how to kill a man.

He kept walking, searching, looking for any sign of Lady Arline. Damn, what he wouldn't give for a bit of moonlight! Sweat trickled down his back as he made his way along, ducking under low lying branches and going around large old trees.

Soon, he came upon Gunther. A very dead Gunther, laying on the ground near a row of thick bramble bushes. Like the others, his throat had been cut. Blood from the gaping wound was still wet. He'd not been dead long. 'Twas then that he heard the voices.

Creeping closer, he heard Lady Arline whispering. She did not sound as though she were distressed. He strained his ears to listen and thought he recognized the man's voice. When he heard the man speak of Castle *Áit na Síochána*, Archie breathed a sigh of relief. Castle *Áit na Síochána* belonged to Rowan Graham. It had to have been Rowan who took the child.

Archie smiled into the darkness, admiring Rowan's ability to not only get into the Blackthorn Keep undetected, but he had also managed to get his daughter out. Rowan would have made a fine shadow man, Archie thought. He would have done the brethren quite proud.

He left them then, as quietly as he had arrived. Lady Arline would be in very good hands amongst the Grahams. Out of harm's way, safe, protected. It would allow Archie time to continue his mission.

SEVEN

T hey rode like the devil was chasing them. And there was a good possibility he was. Once Garrick learned that Lily was missing or the dead bodies of his men were discovered, all hell would undoubtedly break loose. Arline had no desire to be anywhere near Garrick or his men when that happened.

The pain in her ribs was beginning to subside. She no longer wished to die in order to be free from it. Nay, it had lessened to a more tolerable aching blended with a touch of nausea. However, the nausea intensified each time Rowan urged their steed to leap over a small ditch or large felled tree.

Riding across the countryside brought back a flood of memories of her time with the Clan MacDougall. Daniel had been among the men to help take Arline to Stirling Castle. This ride was much like the one she had experienced seven years ago. Jumping over felled trees, racing through icy cold streams, through valleys, and narrow tracks that wound their way through mountains.

The only difference this time was that she was in a good deal of pain and did not have her own horse. Nay, she rode perched in front of Rowan.

Rowan. The man whose image had been burned into her mind for all these many years. The man who had invaded her dreams far too many times to count, more than she cared to admit.

His arms were just as strong and warm as she had dreamt they would be. His chest, just as hard and massive as she had envisioned. And he was just as beautiful as she had remembered, mayhap even more so.

Suppressing the desire to rest her head against his chest had been futile. Before dawn broke across the horizon, she had succumbed to the exhaustion and pain. It was not a blissful, comfortable sleep she experienced. She dozed off and on, jolted back to her senses every time they leapt across an obstacle.

Why on earth did they have to jump like this? Why could they not simply trot across the land, taking their time to gently glide over the hills or through the streams? The answer was quite simple. Garrick. They could not slow down, no matter how badly she hurt. The risk of Garrick catching up to them was far too great.

Arline's time with Garrick Blackthorn left no doubt that he *would* seek retribution for Rowan taking back his daughter and for the men left dead on the forest floor. It wasn't a matter of honor with Garrick, it was arrogance and his warped sense of justice. He felt the rest of the world should all bow in his presence and worship the ground upon which he trod.

The desire to live far outweighed the desire to slow their pace. There would be time to sleep later.

The morning sun had just begun to rise when the group made their way to yet another winding, twisting road that made its way around a small mountain.

When Rowan abruptly slowed their pace to a slow walk, Arline made the mistake of opening her eyes. They were walking along a cliff with barely enough room for a man to walk, let alone these large horses! It was dizzying, nauseating to look down.

Lord almighty, she was terrified of heights! She kept her face buried in Rowan's chest with her eyes closed tightly. She clutched his tunic with both hands and prayed they would not fall down the cliff.

She wasn't ready to die just yet. Mayhap in forty or fifty years, but not today, and not like this.

Rowan chuckled into her hair. "What be the matter, lass?" he asked.

She shook her head against his chest. She was very close to throwing up. To do so would startle the horse, something she wished to avoid at all costs. The thought of the horse startling and the subsequent plummet to her death did nothing to help settle her stomach.

Rowan chuckled again. Apparently, he took some amusement with her distress. If she were not so terrified at the moment, she could have hit him. Why do men laugh at a woman's fear? She certainly would not laugh at him were the roles reversed.

He took note of her trembling and felt guilty for laughing. He cleared his throat and did his best to apologize. "Sorry, lass. I did no' mean to upset ye. We'll be off the cliff verra soon."

She didn't necessarily like his choice of words and worried he may have brought them bad luck by wording it thusly. She clutched his tunic tighter and continued to pray.

"Wheesht, lass," Rowan whispered. "All will be well. I've ridden this road many a time."

Arline took some measure of encouragement with that fact. "How many times?"

"Och! Dozens and dozens," he told her. "And I've only fallen off twice."

In hindsight it was mayhap *not* the best time or place to jest. Arline bolted upright and sucked in a huge breath of air. Her eyes were wide with fear when she looked into his. "Let me down," she demanded. She would rather walk on foot the rest of the way.

Whether it was the look of shock on her face or the death-like grip she held on his tunic, he was uncertain, but either way, he could not resist the urge to laugh.

Anger flashed through those brilliant green eyes of hers. "Ye are an ass!" she told him.

He laughed again.

"A big, ignorant ass!"

His shoulders began to shake as he tried to hold back his laughter.

"A big, ugly, stupid, ignorant ass!"

Arline could hear Frederick and Daniel laughing along with Rowan. "All of ye are big ugly asses!"

The roar of laughter broke through the quiet morning and bounced off the mountainside. It echoed and bounced back, hitting Arline's ears. It sounded like dozens of men laughing and all of them at her.

She hadn't been this angry, well, since last night, first when Garrick had assaulted her and then when Gunther had tried. Were *all* men this unkind? This terribly stupid? This heartless?

She could take no more. A growl started low in her belly as she wound her fist into a tight ball. Before she realized it, she was slamming that fist into Rowan's shoulder. It did nothing but make him laugh even more.

"I hate ye, Rowan Graham!" she seethed.

Rowan could not remember the last time he laughed so heartily. In truth, he hadn't meant to upset her so, but he could not help himself. He found her anger, her bluntness, quite adorable.

"Ye do?" he teased.

"Aye, I do! To laugh at a woman's distress and discomfort," she scolded, "'tis an evil, mean thing to do!"

"I be terribly sorry, me lady," Rowan chuckled. "Ye be quite attractive when yer angry." He surprised himself by saying aloud what he had been thinking.

She had fully intended to berate him further, to tell him what she truly thought. But, his words nearly made her tumble from the horse. *Attractive? What on earth could he mean by that?* She sat dumbfounded, staring up into those beautiful, dark brown eyes of his, at a loss for words.

He was smiling at her. But there was no ire, no disdain in his smile. Mischievous? Most definitely. Genuine? To be certain. But...there was something else...something she could not quite describe.

She chucked it up to being sore, exhausted, and terrified. It made her mind a muddled mess. That, combined with looking at the most handsome, nay *beautiful* face that she'd ever seen, well, it all led to this feeling of uncertainty and discomfit. It was all *his* fault.

It took several long moments before Rowan realized he had said what he had said. He felt his face grow warm and that old familiar feeling of guilt draped itself over his heart.

He hadn't found a woman *attractive* in a very long time. Not since Kate.

His stomach twisted into a large knot. He was looking down at a very angry woman with brilliant green eyes, long auburn locks that looked as though they hadn't been combed in a month. Her face was splattered with mud, her dress torn, tattered and caked with more mud. Her bottom lip was cut and swollen, and a large bruise was forming on her cheek.

The bruises angered him. Were his daughter not waiting for him this very moment, Rowan would have been more than tempted to ride back to Blackthorn Keep and kill the man who had left his mark on her beautiful face.

And yet, he could not deny the fact that he did find her quite attractive. Quite possibly -- if he were so inclined to allow himself to feel such things -- beautiful. Bruises or no, her face was exquisite.

He felt an odd, tingling sensation begin to creep in. He did not like it, not one bit. He shrugged the feelings off as being nothing more than a physical attraction combined with the fact that he hadn't been with a woman in nearly five years. Mayhap all he needed was a tumble between the sheets. Not with Lady Arline, of course, because she was, after all, a lady.

He pushed those thoughts aside and looked away from the angry, yet quite beautiful, face staring back at him. "Do ye think ye'll still hate me once we're off the cliff?" he asked.

Arline cringed. She really wished he would quit using that term *off the cliff*. For every time he said it, she had visions of them falling to their deaths. Frustrated and angry she answered him. "Aye, I will." She *wanted* to hate him, hate him for laughing at her distress, hate him for making her legs quiver. Most of all, she wanted to hate him for calling her attractive for she did not like how that made her feel. All excited and giddy and foolish. It also made her stomach feel as though there were dozens of tiny fish in it all flipping happily about and singing his praises.

"Och!" Rowan said. "I was hopin' ye'd change yer mind, but women, especially attractive women such as ye, rarely change their minds."

There he went again! She could envision the fish in her belly now, swimming about and singing, *Rowan called her attractive! Rowan called her attractive!*

"Do no' do that!" she admonished him.

"Do what?"

As if he had no earthly idea what she meant! "Do no' call me that."

He raised one of those perfect eyebrows of his and looked down at her. "Call ye what?"

"Attractive. Do no' call me that." She tried to look away, but those beautiful brown eyes of his were simply too beautiful to turn away from. They begged to be stared at.

"Attractive? Ye find that insulting?"

Arline cleared her throat before answering. "Nay, no' insulting." *It makes me think of things that canna be.*

"Pray tell then, why canna I call ye attractive?"

She'd die before she answered that question truthfully. The longer he stared at her and the more he used that word, the more inclined she was to leap from the horse and hurtle herself down the side of the cliff. The idea was growing more and more appealing the longer he looked at her.

"Fine," Rowan said. "I shall no' call ye that again."

Why did she suddenly feel so sad and deflated? Why did she not feel relieved?

"I shall call ye beautiful instead."

All the fish in her belly suddenly stopped swimming. They swooned. One collective sigh of bliss and then they swooned. Blasted man! Was he trying to kill her?

"Nay!" she exclaimed. Finally she mustered the courage to turn away from him. If she looked at him again, it would most certainly be the death of her.

Rowan chuckled. For reasons he could not understand, he found himself enjoying the way her face turned red with embarrassment. He enjoyed unsettling her. But more than anything, he was beginning to enjoy the lascivious thoughts that were beginning to bounce around in his head.

He did not want to enjoy them, but enjoy them he did. What, pray tell, would she look like without the mud in her hair or on her face? A vision of the beautiful Lady Arline, naked as the day she was born, flashed into his mind. She was bathing, in the loch, and rivulets of water were cascading down her perfect breasts, her curvaceous hips.

Lord almighty, if he did not get her off his horse and onto someone else's, she would soon know without a shadow of a doubt the effect she was having on his person.

He mulled it over in his mind, mayhap a bit longer than he should have. Would such a thing be so bad? What would it hurt if she did know?

"Be there a reason why I canna call ye beautiful?"

She wished she had the pluck to tell him to go jump off a cliff. Reasoning that he might do just that, just for spite, taking her along with him, she swallowed back that quick retort.

He spoke aloud his conjecture. "Has no man ever told ye that before?"

"Told me what?" For the life of her she could not think.

"That ye are quite bonny. Attractive. And verra beautiful."

The fish woke long enough to have one collective heart seizure and die. Now she was sitting very close to the most beautiful man she'd ever laid eyes on, close enough that she was certain he could hear her heart as it pounded against her breast. And she had a belly full of dead fish.

"I've been told that, before," she answered, trying to sound as if she were told those very things by one hundred different men at least one hundred times a day.

The truth however, was quite different. The last man to tell her she was beautiful was Carlich. Seeing how Carlich had thought of her more as a granddaughter than a wife, she doubted he meant those words with any amount of romantic or lustful inclinations.

Rowan didn't believe her. She was far too agitated and embarrassed for him to believe her. For a woman who had been married before, he found she had an underlying innocence in her countenance and he thought that both strange and endearing.

"Good," he whispered into her hair. He didn't even try to erase his smile when he felt her gasp.

"What is good?" she asked him.

"'Tis good that ye have a man to tell ye such things. Ye need to be told that every day. Repeatedly."

"I do?" she asked him breathlessly. She wondered if he was like this with all women. A man as beautiful as Rowan Graham probably had women falling at his feet all the day long and willing to warm his bed each night. Were she not so afraid of burning in hell for all eternity, she might very well have been inclined to be one of those women.

"Aye," he smiled. "Ye do."

Mentally, she waved goodbye to her good senses and the promise she had made a thousand times to live the rest of her days alone. But before they were completely out of sight, she grabbed them and wrestled them back where they belonged. She could not allow lust to get in the way of her plans to live a blissful, carefree life, one of her own choosing.

Several long moments passed in tense stillness with each of them lost in thoughts, lustful as they were. 'Twas Rowan who finally broke the silence.

"Do ye still hate me, lass?" he asked softly.

"Hate ye?" she asked, forgetting the biting words she had said to him earlier.

"Aye. Do ye still hate me?" he repeated as he gave a nod of his head to their surroundings. Arline blinked once, then again, before she realized what he meant. She took the chance to look around and her shoulders sagged with relief. She could have jumped from the horse and kissed the ground.

At some point along the way, they had left the terrifying side of the cliff and had spilled into a valley. Autumn was just beginning to touch her fingers to the beautiful land that lay before her.

Morning mist clung to everything it touched. Vibrant green leaves still clung to the trees, their ends just beginning to turn, giving tender hints at the golds, reds, and browns that autumn promised. Grass, having long ago turned to seed, waved slowly in the breeze. A deep stream wound its way down from the top of the mountain, through the valley, spilling out to only heaven knew where.

As cold and damp as it was, Arline still found it quite beautiful. It reminded her of home, of her sisters, of her youth. The memories weighed heavily on her heart. She wondered if she would ever see Morralyn or Geraldine again. God, how she missed them!

The air was colder here in the valley, nipping at Arline's ears and fingertips. The moist, cold air made her mud-covered clothes and boots feel even heavier. She craved for nothing more than a warm bath and a place to lay her head.

They crossed the stream and made their way up and through an outcrop of large dark boulders. Arline stiffened and held her breath when she saw the clearing was filled with dozens of men. Her escorts however, seemed quite at ease.

Arline grew tense at the sight of them. Her escorts however seemed quite at ease.

Sensing her tension and fright, Rowan whispered, "Wheesht, lass. These be men who helped us retrieve Lily."

Arline expelled the breath she had been holding and began to search the group for Lily. Dozens of large, serious looking, plaid covered, bearded men surrounded a small fire. She had thought none could look more fierce or imposing than Garrick's men, but she had been wrong in that assumption. These men looked positively menacing.

Rowan, Frederick and Daniel made their way through the rocks and down the small trail that led to the fire. Two bearded men stepped forward and took the reins of their horses. "Graham," one of them said, nodding up at him.

Rowan nodded back and swung down from his saddle. He reached up and grabbed Arline by her waist and pulled her down and set her on her feet. He took a moment to make certain she could stand on her own.

"Are ye well, lass?" he asked thoughtfully and with much concern in his voice.

She really wished people would stop asking that particular question for she could not answer it simply or plainly. "Aye," she told him as she reached out and rested a hand on the saddle. "I am well."

She nearly keeled over when the man who had taken the reins decided at that moment to lead the horse away. Rowan caught her before she could fall completely over.

This time, he did not laugh at her distress. He looked and sounded concerned. "Lass, I do no' think ye be as well as ye wish."

She was fully prepared to argue with him, to explain that she was a grown woman for heaven's sake and completely able to take care of herself and certainly was in no need for him to show her any amount of concern, but her words were stopped short by Daniel and Frederick. Each man stood on either side of her.

"She took a hell of a beatin' from Garrick Blackthorn," Daniel offered.

"Aye," Frederick added. "'Twere it no' for Daniel holdin' me back, I'd have cut the bastard's throat."

Both men looked embarrassed as well as angry for not coming to her aid back at Blackthorn Keep. Arline rolled her eyes at them. "And where would we be now if ye had?" she asked them. "As dead as dead can be, that's where. Ye did the right thing by no' intervening on me behalf. I am alive, and God willin', I'll remain that way fer the foreseeable future. We'll speak of it no more."

"But, me lady," Frederick began. "We need ye to know that we would have stepped in and helped had--"

She cut him short with a wave of her hand. "I said, we'll speak of it no more. What's done is done, lads. All is well *now*."

Daniel was working his jaw back and forth as his red face deepened to a near burgundy tint. "I promise ye this, me lady, that in the future, we'll no' hold ourselves back and let ye take a beatin' again. Next time,"

Arline's brow knitted. "There will be no next time."

Rowan placed an arm around her waist and guided her toward the fire. "We'll let ye rest a spell, warm yerself by the fire."

Arline shook her head at him. "Thank ye, me laird, but I be more concerned for Lily. Where is she?"

'Twas then that a very large, muscular man stepped forward. He had long brown hair, not quite as dark as Rowan's. Brown eyes with just a hint of gold glinted in the morning light. A long scar ran along the left side of his forehead, down the side of his face, disappearing under his plaid. He was as massive and imposing a figure as Arline had ever seen. A chill ran like fingertips down her spine.

"Rowan," the man said as he extended his right arm outward. Rowan took it, grasping his forearm, Rowan pulled him in for an embrace. They patted each other heartily on their backs for a brief moment.

"Caelen, my friend."

Arline stood back, watching the two men. They were more than just friends, Rowan and this man. They were like brothers.

Rowan broke away. "Where be me daughter?'

Caelen shook his head. "Yer daughter be asleep," he answered with a nod over his shoulder.

Both Arline and Rowan looked in the direction Caelen had indicated. There, on the other side of the fire, was a large felled tree trunk resting on the ground. A very large man sat with his back against the tree, his legs spread out before him. On his lap, he held Lily, bundled in a fur like a newborn babe. She was fast asleep with her little head resting against the Highlander's chest. The Highlander looked up at Rowan and smiled.

"She fell asleep not long ago, Rowan," Caelen told him.

Arline thought she detected a note of relief in the man's voice.

"Is she well?" Rowan asked quietly. He resisted the urge to rush to his daughter and scoop her up into his arms. There was no doubt that she was exhausted and mayhap more than a bit frightened. Wishing not to disturb her slumber, he left her alone.

Caelen did not answer immediately. Rowan looked away from his daughter and back to Caelen. The man had his eyes focused intently on Lady Arline.

"Caelen McDunnah," Rowan said. "This be Lady Arline."

Caelen smiled, at least as much as Caelen McDunnah ever smiled. He was better known for fighting than he was for smiling.

"So *ye* be the Lady Arline that Lily speaks so highly of."

Arline gave as much a curtsy as her wobbly and sore legs would allow.

"Lily tells us that ye took verra good care of her," Caelen said.

"As good as I could under the circumstances," Arline told him. Caelen seemed satisfied with Arline's statement. "I am sure Rowan is verra grateful and I ken his people will be grateful fer what ye've done as well."

Arline inclined her head toward him. "'Twas the right thing to do." She could not have turned Lily away any more than she could turn anyone in need away. It went against her nature.

"Ye must be tired, me lady," Caelen said thoughtfully. "We will leave ye to rest a while."

Frederick and Daniel escorted Arline to the fire. Seeing she was in good hands, Rowan and Caelen walked away from the group so they might speak privately.

Once Caelen found a place where they could talk and keep an eye on Lady Arline, he began to fill Rowan in on all that he had learned from Lily.

"Ye've a good daughter, Rowan. She be a verra bright child. She told us much as we traveled here."

Rowan let out a heavy sigh. "Caelen, I did no' want ye to interrogate me daughter! I did no' want to push fer information." He did not want to injure her further by bombarding her with questions or making her relive those terrifying moments when she was with Garrick Blackthorn.

Caelen threw his head back and laughed. "Rowan," he said with a smile. "I did no' interrogate yer daughter. I would have much preferred her to remain quiet on our journey here, but yer daughter had other ideas."

Rowan quirked an eyebrow at his friend. "What do ye mean?"

Caelen let out a quick breath and folded his arms over his chest. "I mean, yer daughter talked non-stop. 'Twas to the point I would have given me right eye fer a few moments of silence."

Rowan chuckled at Caelen. Lily *was* a talker. She was a very inquisitive child and very perceptive. She had no problems with opening up to people, even strangers, *if* she felt she could trust them.

Once trust was earned? Lily could cause even the most stalwart man to lose his mind with all her endless questions and never ending chatter.

"I do apologize fer that, Caelen. Lily only opens up to people she trusts."

Caelen found that amusing. Not many trusted him. "Trust me? Yer child is tetched."

Rowan laughed at his friend. "What did ye learn?"

Caelen took a deep breath in and let it out slowly. "She hates gruel but loves eggs. She thinks cows have funny tongues and sheep are cuddly."

Rowan shook his head. "Caelen," he said firmly.

"She does not remember what happened at yer keep the night she was taken. She only remembers wakin' up on a horse, thrown over a *mean man's* saddle like a sack of flour."

That fit in with what Rowan was able to learn from his people. Somehow, someone had managed to slip a sleeping draught into Lily's tea. They'd also managed to spike the keg of ale that had been served after the evening meal. Once his men had fallen asleep, someone took Lily from her bedchamber and away from the keep.

Rowan's sole focus had been the retrieval of his daughter. Now that he had her back, he could direct his focus to find out who had helped in her kidnapping

"There be more, Rowan." Caelen was reluctant to tell Rowan all he knew.

Rowan braced himself. From Caelen's reticent expression, Rowan knew he was not going to be happy. He nodded his head and bade Caelen to continue.

"Garrick was no' too kind in his treatment of Lily. When Lily woke, she was afraid and had begun to cry. Apparently, Garrick has no patience fer cryin' babes."

Rowan felt a hard jolt in the pit of his stomach. "What did he do?"

"He took a strap to her backside. And when she cried still, he put a gag in her mouth."

Rowan could not remember ever feeling so angry. Not even when he had learned Lily had been taken. Garrick was a large man, as large as Rowan. Though Garrick Blackthorn oft behaved like a spoiled and petulant child, he was still a man full grown.

"I'll kill him," Rowan muttered angrily. "As God is me witness, I will kill that man."

Rowan began to stomp away toward his horse. Caelen stopped him by grabbing hold of his arm. "Rowan, wait!"

"Wait? Fer what? Fer the bastard to take another child? Someone else's child and beat her as well?" Rowan seethed. "Nay, I'll no' give him that chance."

Caelen tightened his hold on Rowan's arm. "Aye, ye'll wait until the time is right. Ye canna go alone," Caelen pleaded with him to listen to reason.

"Let go of me arm, Caelen, or yer likely to lose yer hand."

Caelen was not fazed by Rowan's threat. He knew it was the threat of a very angry father, one who might also be feeling guilty for not being there to protect his daughter in the first place. "Rowan, if ye wait, wait until we get yer child safely back to *Áit na Síochána*, I promise, I will help ye get yer revenge. But now, now Rowan, is *no'* the time."

It was not easy for Rowan to listen to reason. His mind raced with the various ways with which he could kill Garrick Blackthorn. Incensed beyond comprehension, it was all he could do at the moment not to kill Caelen just so he could get to Garrick.

Rowan took a deep breath before turning to look at his daughter.

She was still asleep, but she was no longer in Thomas' lap. Lady Arline was holding her.

The vision of the beautiful woman holding his daughter bothered him. It should be Kate holding her at this moment, not a stranger. And he should not be taking any enjoyment in watching the lovely woman hold his child to her breast with her cheek pressed against the top of his daughter's head.

They looked as though they belonged together, Lady Arline and Lily. The resemblance between the two was uncanny. If a stranger were to make his way into the camp, he would think that Lily belonged to Arline.

But she didn't. She belonged to him and to Kate. He should be the one holding his daughter now.

He had let lustful feelings get the better of him earlier. He had enjoyed the way the woman felt sitting on his lap as they rode across the country. He had enjoyed how her face burned red with embarrassment when he called her beautiful. He had even enjoyed how she had grown angry with him.

But something began to crumble when he saw her holding his daughter, so sweetly, so tenderly. And he damned well didn't like it.

He knew Caelen was right, that they should wait to launch a well-planned assault on Blackthorn. They needed to get Lily back to the safe confines of *Áit na Síochána*. But most of all, he needed to get Lady Arline out of his life and for good, for if he didn't, he feared he and Lily would both become too attached to her for their own good.

He turned back to face Caelen. "Verra well, then, Caelen. We leave now for *Áit na Síochána*. I will seek me revenge once I learn who amongst my clan betrayed me."

Caelen breathed a sigh of relief and let go of Rowan. "I promise ye Rowan, I'll help ye get the bastard."

Rowan said nothing, just nodded his head and walked away. He was too angry with Garrick Blackthorn for having taken his daughter and his mistreatment of her. He was also angry with the vision of beauty sitting on the ground next to the fire, fast asleep and cradling his daughter in her arms.

Thomas came to stand next to Rowan. "I do no' trust that woman," Thomas whispered harshly.

Rowan turned to face him. Thomas was older than Rowan by ten years. He was one of the few men left who had served under his father. Rowan trusted Thomas' good judgment and level headedness.

"May I ask why?"

Thomas ran his tongue across his lips and shook his head. "She is Blackthorn's wife, fer the sake of Christ."

"I believe that marriage was annulled this day, Thomas."

Thomas shook his head in disgust again. "How do we ken that, Rowan? Could all be a ruse to get close to ye, to us, to the clan."

Rowan studied his ginger-haired friend for a moment. Thomas was never one to jump to conclusions or to judge a person harshly. "A ruse?"

"Aye, a ruse. How were ye able to get in and out of the castle so easily? How were we able to get this far without seeing any of Blackthorn's men?"

The same questions had crossed Rowan's mind over the past hours. "Ye think Blackthorn *allowed* us into his keep? And allowed us to escape?"

"'Tis a possibility."

"But why? Why no' cut me throat the moment I entered the keep? Why allow me in to take me daughter? And why did he beat Arline?"

Thomas shrugged his shoulders. "I didna say I had all the answers, just me suspicions. There is something about the woman that I do no' trust or like."

Daniel and Frederick had come to join Rowan and Thomas. Both Daniel and Frederick took offense to Thomas' words.

"I ken the woman, Thomas," Daniel told him. "She be the one that helped Angus and Duncan seven years past. She be a good woman."

"Aye," Frederick interjected. "I ken her as well. She risked her life for two men she had not even met, because it was the right thing to do."

"And she took a beatin' from Garrick because she was tryin' to protect Lily," Daniel explained. "We heard Garrick tell her the marriage was annulled and he was castin' her out. Without escort or means of travel. Lady Arline *begged* him to allow her to stay to take care of Lily until the ransom was paid. Garrick beat her fer it."

Thomas had been listening intently. "He beat her?"

"Aye, and we were about to intervene when one of his men pulled him away. We also heard the man say his *bride* was waitin' fer him." Daniel glanced briefly at Lady Arline before turning back to Thomas. "I think that is why we were able to enter and leave so easily. They were all busy with Garrick marryin' another."

"He annulled his marriage to Lady Arline so that he could marry another?" Rowan was disgusted with the notion.

"Aye, that is what we heard," Frederick told him. After a moment of contemplation, Frederick continued. "I think she be barren."

Rowan's brow knotted in confusion. "Who? Lady Arline?"

Frederick gave a quick nod of his head. "Aye. She was married to Carlich Lindsay fer three years and they had no bairns. And she was married to Garrick fer a year and no bairns. Mayhap that is why he annulled their marriage. Because she was barren."

Rowan's heart sunk. He looked at the woman holding his babe. She had risked her own life for Lily's. How sad it was to think that such a woman as Lady Arline, one who apparently loved children or at the very least cared about them, could not have one of her own.

He thought back to how hard it had been for Kate to make it through her first trimesters. The poor woman had suffered through five miscarriages before they were blessed with Lily. For Kate to go through all of that, only to die a few short months after Lily was born, seemed inherently unfair.

He was always left with an overwhelming sense of sadness whenever he thought of his Kate and all that she missed out on. Lily's first steps, her first words. The first time she fell and skinned her knee.

Lily was surrounded by people who loved and adored her. But still, something was missing in the child's life. A mother. There were things a mother could do for a daughter that a father could not. Such as braid her hair or sing her to sleep. Rowan had tried to do those things, but his talents with braids and singing were sorely lacking.

As he stood watching Lady Arline and Lily he could not make up his mind if he was angry at Lady Arline for taking on the role of mother, or at himself. Selfishly, he had kept his heart under lock and key these past years. The only person he allowed in was Lily. He refused all others entry. And it was not as if no one had tried.

He thought of Lady Beatrice of *Cill Saidhe*. They had met six months ago when the wheel on Lady Beatrice's wagon had broke. Lady Beatrice and her entourage had sought refuge within *Áit na Síochána*. They had stayed the night, left at dawn the next morn, and Rowan had thought he would never see her again.

Beatrice was a bonny woman to look at. She was well-educated, graceful, and elegant. She would have made any man a fine wife. But, she was not his Kate. He had turned down her offer that night to warm his bed. He found himself regretting it the next morning.

However, a few weeks ago he had received a letter from Beatrice, asking if she could take refuge in his home again, but this time, for a more extended stay. Apparently there was a man who very much wanted to make her his wife but Beatrice did not have the same feelings toward the man. She wanted away from Inverness and from the man. Thinking he might be ready to open his heart to another, he agreed to open his home to Beatrice.

She had arrived two weeks before he left for the hunting trip. Aye, she was still as beautiful as he remembered, still as graceful and elegant. But, there was something missing and he had not been able to figure out what that something was, until now.

Warmth.

Aye, she had warmed up to Rowan quite nicely. But Lily was another matter. Beatrice rarely spent any time with Lily. And in those rare moments that she did, there was no outward affection on her part toward his daughter. She had never held his daughter while she slept. She had never played with Lily nor taken her for walks. Those things bothered him.

While Rowan had no evidence that Arline had done any of those things with his daughter, the way she held his daughter said much. Mayhap too much.

Thomas' voice broke through Rowan's quiet contemplation. "How soon do ye wish to leave?"

Rowan had no way of knowing yet if Garrick Blackthorn and his men were following. Deciding it best not to wait and see, Rowan gave the order for them to leave now.

He also decided it might be best if Lady Arline rode with someone else to which she did not argue. Daniel pulled her up to sit behind him while Thomas lifted Lily up into Rowan's anxious arms. He held her tightly in one arm, tucked the fur all around her. She was clinging to the doll Lady Arline had made for her.

Lily stirred, lifted her head and smiled up at Rowan. "Da!"

Rowan returned her smile as he tapped the flanks of his horse. He kissed the top of her head and held her closely.

"Are we goin' home now?" Lily asked sleepily.

"Aye, we are, lassie."

Lily yawned and fought to keep her eyes open. "Good. I missed ye."

"And I missed ye," Rowan told her. "Verra much."

"Is Caelen goin' to go get Lady Arline now?"

Apparently, Lady Arline had made a long lasting impression on Lily. Rowan was uncertain how, exactly, he felt about that. He did not want Lily growing too attached to the woman for he hadn't decided yet what he was going to do with the woman once they reached his keep.

"Nay, Caelen will no' be doin' that, lass, fer we already found Lady Arline. She be ridin' with Daniel."

Lily bolted upright, her bright blue eyes searching for the topic of their conversation. She squealed with delight once she saw her.

"Lady Arline!" Lily shouted as she struggled to get out of the furs.

"Wheesht, lass!" Rowan admonished her. "Sit still."

"But I want Lady Arline," Lily cried.

Rowan let out a frustrated sigh. "Lily, ye need to sit still. Ye can see Lady Arline when we stop."

"But I want her now, da!"

Back and forth the two of them went. Under different circum-stances, Rowan would have sent her to her room until she decided to listen. His daughter had been through one hellish ordeal over the past weeks. Even after he tried to use his sternest voice, Lily continued to cry and plead with him to allow Lady Arline to ride with them.

In the end, it was Lady Arline who settled the matter.

"Lily Graham," Arline said as Daniel pulled their mount next to Rowan and Lily. "Have ye no' missed yer da?"

Lily sniffled and nodded her head.

"And is *that* how ye show him ye missed him?"

Lily suddenly grew quiet and looked quite ashamed. She remained silent, shook her head no and stuck her thumb in her mouth.

"I did no' think so," Arline told her then clicked her tongue and shook her head, looking very displeased with the child.

"I believe yer da has been missin' ye as well, haven't ye?" Arline cast Rowan a faint smile, encouraging him to say something.

Rowan had been staring at Lady Arline, stunned at how easily she had gotten Lily to settle down. Lady Arline raised an eyebrow and tilted her head toward Lily. Rowan cleared his throat. "Aye, Lily, I have missed ye verra much."

Lady Arline smiled and looked pleased with his answer. "There ye have it, sweeting," Lady Arline spoke softly. "So I think ye be needin' to show yer da how much ye've missed him by lettin' him hold ye a while. He went through much to get ye back. I be quite certain he wants to hold on to ye fer a time. If ye act like the wee lady I ken ye to be, when we stop, I'll be holding on to ye fer a spell."

Lily seemed content with Arline's promise and in a matter of moments, she closed her eyes and fell asleep.

Rowan was stunned. Lily was a very determined child, one might even call her strong-willed. There were times when Rowan and Lily butted heads, usually over quite silly things such as eating vegetables and taking baths. On more than one occasion, his daughter left him to question his own sanity and abilities as a father.

But Lady Arline was able to get his daughter to calm herself and fall asleep in a matter of moments and with seemingly little effort. He found it perplexing.

What was it about this woman that left him feeling so bloody confused? There was a calming influence that seemed to ride in the air all around her. He looked around at his men. They seemed… content and unbothered by the events. No one seemed tense or on edge and acted as though they were simply out for an afternoon ride across their lands.

Even Thomas seemed at ease and he was usually the most excitable one of the lot. Was it Arline who brought them this sense of peace and contentment or had they been in the *uisge beatha*? Since the men weren't dancing around the campfire and no one was singing, he doubted they'd been at the whisky.

While Lady Arline's presence might calm his men, Rowan felt anything but calm when near her. She made his heart pound, his blood heat through his veins and his mind turn to all manner of sinfully delightful things he'd like to do with her were the opportunity ever to present itself.

He didn't like it. Not one bit. It made him feel guilty, as if he were not being true to the love he still carried for Kate. He felt that by lusting after any woman he was being disrespectful to what he and Kate had.

True, she had made him promise not to keep his heart to her after she was gone. Kate had wanted him to go on with his life, to love again, to marry and have more children.

He knew he was being foolish, for if Kate were here, she'd smack him alongside his head and tell him just that. Kate would be very upset that he had not moved on.

But he couldn't move on. It was too painful, the guilt all too real. It should have been *him* that died, not Kate. And that was what most of it all boiled down to. He felt guilty that she had to die such a painful and ugly death while he lived.

If he didn't have Lily? He would have taken his own life by now.

Lily was the only thing that kept him going. And Kate's memory and his guilt were the only things that kept him from moving forward.

EIGHT

T hey had ridden well into the afternoon before Rowan called for a rest. Surrounded by trees to the South and west, they now stood in a large clearing. The mist had subsided not long ago and the sun made a grand attempt at trying to burn its way through the clouds. The clouds were winning.

Lady Arline was quite relieved to hear his command. She slid from the back of Daniel's horse without waiting for assistance. Tiny needles of pain raced up from her feet to her knees the moment her feet touched the ground. She stifled a curse, took a deep breath and waited for the pain to pass.

Her legs ached, from her ankles to her buttocks. Her ribs were still quite sore from where Garrick had kicked them. Her neck was stiff from resting her head against Daniel's back, unable to switch from left to right because her cheek throbbed and her eye felt swollen.

Lily was awake and came rushing to Arline's side and flung her arms around her legs. Arline resisted the urge to cry out in pain or to push the child away. Instead, she patted her little head and hugged her back.

"Will ye hold me now, Lady Arline?" Lily asked looking up at her dolefully.

There wasn't a chance on God's earth that Arline could bend over let alone lift the child into her arms. "Soon enough, sweeting. First, let's find a tree."

Rowan was now standing beside them, his arms crossed over his chest as he studied Arline closely. "Are ye well, lass?"

For a brief moment, she thought of telling him and the rest of his men that she would scream if another person asked her that question. "I am good and well, thank ye," she managed to keep an even tone to her voice. "Lily and I will need a few moments, me laird."

Rowan gave a curt nod. "I shall escort ye," he said.

Arline's brows knitted and she felt insulted. "I can assure ye, me laird, that I have no intentions of takin' yer daughter from ye. I can certainly be trusted to help tend to her private needs," she bit out. And she most assuredly did not need any help in that department.

Rowan rolled his eyes at her. "'Tisn't *ye* I worry over takin' me daughter," he explained. "We do no' know yet if any of yer husband's men be nearby."

Arline returned his eye roll with one of her own. "He is *no'* my husband."

"Fergive me." Rowan gave a slight bow at his waist. "Yer *former* husband then. I will no' take any chances of ye or Lily bein' in harm's way again."

"Would we no' have seen them by now?" Arline asked. Clearly she thought it a foolish notion that Garrick's men would be waiting in the woods. If he was going to attack he would have done so by now.

"Mayhap aye, mayhap nay," Rowan said. "But I'll no' be takin' any chances where me daughter is concerned."

Arline shook her head is frustration, took Lily's hand and began to walk away. "Fine, me laird. As ye wish."

She wished she had the strength to stomp away from him. But stomping would have been quite painful and a bit childish. Instead, she ignored him and led Lily toward the tree line. Lily was happily skipping along beside her, clutching her doll to her chest.

"Da," Lily spoke over her shoulder. "I be verra hungry."

"I have cheese and bread in me bag, lass," Rowan told her as he walked not far behind.

"Do ye have any apples?" Lily asked.

"Aye, I do," he told her. His focus was not on his daughter, but on Lady Arline. Any fool could see that she was in a good amount of pain simply by the way she walked -- stilted and stiff.

"The mean people would no' give us any apples," Lily informed him. She sounded upset with that. "All we had was porridge and bread. Sometimes the maid would sneak us cheese."

Rowan's gut tightened. Apparently they had treated his daughter more like a criminal than a child. Silently, he wondered how far they had taken the mistreatment of his child. He doubted there would be much need for asking his daughter many questions. She would tell him everything and would need little prompting.

"Lady Arline gave me her cheese," Lily went on. "She gave me her bread, too."

Arline gave Lily's hand a slight squeeze and smiled down at her. They came upon a large tree, one that would allow them some amount of privacy. After Lily was done, Arline smoothed out the little girl's skirts and sent her around the tree to her father.

"I'll be but a few moments, me laird," Arline called out to Rowan. She wished he would go back to the camp and allow her a few minutes of complete privacy. Truthfully, she wanted a moment alone to let out the tears she'd been holding on to and she did not want anyone to hear her.

Only a moment or two had passed when Arline heard someone from the camp calling out for Rowan. There was no urgency to the man's voice, but Arline took advantage of it.

"Me laird," she told him from the other side of the tree. "I will be fine. Go, see to yer men."

"Nay," Rowan answered, sounding quite determined.

Arline let out a slow breath. "Do you no' have men surrounding the camp?"

"Aye, I do."

"Then I believe I am safe from marauders. Please, go."

Arline heard his heavy sigh of frustration followed by something inaudible.

"Da!" Lily exclaimed. "Ye said a bad word!"

Why she felt some measure of satisfaction knowing she had frustrated him to the point of cursing, Arline was uncertain. But enjoy it she did. Whoever it was that needed Rowan called his name a third time.

Arline took her sweet time. Between the man calling out for Rowan and Lily's loud protests that she was hungry, Arline felt confident that soon he'd relent and leave her.

"Da! Ye said a bad word again. Does this mean ye do no' get any supper?"

Arline covered her mouth with the hem of her skirt so that Rowan could not hear her giggle. "This may take some time me laird," Arline told him. 'Twasn't a *complete* lie. What with the way her legs ached and her side throbbed, it might take some time before she could stand up again.

Rowan let loose with another frustrated sigh. "Fine!" he shouted to the tree. "Do no' leave this spot, me lady. I will take Lily back to the camp, find out why the bloody hell Thomas keeps yelling fer me, and I'll be back fer ye. But *stay put!*"

Arline stuck her tongue out at him as she heard him walk away, rustling through the tall grass. She did not like being ordered about. People had been ordering her about her entire life.

The more she thought on it, the angrier she became. A flood of memories came crashing in over her. First her father with his constant, *children should neither be seen nor heard.* Then Minnie, her maid. *Ladies do no' ride astride. Ladies do no' show skin from the neck down.* Then Garrick, *If ye wish to live, ye'll follow me orders to the letter.*

Would there ever be a time in her life when people, especially *men* did not feel the need to order her about like a child? Would there ever be a time in her life when she could simply do as she pleased without someone telling her she couldn't? She had reached the ends of her patience.

"I will *no'* stay put, Rowan Graham!" she whispered angrily to the tree. In a good deal of pain, frustrated, angry and tired, she used the tree to keep her balance as she stood. She took a moment to smooth out her skirts, wiped away an errant tear and began to walk. Away from the camp.

"I will *no'* be ordered to 'stay' or 'sit' like a dog!" she told the air as she lifted her skirts to make her way around some bramble bushes. She continued her tirade as she walked through a dense thicket of trees, mumbling to herself.

"I'm a woman full grown!" She muttered under her breath. "I'm no' some ignorant fool who doesna ken up from down!"

A moment later, as she stepped through the trees and spilled out into another clearing, she found herself staring into the nose of a rather large horse that stood beside several other large horses.

Panic ensued when she looked up into the eyes of the very large, menacing looking men sitting atop the horses. Without thinking, she lifted her skirts, spun around, and ran back the way she had come.

"I'm an idiot!" she scolded herself as she ran through the woods. "A full-grown, bloody idiot!"

Arline did not take the time to count the number of men on horseback. It could have been thousands for all she knew or cared. Her instinct was to run, as fast as she could, back to the camp to warn Rowan and the others.

Every step and intake of air was a painful reminder of just how badly Garrick had beaten her. But she could not think of that now. She had to warn Rowan, had to make sure nothing happened to Lily.

With her heart pounding and face covered in sweat, she ran as fast as her tired and sore legs would allow. She began to make bargains with God. If He would get Lily and the others out of this alive, she'd never run off in anger ever again. If Rowan told her to stay put, that was exactly what she would do.

She worried over the men Rowan had sent to the perimeters as lookouts. They must have been killed else Garrick's men would not have gotten this close. Arline hadn't taken the time to look into any of the faces to see if perchance she recognized any of them. She had a relative sense of certainty that the men on horseback belonged to Garrick. Who else would sneak up on them like this?

With her heart pounding loudly and her head filled with thoughts of what Garrick was going to do to her, to Rowan and the others, she was paying very little attention to where she was going. As she ran through the trees, her feet slipped on a patch of mud. She fought for balance and when she felt herself slipping, the last thing she could think to do was to scream as loud as she could for Rowan.

R owan was more than frustrated by the time he made his way back to the camp. He handed Lily off to Frederick with orders to feed her before seeking out Thomas. Rowan intended to ring the fool's neck for his constant bellowing.

"What the bloody hell are ye hollerin' about?" Rowan shot out as he walked toward the bank of trees where Thomas stood. He cast a glance over his shoulder toward where he had left Lady Arline. He wanted to get back to her, wanted to see that she was fed something other than porridge.

"Nial McKee and his men be here," Thomas informed him. "I thought ye'd want to ken that."

That was indeed good news. Rowan had expected to meet them earlier and was quite eager to learn what had delayed them. But first, he had to get Lady Arline safely back to the camp.

"Good," Rowan said to Thomas. "Where be they now?" Rowan asked.

Thomas' reply was cut short by Lady Arline's blood-curdling scream.

"Damn!" Rowan spat out as he raced toward the trees where he had left her. He knew he would not find her where he had left her for her scream had not come from there.

The way she had screamed had told him either she had encountered one of Blackthorn's men or a bear or something equally menacing. With his broadsword drawn and fifteen men following fast on his heels he raced through the woods. Breaking through trees and bushes, jumping over felled trees, he raced in the direction he believed the screams had come from.

In no time, he broke through the dense overgrowth and nearly fell down the side of an embankment. A large, torn piece of a woman's dress clung to one of the bushes that grew along the top of the embankment.

Rowan grabbed it and began searching the area with his eyes. He peered over and down the small decline and saw her lying below. For a moment his heart stopped beating when he saw her lying on her back with blood covering her chest.

She had not fallen far, mayhap only ten feet. Thomas, Daniel and Frederick were at his side now and followed his gaze.

Without speaking, Rowan grabbed Frederick's arm for balance and slid down the nature-made wall of mud. Roots of bushes grew randomly through the wall, snagging Rowan's tunic as he slid down to help Lady Arline.

By the time he reached her he was covered in mud and sweat. He rushed to her side, laid his broadsword at his feet as he knelt beside her.

Her bodice was covered in blood. Rowan took only a moment to glance around looking for any sign of Garrick Blackthorn's men. He called up to his men. "She's bleeding! I think she's been stabbed! Look about fer Blackthorn or his men!"

He turned back to Lady Arline who was gasping for breath. "Wheesht, lass," he told her as he removed his dirk from his boot. "I have to check yer wound," he told her as she lay there fighting for breath. Her eyes were wide with what could only be described as abject fear. She was trying to speak. "Wheesht, lass! Was it Blackthorn's men?" His words were rushed and filled with worry. She shook her head and muttered "Nay."

"We'll find the bloody bastard! I swear it!" Rowan whispered harshly. He would kill whoever had hurt this brave woman, the woman who had protected his daughter.

He took the dirk and made a small cut at the top of the bodice. He laid the dirk on the ground, took the bodice between this hands and ripped it to her waist.

Blood was smeared along her neck and chemise. He hoped her injuries were not too grievous. Quietly, he began to pray that she would live, for a multitude of reasons. The most important being he was rapidly developing feelings for her. The most cowardly was the fact that he did not want to have to explain to Lily that her sweet angel had been killed.

He took the top of her chemise in both hands and was about to rip it to get a better look at Lady Arline's wounds. Suddenly, she grabbed his wrist. "Nay!" she squeaked out. Her chest heaved up and down as she struggled for air.

"But, lass, I must see how badly ye are injured!" Rowan told her. He thought it a damned odd time for her to be worried over her reputation or to be modest. The woman had been stabbed for the sake of Christ! Now was not the time to worry over such things. He tried to tear the bodice again when her other hand flew up and grabbed his other wrist.

"Ber--" she closed her eyes, swallowed, and tried again. "Ber-ries!" she managed to work the word out.

"A bear did this?" Rowan asked with wide eyes. He began searching the area with his eyes.

"Nay," she breathed out. "Berries!"

Rowan looked down at her, confusion written in the hard lines of his furrowed brow. "Berries?" he asked, uncertain what she meant.

Arline nodded her head and tried to regain control of her breathing. Her face was red with humiliation. The wind had been knocked out of her when she fell. She had come close to having a heart seizure when she felt herself falling, the fright had knocked the air clean from her lungs.

"What are ye talkin' about lass?" Rowan asked. Had she hit her head as well?

"I slipped. Berries. Up there. On dress. Not blood," Arline told him between breaths of air.

Rowan looked at her dress, bodice, and neck. He glanced up at the side of the embankment. Berry bushes. Several of them. 'Twas then that understanding set in. Arline hadn't been attacked by Blackthorn men. She hadn't been mauled by a bear. She had slipped in the mud, fell, and slid all the way down, smashing berries along the way.

It wasn't blood.

It was berry juice.

She wasn't going to die. At least not from wounds she had received in her fall. But he was sorely tempted to strangle her long, slender neck for scaring the bloody hell out of him!

Her skin had heated, turned red from the top of her head and spread down her neck. She finally opened her eyes to look at him. It took no great level of intelligence to see that he was angry, what with the way he was working his jaw back and forth and the vein that throbbed in his neck. His brown eyes were dark, nearly black. He was taking deep, slow breaths in through his nostrils.

Even angry, he was still a very handsome man.

She cursed the thought and felt her skin heat further.

She wished she had broken her neck in the fall just to save herself from the embarrassment of having him rip her bodice and the anger she saw in his eyes.

He still held the top of her chemise in his curled fingers and she still held on to his wrists. She wanted to die in that moment, as his dark eyes bored into hers.

She suddenly remembered the men on horseback and fought to find her voice. "There are men, on horseback. Many. 'Twas why I was runnin' and fell. I was tryin' to warn ye, to get Lily away," the words tumbled out as she struggled to hold on to what little sense she had left.

Rowan sighed. "Those be Nial McKee's men, lass. Had ye stayed where I told ye, ye wouldn't have been scared half to death and runnin' through the woods!"

It was all simply too much. In less than a day's time, she had been beaten, thrown out of her home in the middle of the night, assaulted, thrown on the back of a horse and carried heaven-only-knew how far across Scottish lands. He had called her attractive and beautiful and tested the limits of her patience. Now she felt like a fool. A complete, utter idiot. He was right. Had she not been so angry at being ordered around like a mongrel dog, she would not be in this situation, with berry juice smeared all over her, the bodice of her dress torn beyond repair, and his hot fingers touching her bare skin.

She couldn't help herself, couldn't contain her frustration or embarrassment any longer. The tears fell, quietly at first but soon turned to waterfalls, streaming down her dirty face, into her ears, and down her neck.

He probably hated her. He'd probably leave her here, alone, to find her own way about. She couldn't blame him if he did. Minnie had been right all those times she warned her that her stubbornness would someday be the death of her.

Her shoulders shook as the tears trickled down her face. She closed her eyes, let loose her hold on his wrists and turned her head away. Crying was for foolish young girls, lasses with dreams, hopes and aspirations. She was none of those things. She was a foolish woman, covered in bruises, mud, and berry juice.

Her eyes flew open when she felt warm hands slide under her shoulders and waist. She looked up and into soft warm eyes staring back at her. He no longer looked angry or upset but she could not describe what she *did* see looking back at her. She supposed someone with far more experience than she had would know what a look like that meant. Realizing her lack of expertise in so many areas made her cry even more.

Rowan lifted her onto his lap and held her. Arline continued to cry as she clung to him, burying her face in the warmth of his chest.

"Cry it all out, lass," he whispered into her hair.

The shock of his statement made her cry all the more. Carlich had been the only man who had ever allowed her to cry. Her father would not allow for histrionics and Garrick certainly would not have put up with tears.

But here, sitting in the mud, was a strong, braw man, a man she barely knew, telling her it was all right to cry was too much. That old familiar feeling, the one of longing for things that could never be began to creep in. Wrapping its long tendrils around her heart, it squeezed and burned, leaving an indelible impression where she did not want it.

While the tears flowed, she heard muffled voices coming from above but paid them no mind. She wanted to stay there, in the mud, with her face hidden in his chest so that Rowan would not have the chance to look into her eyes. If she looked into those big brown eyes again, she'd be forever lost and eternally damned.

W hen she had cried until she had no tears left, Rowan gave her back a gentle pat. "Better, now?" he asked thoughtfully.

Arline nodded into his chest, afraid to move or look up for fear he'd be able to somehow read her mind or heart.

"Good," he said as he gently rubbed his hand up and down her back. He looked up at the wall of earth she had tumbled down earlier and doubted she would be able to make her way back up it.

Their camp sat in a nice, flat clearing and he could not remember seeing any drop offs or embankments near it. Mayhap this bit of land would wind its way around to a spot where she would be better able to climb up.

"Do ye think ye can walk a spell, lass?"

Arline took a deep breath, wiped her wet cheeks with the backs of her hands and nodded again. Her voice had seen fit to leave her, undoubtedly from the embarrassment of having fallen into a heap of hysterical crying.

Very gently he lifted her off his lap and set her bottom on the ground in front of him. He pushed himself to his feet and scanned their surroundings.

Frederick called down to them. "Should we throw down a rope?"

"Nay," Rowan called back to him. As much as Arline tried to argue otherwise, he knew her ribs were seriously injured. He did not want to risk damaging them further by tying a rope around her and hoisting her up. "We shall walk a spell and try to find a spot where the land evens out," he yelled up to Frederick.

Turning his attention back to Arline, he held out his hand. She refused to look up at him. He knelt down and put a hand on her shoulder. "'Tis all right, lass," he whispered.

Arline was playing with the edges of her torn bodice. "I apologize, me laird, fer actin' like a fool."

Rowan chuckled as he took her chin between his fingers and lifted it. Damn, but she had beautiful green eyes. They still glistened from the tears she had shed. Even red from crying they were quite beautiful.

His smile, warm and thoughtful, brought a tickling sensation to her stomach. He was making her look at him, full on, and she realized that she had no desire to stop.

"Do no' worrit overmuch, lass. I'll no' tell anyone if ye promise no' to tell that I panicked, thinkin' ye'd been stabbed, and ripped yer dress."

She burned red again, looked down at her torn, tattered, and filthy dress and realized she must look like hell. "Damn," she muttered under her breath.

He laughed fully then, with his broad shoulders shaking and his head thrown back. Briefly her ire was raised when she believed he was laughing at her distress. But when he looked at her, with those full, chiseled lips upturned and that twinkle in his eye, she knew there wasn't a cruel bone in his gloriously beautiful body. *Damn.*

She wanted very much to have a reason to be angry with him. Wanted desperately to find something about the man to dislike, something that would make the fluttering, nearly giddy sensation in her belly cease.

She could find nothing.

He was perfection personified.

Damn him.

Growling silently, she thrust up her hand and took his. His skin felt warm, nearly hot against her own. Her skin turned to gooseflesh when he lifted her to her feet and she stumbled into his chest. Marble. He was a living, breathing statue of Adonis, carved from marble.

Damn him.

He righted her, winked, took her hand and wrapped her arm around his waist while draping his long arm around her shoulders. "I think we can find a place that might no' be so difficult fer either of us to climb. Are ye sure ye can walk a ways?"

Walk? I'll be lucky if me legs do no' turn to jelly with ye touchin' me like this.

Arline wondered if she would ever find the use of her voice again, felt all the more foolish for nodding her head like a piece of driftwood bobbing in the water. Why did he have to smile *and* wink? Together, side by side, they began the walk back toward the camp.

So when she could find no real faults with him she decided to look at herself. Aye, it was much easier to find faults within herself than with another. Mentally, she began to tick off all the reasons why she could never have the heart of a man like Rowan Graham.

Arline knew she was by no means a homely woman. But neither was she the beauty she felt a man like Rowan would want. She had lost what few curves she had months ago when Garrick had decided to cut her meal rations. She was nothing but skin and bones with very tiny breasts and skin so very pale from lack of exposure to the sun. That's what living as a prisoner did for her. It turned her into a walking skeleton.

She could read and write and figure sums. She could sew a good stitch, paint and draw, but those were the limits of her talents. A man like Rowan needed a woman far more worldly and intelligent.

She chanced a glance up at him as they walked along the flat ground. His long brown hair was windswept, giving him even a more virile and dangerous appearance. Arline was tall, taller than most women, but standing next to Rowan she felt small, tiny, diminutive. Nay, he didn't need her, he needed a tall, buxom, smart, beautiful, witty woman.

Besides, once she was out of danger, she was going to make her way to Inverness, to her sisters. She did not need a man, didn't even want one. At least, not one like her previous husbands.

Soon they made their way to a spot where the ravine came to a hill. It was painful to make the climb but not nearly as painful as it would have been to try to pull her way up a straight wall. She was glad that Rowan was there letting her lean most of her weight against him as they made their way up the hill.

The population of the clearing had increased two-fold, filled with men from the clans Graham, McDunnah and McKee. Rowan quietly explained that they were here to see them safely to his lands.

"We should arrive on Graham lands by the noonin' meal on the morrow," he told her as they walked toward the groups of men.

"And when shall we make it to yer keep?"

"The day after."

Two more days of riding. Two more days without a bath, sleeping on the cold hard ground, or worse yet, atop a horse as it bounded along the land. Arline stifled a frustrated sigh, lifted her chin and tried to pretend that it did not matter.

Rowan wrapped an arm around her shoulder and gave it a slight hug. "I promise ye lass, when we get to me keep, ye can take as many baths as ye want, ye'll sleep in a big, soft, warm bed, and ye'll have something more to eat than cheese and dried meat.

Arline smiled up at him. "It sounds like heaven."

"Castle *Áit na Síochána is* heaven on earth lass."

From the smile and the twinkling in his eyes, Arline did not doubt him in the least.

NINE

Rowan listened intently as his daughter rattled on about her time at Blackthorn Keep. The more he learned, the angrier he became with Garrick Blackthorn.

He also began to grow more intrigued with Lady Arline. Lily seemed to know a great deal about the woman.

"I want sisters, da," she told him as she took another bite of her apple.

Rowan nearly choked on his bread when she said it. "Lady Arline has two sisters. Morralyn and Geraldine. They live in Inverness. But we're no' supposed to tell anyone that," Lily took another bite of her apple.

Rowan raised an eyebrow. "Why is that?"

Lily smacked her lips together, chewed and swallowed. "Because her da is no' nice like ye. That is why she married the mean man, because her da made her."

Rowan was glad his daughter held him in such high regard. Arranged marriages were nothing new. He reckoned that many a young woman thought her parents *mean* when arranging their futures for them. He couldn't rightly say he blamed them.

Although his marriage to Kate had been arranged they had fallen in love very quickly. Kate was beautiful and smart and everything he could ever want in a woman. Rowan knew that most arranged marriages did not end up as happy and full of love as his had.

"Her sisters are bastards," Lily informed him bluntly.

"Lily Graham!" Rowan chastised her. He was more stunned than angry with her. "Where did ye hear such a thing? Is that what Lady Arline called them?"

Lily looked up at him, her eyes instantly filling with tears. "Nay, but isna that what ye call people who be born when their mummy and da are no' married?"

Rowan took a slow breath in. He hadn't imagined having such a sensitive conversation with his daughter, at least not until she was much older. "Some do, but we do no' because it's insulting. We do no' use such language. Ye wouldna want to hurt anyone's feelings, would ye?"

Lily shook her head and looked sincerely regretful. "Nay," she told him. "I be sorry, da."

Rowan patted her little head and gave her a hunk of cheese. "Do no' fash yerself. But remember, in the future, no' to say such things."

"Am I in trouble?" she asked, looking forlorn and worried.

Rowan chuckled. "Nay, yer no'."

That seemed to lift her spirits. She took a bite of cheese. Rowan could sense she was mulling something over in her mind. Lily verified it with her next question.

"So, can I have sisters? Lady Arline has two sisters and she loves them verra much. That is why she married the mean man, so her da wouldna hurt them."

Rowan's brow furrowed. "Hurt them?"

"Aye. If Lady Arline didna marry the mean man, her da was going to cast her sisters out of their house and let them starve in the streets."

Rowan wondered how much of Lily's story was true and how much was the excited workings of a four-year-old child's mind. There was a possibility that there was some truth to what she said but he would wait to make a judgment on Arline's father until after he had heard the truth from Arline.

"Lady Arline didna want her sisters to starve or be hurt. She hid them, in Inverness so her da canna find them. He's no' nice like ye."

She finished her cheese but not her story or her questions. "Ye wouldna do that, would ye da? Throw me sisters out if they were born on the wrong side of the blanket?"

Rowan nearly choked again. "Where on earth did ye hear *that*?" he asked, hoping she hadn't heard it from him.

"Mrs. McGregor!" Lily said. "That is what she says about bastards. And ye told me I couldna say that word, bastards, anymore."

It was all he could do not to laugh and cry at the same time. He took a moment to calm his nerves, making a mental note to have a talk with their cook, Mrs. McGregor, just as soon as they returned home. "Lily, I do no' want ye to use that expression again."

She looked glum and confused. "So what *should* I say?"

Rowan let out a frustrated sigh. "Ye shouldna say anythin' about someone's--" he searched for the appropriate words, words that a four-year-old could understand. "Ye shouldna say anythin' about whether a person's parents were married or no', fer it does no' matter."

Lily thought long and hard. "Because ye must judge a man by his character."

Rowan smiled proudly at his daughter. She was smart, wise beyond her four years. "Aye, ye have the right of it."

"So can I have sisters?"

He sighed. This child was going to be the death of him. He would love to give her sisters -- legitimate sisters. But that would require marrying again. Rowan doubted he would ever be able to give his heart to another woman, doubted he could ever love another woman as he had loved Kate.

Guilt crept in. Was he being a selfish man by not giving Lily a mother and brothers and sisters? There were so many things he wanted to give his daughter, chief among them a family.

He also wished for his daughter to grow up in a time of peace and prosperity, a time where children were not kidnapped or worrying over when their next meals might come.

The Black Death had nearly destroyed his clan. Left with only a handful of loyal men and women, Rowan was doing his best to rebuild his clan, his home and his life. Though they did not struggle like many other clans, they were by no means out of trouble.

Many of the crofters' huts scattered across his lands remained empty, their original inhabitants now dead. Without anyone to tend to them, the little houses were slowly decaying and falling apart. And without enough people to tend the lands, their harvests were, to say the least, reduced.

Still, they had plenty of meat to get them through the roughest of times. Gradually over the past year, they had increased their numbers by inviting those less fortunate to come live among the Clan Graham. A rag-tag bunch if ever he saw one, but still, they were loyal people, glad to have a home and way to make a living. They had come from all parts of Scotland, many with just the clothes on their backs and empty bellies. There was not a clan left untouched by the Black Death and several were wiped out completely.

"Well?" Lily asked him as she tossed the remains of her apple into the fire, disrupting Rowan's thoughts.

"Well, what?" His mind had wandered and he could not remember her question.

"Can I have me some sisters or no'?" She pursed her little lips together and gave him a stern look.

He sighed again, ran his hand over his face and searched for the appropriate words. Having found none, he fell back on the age old answer parents give children when they don't have a better one. "We'll see."

Lily seemed satisfied with that answer but Rowan knew she'd ask it again and again until either he forbade her to ask it again or gave in. That was how she got her very own pony: sheer relentlessness.

"I need to speak with Lady Arline," Rowan said as he pushed himself up from the log he'd been sitting on. "Ye stay here, with Thomas. And do no leave or go runnin' off."

"I want to see her too!" Lily exclaimed.

"Nay," Rowan told her. "No' yet. Ye may see her verra soon. Do as I told ye, child."

Her bottom lip jutted out and she crossed her arms over her chest. It was her way of warning her father that an argument was about to ensue -- *if* he were to allow it.

"A bird will come along and leave droppins' on that lip if ye are no' careful," he told her.

Lily giggled at his retort.

"Now, go stay by Thomas," Rowan told her, giving his head a nod in Thomas' direction.

Lily slid off the log and ran to Thomas for which Rowan was exceedingly grateful. He was in no mood to argue with his daughter. He imagined it would be days, if not weeks, before things returned to normal for any of them.

After he made certain Lily was in Thomas' good care, Rowan went to the tent that had been erected for Lady Arline and Lily to use. Without thinking to ask for permission to enter, he lifted the flap and stepped inside. It took a few moments for his eyes to adjust to the darkness of the tent. He was not prepared for the sight before him.

"God's bones!" he exclaimed, startling Lady Arline.

She was sitting in the corner of the tent with a bowl of water on the ground in front of her. She had pulled the top of her chemise down to her waist and was washing her neck with a wet cloth.

It was not her nakedness that caused his outburst. It was the large bruise that ran from under her arm down to her tiny waist that made him curse. It was dark purple and wrapped its way around her lower back and stomach. Rowan swallowed back the anger that sprang from his stomach.

Arline's eyes grew as wide as trenchers when she heard his voice. She covered her breasts with her arms. "Do ye no' give a woman a warnin' that ye be comin' into her tent?" she shouted at him. Her skin warmed and went crimson. "Have ye no manners? Turn around, man!"

Rowan shook his head in disbelief. "Ye be injured, lass."

"I ken that, Rowan! Now turn around!"

"Ye need someone to look at yer ribs," he told her as he took a few steps forward.

Her eyes grew wider, astonished that he refused to leave. She was half naked for heaven's sake! Could he not see that?

"Me ribs are fine. Now I ask ye again to leave!"

He wasn't about to. He took another step and knelt down beside her. "Nay, I'll no' leave until I've checked to see if yer ribs are broken." He reached out to touch her.

Arline smacked his hand away angrily. "Ye'll do no such thing, Rowan Graham!"

Rowan paused and looked into her very frightened eyes. "Let me see," he said sternly.

"Nay! Go away!"

"Nay."

"Yer no' a man, yer a beast!" she seethed, wrapping her hands and arms tighter around her torso.

Rowan chuckled and shook his head. "That may be, lass. Ye needn't worry that I'll seduce ye. I simply want to make certain ye have no broken ribs."

Her eyes turned to slits and her chest heaved in and out. "Och! As if I'd *let* ye seduce me any more than I'd let ye grope about me person lookin' fer broken ribs that are no' there!"

Rowan bent his head forward to whisper in her ear. "Are ye worried ye might enjoy my seducin' ways?"

Her mouth fell open but her words were lodged somewhere in her throat. Extracting them was impossible at the moment for he chose that moment to begin gently examine her ribs with his hot fingers. Too stunned to move or to speak, she sat as still as a stone while her skin turned to gooseflesh.

There were a thousands things she wanted to say to him and twice as many things she wanted to do to him. He was close enough to kiss, close enough to smell his skin, all clean and manly. Close enough that were she one of those wanton harlots Minnie had warned her about, she could have thrown him on his back and had her way with him.

"I do believe ye are at a loss fer words, lass," Rowan whispered in her ear as he continued to gently press around her ribs. "And I do no' think yer breathin' proper."

Breath? Think? Speak? All impossible to do when he was touching her. Granted, his touch was meant to inspect for broken ribs, but, she was certain if he were touching her for the purposes of seduction, her heart would have stopped altogether.

Beast! Brute! Bastard! Beautiful, handsome, dastardly man! Aye, if her tongue was not so dry and her body not all tingly and her mind not filled with all sorts of lustful thoughts, she would have called him all those things and slapped him silly for making her feel so unsettled and confused.

Time passed as slowly as molasses in wintertime. She felt light-headed and her lungs felt as though they would burst at any moment. She had to will herself to take in a breath of air and then another and another.

"I do no' think ye have any broken ribs, lass," Rowan said as he grabbed the drying cloth that lay next to her. Carefully, he unfolded it and wrapped it around her shoulders.

For a brief moment, she felt quite disappointed that his fingers were no longer on her skin. He sat down a few steps away from her.

"Why did ye no' tell me ye were so injured?"

Odd. The further away he was from her the easier it was to speak. But let him get close enough to touch and she turned into a mindless puddle of goo.

"Ye kent I was injured," she said, attempting to sound as nonchalant as possible. Her stomach was still all aflutter and she had to focus on speaking coherently.

"Aye, but I didna ken it was *that* bad. Ye should have said somethin'. We could have slowed our pace and allowed ye time to rest."

While that would have indeed been a glorious luxury, it was one they could not have afforded. "And risk Garrick's men catchin' up to us? I think no', me laird. Stopping would have served no purpose other than riskin' yer life, Lily's life, and the lives of yer men. A few bruises were no' worth takin' such a risk over."

"'Tis more than just a few bruises, lass. Ye've had the hell beat out of ye."

Arline took a deep breath in and let it out slowly. "We could go

123

'round and 'round about this but 'twill change nothin', me laird. What's done is done. We're now safely on yer lands and ye'll be home soon."

He knew she was right. Talking about it would change nothing. "Aye. But in the future, I'd appreciate it if ye'd no' try to be so damned noble and tell me if yer needin' something."

Future? What future? As soon as she could get her funds from her father she would be on her way to Inverness to get her sisters. "I plan on never bein' in such a predicament as this, ever again, me laird."

Each time he saw her swollen and bruised cheek, it made his hatred for Garrick Blackthorn increase a hundred fold. She had risked her health, her own life, for Lily. Rowan realized that the only other woman he knew who would have done such a thing was Kate.

Arline looked so damned proud and vulnerable at the same time. The candlelight flickered in her green eyes and cast streaks of gold in her auburn hair. She was a beautiful woman, albeit a bit on the thin side. Nothing a few good meals could not cure.

There was a recognizable longing in the green eyes that stared back at him. As much as he wanted to take her in his arms and begin kissing her from the top of her head to the tips of her toes, he knew he could not. They were both in far too vulnerable a state to start down that road.

He held his breath, gave her a quick nod and quit the tent before he did just that.

N ight had fallen, their bellies were full as they sat around the fire, decidedly glad to be back on their own lands. No longer worried about his daughter's safety, or Lady Arline's, Rowan was able to relax for the first time in weeks.

"When will we be home, da?" Lily had asked that question a hundred times over the last few days. He would not chastise her for asking because it was better than her pleading with him for sisters.

Rowan sighed as he pressed her head against his chest. "I've told ye again and again, we'll be home before the noonin' meal on the morrow."

Lily yawned, thrust her thumb into her mouth and began twisting a ringlet of hair around her finger. "And the mean man won't bother us anymore?"

Rowan's stomach lurched as if he'd just been kicked. "Nay, Lily. Ye needn't worry over him ever again."

"I want to sleep with ye, da," she said quietly.

He could not rightly blame her for not wanting to be alone at night. In truth, he did not want his daughter out of his sight. "Ye can sleep in my room fer a time after we are home."

"But I want to sleep with ye tonight."

Rowan tilted his head to get a better look at her face. "Tonight? Nay, not this night. Ye'll be sleepin' in the tent with Lady Arline."

Tears filled Lily's tired eyes. "But I'm afraid, da."

His stomach tightened again. "I'll be right outside the tent, lass. I promise, I'll no leave ye."

Arline had been fighting sleep, sitting next to Rowan and Lily. She yawned and tried to stretch, but it was too painful. "I can sleep outside the tent, Rowan. Lily needs her da. 'Twill be all right."

"I want Lady Arline too!" Lily cried.

There was no way on God's earth he was going to allow Arline to sleep on the cold ground. "Nay," he said to Arline. "Ye'll sleep in the tent, with Lily. I'll be right outside it."

Large tears streamed down Lily's face. These were not the tears of a child not getting her way. These were real tears of distress and fear. Rowan wrapped his arms more tightly around her and began to whisper words of comfort in her ear. "Lily, I promise I'll no' leave ye."

"But what if the mean man comes again? What if he takes me and Lady Arline again?" she began to sob uncontrollably.

Rowan looked to Lady Arline for help, but she had tears in her own eyes. "Lass," he said to Arline. "Why are *ye* cryin'?"

Arline wiped her cheeks with the backs of her hands and choked back her tears. Her words came spilling out almost as rapidly as her tears. "Because Lily is cryin'! She's scared and tired and cold and she's missed her father and she should never have been put in this situation to begin with! Garrick Blackthorn is an evil bastard and I hope he someday burns in hell!"

One crying female was enough to set his teeth on edge. Two crying women was more than any one man could handle. *God's teeth! They're going to be the death of me.*

"Wheesht, now lassies," Rowan said as he cradled Lily in one arm and Arline in the other. "I swear, ye needn't worry over anythin'. Me and me men will be guardin' ye with our lives, I swear it."

His promises and soothing words fell on deaf ears. In a matter of moments, both Lily and Arline were inconsolable. Lily reached out and grabbed Arline around her neck and scooted to her lap.

"I wanna go home!" Lily cried. "I wanna sleep in yer bed!"

Arline had no home to cry for, no home that she longed for or missed. She had nowhere on this earth to go to and that realization hit her hard. There was no way to hold back the flood of tears.

Thomas, Frederick, Daniel and several of the other men jumped to their feet, looking at Rowan as if he were some grand bastard.

"Rowan," Thomas said, sounding quite alarmed and looking even more distressed. "Lily simply wants her da!"

"Aye," Frederick added. "Sleep with the babe, Rowan. She's frightened."

"But she wants both me *and* Lady Arline!" Rowan tried to explain.

"And ye canna sleep in the same tent with Lily?" Thomas asked as if Rowan had lost complete control of his mind.

"Well, nay! 'Twould be inappropriate!"

"Och! No one here thinks ye'd be tryin' to seduce the lady whilst yer child is sleepin' next to ye!" Thomas said. He continued to look at Rowan as if he had lost his mind.

"But--"

Arline spoke up. "Are ye worried *I'll* seduce *ye?*" she said through sobs.

Rowan had reached the end of his patience. He rolled his eyes, took his crying child from Arline and stood. "Fine! But if yer reputation is ruined ye'll have no one to blame but yerself!"

Shifting Lily into one arm, he held out the other for Arline. She sobbed, wiped away more tears and took his hand. Lily continued to cry as Rowan led them to the tent. "Wheest, Lily," Rowan whispered. "I'll be sleepin' in the tent with ye and so will Lady Arline."

Wiping her face and nose on Rowan's tunic, Lily sniffled and sobbed out a thank you. Thomas had beat them to the tent and now stood at the entrance, holding the flap open as if he were some Roman squire. Thomas tossed a wink toward Rowan before standing at full attention, with his shoulders thrown back and eyes forward. Thomas saluted the trio as they walked inside.

Rowan found little humor in Thomas' dramatics. In truth, he had very little good humor left in him at the moment.

Arline removed her cloak and stepped to the spot closest to the outer wall of the tent. She lifted the furs, slid in between them and held the fur up, waiting for Rowan to set Lily down.

At the sight of Arline laying on the pallet, with her torn bodice exposing her chemise and bare skin, the fur in her hand, smiling and waiting, made his groin ache with want. He stood, with his child in his arms, staring down at the beautiful woman and wished he could hand Lily off to Thomas for a few hours.

Swallowing down the guilt-ridden lust, Rowan cleared his throat and dropped to his knees. Lily scrambled from his arms and nestled in next to Arline. Two smiling faces looked up at him.

The two of them looked happier than a bird with two worms.

Nay, they hadn't played him like a fine flute or harp. They were simply two exhausted individuals who had been through far too much in the past weeks.

He felt more than a bit of pride in the fact that they needed him to chase away their fears. He was a comfort to them and in return, he felt his own sense of comfort in knowing that he was needed.

Unfastening his belt, he laid his broadsword down next to the flap of the tent and blew out the candle that sat on the small table. He felt his way around in the dark until he found his daughter's head. She giggled as he slid in under the warm furs. Lily grabbed his neck and pulled until he scooted closer to her and gave him a kiss on his cheek.

"I love ye, da," Lily whispered around the thumb in her mouth. Rowan kissed the top of her head. "I love ye, Lily Graham. Now, wheesht and let us get some sleep."

Lily snuggled in closer and was soon fast asleep.

Rowan lay with his hand resting on Lily's chest, listening to the gentle sounds of his daughter's soft breathing. Occasionally, she would shudder a sigh, the remnants from all her earlier tears and sobs. Occasionally, Lady Arline would mimic Lily's shudders.

Arline's hand was resting on Lily's stomach, just a hair's breadth away from Rowan's. He had to swallow back his own tears.

Before Kate had died, they would lay in bed with Lily between them. Just looking at her, watching her breathe and coo and smile back at them. A week before Kate became ill, Lily laughed for the first time. The memory was as vivid as the moment it had happened. He had been making silly faces and noises at Lily. When he had made a particular silly sound, the babe laughed. Kate begged him to do it again. For nearly an hour he had repeated the silly words and sounds, just to hear both Lily and Kate laugh.

That was how his life should have remained. With him and Kate raising Lily together. With Kate's laughter filling the keep to the rafters. The two of them, together, chasing away Lily's bad dreams.

His memories were broken by the sleepy sound of Arline's voice. "Thank ye, Rowan," she whispered as she snuggled closer to Lily.

Their hands touched then. Desperately he wanted to take Arline's hand in his, just to hold. 'Twasn't a lust-filled desire, but one born of a broken heart. Until this moment he hadn't realized just how badly he missed Kate and the void she had left in their lives. As his skin touched Arline's hand, ever so slightly, it felt as though his heart had been ripped from his chest and thrown against a wall. That was how he had felt when Kate had died, with a hole in his chest where his heart had once beat happily.

Rowan's voice was lodged in his throat and he could not respond to Arline. He swallowed back the tears of remorse and regret. Tamped it all down, hiding it deep in his belly. If he tried to utter any words, he knew he would break down and sob like a bairn, like Lily and Arline had done earlier.

He remained mute, unable to move, to speak. With his eyes closed, he forced his lungs to take in air. He would save his tears for later, for a time when he was alone in his bedchamber back at his keep.

Rowan was not certain he enjoyed the stillness of the night for it made it far too easy to think. The sounds of crickets and tree frogs carried on the air outside the tent. He could hear the low, muffled voices of his men as they sat around the crackling fire. Lily's breathing, blended with Arline's and his own, gave him a sense of something long forgotten.

In that moment between wakefulness and sleep, a sense of peace fell over Rowan, draping over his soul and heart. How long had it been since he'd felt *at peace* with anything?

'Twas then that he realized Lady Arline had draped her hand over his. Long slender fingers curled and tucked into his palm.

Whether he dreamt or not, he neither knew nor cared. He no longer felt quite so bereft and alone. The hole in his chest, left empty, cold, and bare for four long years, no longer felt quite so empty.

R owan was roused from his sleep at some point near dawn by his daughter climbing over him. Lily was whispering that she had to pee. Rowan was about to grudgingly open his eyes to help her when he heard Frederick speaking to her in hushed tones. "Let yer da sleep a bit, wee one. Uncle Frederick will help ye."

Knowing Lily was in good hands, Rowan kept his eyes closed and drifted back to sleep. He'd reward Fredrick handsomely for his kindness later. The worry of the past weeks, the relief at finding his daughter not only alive, but well-cared for, and their subsequent late night escape had finally caught up with him.

Sometime later, he woke to the sound of his daughter laughing just outside their tent. Remembering she was in good hands, he did not rush to leave the warm pallet, the furs, or the wonderfully warm body that was lying very close to him. Her exquisitely round derrière nestled into a groin that was quite happy to have it there. Her soft back snuggled nicely against his torso and she was using his other arm as a pillow. As the fog of sleep slowly lifted, he realized his arm was wrapped around her waist with his hand tucked quite nicely under her side, holding her tightly against himself.

God's teeth, but he did not want to move from this piece of heaven-on-earth, not yet, not for some time.

He should do the honorable thing and remove his hand at once and quit the tent. He should not be taking such wicked enjoyment from a sleeping and unaware woman. His mind should not now be filling with thoughts of bare skin against bare skin and soft, supple lips pressing against his. And most assuredly he should not be thinking about what it would feel like if he were to roll her over on her back right now and make slow, sweet, passionate love to her.

For the first time in a very long time, Rowan decided against doing the honorable thing. Nay, he chose the wretched, rapscallion path that only a rakehell would take -- he held her tighter.

Much to his delight and pleasure, Arline sighed contentedly and snuggled in even closer. She rubbed her cheek against his arm much like a cat does when it's demanding to be petted.

They lay there side by side for a long while. Arline lost to whatever peaceful dreams she might be having and Rowan lost to the wretched and despicable images flashing in his mind, shamelessly and with abandon.

He should leave, find a loch to jump into, find a kirk, throw himself at the altar before God and beg for forgiveness. And unequiv-ocally, he should *not* lift his head and kiss the side of her neck as he was now doing. God help him, he was a bastard.

"Nay," Arline grumbled a sleepy protest and pulled the fur around her shoulder. It was far too warm under the furs. And it felt far too good curled up next to Rowan. She liked the way his arm felt, so protective and warm, draped over her waist with his hand tucked under her belly. And the way his lips felt as they left a trail of kisses on her neck. "Let me sleep, just a while longer," she mumbled, still half asleep.

Kisses. On. Her. Neck. Lord above, he was kissing her neck! She went stiff as a tree trunk, her eyes flew open, wide with wonder and amazement. Och! The kisses felt too good to be real! Mayhap, she thought, she was still asleep and this was but a dream, a wonderful, glorious dream.

She slammed her eyes shut for she positively did not want the dream to end. And if the kisses were real? She did not know what she would do. Probably die from the embarrassment of having enjoyed them far too thoroughly for a refined and dignified lady.

The kisses stopped, far too abruptly for the harlot and wanton woman who seemed to have taken up residence inside her body. Ever so slowly, she opened her eyes again.

Nay, 'twas not a dream. Rowan was lying next to her, his arm wrapped rather divinely around her waist, his fingers tucked in under her side. Aye, the wanton was alive and well and no matter how hard she wished she would go away, the wanton refused.

Battered, beaten, bruised, and yet she somehow managed to find the ability to lose herself in lustful, sinful thoughts. She had not protested the kisses, hadn't pushed him away haughtily, like a true and dignified lady would do. Nay, she relished in them, took great delight in the way his soft, warm lips felt against her neck, the way her skin turned to tingly gooseflesh.

I'm goin' to burn in hell, I just ken it! she thought to herself. Och! How she wished Minnie were still alive and here to give her good council. *Bah! To the devil with Minnie!* she heard the wanton say.

Aye, I'm going to burn in hell.

As she lay there contemplating where her soul would eternally rest and how she could keep it from burning in hell, she could hear Rowan's gentle snoring.

Suddenly she felt quite dejected and pathetic. He was sound asleep and had not realized what he had just done. Her stomach lurched at the next thought that entered her mind. He hadn't kissed *her,* but some woman, some vivacious, curvy, buxom and beautiful woman of which he dreamt. Mayhap, he had even been dreaming of his wife.

This was her lot in life. None of her husbands had wanted her in the physical sense, and apparently neither did the man who slept right next to her, with an arm draped around her waist. For reasons she had never quite been able to understand, men simply did not want her, did not, could not, or would not desire her.

A miserable sigh passed through her lips. With a heart full of melancholy, she carefully lifted away the furs, then Rowan's hand and quietly crawled away from him. She ran her fingers solemnly through her hair. She kept her back to him for she knew, if she took the chance to look at him, she would cry like a bairn. She'd done enough of that of late.

She shook the dried mud out of her boots, tugged them on and stood. She looked down at her torn dress and shook her head. Thankfully, her cloak would serve both as a means to keep warm and a way to cover her torn dress.

Without looking back, or down at the beautiful man slumbering on the floor, Arline quit the tent.

TEN

There was no doubt in Rowan Graham's mind that he was a dishonorable reprobate as well as a coward. He had taken liberty with a sleeping and unaware woman, then, when she roused, he feigned sleep just to avoid her *knowing* he was a dishonorable reprobate and a coward.

He waited a good long while before he *pretended* to wake, even going so far as to stretch and groan loudly. Aye, he was a coward.

As he had lain in the empty tent he thought about Arline. He was growing more fond of her as the hours passed. She *was* a good woman even if she did have a way of saying whatever was on her mind. He found he liked her blunt and straightforward manner.

Lily was quite attached to her as well and if his gut was correct, Arline was attached to and fond of Lily. He couldn't be completely certain just yet, but Arline seemed to genuinely care for his daughter, almost like a mother would.

It was, of course, too soon to tell. Mayhap theirs was a bond formed out of the need for survival while at Blackthorn Keep. Mayhap Arline was this way with all children. He wondered how Arline would be with Lily if she were to see her every day, on a more permanent basis and less stressful and traumatic conditions. Would she still caress Lily's hair? Would she still worry and fuss over her? Would Arline still insist, even in the face of adversity, that Lily mind her manners?

There was only one way to find out and that was to ask Arline to stay with them, live with him and Lily and his clan. How would Arline respond to such an offer? Again, there was only one way to find out. He would have to ask.

Shoring up his courage, he finally left the tent. His men were busy breaking down their camp. Arline and Lily sat on a log near the fire. Arline was running her fingers through Lily's hair, apologizing for the fact that she did not have a proper comb.

"I like how ye comb me hair, Lady Arline. Ye do no' hurt and pull it like da does," Lily informed her. As Arline combed Lily's hair, Lily pretended to comb her doll's non-existent hair with a twig.

A radiant smile formed on Arline's lips. "I'm sure yer da does the best that he can, sweeting. Ye should be grateful that ye have a da who at least tries."

Lily thought hard for a moment. "Did yer da comb yer hair?" she asked innocently.

Arline's smile quickly faded. Her father was a subject which she did not enjoy discussing. "Nay, lass, he did no'."

"Did yer mum comb yer hair?"

Arline smiled woefully. "Aye, when I was little she did.'"

"Do ye miss her?"

Arline nodded. "Aye, I miss her verra much."

Lily looked sad and forlorn. "I didna get to ken me mum, but I still miss her. Me da says she was pretty, like me, and verra smart. He loved her verra much."

Arline's shoulder sagged slightly. *Aye, 'twasn't me he kissed this morn. 'Twas his wife.* She did not hold his actions against him. If he loved Lily's mum as much as Lily believed he did, then he probably missed her terribly.

Arline fished a handkerchief from the pocket of her cloak and began to gently wipe Lily's face. "I ken," she said softly. "Ye've told me that before. Ye are verra blessed to have a mum and da who love ye so much. And 'tis all right to miss yer mum, even if ye never knew her."

Lily was quiet for a time before she asked her next question. "Lady Arline, am I bad because I wish I had a new mum?"

Arline tilted her head slightly and looked into Lily's bright blue eyes. The child looked sad, regretful, almost guilty. "Nay, sweeting, that isn't bad. Do no' feel yer doin' somethin' wrong by wantin' a mum."

Rowan's heart began to shatter as he listened to his daughter talk about wanting a mother. It made him feel guilty. He had spent so much time mourning Kate's death that he forgot to live. Aye, he woke each day, went about his daily routine and business, but he wasn't truly *living* his life. He was merely existing.

At every possible opportunity, he had told his daughter how wonderful and beautiful and smart her mother had been. He had been so focused on not forgetting Kate that he could not see what was in front of him. By sharing all his memories with Lily, he was constantly reminding her of what she did not have.

Had he been paying attention, he would have realized sooner that his little girl was hurting. She wanted a mum, but because of his constant reminders, she felt guilty.

He could have dropped to his knees then, and thanked the good Lord for putting Arline in their lives, especially Lily's. Arline had lost her mother at a young age and could very well understand how Lily felt.

He would pretend he had not heard their conversation. Painting a smile on his face, he walked to them and cheerfully greeted them good morn. Lily smiled as Rowan lifted her into his arms.

"Da! We saved ye some bread and an apple!" Lily said as she hugged him tightly around his neck.

"Ye did? Well, thank ye kindly, lass," he said as he kissed her cheek.

"Aye," Lily nodded. "Ye must have been tired. Ye slept a verra long time."

'Twasn't necessarily incorrect. He had gotten more sleep last night than he had in weeks. "I was verra tired," he told her, wanting very much to change the subject.

"Are ye ready to go home this day, Lily?" he asked, bouncing her up and down in his arm.

"Aye! And I do no' want to leave it fer a long, long time."

He could not say that be blamed her or disagreed. He'd like to return home, take a nice hot bath, and climb into bed for at least a sennight. Duties, however, would bar such a luxurious holiday.

"I agree," he said as he set her on her feet before summoning the courage to at last speak to Arline. There were a hundred questions he wanted to ask but fear and good manners prohibited asking them. "Are ye ready as well, me lady?"

Arline dusted her skirts and stood. Rowan thought he detected a blush rising in her cheeks. "Are ye well, me lady?"

"Aye, I am," she told him. After embarrassing herself inside the tent earlier, she had no desire for small talk. "Who shall I ride with this morn?"

Lily answered before Rowan had a chance. "Ye can ride with me and da," she said cheerfully.

Another blush rose to her cheeks. That was the *last* thing she needed to do. "I'm sure that is too many riders fer yer da's horse, Lily."

Rowan wanted the opportunity to speak with Arline before they arrived as his keep. "Lily," he said as he lowered to one knee. "I need ye to ride with Thomas fer a time." He spoke is a low, soft voice. "Just fer a little while. I want to speak with Lady Arline."

Lily's lip jutted out and she looked genuinely worried. "But I feel better when I be with ye both."

It would take much time, encouragement, and reassurance before Lily felt unafraid. Silently, he cursed Garrick Blackthorn and the men who had taken her, terrified and hurt her. They had taken away his daughter's sense of security.

"Rowan," Arline said as she came to stand beside them. "I can ride with Frederick. Lily needs her father now."

"But I want ye both," Lily repeated before thrusting her thumb into her mouth.

Lily was genuinely worried and frightened, both Rowan and Arline could see that. She was far too young and it was far too soon to expect her to just push aside her fears and move on.

"Lady Arline," Rowan said as he stood. "I do believe me horse can handle the three of us. That is, if ye do no' mind holding Lily on yer lap while we ride."

It was difficult enough to deny Lily much of anything, considering the circumstances. It was also ridiculously difficult to tell Rowan no, especially when he looked at her with those big brown eyes. Mayhap with Lily riding with them, Rowan would be less inclined to be as devious and mischievous as he was when they made their way down the side of the cliff.

"Fine," she finally answered. "We shall ride together." She shot Rowan a stern look that warned him that he should be on his best behavior.

Alternating their speeds between a full out, terrifying run and trotting, they would make *Áit na Síochána* in a few hours. Arline could not wait to be off the horse. When she reflected on the number of times she had actually ridden a horse over the past eight years, it registered in her mind that they had been less than pleasant experiences. Seldom was she able to simply enjoy a nice, leisurely pace.

They stopped once to stretch legs and empty bladders. While they allowed the horses to rest, Frederick and Daniel chased Lily around a large boulder, much to the little girl's delight. It was not easy for a child like Lily, so full of energy and spunk, to sit for hours on a horse.

Rowan wanted a few moments alone with Arline, to discuss the possibility of her staying amongst his clan. She was standing in the tall grass rubbing the back of her neck. He watched as she tried to stretch the kinks out, the movement causing her to wince. He still worried over her injuries and hoped the breakneck speeds they had been taking hadn't made them worse.

"Me lady," he said as he walked toward her. "Mayhap a walk will help stretch yer muscles? That is, if yer ribs and bruises are up to it."

Arline took only a moment to contemplate his suggestion. Mayhap taking a walk would help. It certainly could not hurt any more than the bone jarring ride atop the horse.

"I think that be a verra good idea," she said.

Rowan gave a slight bow and offered her his arm. She cringed inwardly at the thrill that raced up and down her spine as she placed her hand on his arm. The wanton was back. She wondered if by chance a priest resided at Rowan's keep. Mayhap it would take a priest to exorcise the wanton out of her system.

They walked through tall grass, not wandering too far from the men and Lily. The breeze tickled the tall grass, the trees and Arline's hair. The sun shone brightly against a beautiful cloudless blue sky. The sound of Lily's happy laughter and the twittering birds blended together. Though it was a perfectly beautiful day, much tension still hung in the air. Arline supposed that tension would not wane until they were safely ensconced behind the walls of the Graham keep.

They walked in silence for a time before Rowan finally rallied the courage to bring up the subject of her future. "Lady Arline," he began. "Have ye given any thought to what ye might do, now that ye no longer be married to Garrick?"

Had she given it any thought? An amused smile came to her lips. That was all she had thought of for the past year. "Me sisters are in Inverness. I would verra much like to go there, to live with them." Until a sennight ago, just thinking about Inverness would bring an excited flutter to her stomach, she would even dance gaily about her room with uninhibited excitement.

But now, when she said it aloud, it did not make her giddy or breathless with anticipation. Something had changed in her these past weeks. Lily. She would miss the little girl terribly, but, going to Inverness was the only plan she had.

"I see," Rowan said, looking at the tree line that lay ahead. "And is it *verra* important to ye, to go to Inverness?

Until Lily had come into her life, going to Inverness had been the only thing that kept her from losing her mind. Still, what other option did she have? She certainly would not return to Ireland, that was out of the question.

"Me sisters are there, ye ken," she told him. "I miss them verra much. I have no' seen them in over a year." She hadn't seen them since the night she snuck out of her father's home and into the village where Morralyn and Geraldine lived.

"Lily mentioned them," Rowan said. He did not divulge the extent of the conversation.

Her father had known for years that Arline had been sending the two young women money each month. He had been well aware of how much Arline loved them. Orthanach had threatened to send her sisters far away, had promised she'd never lay eyes on them again if she continued to refuse to marry Garrick.

Knowing her father as she did, she knew he was not bluffing. So she had written to her former stepson, Phillip Lindsay, and begged him for help. Phillip had responded quickly and generously by sending ten of his best men to take Morralyn and Geraldine to Inverness. Phillip had friends there and made arrangements for Morralyn and Geraldine to stay as long as needed. Arline knew she would never be able to repay Phillip. She would be forever in his debt.

"Lady Arline, I ken how much ye surely love yer sisters," Rowan stopped and turned to look at her. "But I have a proposition fer ye, that I'd like ye to consider."

Arline tilted her head with curiosity and more excitement than was proper. She told herself he said *proposition* and not *proposal.* They were two entirely different things.

He took a deep breath and let it out slowly. "I owe ye a debt that I can never begin to repay."

"Och!" she said with a wave of her hand. "Do no' worry overmuch, me laird."

"Nay, 'tis important that ye ken how grateful I am to ye, Arline. Ye risked much in takin' care of Lily."

"'Twas the right thing to do, me laird," she told him. Truthfully, she had enjoyed taking care of Lily. For the first time in a very long time,

Arline finally felt like her life had a purpose, albeit a temporary one. Lily was a precious child, one she had grown quite fond of. The thought of leaving her left an emptiness in her heart that she had not thought possible.

"So ye've said before," he flashed her a smile. Resisting the urge to tuck a loose strand of her auburn hair behind her ear, he clasped his hands behind his back. "But be that as it may, me daughter has grown quite fond of ye. She will be verra sad to see ye leave." *I've grown fond of ye as well.*

A warm smile lit her face. "She is a precious child."

"Aye, that she is," he agreed. "I fear I make a miserable mum for her," he chuckled. "I've treated her more like a lad than a little girl. She needs the influence of a proper lady. Someone who will teach her all the things a proper lady should know."

Arline's spirits and hope began to soar. She threw a rope around them and tugged them back to earth. Certainly he did not mean... Nay, he could not mean to propose. She gave a mental shake of her head.

"So me proposal is this," he said, standing a bit taller. "I would like ye to stay with us at *Áit na Síochána* as a governess for Lily. Ye'll be given a fine room near Lily's and anything ye might need to teach Lily."

Spirits and hope plunged downward, along with her heart and lodged themselves firmly into the soil beneath her feet. Of course he hadn't meant what she had found herself wishing for. He didn't want a wife, or at least not her as a wife. 'Twas a ridiculous notion to begin with. What man proposes after but a few days of meeting someone? She felt like a ridiculous fool for having thought it.

"I ken ye wish to be with yer sisters, me lady."

She could only nod her head in affirmation. The ability to form words had fled.

"So me proposal is this. Ye stay at *Áit na Síochána*, fer at least a month, to act as Lily's governess. If, after the end of that month, ye find ye do no' wish to stay on permanently, then I shall give ye escort to anywhere ye wish to go."

The wanton screamed for her to agree. If he didn't want her as a wife, mayhap he'd desire her as a mistress. She took a deep, steady breath and mentally pushed the wanton into the earth along with her heart and hopes. Reminding herself she did posses *some* amount of pride and dignity.

This was not a decision that could be made lightly. It would require a good deal of thought and consideration. She did have her sisters to consider. They were hiding in Inverness and Lord only knew how they were faring. It had been months since last she'd heard from them or been able to write to them. Garrick had stopped allowing her to communicate with anyone, especially her sisters.

She would write to them as soon as she reached *Áit na Síochána.* If they were well and good, then she would consider Rowan's proposition.

"May I have some time to think on it, me laird?" she asked.

"Aye," he said with a nod. "However, I fear ye may no' be able to say *no,* once ye see *Áit na Síochána.* It has a way of stealin' yer breath and yer heart at the same time," he told her, flashing that brilliant and perfect smile.

Much like the man who rules over it, she thought.

ELEVEN

Castle *Áit na Síochána* lay on the horizon. It was just as beautiful as Rowan had described and, as promised, its majesty and beauty did take her breath away.

They had stopped at the top of the hill to gaze down at *Áit na Síochána*. The road leading to the castle wound ever so slightly, following the lay of the land. A few crofters' huts were scattered here and there on either side of the road. At the end stood the castle she had heard so much about, first from Lily, then from Rowan.

Three stories tall, created out of large blocks of gray limestone, it stood seemingly impenetrable at the edge of a very large loch. The loch surrounded the castle on three sides. The only way in was the road they traveled, or by boat.

A massive thick curtain wall spread from east to west. Beyond that was another wall that surrounded the keep in its entirety. Enormous square towers stood on each corner of the wall, towering high above the keep itself.

"Ye didna exaggerate, Rowan!" Arline said breathlessly. "It *is* beautiful."

Rowan smiled in agreement. He had both arms wrapped around

Arline, who was holding a sleeping Lily in her arms. He gave them both a gentle squeeze before giving a tap to move their horse forward.

They rode down the road quickly, with each of Rowan's men following close behind. The level of excitement amongst Rowan and his men was palpable. They were glad to be home and Arline felt it clear to her toes.

That old familiar sensation of longing draped over her heart. She hadn't felt at *home* in a very long time. The one and only time she felt at peace or at home was when she was married to Carlich Lindsay. That now seemed a lifetime ago.

She wondered if she would ever feel that way again. Aye, Rowan had generously made her an offer to stay at *Áit na Síochána* to be Lily's governess but doubts about whether to accept that offer or to turn it down lingered. Being Lily's governess meant being in constant contact with Rowan. It would help if he weren't so decidedly handsome!

She'd been going back and forth between yes and no since he'd made the offer. It wasn't until she saw *Áit na Síochána* that she made up her mind.

"Rowan," she whispered over her shoulder. "I'll take ye up on yer offer to be Lily's governess. I will give ye one month."

He was glad she couldn't see his face for that way she could not see the sheer joy on it. He was still uncertain where exactly he wanted their friendship to lead him. All he knew with any amount of certainty was that he did not want her to leave.

She had grown quiet and she looked distant and removed. "Ye miss yer sisters."

"Aye, I do. Verra much." To say she missed them was a tremendous understatement. But it went beyond just missing them. There was still much guilt that she harbored over her father's mistreatment of them. Orthanach would never try to atone for his sins so Arline did her best to atone on his behalf. Why her sisters should be punished for their father's misdeeds made no sense to her.

An idea began to form in Rowan's mind. He seriously doubted Arline would be able to live here beyond the month without her sisters. They were a very important part of her life and even a fool could see how much she loved and missed them.

"I have another request, me lady."

"Aye? And what would that be me laird?"

"One," he whispered into her ear. "Ye quit with the 'me lairds'. I'm no' a laird, I'm the chief of Clan Graham. Please, call me Rowan. Everyone else calls me by me given name. I'd like ye to do the same."

Arline felt her cheeks flush and grow warm. It seemed a very personal thing to do, to call him by his given name. It had taken the entire first year of her marriage to Carlich before she felt comfortable enough to call him by his. Using first names bespoke of a certain level of intimacy.

He *had* seen her half naked. He *had* touched her bare skin -- albeit to look for injuries. Rowan Graham was the first man to ever see bare skin below her décolletage. Supposing that was indeed a level of intimacy, one she'd never had with any other man before, calling him by his given name seemed appropriate under the circumstances.

"I agree," she told him. "Is that all?"

"Nay," he said. "I should like to see ye smile more."

Her brow knitted. The man was plainly daft, evidenced in what she found to be a rather odd request. "Yer daft."

He laughed at her. "I've been told that before."

Soon, they reached the large wooden gate of the outer wall. The four men standing atop that wall called down a welcome to Rowan and the others as the gate opened. They rode in silence until they reached the second wall and gate.

It flew open and loud cheers went up. Dozens of people came rushing toward them, all calling out to Rowan and the men. Arline took note of the relieved and happy faces of Rowan's people.

Lily woke to the sounds of the cheering crowd. She sat up, threw back the fur that covered her head and looked about. "We're home!" she exclaimed gleefully.

Before Arline realized what was happening, someone grabbed Lily down and enveloped her in a big hug, whisking her into the keep. "I think they be glad to see us, lass," Rowan whispered into her ear.

He swung himself down from their mount only to be assaulted by crying women fighting for a chance to hug him and men slapping hands on his back and arms.

Arline had never witnessed such a thing as this before. Stunned by the outward displays of emotion, she sat rigid on the back of the horse. For a brief moment, she thought of stealing Rowan's horse and fleeing.

Rowan did not give her time to escape. His hands were around her waist and lifting her down to stand beside him before she could blink.

"Selina!" Rowan called out as he took Arline's hand in his and led her up the steps of the keep. As they reached the entrance a young lass of no more than seven and ten pushed her way through the crowd.

"Selina!" Rowan greeted the young woman with a smile and grabbed her arm. With Arline on one arm and Selina on the other, he pushed his way through the crowd.

Carefully, he guided them down the steps that led to a large and immaculate gathering room. Massive chandeliers hung from the beamed ceiling. Two equally massive fireplaces mirrored each other on opposite walls. Over each mantle hung the Graham rampant with two crossed broadswords.

Several women stood near the fireplace to Arline's left and they were all taking turns hugging Lily. "Och, lassie!" one of the older women said. "We be so glad to have ye home!"

Lily was all smiles and seemed quite happy with the attention being given her.

"Are ye hurt, lassie?" an older, short, stout woman with her gray hair in a loose bun at the nape of her neck asked.

"Nay," Lily told her. "I was verra scared though. But Lady Arline took verra good care of me!"

Arline was not given much time to take it all in. Without knowing who it was that had aided in Lily's kidnapping, Arline did not feel she could trust any of these people.

"Selina, this be Lady Arline." Rowan smiled as he introduced the two women, pulling Arline's attention away from Lily.

"Lady Arline, this be Selina. Selina, I want ye to take verra good care of Lady Arline. Give her my mother's auld room, see to it that she has as many baths as she wants. And find the healer to tend to her injuries." Rowan was rattling off orders in such a rapid succession that Arline found it difficult to keep up.

"I should see that Lily is settled first, Rowan," Arline interjected.

Rowan stopped, tilted his head slightly and stared at her as if she were some curious new being he'd never seen before. "Nay, lass. There are plenty of people here to see to Lily's needs. Ye need to see to yer own first."

Arline stepped closer, tugged on his tunic so that he would bend low. Whispering in his ear, she said, "But Rowan, did ye no' say that ye have no idea who helped aid in Lily's kidnappin'? What if they try again?"

Rowan smiled and gave Arline a pat on her shoulder. "Lass, I have me most trusted men, Frederick and Daniel, guardin' me daughter."

"But I'd feel better if --"

Rowan cut her off before she could continue her protests. "Arline, *I'll* be guardin' her as well."

He watched as Arline's shoulders sagged with relief and it made him smile all the more. "Now, ye go with Selina. She'll see that yer settled. We'll talk later, after the evenin' meal."

He turned then to Selina. "I want ye to take verra good care of Lady Arline. She took verra good care of me daughter and I owe her much fer that. She's been through quite an ordeal these past days. See if ye can find some dresses fer her and if ye canna find them, make them."

"I'll take good care of her, Rowan, I promise!"

Just as Selina took Arline's arm to take her away, a woman's voice called out from somewhere behind them.

Arline turned to see a beautiful woman with raven black hair descend the staircase. She wore a magnificent gown made of burgundy damask that trailed down the stairs behind her. The dress clung to her almost like a second skin. And she showed more bosom than Lady Arline could ever hope to own.

Even if she had not been covered from head to toe in mud, muck, grime and berry juice, Arline would still have felt just as inadequate as she now did. The woman was stunning, elegant, graceful.

The woman ignored Lily and the women fawning over her, did not so much as give them a nod of her head. She came straight to Rowan.

"Rowan! Och! I was so worried over ye!"

When the woman flung her arms around Rowan's neck, Arline wanted nothing more than to pull out every last strand of her raven black hair. She pulled the feeling back quickly. She knew she had no claim to any man, let alone Rowan Graham.

Rowan's face held an odd expression. One of frustration blended with confusion. "Beatrice," he said as he pulled her arms away and took a step back. "Why are ye still here? I thought ye were goin' to Edinburgh?"

Beatrice stuck her bottom lip out, as if she were wounded and hurt. Most men might have found that pouting lip quite attractive. Rowan wasn't most men.

"I could no' have left ye in yer time of need! I was so worried over ye that I delayed me trip. Fer ye, Rowan." Her voice was as smooth as silk as she batted her lashes up at Rowan.

Rowan raised his voice. "Lady Beatrice of *Cill Saidhe*," he said as he stepped toward Arline. "This be Lady Arline." He smiled proudly down at Arline. "She helped to care fer Lily."

Beatrice stepped forward and gave Arline an elegant curtsey. "'Tis me pleasure, me lady."

Although Beatrice curtsied elegantly and made a grand attempt at being congenial, Arline caught a glimmer of something in the woman's eyes. Arline also took note that not once since entering the room, did the woman ask after Lily.

"Me lady," Arline said, returning the curtsey.

There was something about this woman that Arline disliked. Mayhap it was the fact that the woman was stunningly beautiful, with a beautiful gown and perfectly kempt hair, all of which made Arline feel even more lacking than she usually felt. Mayhap, Arline thought, she was simply exhausted and had jumped to a conclusion about the woman.

Or, more likely than not, it was the way the woman draped herself around Rowan that made her want to scratch those beautiful blue eyes right out of their sockets.

Sleep. Arline thought. *I just need a bath and sleep. Yer bein' ridiculous. The woman has done nothin' to deserve yer rudeness!*

"'Tis me pleasure as well, me lady," Arline said, forcing a smile to her lips.

"Yer Garrick Blackthorn's wife, are ye no'?" Beatrice asked.

Her question, though hidden behind a veil of politeness, made the hair on the back of Arline's neck stand. "Nay, I am no longer married to Garrick Blackthorn."

Beatrice was stunned by the news. She pressed her delicate fingertips to her neck. "Nay? Be he dead?"

Arline stood straighter and thrust out her chin. "Nay, he is no'."

Confusion and curiosity lit behind Beatrice's eyes. "Then, how --"

Rowan did not allow Beatrice to finish her question. "Beatrice, now is no' the time." He did not want to bring any further embarrassment to Arline. She certainly did not need to be interrogated by Beatrice.

"Selina," Rowan began. "Please take Lady Arline above stairs as we discussed."

Selina gave a quick curtsy and pulled Arline away. Arline waited until they were out of earshot of the rest of the gathering room before asking about the beautiful Lady Beatrice. "Who is that woman?"

Selina's smile quickly evaporated. She cast a quick look over her shoulder at the woman in question. "Lady Beatrice?"

"Aye, Lady Beatrice."

Selina cleared her throat before answering. "She be a friend of Rowan's."

Friend? That could be taken any number of different ways. From the expression on Selina's face, the term was probably the most polite way of describing her as Rowan's lover. The thought made her heart feel tight, constricted.

They made their way up the curved and narrow staircase which spilled out onto a large landing. Selina remained quiet as she led Arline down the long narrow hallway.

"Lady Beatrice," Arline murmured softly. "She is Rowan's lover?"

Selina's eyes grew wide with disgust and surprise. "Och!" she exclaimed loudly before leaning in to speak to Arline in hushed tones. "She *wishes* she were his lover!"

Arline's interest was thoroughly piqued. She feigned ignorance and bade Selina to tell her more.

"My mum taught me that if I dunna have anythin' nice to say, then I shouldna say anythin' at all." Selina was reluctant to tell Arline anything that might be construed as inappropriate or rude.

Selina stopped midway down the hallway and opened the door to a nicely appointed bedchamber. A large canopied bed sat to Arline's right and directly opposite the bed was a fireplace. The room had not been used in quite some time and all the furniture, save for the lovely bed, was draped in white sheets.

"It has been some time since anyone has used this room, me lady," Selina said as she walked to the windows and pulled back the heavy furs that covered them. Though it was a rather gloomy day, the breeze that rushed in helped to remove some of the musty smell that filled the room.

Together, they began to remove the sheets from the furniture. Arline could not keep her curiosity at bay any longer.

"Selina, if yer mum *hadn't* taught ye to hold yer tongue if ye hadn't anythin' nice to say," Arline tried to sound as nonchalant as she could. "What *would* ye say about Lady Beatrice?'

Selina giggled as she snapped the dust from the sheet that had been hiding a beautiful writing desk. "Well, if me mum hadna taught me that, then I'd be tellin' ye that I do no' like Lady Beatrice."

Arline raised an eyebrow and felt some measure of satisfaction knowing she was not alone in her feelings for Lady Beatrice. "And?"

Selina folded the sheet and reached for the one that Lady Arline was holding. "Me lady, I do no' like to speak ill of someone who is no' here to defend themselves."

Instantly, Arline felt guilty for having asked. She detested gossip and felt precisely the same way as Selina when it came to speaking about someone behind their back. And what did she care about the relationship between Rowan and Beatrice?

So what if she had wakened this morning, wrapped in his strong, protective arms? And what did it matter that he kissed her neck? He had been asleep after all. She couldn't hold anything a sleeping man did against him.

She had done her best to convince herself that none of that had mattered. And she wasn't about to read anything into his offer of a safe home and a position as Lily's governess. Arline needed a home and Rowan needed someone to care for his daughter. There was nothing more to it than that.

As they set the room to rights, shaking the dust from the sheets and airing out the room, Arline answered Selina's questions on how she came to be at Castle Áit na Síochána.

Arline kept her answers short and to the point. Her story did not take long to explain and she was glad that Selina had not asked too many questions.

"Well," Selina said as she looked about the room. "While yer in the bathin' room, I'll bring ye clean sheets and blankets. I'll see about findin' ye some clean clothes as well."

"Bathin' room?" Arline asked.

"Aye, we have a room below stairs, just off the kitchens, where we do all our bathin'," Selina explained. "We have six tubs there. It saves on us havin' to tote tubs and buckets of water up and down the stairs."

Arline thought it an ingenious idea and could not wait to see it. She followed Selina out of the room and down a different set of stairs. These were a bit wider and well lit from sconces that hung on the walls every few feet.

The stairs took them into a very small area next to the larder and kitchen. Arline could hear a bustling of activity coming from the kitchen. They continued down a narrow hallway lined with many heavy wooden doors. Selina opened the second door to their right. The humidity hit Arline's face the moment she stepped inside.

The room was quite large, with tall ceilings and wood floors.

151

There were gaps between the wooden planks which Arline found odd. A wall ran down the center of the room dividing it in half. There were three tubs on each side, a large fireplace with an enormous pot hanging over the fire. It resembled the pots one would find in the laundries.

Several chairs were scattered about the room along with low tables and shelves. Selina led Arline to the tub room on their right. "This side is fer the women, the other side fer the men," Selina explained. "I'll grab a bucket and start fillin' the tub."

"I'll help ye," Arline said as she followed Selina to the fire.

In a short time, the tub was filled with hot, steamy water. Selina took a vial from one of the shelves and added a few drops of scented oil to the water. Arline breathed in deeply, all at once feeling both happy and relaxed. "Lilies?" she asked, recognizing the scent almost immediately.

"Aye," Selina said with a smile. "We collected them from the loch in the summer. We have other scents ye can try later. Lavender, blue bell, marigold. If ye have a scent ye like, I can make it fer ye."

Arline hurried out of her clothes, unable to wait any longer to soak in the hot, steamy water. "Ye make them?"

"Aye, I do." Selina smiled proudly. "I learned at me mum's hip!"

Arline draped her cloak, dress and chemise on the back of a chair and anxiously stuck one toe into the tub. It was a bit hot, but she was not about to complain. Her bones and muscles ached.

Carefully, she slid into the tub. Almost instantly, the water began to soothe her achy muscles and tired bones. "Heavenly," she murmured as the water worked its magic.

She sat soaking for a time, enjoying the sleepy feeling as it crept in. She could have stayed here until the morning, as long as the water was warmed.

Selina helped her to bathe and wash her hair. It took some time before the water began to cool and Arline enjoyed every moment of it.

Far too soon for her liking, she was scrubbed clean from head to toe. The mud and muck was washed from her hair and she felt better than she had in days.

As Selina was rinsing the last of the soap from Arline's hair, a young girl, came rushing into the bathing room.

"Selina!" the girl said, out of breath and panting. "Mrs. McGregor needs ye straight away!" The girl sounded panicked.

"Is it Lily?" Arline asked as she hurried to rinse off.

"Nay, m'lady," the girl said curtly. She shot Arline an odd look, as if Arline had no right to ask such a question.

"Och!" Selina said, patting Arline's shoulders. "Never ye mind it, m'lady. Mrs. McGregor is always fashin' on about somethin'. She be the head cook here and is always in a fit over one thing or another." Selina poured another pitcher of clean water over Arline's hair.

"But, Selina, she said *now*. Ye are to drop everythin' and come see her immediately." The girl cast a look of reproach toward Arline. "Do ye ken how to bathe yerself?" the girl asked, her words sharp and clipped.

"Of course I ken," Arline answered calmly. She could not figure out why this girl seemed so angry or bitter toward her.

"Come now, Selina," the girl urged. "She's fit to be tied."

Selina rolled her eyes and let out a frustrated sigh. "Go tell her I'll be right there."

"*Now,* Selina," the girl folded her arms over her chest, looking quite upset with the both of them.

"Selina, go. I can make my way back to me room," Arline told her.

"Are ye certain, m'lady?" Selina asked.

"Aye. Just hand me a dryin' cloth and I'll be fine."

Selina nodded, grabbed a drying cloth from a peg on the wall and handed it to Arline. "I'll see what has Mrs. McGregor in such a fit and I'll come to help ye straight away. They should have put yer room to rights by now."

"Thank ye, Selina," Arline said as she stood and climbed from the tub. She wrapped the drying cloth around her shoulders and smiled at Selina. "I do thank ye, fer all of yer help, Selina. Now go, before ye get into trouble with Mrs. McGregor."

TWELVE

Arline managed to find her way back to her room after her bath. She was rather surprised to find that her room had not been *put to rights* as Selina had promised. There was no fire in the hearth and no clean linens or blankets on the bed. It looked exactly as it had been left.

She dropped her cloak, dress, and chemise on the bed and looked about the room. Had someone thought to at least bring the wood and kindling, she could have started her own fire. There wasn't so much as a candle for her to light.

Mayhap Selina was having a difficult time finding something suitable for her to wear. Arline felt certain that Selina would appear at any moment, her arms filled with clean clothes and linens, and a sensible explanation.

With no fire to help dry her hair, she felt cold. The room, devoid of any warmth, left her with a sense of longing. She had lived a solitary existence in a castle full of people for many months and this room left her feeling as though she were back at Garrick's keep.

Drawing the drying cloth around her shoulders for warmth, she explored the room. The drawers in the writing desk were empty, as was the large cupboard that sat in the corner by the fireplace. She had the same results with the trunk at the foot of the bed. Nothing to even hint that anyone had ever lived in this room.

She sat in the chair at the writing desk and took the drying cloth to her hair. Her skin turned to gooseflesh as she attempted to dry her long locks without knotting them. After a time, the cool air coming in through the open windows became far too chilly. She went to the bed and pulled on her cloak. At least it was some form of warmth.

The longer she was made to wait the more frustrated she became. She walked around the room, trying to keep warm, and trying to convince herself that she had not been forgotten.

Rowan had been far too much of a gentleman to have forgotten her, hadn't he? Had he not made sure she had food aplenty and was warm on their journey here? He had.

Mayhap something was wrong. Mayhap someone had slipped another sleeping draught into the ale and someone was, at this very moment, making their way out of the keep with Lily!

She was about to rush out of the room and below stairs when the door flew open. At first, she felt a great sense of relief until she saw who it was that was entering.

"Lady Beatrice," Arline said unable to mask her surprise.

Beatrice entered the room in a great hurry, shutting the door behind her before hurrying to Arline. The woman looked positively beside herself with worry.

"Lady Arline!" Beatrice exclaimed, taking Arline's hands in hers. "There is no' much time to explain, but I need ye to come with me!"

Arline's first thought was that something was wrong with Lily. Her heart began to pound against her breast. "Is it Lily?" she asked worriedly.

"Nay, Lily is in good care," Beatrice said as she tried to pull Arline to the door.

Arline would not move until she knew what had brought the woman here in such a frenzied state. "What is the matter, Lady Beatrice? Is the keep under attack?"

Beatrice stopped pulling on Arline and looked over her shoulder at the door. "Nay, the keep is no' under attack. 'Tis ye that I worry over! Please, I beg ye to come with me. I promise I'll explain meself, but I need ye to hurry."

Arline stood her ground. "I'll no' leave this room until ye tell me what is the matter."

Beatrice let out a frustrated breath and took Arline's hands again. "'Tis Rowan."

Arline's brow drew into a knot. "Rowan? Is he ill? Injured?"

Beatrice shook her head. "Nay, he's no' injured. And I suppose one could say he's ill, but 'tis an illness of his own doin'."

"I don't understand," Arline said. The woman wasn't making any sense at all.

"Rowan has fallen back into the bottle, me lady."

Rowan? A drunkard? Nay, she could not believe that.

Beatrice gave Arline's hands a gentle squeeze. Worry was etched across her beautiful face and she seemed quite sincere. "Lady Arline, I ken it be hard to believe, but Rowan, he has no' been well since his Kate died. He'll go months without so much as a drop of anything stronger than weak wine. Then something happens and he takes up the whisky. Och! When he's no' drinkin' he is the kindest man ye'd ever meet! But when he's in the bottle? Och! He's not himself. He turns mean and angry."

Arline felt her heart crack. The poor man! He still grieved over losing his wife and that grief led him to drink. "I should go to him!" Arline said and started toward the door. Beatrice stopped her.

"Nay!" Beatrice cried out. "Ye must stay away from him!"

Rowan had done so much for her. How could she in good conscience leave him alone in his time of need? "Mayhap if I talk to him--"

Beatrice stopped her. "Nay, ye don't understand. 'Tis *ye* that he is mad at."

"Me?" That made absolutely no sense. Arline had done nothing to earn his ire.

"He is below stairs, in his library, drinkin'. I had to leave him to come warn ye. I dunna ken why he is so angry with ye, me lady, but he is. Out of his mind. He keeps calling ye--" she paused as if the words were too painful to say.

"Calling me what?" Arline wasn't sure she wanted to know the answer.

"I'm sorry, me lady, I truly am. Ye must no' take it to heart. When he is drinkin' he canna control his tongue or his fists."

Arline shook her head as if doing so would bring some clarity to the moment. "Lady Beatrice, please, tell me what he said."

Beatrice took a deep breath and cast her eyes to the floor. "He's calling ye Blackthorn's whore."

He might have well slapped her across the face, the shock was the same. *Blackthorn's whore?*

Beatrice wasn't finished. "I'm so verra sorry, me lady. But he is so angry. He says ye may well have helped take care of Lily, but ye were still married to Garrick Blackthorn and still his whore. I left and came to ye as quickly as I could because he was talking about tossing ye into the dungeon. He says he doesna feel he can trust ye."

Arline felt numb, cold to her bones, and very much alone. She knew, from the many nights she had listened to her father drink himself into a stupor, that men said things while drunk that they would never say during a sober moment. And sometimes they spoke their true hearts.

Rowan apparently thought very little of her. Had he made the offer of a home and position caring for Lily so that he could keep a close eye on her? Did he think she was a spy, working to gain knowledge for Garrick.

"I truly did no' want to tell ye this, me lady. It breaks me heart to do so. He'll be fine in a few days. But ye must stay out of his sight until he's done with the drink."

Arline was too stunned, far too hurt to utter a sound.

"We have a room fer ye, above stairs. He never ventures up there and ye'll be safe. Fer now, he's ordered that we treat ye more prisoner than guest. We canna give ye any clean clothes, ye canna come to the gathering room fer yer meals. If he sees ye, he is liable to order ye tossed in the dungeon."

She had traded one prison for another. "How often does he get like this, Beatrice?" Arline mumbled.

"Och, only every other month."

Every other month? How could she spend every other month in hiding while she was supposed to be here taking care of Lily? Lily, the poor babe. What pain must the poor babe suffer through when her father was like this?

"What of Lily?" Arline asked.

"Och! He'd never hurt her, no matter how badly he drinks. He loves that child more than anything."

There was some relief in knowing that. The poor child. How could a man as kind and honorable as the one she had come to know these past few days turn into such a monster?

Blackthorn's whore. Is that what he truly thought of her? It made her ill to think that he did. She felt angry and hurt and violated. Even more so than when Garrick had beat her senseless and tossed her out of his home.

"He'll be fine a few days, me lady. But fer now, we must keep ye safe and hidden."

Mindlessly, Arline grabbed her dress and old chemise and followed Lady Beatrice out of the room and to the third floor. It was so very difficult to wrap her head around the prospect that the man she had come to care so much for was in truth a drunkard and a mean one at that. How could he think such things about her?

They made their way down a long narrow corridor. Arline could tell that Beatrice was doing her best to make her feel better. "Please, me lady, do not worry over it. Just a few days, and ye'll see, he will be his old self again."

Arline wondered which Rowan was the true Rowan? The kind, handsome, tender, honorable man or the mean drunk? She'd only known him but a few days so she could not rightly answer that question at the moment.

They finally reached their destination. Beatrice opened the door and led Arline inside. It was a very small room. But at least here, she had blankets. Small comfort but a comfort nonetheless. An old chair sat in the corner, the pallet and blankets along one wall. A few trunks sat along the opposite wall and in the center of the room was a brazier. It might not have been as open and spacious as the room she had just left, but at least she would be out of Rowan's path. And there were the makings for a fire.

"Me maid, Joan, will bring ye a meal verra soon, me lady," Beatrice said from the door. "I ken it be not much of a room, but here, ye will be safe."

"What of Lily? I was to take care of her," Arline's voice began to crack.

Beatrice smiled thoughtfully at Arline. "She's in good hands, me lady. Selina is taking care of her." Beatrice left, quietly closing the door behind her.

Arline stood in the center of the tiny room feeling lost and hurt. Knowing Selina was taking care of Lily lightened Arline's heart somewhat. But still, she wished she could go see for herself that Lily was doing well.

Arline could sense that the people here did care a great deal for Lily. The women had practically smothered the child with hugs and kisses earlier.

But what of the one person here who had slipped the sleeping draught into the ale? Could that person still be lurking about, only pretending to have good feelings toward their chief and his child? Would that person be foolish enough to try again?

With Rowan deep in his cups, *now* would be a perfect opportunity for them to strike again.

She grew quite angry. How could Rowan lower his defenses at a time like this? How could he drink himself into a stupor when the traitor had yet to be found? What was the man thinking?

Pacing the room, which was no more than eight steps by eight steps, Arline chewed on her thumbnail and tried to work the events out quietly. The more she worked them over in her mind, the angrier and more hurt she became.

The evening meal would be served soon. She decided that she would wait until then before she left the room. If Rowan was drinking as heavily as Lady Beatrice had described, more likely than not he would pass out before too long.

Hopefully Joan would arrive with a tray soon. As soon as she could, she would make her way through the keep to find Lily, just to make certain the child was, in fact, well.

A tear fell down her cheek when she thought of how kind he had been. How could she have been so foolish to believe he was any different from any other man she had known? Were it not for Carlich showing her that men could in fact be kind, she would never have believed it possible.

In a few days, once Rowan climbed his way out of the bottle, Arline would go to him and ask for the escort to Inverness. He would be much easier to deal with sober. There was no sense in poking a stick at the hornet's nest for she knew she'd be stung repeatedly. He'd toss her into their dungeon and heaven only knew how long he would keep her there.

Not much time had passed before there was a knock on Arline's door. She opened it cautiously. A young woman, mayhap in her early twenties, stood in the hallway with a tray in her hands. She was a very pretty young woman, with dark blonde hair and bright blue eyes.

"I be Joan, me lady," she said with a curtsy.

Arline opened the door to allow the girl to enter. Joan sat the tray down on one of the trunks without saying a word.

"I thank ye kindly, Joan."

"I wish it could be more, m'lady, but with Rowan in such a foul mood and the larder near empty, 'tis the best we can do." She hurried to the door.

"The larder is empty?" Arline asked.

"Near to empty. The clan is still trying to make up fer all that was lost four years ago."

The Black Death. There wasn't a clan in all of Scotland, or people anywhere else, that had not been affected by it. Arline had not realized the toll it had taken on Clan Graham until now. It had to have been horrific if their larders were still bare after four years. Mayhap that was one more reason why Rowan drank.

"I managed ye some tea, m'lady, and a bit o' bread," Joan said apologetically. "They try to feed the bairns and wee ones first, ye ken."

Arline felt her heart begin to crack even further. These poor, poor people! "Thank ye again, Joan."

Joan gave a sad nod and left the room. Arline closed the door behind her and barred it.

No wonder Rowan had come to rescue Lily. He hadn't possessed the funds to pay the ransom.

She was left feeling even more confused. How could a man like Rowan be a drunkard? He had risked everything to rescue his daughter, not because he was selfish and didn't want to pay the ransom, but because he could not. Rather than risk his daughter's life when Garrick found he could not pay, he risked his own life to save hers.

That was not the mark of a drunkard or a lout. That was the mark of a man with a heart, with conviction and honor. A man who loved his daughter.

Suddenly, she found she could no longer be angry with him. There was a distinct possibility that the man drank to dull the pain, the hurt left behind in the wake of the Black Death. How could she blame him? How could she hold anything against the poor man?

He'd lost his wife, a good number of clansmen, and had nearly lost his daughter. 'Twas no wonder the man drank.

She decided that she could no longer be angry with him. She would wait until he had sobered up and then she would have a good long talk with him. She would offer whatever assistance she could to help his clan grow and prosper. She could be more than just a governess, she could be his friend.

There was plenty of money being held in her name. In just a few short months, she would turn five and twenty and demand that her father turn the funds over. She would not use the money to travel the world. Instead, she would offer it to Rowan as a gesture of goodwill, of thanks for offering her a home.

She could not hold anything he had said in a drunken rage against him. Chances were he was not angry with her, but with himself and the lot life had dealt him.

With her mind made up, she went to the trunks and removed the linen to see what Joan had managed to procure for a meal.

Porridge. Bloody hell.

H aving bathed and donned fresh clothes, Rowan entered the gathering room with a bounce in his step and a smile on his face. With great anticipation, he looked forward to seeing what Lady Arline would look like with clean hair and a fresh gown. Clean or dirty, the woman fascinated him.

The room was already filled near to capacity when he entered. His men, some with wives, some with women who hoped to someday be their wives, were milling about the room or already seated. The smoky air was filled with the sounds of laughter, giggles and chatter.

Ever since Kate's death, Rowan had dreaded the evening meals. He missed having Kate sitting beside him, missed sharing his day with her over a fine meal.

But tonight, he actually found himself looking forward to the evening meal. Lady Arline had begun to fill the void in his life. It made him feel young again, more alive and excited than he had felt in more than four years. Though he was still unsure what he exactly felt for her, he could not deny that he was growing genuinely fond of the woman.

His smile instantly faded when he saw that Lily was already seated at the head table, in her usual spot to his right. What frustrated and angered him so was the fact that Lady Beatrice was sitting in the spot to his left. He wanted Arline there, beside him, not Beatrice.

Working his jaw back and forth he made his way toward the high table. He would not embarrass Beatrice by asking her to move, but come the morrow, he would make certain that she understood where the two of them stood. He'd make damned certain she was completely clear on the subject and that she would never sit in that seat again.

He made his way up the three steps and to his seat. Lily scrambled down from her chair and flung her arms around his leg before he could sit.

"Da!" she exclaimed happily. "I missed ye!"

Rowan scooped her up into his arms and gave her a big hug. "And why would ye be missin' me? Ye just saw me no' more than an hour ago."

Lily giggled and gave him a peck on his cheek. "I always miss ye."

He patted her back and set her down on the bench. He sat down beside her and turned finally to Beatrice. "Lady Beatrice," he said, trying as best he could to mask his anger.

"Rowan," she said with a lady like nod of her head. "'Tis good to see ye."

He could not say the same thing and refused to lie about it. He was not happy, not happy at all, to see her sitting at the high table, without his invitation.

"I trust ye are pleased with how well the keep ran in yer absence?" Beatrice asked.

Rowan continued to clench his jaw, swallowed down the myriad of things he wanted to tell her. "My keep *always* runs well in my absence. I've good people here."

She had been fishing for a compliment and he was not about to give her one. A look of disappointment flashed in her eyes, quickly replaced with a smile. "Ye do, Rowan, ye do."

Beatrice took a drink of ale. Rowan was looking about the room, his expression growing more sullen as the moments ticked by. He could not find Arline anywhere.

As if she could read his mind, Beatrice spoke. "I believe ye be searchin' fer someone who is no' here."

Rowan cast an angry glance at her before taking a drink of ale.

"Do no' worry, Rowan. Lady Arline is safely tucked away. She was too exhausted, too tired this night to attend the meal. I'm sure she'll be fine after a good night's sleep."

Some of his anger subsided. It made perfectly good sense that Arline was tired. He made a mental note to check in on her later.

"I had Joan take her a tray. Joan tells me that Arline did eat and she's now resting quite comfortably."

More of his anger faded. He was relieved to hear that Arline had eaten. The woman was nothing but skin and bones. He worried over that and those awful bruises on her torso. "And the healer?"

Beatrice took another sip of ale before answering. "Lady Arline is quite well. All she needs is a few days rest."

The kitchen staff began bringing trays of delectable foods to the tables.

"Venison! Sweet cakes!" Lily squealed happily. "I be verra hungry da."

Rowan ran a hand over the top of Lily's head and smiled as she stuffed a bite of venison in her mouth. He'd let her eat whatever she wished this night, for he knew it had been quite some time since she had eaten anything more than porridge or bread and cheese and apples. His stomach tightened when he thought of how poorly his daughter -- and Lady Arline -- had been treated.

He found his appetite waning. More than anything he wanted to go to Lady Arline, to see with his own eyes how she fared. But if she was resting, it would be rude of him to interrupt. He decided he would let her sleep for now. But in the morning, he would go to her, just to see for himself.

G etting Rowan Graham to fall in love with her had turned out to be a daunting, if not an impossible task. Most men fell over their own feet to get to Beatrice. But not Rowan. The fool.

It took a great deal of effort on her part, not to dump her trencher on top of Rowan's head. Could the man not see how badly he needed her? Could he not see what a value she was to him, to his people?

She needed him to see what a wonderful wife she would make, needed him to find her irreplaceable.

It was not his heart that she desired. Nor did she crave to join with his magnificent body. Those two needs and desires were currently being met by a man much younger than Rowan Graham. Aye, he might not exude the same power as Rowan, or the same level of sexual experience. Still, there was something to be said for stamina.

There were other things that only Rowan Graham could give her.

Beatrice had tried every feminine wile she could think of and none of them had worked. The stupid man was still so in love with his dead wife that he could not see what was standing in front of him. Or, right beside him.

She knew she had been taking a chance by taking the seat next to his without an invitation. She had hoped that by seeing her in that spot, it would help give him a nudge in the right direction. At the very least, get him to start thinking of her as a potential wife.

Her boldness hadn't even elicited a smile. Nay, instead, he had looked quite angry to see her there. It was all that blasted Lady Arline's fault. How in the bloody hell did the woman still live? She was supposed to be dead. And if not dead, then on her way back to Ireland.

But nay, somehow the whore lived and found her way here. Rowan had been somewhat evasive in his answers when she had spoken with him earlier. *She needed our help, so we gave it. Were it no' fer Arline, Lily may be dead. I owe her a great debt, Beatrice.*

She had been afraid to push the matter further until she heard Lily. The brat spoke of nothing but *Wady Awine.* Lady Arline this, Lady Arline that. As if the ugly wench was some kind of mythological goddess come to life.

Bah! The child was witless and took up far too much space in her father's heart. But then, it wasn't his heart Beatrice wanted or needed. Just his hand in marriage.

She watched Rowan out of the corner of her eye. He was focused intently on his daughter, hanging on every word that came out of her mouth. It was as if Beatrice wasn't there, as if she did not exist or were of no import at all.

One way or another, Rowan Graham was going to marry her. If he wouldn't come willingly, slobbering all over her like most men did, then she had no problem in deceiving him into asking for her hand.

Rowan Graham was honorable. That was Beatrice's biggest obstacle, yet, in the end, it would be her greatest weapon.

THIRTEEN

Arline could not remember falling asleep. She awoke with a dull throbbing headache. Cursing under her breath, she threw back the covers and rolled off the pallet. With no windows in her room, there was no way to tell if she had been asleep for a few hours or a few days.

Rubbing the sleep from her eyes, she stood and tried to stretch her aching muscles. There was no fire left in the brazier. Cold black coals were all that remained. It was a sign that she had been asleep for several hours.

The room was cold, frigid and made her bones ache all the more. There was not much wood or kindling left, but there was enough to help take the chill out of the air. In no time, she had a decent enough fire going.

Her stomach growled. She had refused to eat the porridge last night. There wasn't so much as a crumb left of the bread. There was nothing in her room with which to make tea. What she would not give for a dram of whisky and a piece of venison.

She took her cloak from the peg and wrapped it around her shoulders before sitting down beside the fire. How long would she have to live like this? Could she last several more days with nothing but bitter tea and stale bread?

As she sat gazing at the flickering flames in the brazier a knock came at her door. She flew to her feet, unbarred the door and opened it, hoping that whomever was on the other side was holding a tray of food. She was so hungry that she would not turn away a bowl of porridge, no matter how she detested it.

It was Lady Beatrice and her hands were empty.

"Lady Beatrice!" Arline said as she opened the door and bid her entry.

"Lady Arline," Beatrice said as she floated into the room. "How fare ye this morn?"

Arline's stomach growled her answer. She felt her cheeks grow warm with embarrassment.

"Ye poor thing! I be so sorry for this ill treatment. I've heard how kind ye were to Lily. Ye deserve better treatment, me lady."

Arline waved her hand as if to say not to worry. "How is Lily this morn?" Arline wanted nothing more than to go to the child, wrap her arms around her, and tell her that all would be well.

"She is well. She adores Selina. They get along quite well."

Arline had seen neither hide nor hair of Selina since yesterday. She supposed that Selina was busy caring for Lily while Arline was locked away like a thief. Although she hadn't spent much time with Selina, she felt Selina could be trusted. But Beatrice? She was not sure.

Arline's first impression of Beatrice had been one of immediate and intense dislike. Now that she had had ample time to think on it, Arline began to think those feelings were the result of her own jealousy. Beatrice seemed sincere and to genuinely care about her.

"And how does Rowan fare today?"

Beatrice's smile faded. She took a deep, sad breath and shook her head. "No better. He started drinkin' the moment he woke up this morning. And he's been at it all day."

Arline's eyes grew wide with surprise and shame. "All day? How long did I sleep? What time is it?"

"Och! Do no' worry over it, me lady. Ye had been through such a trial of late. We thought it best to let ye sleep. It is well past the noonin meal."

No wonder her stomach was growling so intensely. That also explained the headache she had wakened with. She always got a headache if she slept too long. "I apologize, Lady Beatrice. I'm not one to sleep the day away."

Beatrice smiled warmly at her. "After what ye've been through? No one could blame ye fer sleepin'. Now, I must hurry. I will have Joan bring ye another tray."

Arline thanked her for her kindness. "I hate to be a bother, but I could truly use a clean dress. Do ye think ye could arrange it?"

"I shall do me best, but I can make no promises. Rowan is still in a rage over ye today. He did ask where ye were. I told him ye were no' feelin' well. If he finds ye, I'm certain he'll order ye to the dungeon. I fear he is no' getting any kinder in his regard toward ye. He keeps referrin' to ye as Blackthorn's whore, calling fer ye to be flogged fer bein' a spy."

Arline pursed her lips together. Last night she had been convinced he drank to dull his pain. She refused to give in to her urge to go and find him and clobber him over the head with something heavy.

"I can assure ye, Lady Beatrice, that I be no spy."

"I believe ye, me lady. But Rowan? He canna think straight when he is like this. He seems worse this time. Much worse."

Arline raised an eyebrow. "How so?"

"Well, he took three women to his bed last night and that is so unlike him. Most times, he does no' pick up the bottle until after the noonin meal. I worry that this time, he might no' stop drinkin'."

Not stop? He had to stop. He had to think of his daughter, his clan. "Ye canna be serious?"

Beatrice looked quite sorrowful. Her shoulders sagged and tears formed in her eyes. "I am. He's no' ever been this bad before. I tried talkin' to him, but me words fell on deaf ears. He will no' listen to me, or to Frederick and Frederick be his most trusted and valued friend. Frederick is just as worried as I."

These people knew their chief, their friend, far better than Arline.

She supposed they'd known each other for years. If his best and truest friend was worried, then mayhap Arline should worry.

"I say we wait a few more days, me lady. And if he doesna stop his drinkin', we'll make arrangements fer ye to leave, to go back to Ireland."

"Nay!" Arline exclaimed. "I will no' ever go back to Ireland."

Beatrice looked puzzled by Arline's statement. "No' go back? But why?"

Arline had no desire to confide in Beatrice. It was far too embarrassing and humiliating to explain. "I have me reasons. I will no' go back. But if Rowan does no' stop this time, then I shall leave. But I'll no go back to me father."

"Then we shall find ye safe haven elsewhere," Beatrice said. "But fer now, please, do no' leave this room. I fear fer yer life, me lady, I truly do."

With that, she left Arline alone to ponder her situation.

Her dreams of belonging to a family such as Rowan's was rapidly dwindling away. Of course, she still had her sisters, Morralyn and Geraldine. The funds their father held for Arline would be enough to see they lived comfortably for the rest of their days. Nay, they wouldn't live a life of luxury but neither would they live a life of want and need. Her heart stung with missing them. Mayhap she should just go to Rowan now and ask for the escort to Inverness. But nay, he was drunk, mean and threatening to have her flogged! There would be no way to have an intelligent conversation with him in his current state.

Such a fool she had been to think, even for a brief moment, that she could live here, among the people of Clan Graham. She had begun to care a great deal about Rowan, Lily and even his men. She had hoped that his people would welcome her, if not with open arms then with the possibility of forging friendships.

Her mind began to wander to something else Beatrice had said. Rowan had taken three women to his bed last night. Three! The thought made her cheeks burn red and her anger bubble up again. She could barely imagine what it would be like to be with one man. She couldn't imagine what such an intimate act would be like with two additional women. An involuntary shiver ran down her spine.

Mayhap Rowan Graham wasn't the honorable kind man she believed him to be. Mayhap he was just as morally bankrupt as her own father. It was that bright smile of his, that more than beautiful face and those dark brown eyes. He hid behind a façade of beauty, but deep down, underneath it all, he was just as depraved and ruthless as most other men she had known.

"I be an utter fool," she mumbled aloud as she began to pace around the cramped room. "A complete and utter eejit!"

Rowan was worried when Arline had not appeared in the gathering room that morning. Believing she was still mending from her injuries and far too tired to make it down the stairs, he went about his normal daily routine.

He and his men took to the training fields for a few hours. They had to maintain a level of preparedness in case Garrick Blackthorn decided to reclaim some of the dignity he lost when Rowan was able to gain entry into his keep and retrieve his daughter.

Knowing Garrick Blackthorn as he did, Rowan wouldn't put anything past the man. Garrick was a full-grown man, but still acted more like a spoiled child. There was seldom any sense to be found in anything the idiot did.

Part of Rowan wished that the fool *would* attack, just for the opportunity to kill the bastard. He relished the thought of cutting his throat or running his broadsword through his gut.

But the more sensible part of him knew that the clan might not be able to withstand such an attack. The number of fighting men was nowhere near what it had been before the Black Death. He had been slowly rebuilding the numbers, offering home and hearth and the promise of a future to men who had also lost much four years ago. It was a slow process.

The men he did have were well trained and loyal and he knew he could count on each and every one of them. But they did not have the numbers to equal Garrick Blackthorn's.

Rowan was not completely without hope. If Blackthorn trained his men in the same manner he treated people, with no respect or dignity, then he probably had a group of lazy warriors whose fealty was to their own necks.

He had spent a good portion of the afternoon in his library with Lily asking one question after another. Very few of them could he answer. Most of them were in regard to Lady Arline.

"But *when* will she get better? And when can I see her?" Lily asked as she sat on the edge of his desk playing with the doll that Arline had made for her.

"I do no' ken, lass. But she has been through much and needs her rest."

Lily didn't care for his answer. "I was through much too! And look! I'm all better!"

He could not argue with her reasoning. But he knew that children tended to be far more resilient than adults.

"Aye, and I be verra glad ye are all better," he told her as he added numbers in his ledger.

"So why isn't Lady Arline better? I miss her. Lady Beatrice won't let me go see her. Why can't I?"

Rowan let out a frustrated sigh, set down his feather and looked at his daughter. "Lily, ye must understand that Lady Arline was seriously injured and it will take a few days to recover."

"Have ye seen her?"

"Nay, I have not." And it wasn't for lack of wanting to. He was simply giving the lass time to rest. But still, he was growing concerned as the hours passed by without seeing her.

"I miss her, da," Lily said, pulling her lips into a pout. "She took good care of me."

Rowan knew his daughter was genuinely concerned for Arline, for he had similar concerns.

"I tell ye what, lass," Rowan said as he scooped Lily up and into his arms. "We will give Lady Arline another day to rest and if she is still not well, we shall go and see her."

"Do ye promise?" Lily asked as she rested her head against his chest.

"I do so promise," Rowan whispered. "She'll be better soon, so ye needn't worry. 'Tis nothin' some good sleep won't cure."

He prayed that he was right.

L ater that afternoon, Rowan called for Frederick, Daniel and Thomas for a meeting in his library. They had much business to discuss, the primary concern being who had tainted the ale with the sleeping draught.

Rowan sat behind his desk as the three men stood before him.

"Have ye learned anything since our return?"

"Nay, Rowan, we have not," Thomas answered. "I've been askin' the womenfolk and so far, nothin'. Mrs. McGregor seems to be as puzzled as the rest of us as to who might have done this. But, it would be quite easy to slip into the cellar and taint the ale. 'Tisn't like we keep it guarded."

There had never been a need to keep the ale under guard. No one, least of all Rowan, would ever think such an act necessary. His clansmen were good, honest people. Many were related by blood, but others had come from nearby clans that had been decimated by the Black Death. There were even a few from as far away as Inverness.

Concern was etched in the lines of his face. Had he unwittingly opened his home to a traitor? Or worse yet, traitors? Why would anyone do such a thing? Had he not offered them a safe home? Did he not treat each among them with respect and dignity?

"Have any of ye any suspicions?" Rowan asked.

The men cast furtive glances at each other. Rowan sensed they were afraid to speak their minds, which he found rather odd. Each of them looked very uncomfortable.

"I get the feelin' ye be afraid to speak yer minds, lads."

Frederick cleared his throat and shifted from one foot to the next. "None of us want to suspect our own, Rowan."

"Neither do I, Frederick. But someone within these castle walls tainted the ale and kidnapped me daughter. We need to find out who it was. Who is to say that they might not make an attempt again?"

"Do ye really think it be one of our own, Rowan?" Thomas asked.

While he did not like the thought, it was a possibility. "I dunna what to believe at this point, Thomas. I dunna want to think it be one of our own."

Daniel finally spoke. "Do ye think it be one of those that ye opened yer home to? Someone not born within the clan?"

Frederick turned and looked at Daniel, visibly angered by his question. "I was no' born within this clan, and neither was me brother Ian. Do ye accuse us?"

"Nay, I do no'!" Daniel snapped. "But at this point, no one is above suspicion. Do I think ye or yer brother were involved? Nay, I do no'. But *someone* did betray us, all of us."

Frederick looked as though he were ready to snap Daniel's neck. Frederick had come to live among the clan when Rowan and Kate first married.

"If I thought, even for the briefest moment, that any of *ye* were involved, ye would no' be standin' here before me," Rowan said as he looked Frederick in the eye. "I trust the two of ye with me own life and the life of me child." He paused a moment to allow his words to settle in. "But Daniel is still correct. Someone here *did* betray us and we need to find out *who*. We can worry about the why of it later."

Thomas offered his own opinion on the matter. "Aye," he said as he patted Frederick on the shoulder. "I feel the same as Rowan. I trust ye and Daniel, without question. But the fact remains we have to find out who did this."

"Keep doin' what yer doin'," Rowan told them. "Keep yer eyes and ears open. I'd concentrate first on those who are newest here. They verra well could have been sent by Blackthorn to do this. As of this moment, no one is above suspicion save the four of us in this room."

"Does that include the ladies Arline and Beatrice?" Thomas asked as he folded his arms over his chest.

Rowan's stomach tightened at the notion. "Need I remind ye that Lady Arline was no' here?"

"Nay, I ken that. But, how do we ken that she wasn't sent to finish what was started?"

Rowan cast him a look of derision. "At the point we met Lady Arline, she was plannin' on stealin' Lily away, to protect her from Garrick. The man didna ken we were comin' fer me daughter, so how could they have planned such a thing?"

"We dunna ken any such thing, Rowan," Thomas replied sternly. "I keep askin' meself how it was that ye were able to get into his keep so easily? 'Twas almost as if he was expectin' ye."

Rowan had thought they had settled this matter days ago. "Lady Arline *is* above reproach. Need I remind ye that she helped save Angus McKenna's and Duncan McEwan's necks seven years ago?"

In Rowan's mind that was enough to disqualify her as spy and traitor. Thomas however was not so inclined to remove Lady Arline from the list of suspects.

"I ken what she did fer Angus and Duncan. But much can happen in seven years, Rowan."

Rowan was growing impatient with Thomas' theory. "So ye believe do ye, that Garrick Blackthorn, known whoreson and spoiled bastard, allowed us into his keep so we could take Lily back? And ye believe that Lady Arline allowed him to beat the bloody hell out of her just so she can gain entry into our keep? Fer what purpose, Thomas? To steal Mrs. McGregor's recipe for meat pies?"

Thomas rolled his eyes. "Nay, no' to steal Mrs. McGregor's recipes."

"What then?" Rowan asked, holding his palms upward. "It makes no sense, Thomas."

"None of this makes much sense, Rowan," Daniel said. "I believe Garrick Blackthorn was no' hurtin' fer money, or anythin' else fer that matter. He outnumbers us two to one. His clan was no' hurt nearly as bad as ours and many others. If it's yer coin he wants, why no' just attack and take it? Why kidnap Lily fer ransom?"

Rowan thought that to be a very good question. He pondered it for several long moments. "Let's look at what we do ken," he said as he stood and went to the fireplace. "We ken that Garrick is a spoiled man. A boy trapped in a man's body. We ken that he has plenty of fightin' men, more men than we. We ken that someone here aided in the kidnappin' of me daughter," he paused and clasped his hands behind his back and thought.

"We also ken that he annulled his marriage to Lady Arline," Daniel offered. "But why? They were married for over a year."

"What has that got to do with anythin'?" Rowan asked, growing perturbed with how they kept coming back to Lady Arline.

"I find it curious is all," Daniel said.

"She's barren," Frederick said with a shrug of his shoulders. "Garrick was no' her first husband. She was married to Carlich for three years and no children came of that marriage. 'Tis the only thing that makes sense. He annulled the marriage because she could no' give him an heir."

Rowan was growing more and more frustrated with the topic. In his heart, he knew Lady Arline had nothing to do with the kidnapping. "Again, I ask ye *why* that be important."

"It may no' be important as it pertains to the kidnappin'. But it may be important fer *ye* to ken that," Thomas replied.

"Me? Why would I care if she be barren or no'?" Rowan unclasped his hands and rested them on his hips.

"Och! Rowan, we all saw how ye were lookin' at the lass on our journey home," Thomas said with more than a hint of frustration to his tone.

"Yer daft. I have no idea what yer referrin' to, Thomas," Rowan snapped at him. Aye, he had fond feelings toward the woman. But he was not yet ready to admit to anyone that there might be more to his feelings than just a fond admiration or gratitude for what she had done for Lily.

Thomas harrumphed. "And yer daft if ye think no one could see how yer eyes lit up whenever ye saw her. I only say this fer yer own good. Ye could never marry that woman."

Rowan's fury erupted. "Marry her? Who said anythin' about me marryin' anyone? We're talking about who betrayed us and helped kidnap me daughter!"

Thomas let out a sigh. "I was merely pointin' out the obvious. Lady Arline be barren and ye be lookin' at her all calf-eyed. I feel it me duty to also point out that ye canna marry a woman known to be barren."

In two strides, Rowan was standing eye to eye with Thomas. "It is none of yer business how I feel about Lady Arline, or any other woman fer that matter," he said through gritted teeth. "And if I were inclined to ever marry again, it will be a woman of me own choosin', barren or no'."

Thomas would not back down. "Am I or am I no' one of yer advisors? Have ye no' always relied on me opinion? I merely be pointin' out facts, Rowan. Facts ye might no' be able to see because yer smitten with the lass." Thomas reached out and placed a hand on Rowan's shoulder. "Ye canna deny that ye are, no matter how loudly you voice it otherwise. I be simply tryin' to help ye see things from all angles. Ye need a son and she canna give ye one."

As much as he hated to admit to it, there was truth in Thomas' statements. Aye, he *had* grown quite fond of Lady Arline. And if she were barren? As much as he wanted to deny it, it mattered more than he cared to admit.

He could not deny wanting more children. When he and Kate had first married, before they realized the trouble she would have getting with child and carrying one to full term, they had both wanted a very large family. Kate thought six of each would be a perfect number and Rowan agreed.

Still, it was far too soon to think of such things. He had a strong desire to get to know Lady Arline. She was a fine woman of good character, still, there was much he did not know of her.

Mayhap, he told himself, in the end, they were destined to be nothing more than good friends. That in and of itself would not be a bad thing, to have her as a close personal friend.

His heart, however, didn't believe a word his mind was telling him.

W hen Arline did not appear in the gathering room for the evening meal, his worry intensified. He grabbed Frederick from the crowd and pulled him into the hallway where they could have a more private conversation.

"Frederick, have ye seen Lady Arline this day?"

"Nay, I haven't, Rowan," Frederick said as he studied Rowan closely. "Do ye wish me to go and find her?"

"Aye, I do. I'd like to ken how she fares. I'm told she is not feeling well. And see if ye can find the healer."

Frederick gave a nod and left Rowan standing alone in the hallway. He had sent for the healer three times and each time a message was brought back that she was busy tending to other clansmen and would come to Rowan as soon as she was able.

If the lass was still ill on the morrow, he would go to her then. He'd quit fooling around with messages and messengers. With that decision made he returned to the gathering room.

Beatrice sat at the high table again, occupying the same seat as last night. Time had slipped away from him today, what with training, his meeting with Thomas, Fredrick and Daniel and his other duties. He had forgotten all about speaking with Beatrice.

Lily wriggled her way through the crowd and took Rowan's hand. The little doll that Lady Arline had made for her was tucked into the crook of her arm. Lily hadn't been without the doll since the night he took her back from Garrick.

Lily looked very excited about something. "Da!" she said gleefully. "Red John's dog had puppies! He let me see them today!"

Rowan smiled as he scooped Lily into his arms. "That is excitin' news!"

Lily nodded her head vigorously, her little ringlets bouncing. "He says I can have one if I want!"

Rowan stopped dead in his tracks. He would strangle Red John for making such an offer without speaking to him first. "He did, did he?"

Lily nodded her head again. "Aye! He said I can pick whichever one I want, as soon as they're weaned!"

Rowan made a mental note to visit his stable master first thing tomorrow morning. He didn't feel that Lily was old enough yet for the responsibility that a puppy would require. Not ready yet to have this battle with his daughter, he chose to change the subject. He walked down the pathway toward the high table. "What else did ye do this afternoon?"

She paused, tilted her head and thought hard for a few moments. "I played with the puppies. Jinny and Robert played with them too. One of the puppies peed on Robert's hand!"

Rowan smiled as he set his daughter on the bench before taking his own seat. "And what did Robert think of that?"

"He wasna happy, but Jinny and I laughed. Red John told us that it wasna polite to laugh at someone in distress." Lily smoothed out the skirt of her blue dress and set her doll on the table beside her trencher.

"Red John is right, Lily. 'Tisn't polite nor honorable to laugh at someone in distress."

Having had enough of being ignored, Beatrice cleared her throat. "Good evening, Rowan. Lily."

Rowan turned and gave Beatrice a slight nod. "Lady Beatrice."

"I think ye'll like tonight's dinner. I had cook make all of yer favorite dishes." Beatrice smiled warmly and rested her hand on Rowan's arm. "I hope that meets with yer approval, Rowan."

Beatrice would not be the first woman who tried to bribe her way into a man's heart with food. "Thank ye," he said curtly, not impressed with her charm.

The tables were soon laden with venison, pheasant, fruits, vegetables and all manner of delectable foods. Rowan continued to ignore Beatrice as he ate in silence. He could feel her watching him out of the corner of her eye. As the moments went on he could feel her frustration growing.

He caught sight of Frederick then, coming down the aisle toward him. His face was unreadable. Frederick climbed the stairs, came to Rowan's side and whispered in his ear.

"I didna get to see her, Rowan, but I did talk to her maid."

"And?" Rowan was certain he was not going to like the answer.

Frederick hemmed and hawed for several long moments, as if he was uncomfortable giving Rowan the information.

"Out with it, Frederick," Rowan told him as he leaned back in his chair.

"Lady Arline is indisposed."

Rowan raised an eyebrow and waited for Frederick to continue. When he was not forthcoming with more information, Rowan let out a frustrated breath and stood. He took Frederick by the arm and stepped away from the table.

"What do ye mean, she's *indisposed*?"

Frederick cleared his throat. He looked both embarrassed and frustrated. Finally, he blurted out the answer. "She got her monthly courses and is sufferin'."

Rowan blinked once, then again. His Kate had always had a horrible time with her monthly courses. Sometimes her cramping was so bad that she would vomit. "I see," he said quietly. "And what of the healer?"

Frederick ran a hand across his beard. "The maid says the healer has been to see her and that she reports Arline will be well in a few days. They say no' to worry overmuch."

Rowan was not satisfied with that answer. "And why, pray tell, has the healer no' come to see me?"

"I dunnae, Rowan. But I did tell the maid to relay yer message that ye wish to speak to Ora as soon as she comes back. She's out helpin' someone with the ague right now."

Rowan supposed that he would have to wait. The ill took precedence over his desire for information on how Arline fared. Still, he was left with a very uncomfortable feeling in the pit of his stomach.

"Go back and tell the maid that I *will* see Lady Arline first thing in the morn. I dunna care how ill she is, I will see her."

Frederick nodded and quickly left to deliver the message. Rowan returned to his seat to finish his meal.

"Is something the matter, Rowan?" Beatrice asked.

He was uncomfortable discussing Lady Arline with Beatrice. Rowan knew that Beatrice wanted more than just a friendship with him. She wanted far more than he could ever give. He knew that very soon, he would have to let her know truthfully how he felt. "Nothin' to concern yerself with, Beatrice."

"'Tis Lady Arline ye worry over."

Rowan hid his surprise by taking a pull of his ale. "Aye, I do."

Beatrice appeared not to be bothered by his statement. "She is a verra nice young woman. I saw her earlier today."

He was not sure if he should be bothered or glad. "And how did she fare?"

Beatrice took a delicate sip of wine before answering. "I do no' know if it is me place to speak on the matter of Lady Arline."

Rowan had the sense that she wanted to tell him something but worried he might not like the answer. Mayhap she was just as uncomfortable discussing feminine matters as Frederick.

"Beatrice, ye ferget I *was* married fer a time. Things such as monthly courses and the like do no' make me blush like a maiden. 'Tis the natural course of things."

Beatrice response was not what he had expected. "I'm sure I do no' know what ye are speakin' of."

Rowan chuckled. "I already ken that Lady Arline is sufferin' from her monthly courses. 'Tis why she is no' joinin' us this night."

Beatrice looked genuinely surprised by his statement. "Sufferin'? She was no' sufferin' when I saw her last."

He found that quite curious. "How *did* ye find her?"

Beatrice let out a heavy sigh. "Rowan, I think ye be smitten with the young woman. I'll no' speak unkindly about her, fer ye wouldn't believe me, no matter what I said."

Rowan's brow furrowed, his curiosity rising. "Ye think I be smitten with her?"

Beatrice took another sip of wine. "Aye, I do. And I canna say that I blame ye."

Silently, Rowan wondered who else believed he was smitten with Lady Arline. He thought he had done a fine job at masking his feelings as they pertained to Arline. Apparently he needed to work on that.

"Beatrice…"

She smiled and stopped him with a wave of her hand. "Rowan, ye needn't worry that I be jealous of Lady Arline. She is a pretty young woman, but," her words trailed off.

"But?"

"I truly do have only yer best interests at heart. I do value our friendship, Rowan. I've given up all hope of us ever having more than just a friendship. Ye do no' love me and ye never will. I ken ye couldn't marry a woman ye did no' love."

Rowan sat is stunned silence. While he was glad that the topic had finally been brought up, he was shocked at her honesty and the fact that she seemed at ease with discussing the matter.

"Beatrice, I never meant to lead ye astray,"

Beatrice's laugh was honest and genuine. Mayhap there was more to Beatrice than just a beautiful face and elegant demeanor.

"Rowan," she began, touching his arm again. "Yer sense of honor is commendable. Ye never led me astray. Och! I had hoped something more would grow from our friendship, but I'm no' a young and naïve lass and ye needn't worry over hurtin' me. We are both adults. Me heart is quite intact."

Rowan smiled at her then. He appreciated her honesty and straight forwardness.

"Now, with that said, I do think ye need to tread lightly with Lady Arline."

"How do you mean?"

"I mean the lass might not be all that she appears to be. Now, I'm no' sayin' she be evil or wicked. But I feel like the lass be hidin' somethin'. What that is, I dunnae. 'Tis just the impression I get from her that mayhap, she truly does no' wish to be here or to be takin' care of Lily."

Rowan found that difficult to believe. Arline had displayed nothing but genuine fondness for his daughter. He looked over at Lily who was pretending to feed her doll.

"Rowan," Beatrice said, lowering her voice. "I do no' doubt that Arline cares for Lily. But I do no' think she truly wants to be her governess. I fear she is afraid to tell ye that fer fear of hurtin' ye."

Rowan cut a piece of venison and shoved it into his mouth. He did not want to believe that Beatrice was right. He wanted Arline to be happy here. He wanted her to feel as though she were part of his clan. He wanted her to be an important part of their lives. He wanted …. He wanted Arline.

His appetite for food quickly vanished when he thought of how he truly *wanted* Arline. He set his knife down and pushed the trencher away. He wanted her. But whether it was simply physical desire or the need and want of something more, he could not say with any amount of certainty.

Beatrice continued on but he paid no attention to her. His mind was on a certain auburn-haired woman above stairs. On the morrow, he told himself, he would go to Arline. He would find out from her own lips whether Beatrice spoke the truth.

If Arline did not want to be here, if she was wholly homesick, then he would give her the escort he had promised. If not, well, he was unsure where to go from that point. The easiest thing would be to step back and allow their relationship to take a slow, steady, natural course.

When he found himself praying -- something he did not do on a regular basis anymore -- praying that Arline would want to stay, he knew his heart was in trouble.

FOURTEEN

Four long days and three cold, lonely nights had passed since Arline had first arrived at the Graham Keep. With the fourth cold night just an hour or two away, Arline was growing angrier and more frustrated with the current conditions.

Were it not for Lady Beatrice and Joan visiting her several times throughout the day, Arline was quite certain she would have gone stark raving mad by now.

According to Beatrice, Rowan was still soaking at the bottom of a whisky bottle and his anger toward her was growing worse as the hours passed by.

Depending on the hour, he either wanted Lady Arline labeled a traitor to the crown and tossed into the dungeon, or, worse yet, declared a witch and burned at the stake.

Just what she had done to deserve his anger or mistrust she could not fathom. Over and over, she searched her memory for something, no matter how miniscule, that she might have said or done on the journey here that would have made him hate her so much.

And hate her he did. Vehemently and passionately, according to Lady Beatrice.

He had ordered that Lady Arline go nowhere near his daughter.

He had ordered her locked away, fed nothing but bread and porridge. And this morning? He had declared, much to her horror, that she was no longer allowed the comfort of wood for her brazier. He wanted her to suffer, to suffer intense ignominy. She was Blackthorn's whore. There had even been talk that he would have that moniker branded to her forehead!

She paced around her cold room, chewing on her thumbnail, wondering what she had done to anger God so much that he had placed her *here* to suffer so.

And what, pray tell, had she done to deserve Rowan Graham's disdain and hatred? Had she not done everything in her power to keep his daughter safe? Had she not helped them escape Blackthorn Castle? And not once, the entire time they rode to Clan Graham lands had she complained of anything. Not her bruised and battered body, the lack of hot water nor good food. She had even gone so far as to give up her dream of going to Inverness to live the rest of her life alone, save for the company of her sisters.

At one point, she had even pondered giving the funds her father held for her to Rowan so that he might build up his larder and help his clan return to the same great power they had been prior to the destruction left by the Black Death.

The more she paced, the angrier she became.

Patience, Lady Arline, Beatrice had told her repeatedly. *'Twill all be over soon.*

Joan knocked at her door with her evening meal. It came as no surprise to Arline to find the usual fare of stale bread, porridge and that God awful bitter tea.

Arline thanked Joan and sent her on her way. Tonight, she didn't bother with asking how Lily was getting along or how drunk Rowan was. The answers were always the same. Selina was caring for Lily and Rowan was drunk and angry.

Arline sat down on the little stool, staring at the tray. Porridge. God in heaven how she hated porridge!

Anger rose from her belly to her fingertips. She took the tray and slammed it against the wall. She had reached the end of her patience.

"If Rowan Graham has a problem with me, he can tell me to my face!"

She flung open the door with such force that it slammed against the wall with a loud thud as she stomped out of her room and down the hallway.

She was going to put an end to this nonsense, demand an explanation and the opportunity to defend herself against his accusations.

Muttering curses and blasphemies all the way down the hall and stairway, Arline went in search of Rowan Graham.

R owan was beginning to question his first impression of Lady Arline. He had believed at one point that she was an honorable woman of strong moral character. But after days of her refusing to leave her chamber, he began to question his first impression of her.

He had tried to see her before the evening meal. He had gone to her room, but the door was barred. He knocked several times, had almost begged her to allow him to enter. Finally the bar lifted, but it was not the Lady Arline, but Joan who answered the door.

"She be sleeping," Joan told him in a hushed whisper as she stepped into the hallway.

Joan was a petite woman and Rowan was able to make out Lady Arline's sleeping form in the bed by looking over her blonde head.

"Sleeping? Is she well?"

Joan closed the door and led Rowan a few steps away. "Pardon me fer bein' so blunt, m'laird, but I think the lass be depressed. She will no' see anyone, no' even ye."

Rowan could not hide his confusion. "Why will she no' see me?"

Joan seemed reluctant to answer his question. "I really canna say, m'laird. Ladies, ladies like Lady Arline, often behave strangely and do things that make no sense to the rest of us."

Joan left him there, perplexed and at a loss. He took Joan's words to mean that mayhap the *lady* was behaving like a spoiled child.

Now he sat behind his desk in his library, only half listening to Frederick and Daniel. Their investigation had turned up no new leads. Rowan was growing frustrated with their daily reports that held no information. He was half tempted to pull every single member of his clan into the courtyard and interrogate them one by one.

"Did ye hear me, Rowan?" Frederick asked as he stood before Rowan's desk.

"Aye," Rowan answered sharply. "Ye have no new information. The same as yesterday and the day before."

Frederick and Daniel looked at one another each man thinking along the same path: Rowan was growing frustrated.

"Rowan, I may not have learned who tainted the ale, but I am growing quite concerned about Lady Arline," Daniel said.

Rowan finally looked up at him. "What of Lady Arline?"

"Well, it seems she's gaining a reputation around the keep as being...well, difficult."

Rowan looked at each man for a moment as he worked his jaw back and forth. "Difficult? How do ye mean?"

Neither man wanted to tell Rowan the gossip they were hearing as it pertained to Lady Arline. Neither man believed what they were hearing, but still, it was quite disturbing.

Frederick knew he had to tell Rowan about the gossip floating around the keep. "Someone is spreadin' rumors about her Rowan. They say she refuses to eat, to leave her room, that we're all beneath her. They say she cries all the time. There be another rumor that she wants to go back to Ireland, to her da and that ye are refusin' to allow it." There was more, much more that he had heard and he did not relish telling his chief, but knew he must. "They be referrin' to her as Blackthorn's whore."

Rowan shot to his feet his eyes filled with anger as well as surprise. "Blackthorn's whore?" He was astounded. He could not imagine his people saying such things.

"Aye," Daniel said reluctantly. "I do no' believe the rumors, Rowan. Ye ken how I feel about Lady Arline. She's a fine woman, but some-thin' is afoot here."

Rowan had had enough. He hadn't seen the woman in days, now he learns that his clansmen are using disparaging remarks against her.

Aye, Daniel was correct. Something *was* wrong and he was going to find out what it was.

A rline had made her way down the stairs and into the hallway outside the gathering room. A very large young man was walking in her direction. She stopped him and asked where she might find Rowan.

"Down the hall," he said, with a nod over his shoulder. "Second door on the right. He's in his library."

Arline thanked him. "And be he drunk this night?" she asked tersely.

The man looked at her as if she were insane. "Drunk? Nay, me lady."

"He is quite sober then?" she asked, only for clarification sake.

"Aye, me lady," the man answered politely.

She thanked him again, lifted her cloak and skirts in both hands and rushed off to find him.

Her anger had reached a boiling point by the time she had stopped the man in the hallway. When she learned he was finally sober, she felt some of that anger ebb. At least now she could have an intelligent conversation with the man.

She rushed down the hallway and found the second door on the right. She paused only long enough to take a deep breath to steady her nerves. Without knocking, she flung the door open.

R owan didn't know at first just what had hit him in the front of his skull. He had just reached the door to his library when it flew open. The edge of it hit him squarely between his eyes. It had opened with such force that it caused the air to stir and papers on his desk went floating to the floor.

The shock of being banged in the head with the edge of the door made him take a few steps back. Frederick and Daniel flew to his side to catch him in case he fell. They stood on either side of Rowan, holding his arms, with mouths agape.

"Rowan!" Daniel exclaimed.

Rowan shook his head which only made it hurt worse. "What the bloody hell?" he stammered, as he tried to focus his eyes.

Lady Arline stood in the doorway. She'd gone as pale as a sheet, her fingers touching her lips as if she were trying very hard not to scream.

"Och! Rowan, I be so terribly sorry!" she said from behind her fingers.

He shook his head again and shrugged Daniel and Frederick away. "Damn it, woman!"

Tears instantly welled in her eyes. She looked positively terrified. Even through his slightly blurred vision he could see that she was upset and afraid. He immediately felt bad for having cursed and yelled at her.

"I be sorry," he said through gritted teeth. "Ye caught me unaware and, bloody hell, that hurt!" He rubbed his forehead with his fingers. "I be sorry fer yellin' at ye."

"I'm sorry fer hittin' ye with the door," she murmured.

He took another step back and bade her to enter with a wave of his arm. "Please, come in."

Arline hesitated a moment, took a deep breath, threw her shoulders back as if she were steeling herself for something. Lifting her cloak and skirts, she finally entered the library.

She noticed the papers scattered around the floor in front of his desk. Rowan noticed them too.

They bent at the same time to pick them up.

Her forehead collided with Rowan's as they bent to retrieve them.

"Och!" Arline exclaimed as she took a step back and stared at him. He looked to be in a good deal of distress, rubbing his forehead, holding his breath. She nearly lost control of her bladder at that point.

She'd come to fight it out with him, not assault him.

"Rowan, I--" she didn't know what to say. She took a step toward him.

"Nay!" Rowan snapped. "Stop before ye kill me!"

Her eyes grew wide with horror as she stood as still as a statue. *Oh, lord, help me.*

Rowan let out an exasperated breath, took her hand and sat her in the chair in front of his desk. He remained quiet as he rubbed his forehead and tried to gather his thoughts.

They sat in tense silence for quite some time before Rowan finally spoke.

"Lady Arline," he said as calmly as he was able. "I take it ye have somethin' ye need to discuss?"

Arline swallowed hard as she tried to dislodge her voice from her throat. She was studying him closely. For a drunkard, he certainly looked quite healthy. She had expected to see the remnants of a four-day drunk, red and bloodshot eyes, an unshaved face and trembling hands. Instead, she saw the same handsome, strong and well kempt man she had seen days ago. It made no sense, no sense at all.

"Well?" Rowan asked after a considerable amount of silence passed between them.

Arline shook her head slightly. "Yes?"

"Why are ye here?" he asked. She seemed quite distracted.

"Och! That!" she said, scooting closer to his desk. "Yes, I did in fact wish to see ye, Rowan."

Rowan glanced at Daniel and Frederick. They looked just as confused as Rowan felt. She was acting quite odd.

Arline spotted the remnants of a tray of fruits, cheeses, meats and breads on the corner of Rowan's desk. Just sitting there. How could they let food go to waste like that when their larder was lacking? They could at the very least give it to the poor children!

"Lady Arline?" Rowan asked, breaking her train of thought.

"Yes?" she said, glancing back at the tray.

Rowan finally noticed that she was indeed quite focused on the tray of food. More than once she licked her lips and swallowed hard.

"Lady Arline," he repeated as he took the tray and slid it in front of her. "Would ye like somethin' to eat?"

She licked her lips again with a look of longing in her eyes. "Nay, thank ye. Mayhap ye should give it to the children."

Rowan thought it an odd request, but then she was acting out of sorts. "Me lady, please, tell me what it is that ye needed to discuss with me."

With tremendous will, Arline pushed the images of the food from her mind, took a deep breath and proceeded to tell Rowan Graham just what was on her mind.

"While I do appreciate yer kind offer of a position here, among yer people, I am afraid that I canna continue on like this, me laird. I do no' ken what I did that angered ye so, or made ye turn to drink. Whatever it was, I will apologize fer it, here and now. But, I'm afraid I canna go on like this. While I am glad fer a roof over me head, and the pallet ye provided and the fur, it is no' quite enough to keep the cold out. A few pieces of wood at night would have been sufficient. And to say ye want me here as Lily's governess, then to forbid me to see her, well, that just doesna make any sense, me laird, no sense at all."

Rowan tried to ask her what the bloody hell she was going on about, but she did not give him time to ask. She went on, occasionally distracted by the food on the desk.

"I am no' sayin' that ye need to drape me in the finest fabrics, but to deny me even the use of a bone needle to repair me dress? I would think even prisoners get to repair torn clothes! And to call me the things ye've been callin' me? I canna abide that either me laird. I simply canna remain silent. All that I ask of ye is an escort to Inverness. I realize now, that ye dunna want me here, and that is all well and good, though it does perplex me why ye asked to begin with. And I still dunna ken why ye hate me so much! I be no spy. And I'm no' a witch either!" She took a deep breath, licked her lips again, and went on. "And the porridge! Och, I hate the bloody porridge! But I eat it, just to keep me strength up mind ye. I mean, I canna eat bread just twice a day and expect to survive!" She took another deep breath and wiped an errant tear from her cheek.

The last thing she wanted was for Rowan Graham to think he'd broken her spirit. She'd be damned if she would allow it to happen or allow him to know it.

"I ken there be a good man in ye, somewhere, me laird. I've seen him, I have. With me own eyes. Please, I will beg ye if I must, but please, at least give me a horse!" The memory of the night Garrick threw her out of his keep sent shivers down her spine. She sent a silent prayer up to heaven that Rowan would at the very least, allow her a horse when he tossed her out.

Her emotions were getting the better of her. She took deep breaths to steady her nerves. Her hands trembled and she began to feel light headed. She sat in silence, waiting for Rowan to respond.

"Me lady, I have absolutely no idea what yer goin' on about," he said as he leaned forward in his chair.

Arline rolled her eyes at him. Was it possible that he'd been so drunk that he could not remember any of his directives or orders? "I am wantin' to ken why ye are so angry that ye won't let me mend me dress, why ye took the firewood and brazier away, why ye refuse to let me see Lily, why ye only give me bloody porridge and stale bread twice a day! And why the bloody hell you keep callin' me Blackthorn's whore!"

He sat there in silence, as astonished as he was confused. His voice cracked ever so slightly when he finally spoke again. "Arline, I never did any of those things to ye."

The tears fell, one by one, down her cheeks. "Nay, ye had others do it fer ye."

The accusations appalled him. He started to stand, changed his mind, and sat back in his chair.

"Has the healer, mayhap, given ye somethin' that might make ye a little daft?"

It was Arline's turn to be confused. "Healer? I've no' seen the healer, me laird."

He tilted his head ever so slightly. "Did she not give ye something to help yer ribs when ye first arrived?"

"Nay. I tell ye, I've no' seen the healer at all."

Worry began to settle in the pit of his stomach. "And why have ye no' joined us fer any of the meals?"

She scrunched her brows together. The man was daft. "Me laird, I was told I could no' join ye at the meals. I was told to stay out of yer way because ye were so angry with me."

Rowan remained silent, the anger boiling up inside him.

He studied her closely. She seemed perfectly lucid and sincere. He detected no lies, nothing disingenuous on her part. She truly believed everything she was telling him. He noticed then that she was wearing her cloak. It had not been washed for it still bore the mud and berry stains from her fall down the side of the ravine.

"Lady Arline, why are ye wearin' yer cloak?"

"To stay warm," she sounded somber and embarrassed. "And to cover me dress. Ye'd no' allow me to wash it or mend it."

"Show me."

Was the man truly insane? Had he drunk himself to insanity? Fine, if he wanted proof, she'd show him. She scooted the chair back and stood before him. She undid the ties of her cloak and pulled it open.

The torn bodice hung limply at her waist. He could see where she had tried to remove the berry stains on her chemise for they were faded somewhat.

Feeling as though she were some oddity on display, she burned crimson. She pulled her cloak closed and hugged herself with it and sat back down.

Rowan saw her look at the tray of food again. "When was the last time you ate something other than porridge and bread?"

"The cheese and apples ye gave me when we were comin' here."

"And yer last good meal?" His jaw was beginning to ache from grinding his teeth.

"Me last good meal? I suppose it was right before I married Garrick," she said trying to add some levity to the room. She failed miserably.

Rowan shot to his feet and gave Daniel and Frederick a few orders. "Go now, to the kitchen. Find her some food, anything but bread and cheese!" He came around the desk and stood next to Arline. "And I want every last person in this keep assembled and in the gathering room *now*."

Daniel and Frederick left to do his bidding. Rowan gently took Arline by the arm and guided her to the chair next to the fireplace.

"Lady Arline, I most humbly and sincerely apologize fer the way ye've been mistreated." He went to the desk, grabbed the tray and brought it back to her.

Rowan sat down on the stool in front of her and held the tray out for her and urged her to eat.

"Nay, me laird," she whispered and turned her head away.

"Why will ye no' eat?"

"Give it to the children, me laird. They need it more than I." She was exceedingly glad to see the old, sober Rowan had returned. There was no hint of the drunkard or the angry and belligerent man she'd been warned to stay away from.

"Quit *me lairding* me and eat, lass." He was growing more and more frustrated with her refusal.

"Nay!" Arline shook her head. She would have loved nothing more than to devour every morsel left on the tray, but her conscience would not allow her to. "Please, give it to the children."

He took a deep breath and let it out slowly. "The children have eaten." They were going around in circles.

She gave him a look of pity, one that said, *Och! Ye poor, poor man.* She placed a cold palm on his cheek. "I ken that yer larder is bare, me laird. 'Tis nothin' to be ashamed of. Many clans have fallen on bad times. I canna take food out of the mouths of children."

He placed the tray on his knees, dumbfounded, perplexed, and growing angrier by the moment.

"Arline," he said, trying to keep the angry edge out of his voice. "Ye have been sorely mistreated,"

Arline removed her hand and placed it in her lap. With downcast eyes, she said, "Ye could no' help it, me laird. Ye were too drunk to ken what ye were doin'." She wiped her face on the sleeve of her cloak, unable to look at him.

197

"Drunk? Who the bloody hell told ye that?" He could no longer shield his anger.

Arline blinked as she looked up at him. "Lady Beatrice and Joan. 'Tis why ye've treated me so poorly. Ye could no' help it. 'Tis why yer larder is bare, because ye drink too much and canna hunt or lead yer clan to prosperity."

He was too stunned, too angry to speak. He stood, sat the tray on the stool he had just occupied and turned away. He did not want her to see the fury as it boiled in his blood.

Beatrice.

It all began to make sense to him. Beatrice had lied to him and to Arline. Somehow, she had managed to convince Arline that Rowan was a drunkard. A drunkard who would take away her food, wood for her fire, and not even allow her a bone needle.

"I be truly sorry for speakin' of it, Rowan. I did no' want to embarrass or humiliate ye. Me da sometimes drank far too much, but I think he drank fer different reasons than ye. Please, do no' think that I hold ye in low esteem." In truth, she could not continue to be angry with him, even after all he had done. If anything, she pitied the man, felt ever so sorry for him.

Arline believed he was driven to drink after the loss of his wife. It was a pain he could not vanquish without the aid of whisky. 'Twas a shame, really, for she believed that if he were able to put the bottle down, he could be a remarkable man and leader. The poor soul.

She had been so furious with him, just moments ago, that she could have beaten him over the head with a chair. Had he been drunk when she entered his library she might very well have done just that.

Standing before her was a proud man, the man she had grown to care so much about. The father of an innocent little girl who worshiped the ground he trod upon. The anger had slowly begun to evaporate when she caught sight of *that* man.

"I be no' angry with ye, Rowan. Ye couldna help yerself."

The pity he heard in her voice intensified his anger. He held no animosity toward Arline. Nay, his fury and rage he would reserve for one woman and her maid. His hands balled into fists. Never in his life had he ever wanted to physically harm a woman. Until now. This was beyond the pale.

He took several deep breaths before turning to look at her. The pity she held for him was plainly evidenced in her teary eyes and the faint, sad curve of her lips.

"Arline," he cleared the anger from his throat and began again. "Arline, I can assure ye that me larder is no' bare. Our children do *no'* go hungry, I most certainly am *no'* a drunkard, and I would *never* call ye Blackthorn's whore." His words were clipped and angry.

He could see from her expression that she did not believe him. "Would ye like to see the larder? Would ye like me to bring the clansmen and children in one by one to tell ye that I speak the truth?" He paused and shook his head. "I swear to ye that I speak the truth."

He went to her then, bent to one knee and took her hands in his. "Ye've been lied to, lass. I have been worried over ye to the point that I canna sleep at night. Lady Beatrice has lied to us both. She told me that ye do no' like it here, that ye want to go back to yer da, to Ireland."

Arline stared blankly into his brown eyes. He was pleading with her to believe him. There was such sincerity to his voice. She desperately wanted to believe him. It was difficult to believe that Lady Beatrice, the woman she thought her only true friend here would lie. Arline had thoroughly believed that only men were devious and masters of manipulation. The thought of a woman behaving in such a manner never entered her mind.

Something in his eyes, the firmness of his voice, the quiet turmoil she saw simmering just under the surface of his calm exterior made her believe he was telling the truth.

The sudden realization that she had been lied to, had been made to believe all the ugly, horrible things said about him left her feeling as though a wall of stone had just crashed onto her shoulders. She felt guilty and ignorant and terribly naïve all at once.

She covered her mouth with the palm of her hand to stifle the cry and the curses that threatened. "I'm a damned, bloody fool."

Relief washed over Rowan when he saw clarity dawn in her wide eyes. He chuckled softly, squeezed her shoulders and smiled. "If ye be a damned, bloody fool then I am a thousand times worse." He shook his head and let go of her shoulders. "I should never have believed the things Beatrice was telling me. I should have demanded that ye see me. Earlier, when I came to see ye, I should have broken down the door and made ye speak to me."

Arline's eyebrows drew inward. "Ye came to see me? When?"

"Not more than a few hours ago. Right before the evening meal. I knocked and knocked but ye didn't answer. Joan finally came to the door and told me ye were sleepin'."

Beatrice and Joan were far more devious than Arline would have given them credit for. "Rowan, I was no' sleepin' and I didna hear ye knock. Which room did ye visit?"

"The room I gave ye four days ago, lass. Me mum's auld room."

Her mind began to race with all the events of the past few days. Outrage began to build from the depths of her belly. "Lady Beatrice moved me out of that room days ago, Rowan. I've been stuck in a tiny room on the third floor. I've been sleepin' on a pallet amongst empty trunks. They came today and took the brazier away, sayin' 'twas by yer command. If ye had knocked on the proper door, I would no' have turned ye away. I would have hit ye over the head with me chamber pot!"

He chuckled again as he rubbed his fingers along his forehead. "I do no' doubt it! Is that why ye came chargin' in here earlier? To beat me senseless?"

Shame turned her face beet red. "Aye," she whispered, feeling all the more guilty and ashamed for having been so easily duped.

Rowan patted her shoulder and smiled. "I canna say that I blame ye. I reckon I'd have felt much the same way."

He offered her the tray of food once again. This time she took it, placed it on her lap and ate without question, without restraint. "Would ye like somethin' to drink lass?"

With her mouth full of cheese, she nodded her head. "A dram of *uisge beatha* would be verra good," she answered, plopping a plum into her mouth.

Rowan's brow quirked with surprise. "Ye like whisky?"

Arline nodded in affirmation as she tore a hunk from the loaf of bread and stuffed it into her mouth. "Ye ferget, I be Irish. We're weaned off our mum's breast and onto the *uisge beatha*."

She took a knife from the tray, found a relatively clean spot on her cloak to wipe it clean. *Butter!* She could have cried tears of joy over the butter alone. She slathered a dollop onto a piece of bread and popped it into her mouth. Manners be damned, she was hungry!

Rowan returned holding a bottle of whisky in one hand and a mug in the other. Arline set the knife down, brushed crumbs from her fingers and took the bottle.

"Thank ye, Rowan!" she smiled and took a drink from the bottle. A moment later, she sighed a most contented and blissful sigh as the whisky spread from her belly to her extremities, leaving her feeling warm and happy.

The look of bliss on her face, that happy, contented sigh reminded Rowan of the sounds a woman -- or a man -- made after a good round of loving. It made his groin ache.

Arline took another drink from the bottle and sat it at her feet. "'Tis no' bad whisky, fer a Scot that is."

He did not take her statement as an insult toward Scots. She was a woman just as proud of her heritage as he was his. Though Rowan felt Scots made much better whisky, he would not argue the point with her now.

She took another drink from the bottle and handed it back to him. "I best be careful with that. I've not eaten well in some time and have had nothing but that awful bitter tea ye all are so fond of."

Rowan had no idea what she meant. "What bitter tea?"

"Och! That tea Joan kept bringin' me. 'Tis bitter and tastes like the devil himself peed in it!" She giggled at her own jest as she ate another plum.

Rowan was just about to ask a question as it pertained to the tea but Frederick walked in, carrying a tray of food.

"I be sorry, Rowan, but Mrs. McGregor was no' verra happy," Frederick said as he brought the tray to Lady Arline. Rowan took the now empty tray from her so that Arline could take the tray from Frederick.

"What do ye mean, she be no' verra happy?" Rowan asked. Frederick glanced at Arline then back to Rowan. Rowan could tell there was something Frederick wanted to say but did not want to say it in front of Lady Arline.

Rowan stood and pulled Frederick aside. In a low voice he asked him to clarify what he meant.

"Mrs. McGregor said she'd no make anything special fer," he glanced at Lady Arline before continuing on in a whisper, "fer Blackthorn's whore."

Rowan began working his jaw back and forth. He was long past the ends of his patience, ends that were, in fact, completely out of sight.

"I made the tray meself, fer she absolutely refused."

"Why do they dislike me so?" Arline's voice, trembling slightly, broke through the stillness of the room. She had heard their conversation. *Blackthorn's whore.* It was like a dull knife cutting through her heart. She set the tray on the floor, unable to touch another bite of food. She felt sick and betrayed and for some reason, unworthy, though she knew that to be unwarranted.

Neither Rowan nor Frederick had an answer. She had done nothing to any of the clansmen to deserve their unkind words or mistreatment.

"Daniel has everyone in the gathering room," Frederick said after several moments of tense silence passed.

"Go," Rowan said, his attention and eyes focused intently on Lady Arline. "I shall be there shortly."

Frederick gave a quick nod before quitting the room. Rowan and Lady Arline stared at one another for quite some time. There were a thousand things he wanted to say to her but knew now was not the time. He wanted to take her in his arms and apologize, beg for forgiveness. Had he been paying closer attention to his instincts none of this would have happened.

Swiftly he went to her, knelt and took her hands again. "None of this is your fault, I want ye to ken that. While I am certain Lady Beatrice is behind all of this, I need to speak with my people."

Arline sighed and shook his hands loose. "Why? What will it matter, Rowan. They do no' want me here."

He searched for the right words, a way to explain to her that they only felt this way for two reasons. One, someone had used lies to sway their way of thinking and two, they did not know her.

"Lady Arline, are ye going to just sit back and let Beatrice win?"

"What do ye mean?" she didn't appreciate the accusatory tone in his voice.

"If ye do no' go out there, to the gathering room with me, with yer head held high, then Beatrice wins. If ye hide, it will look as though ye have somethin' to hide or that yer ashamed of yerself."

"Go out there? To the gatherin' room? With ye? To face all those people?" She shook her head. "Nay, I will no' do that. They've made up their minds, Rowan. They do no' want me here."

He took her hands in his again. He liked the way her long delicate fingers felt wrapped around his. "The Lady Arline that I met last week would no' let a woman like Beatrice get away with such behavior. The Lady Arline that I know would stand up to her, toe to toe, and no' back down." He squeezed her hands again. "And mayhap," his voice turned playful, "she might even beat her over the head with a chamber pot!"

Arline could not help but join in his laughter. She knew he was right. If she hid, she would look guilty. Her crime? Weakness. No matter what rumors may be floating around the castle, whether there was any truth to them or not, the rumors would take hold and it would take a lifetime to dispel them.

If she truly were to try to make this her home, she could not back down, could not run and hide.

Until a few moments ago, she was thinking of nothing else but going to Inverness. Now, when he looked into her eyes, she wanted nothing more than to stay.

"Verra well then," she said as she stood and threw her shoulders back and her chin up. She place a hand on Rowan's arm, took a deep breath and bade him to lead the way.

"But I do no' want ye gettin' mad at me if I *do* hit Beatrice with me chamber pot."

Rowan's lips curved into a warm smile and his eyes lit with a mischievous twinkle. "Nay, ye'll hear no objection from me."

E very man, woman and child who lived within the walls of the keep or within walking distance, was brought into the gathering room. Curious whispers and inquiries flittered through the air. Some complained of the lateness of the hour while others grumbled they were being made to wait.

The crowd grew silent and parted when Rowan entered the room with Lady Arline on his arm. His steely glare and clenched jaw left no room for doubt as to his mood. He was furious and cared not who knew it.

He had his men spread throughout the room. Their sole purpose was to watch and listen and wait.

With an air of gentle grace and dignity that belied her torn and dirty clothes as well as her nervous stomach, Arline held on to Rowan, gaining strength from his countenance. As long as he was here, beside her, she felt she could face anything. Even an angry horde of people who did not want her here.

She stared straight ahead, refusing to look at those people who lined the aisle. Rowan led the way up the stairs. The tables had been raised after the evening meal. The only thing that remained on the dais was his high-backed chair. With his hand on her elbow, he helped her sit in *his* chair.

It was a blatant display, to show his people that *he* was in charge and that he felt an intense level of respect for Lady Arline. Should anyone have previously doubted it, now there was no question.

Rowan stood beside her with his hand on her shoulder and scanned the crowd. Two people were conspicuously missing from the congregation. Beatrice and Joan. Rowan waved two fingers at Daniel who made his way at once through the crowd and up the stairs. Rowan leaned in to whisper in his ear.

"Ye go and find Beatrice and Joan. Do no' let them out of yer sight."

Daniel nodded and left the room in a hurry. Several sets of eyes followed Daniel out of the room before turning their attention back to Rowan.

Rowan waited, several long moments, before he began to speak to his people.

"Who among ye have sworn allegiance to me as yer chief and to Clan Graham?"

Every hand in the room raised, some hesitantly, others more immediate.

"Who among ye question me judgment?"

All hands slowly lowered and quizzical expressions stared back at him. "None?" he asked loudly. "None of ye question me judgment as yer chief?"

He paused, waiting for a moment to see if anyone did in fact question his judgment. When no hands went up, he nodded his head approvingly.

"Raise yer hands if ye have had the pleasure of meetin' Lady Arline."

His people looked at him curiously. A few of them harrumphed at the mere mention of her name. Besides his men, the only hands to be raised were Selina's and one of the kitchen maids, whose name Rowan could not remember.

"Two? Is that all?"

People began to whisper to one another, wondering where Rowan's line of questioning was headed. He raised his hand and a hush fell over the hall.

"Out of all of ye, only two in this room have met Lady Arline in person." He shook his head, disgusted with each of them.

"You," Rowan said, pointing to the kitchen maid. She looked startled at being pointed out. "How much time have ye spent with Lady Arline?"

The young girl looked at Mrs. McGregor as if she sought permission to answer. "Nay!" Rowan barked at her. Everyone in the room jumped at the sound of his angry voice. "Do no' look at Mrs. McGregor. Look at *me*."

He could see her tremble. She stammered, "I dunnae--" she cast a furtive glance at Mrs. McGregor then turned her eyes to the floor.

"Five times? Ten? More?" Rowan demanded.

"I do no' think it was that many," she mumbled.

Rowan gave Arline's shoulder a gentle squeeze. They had spent a few moments speaking about the events of the last days before they had come into the gathering room. She had already given him a list of people she had met and her impressions of them.

Swiftly, he left Arline's side and bounded down the steps. "Come here," he said to the maid. Hesitantly, the girl stepped through the crowd and came to stand before him. He reckoned she could not be more than four and ten. "What is yer name?" he asked sharply.

"Bridgett," she murmured.

"I ask ye again, Bridgett, how many times have ye met with Lady Arline?"

She whispered her answer so softly that Rowan could not hear. He already knew the answer, but needed her to say it loud enough for the entire room to hear. "How many?" he demanded.

"Once."

"Once?" he asked with a nod of his head. "Tell me, Bridgett, how much time did ye spend with the Lady?"

She was staring at her feet, twisting her fingers together. "I - I do no' remember."

"Well, was anyone else in the room with ye and Lady Arline?"

Rowan was growing frustrated with the girl's hemming and hawing. He was about to ask her again, when a voice piped up from the crowd.

"I was there, Rowan."

He looked up to see Selina making her way through the crowd. Selina ignored the whispers as she walked by them. "I was there."

"Can ye tell me what happened at that meeting?"

"Aye, I can. It was the afternoon ye brought Lily home. I was in the bathing room, helping Lady Arline. She was very sore, covered with all those ugly bruises. I was helpin' her wash her hair because it hurt for her to raise her arms," she cast a smile at Lady Arline. "She would no' admit to bein' in pain, but I could tell that she was."

"And how was Lady Arline behaving?" Rowan asked.

Selina's expression changed to one of confusion. "How do ye mean?"

"Well, was she rude? Did she make a fuss? Was she complainin'?"

Selina's eyes grew wide with shock. "Nay! Nay! She was verra nice. She kept tellin' me *thank ye,* and was tryin' to convince me that she could do it herself. But every time she raised her arms above her head, well, I could see as plain as the nose on yer face now, that she was hurtin'. Those bruises were awful, Rowan."

Rowan nodded his head and bade her to continue.

"Well, we were almost done. I was takin' good care of her, like ye asked me to, when Bridgett came runnin' into the bathin' room sayin' that Mrs. McGregor needed me straight away." Selina cast a look of reproach at Bridgett, who had grown unusually quiet. Normally the girl was a chatterbox.

"And then what happened?"

"Well, Lady Arline told me to go before I got into trouble with Mrs. McGregor. She insisted. So I gave her a towel and we left."

"I see," Rowan said. He turned his attention back to Bridgett. "Does Selina tell the truth, Bridgett?"

The girl shrugged her shoulders and refused to answer.

Rowan took a few steps away, paced for a moment before turning back to his people. Some of them looked perplexed by his line of questioning, others, more than a handful, looked quite upset and angry. They were staring at Arline with disdain.

"I would like to know *why* ye have all acted like fools. I would like to know *why* ye all are so set on dislikin' a person ye've spent no time with. I'd like to know *who* ordered Lady Arline to be treated so poorly, feedin' her nothin' but porridge and stale bread, takin' the room *I* gave her away and stickin' her in one of the storage rooms on the third floor. I would like to know *why* she was no' given clean clothes. I would like to know *why* and by *whose* order ye all decided to treat her with no respect at all!" His voice grew in direct proportion to his anger.

"This woman," he turned then to look at Arline. She sat with her hands folded in her lap, her face filled with embarrassment and sadness. It made him all the more angry to see her in such distress. "This woman," he began again, lowering his voice slightly. "She has done nothing to deserve this kind of treatment. She protected my daughter, Lily, as fiercely as if she were her own. She took a beatin' from the hands of Garrick Blackthorn while tryin' to protect my daughter. I owe her -- we all owe her -- a great debt, a debt that I can never begin to repay her."

Shaking his head, he turned back to his people. "I canna begin to reason *why* ye all would behave so poorly!"

Tears began to stream down Selina's cheeks. "Rowan, I didna *want* to!"

With his brow line with confusion, he looked down at Selina. "Then *why?*"

Selina cast a backward glance at someone in the crowd. Rowan pretended he hadn't noticed. "Tell me, Selina. Why did ye do this?"

"Because I was afraid," Selina cried.

"Afraid of what?" he asked gently, giving her a moment to answer. "Or should I ask *who?*"

Selina wiped away her tears with her trembling fingertips. "She said if we didna help her she would go to ye and have us tossed from the clan! That ye would believe anythin' she said because ye hold her in such high regard!" her words came tumbling out. "We canna leave the clan, Rowan! Me mum, she's no' well and canna work like she used to. I have little brothers and sisters. We love it here!"

Rowan did not doubt that Selina had acted out of fear. The more he learned of Beatrice's lies and deceptions, the angrier he became.

Though he was quite certain he knew it had been Beatrice who had made the threats and terrified the lass, he needed her to say it aloud.

"Who, Selina? Who threatened ye?"

"Mrs. McGregor!" she blurted out.

"Shut up ye ungrateful wench!" the aulder woman screeched as she made her way through the crowd. She looked positively incensed as if she were ready to scratch Selina's eyes out. Her face was deep red, her auld blue eyes filled with contempt and hatred. Thomas grabbed her by the arm before she could get too close to Selina.

Rowan felt as though he had been kicked in the gut. His eyes shot to Mrs. McGregor who was standing near the back of the crowd.

Mrs. McGregor? He found it difficult to believe she was behind this. He thought it had been Beatrice. Mrs. McGregor had come to them more than a year ago, after the death of their longtime cook. Mrs. McGregor was an excellent cook and ran her kitchen with an iron fist.

"Mrs. McGregor?" he asked, stunned by Selina's accusation. "Is this true?" Rowan directed his question at Mrs. McGregor. She refused to answer, her countenance awash with a haughtiness and derision he'd never witnessed in her before. She struggled against Thomas' grip, a few strands of her graying hair coming loose from the bun at the nape of her neck.

"How could ye do this?" Rowan asked. "I do no' understand how ye could treat anyone with such vulgar disrespect."

The fact that it was a rhetorical question slipped by Mrs. McGregor.

"Respect *her*? I think not!" the aulder woman's voice broke through the silent crowd. "She's Blackthorn's whore and I'll show her no respect! She doesn't deserve it!"

For a moment, just a brief moment, Rowan was so enraged that his head swam. Regaining his composure, he gestured for Thomas to bring the woman to him.

"Why?" he ground out.

She looked at him as though he had lost his mind. "Because she be Blackthorn's whore! She comes here tryin' to worm her way into the clan, all high and mighty, like she's the chatelaine, wantin' everyone to ferget *who* she is! 'Tis no' right!"

Had Mrs. McGregor been speaking of Beatrice and not Arline, he would have understood her displeasure and line of thinking. The woman wasn't making a bit of sense. Her accusations were unfounded and he knew not where she had come up with them.

"How can ye say such things when ye have no' spent any time with her?"

"Bah!" Mrs. McGregor spat out. "I do no' need to spend any time with the likes of her! I ken her kind well enough."

Rowan took a step forward and leaned down so that she could see just how angry he was. "Did anyone help ye come to these conclusions? Did anyone put these thoughts into yer mind? How can ye judge a woman ye've never met?"

She clamped her mouth shut. Without a doubt she was holding something back, but what, he could only imagine. He was left to believe that Beatrice had put these hateful thoughts into his cook's mind.

When next he spoke, his words were blunt, sharp, and left no doubt in anyone's mind how he felt about their behavior. "Take her to the dungeon," he ordered Thomas.

Arline shot to her feet and shouted her objection. Everything in the room came to an abrupt halt. "Nay!" she said again as she ran down the steps and came to stand beside Rowan.

Rowan spun around, his eyes filled with astonishment. Arline was upset, but not with Mrs. McGregor. She was upset with him.

"Rowan," she said as she placed a hand on his arm. "Please, do no' put her in the dungeon!"

"Why the bloody hell no'?" he barked out angrily.

"Because it's cold and wet and filled with rats! Ye canna do that to a woman!"

"Do no' defend me!" Mrs. McGregor shouted. "I do no' want any help from the likes of *ye*!"

Arline ignored the woman, her focus at the moment was on

Rowan. "Rowan, ye canna lock her away like an animal, just because she has a preconceived notion of me."

Rowan tried to steady his breathing and his voice. "'Tis no' her notions that I'm punishin' her fer! 'Tis the way she treated ye!" His intent was not to keep the woman there indefinitely. Just long enough to make her understand that she was not in charge of his keep or his people. He was also using it as a means to gain information. A stay in the dungeon might get her to open up and tell them what he was certain he already knew. Beatrice was behind this.

"Aye, she treated me poorly but 'tisn't like she stabbed me or poisoned me or tried to kill me!" Arline pleaded with him to listen to reason.

What Mrs. McGregor said and did next nearly cost her her life. She wriggled free from Thomas' grasp. Her hand flew out before anyone had time to respond. Her hand landed with a loud smack across Arline's face. It landed with such force that Arline's head turned. "I said, do no' defend me! Do no' pretend that ye care what happens to me. I'd rather rot in the dungeon than have a whore such as ye act on me behalf!" With her face contorted and twisted with anger, she spat on Arline's dress.

Arline's hand flew to her burning cheek, her eyes wide with shock and incredulity. The last person who hated her this much had been Garrick.

A growl formed deep in Rowan's throat, it echoed across the stunned crowd of people. Daniel came to help Frederick pull the violently angry Mrs. McGregor out of the room before Rowan could put his hands around her neck and strangle her. They took her out of the room kicking and screaming, cursing the ground Arline trod upon. It was an embarrassing spectacle, one he was not used to witnessing. What the bloody hell had happened to his clan?

Then he realized not *what*, but who.

211

FIFTEEN

After Mrs. McGregor was pulled from the room, Rowan turned his attention to Lady Arline. Guilt ridden over the way his cook had behaved, he was at a momentary loss for words.

Selina stepped forward to offer her help. "Rowan, Lady Arline," she said quietly. She stood before them looking forlorn and ashamed. "I hope ye can forgive me."

Arline was still holding her cheek, unable to believe what had just transpired. With an unsteady voice, she gave Selina the forgiveness that she deserved. "Selina, do no' worry it. Ye acted out of fear and that is understandable."

"Arline, are ye hurt badly?" Rowan finally uttered as he took her hand away and examined her cheek.

"I think me pride is hurt worse than anythin'. Though I wish she hadn't chosen the same cheek as Garrick had."

His stomach tightened and his heart felt constricted with the mention of Garrick's name. It had been more than a week since he had taken Lily from Blackthorn and brought Arline here.

"Rowan, please, let me take Lady Arline above stairs, to her room, the one *ye* gave her, no' the one Beatrice put her in. I do have a clean dress fer her and I have been workin' on makin' her one, even though Mrs. McGregor told me no' to."

"In a moment, Selina. But first, I must address the clan." To Arline he said, "Are ye sure ye are well?"

"Aye, I've been hit harder and by much bigger men," she said, trying to add some levity to the situation but falling short.

While he would love nothing more than to see to it that Garrick Blackthorn suffered greatly for all he had done to Arline, right now, he had to focus on his people.

Raising his hand, he spoke above the murmur of the crowd. "We are no' done here yet," he said firmly. He took a step away from Arline and Selina to address his people.

"Hear me and hear me now," he called out to them. "Some of ye may think ye did the right thing by listenin' to Mrs. McGregor or others when they spoke harshly of Lady Arline. But those people do no' ken the truth. They do no' ken all that Lady Arline suffered in order to care fer Lily. As I told ye earlier, I owe Lady Arline a great debt. She deserves much more than what some of ye have shown her. From this moment forward, ye will treat her with kindness, dignity, and respect. I will expect nothin' less from any of ye. And if ye canna show her this, canna show her how great the people of Clan Graham are, well, ye may either leave now or go join Mrs. McGregor in the dungeon."

L ady Arline had insisted that she see Lily with her own eyes. Rowan gladly granted her request. Lily had been asleep when Rowan, Arline and Selina had quietly entered the room.

The tension and worry left Arline the moment she saw the sleeping babe. Her shoulders relaxed as she smiled warmly at the little girl.

"We keep a candle lit throughout the night," Selina explained in a soft whisper. "I've been sleepin' here with her, but she always gets up and goes to Rowan."

Arline stepped softly and knelt beside the bed. Lily was curled into a little ball, with her thumb tucked in her mouth and a lock of hair wrapped around her finger. Tenderly, Arline swept away the curls from Lily's forehead to get a better look at her face.

Arline's heart was an odd blend of joy, relief, and regret. She was happy and relieved to see the sweet child, to know that she was well and that Selina had been taking good care of her. The regret came from not having a child of her own.

As she knelt beside Lily, she wondered how it was possible to love someone as much as she loved and adored this sweet babe. She knew it was silly and probably quite dangerous to love the little girl this much.

Her thoughts turned to her sisters, Morralyn and Geraldine. It had been months since she'd received a letter from them. After the death of her father-in-law, Garrick had forbidden her to have any contact with anyone. She imagined that if her sisters had sent letters, Garrick had destroyed them. She prayed they were well and on the morrow, she would write to them, letting them know where she was. Mayhap Rowan would allow them to come here. Mayhap it was too soon to ask such a favor as that. But Arline knew that her heart and worries would not settle fully until she knew how her sisters fared.

Rowan rested a hand on her shoulder, quietly breaking her reverie. She glanced at him over her shoulder but said nothing. She stood and followed him and Selina out of the room.

"Lily will be verra happy to see ye," Selina said with a smile. "She has done nothin' but ask after ye, wantin' to see ye."

Knowing Lily missed her lifted her spirits somewhat. She looked up at Rowan and smiled. "Thank ye fer lettin' me see her."

She noticed he had a peculiar look on his face, as if he were lost in his own thoughts. "Are ye well?" she asked him.

"Aye," he answered quietly. He cleared his throat before speaking again. "Me room is right next to Lily's," he explained. "Me mum's auld room is just across the hall."

Arline hadn't known where Lily's room was in correlation to the one she had first been given when she arrived. It was good to know that she was so close. But knowing Rowan's room was just a few steps away left her with an odd, tingling sensation she felt clear to her toes.

"I leave ye in Selina's care," he told her, his deep brown eyes twinkling in the light of the torches. "But should ye need anythin', I am but steps away."

Arline swallowed hard and tried to chase away the sinful and lust-filled mental images that popped into her mind. She gave him a small curtsy and a nod, for she didn't dare speak. They stood for a time, gazing into one another's eyes.

Finally, he bowed to her, and left without saying anything. She didn't breathe again until she saw his magnificent form disappear around the corner.

H ad he remained in her presence any longer, Rowan would have made a fool of himself by taking the woman in his arms and kissing her soundly.

Something had happened to him as he watched this woman he barely knew, kneeling before his sleeping daughter. The love she felt for his child was undeniable and unmistakable. Arline had made no attempt to hide her adoration. Her eyes had brightened, her smile so very tender, and her caress as gentle and tender and delicate as a spring breeze.

He was genuinely touched by Arline's quiet display of affection toward his daughter. Her feelings were real, honest, and genuine. When Arline had gently swept away Lily's errant curls, he could have sworn she was touching him instead. He felt it to the very depths of his soul and the act, so sweet and tender, had stolen his breath.

For days he had battled with his conscience, worried that he was being untrue to Kate. Having feelings for another woman left him feeling like a cad, an adulterer.

And then, in the hallway, when Arline's bright green eyes gazed into his, he felt his heart being tugged in her direction. During that long moment of silence, as he stared at this beautiful woman who was so kind, smart, and strong, he could hear Kate's voice, like a whisper in his ear. *Do no' keep yer heart to a dead woman.* He almost jumped from his skin.

So he left the beautiful woman there in the hallway, for he knew he would not be able to keep from kissing her and spilling his heart to her.

He needed time to think, to ponder, to come to grips with these growing feelings toward her. How could he explain them to her if he didn't quite understand them himself?

There were other important things that he had to address before he could even begin to consider a relationship with Arline. First, he had to deal with the thorn in his side that was named Beatrice.

R owan met Daniel and Frederick in the hallway around the corner. "There ye be!" Daniel said, sounding quite relieved to have found him.

"Where the bloody hell is Beatrice?" Rowan asked through clenched teeth.

Daniel and Frederick cast worried looks at each other before Daniel answered the question. "That be why we were lookin' fer ye. Yer no' goin' to like this, Rowan. Mayhap ye want me and Frederick to deal with her."

His lips pursed and his brow drew into a knot. "Nay. Tell me." He was growing quite weary of the turmoil Beatrice had brought to his home.

"She has taken up residence in Kate's auld room."

Fury erupted behind Rowan's dark eyes. No one, *no one* was allowed in Kate's rooms. They were off limits even to Lily. Who the hell did this woman think she was?

He had afforded her a very nice room at the other side of the keep, just two corridors down. Why she felt it appropriate to take the rooms meant for his wife, he did not know, nor did he truly care at the moment.

He spun on his heels and headed around the corner. Kate's rooms were next to his. They were connected but each had their own entrances off the main hallway.

How Beatrice had been able to take over Kate's rooms without his knowledge or notice made him furious. Quite frankly, he had had enough.

When he threw the door to Kate's room open, it banged loudly on the wall and bounced back. He caught it with his hand, flipped it open again and stepped inside.

Beatrice was sitting beside the fireplace with some small piece of needlework in her hands. Her eyes grew wide with fear as Rowan entered the room. Joan had been sitting next to Beatrice but when Rowan started forward, Joan leapt to her feet to stand beside her.

"What, do you think, ye are doin' *here.*" Rowan's voice was laced with fury and 'twas all he could do not to lift her up and toss her out of the window.

He looked about the room. Beatrice's had her things spread on Kate's dressing table. She had *her* clothes hanging on the pegs. Rowan felt just as violated as the moment he learned Lily had been taken.

Beatrice feigned ignorance. "Why, whatever do ye mean?"

He couldn't contain his anger any longer. He was at her in three steps, grabbed her by her arms and lifted her to her feet. Between gritted teeth, he spoke. "Who said ye could be in here? Who said fer ye to take over me wife's rooms? By what authority do ye take such liberty?"

"Liberty? I did no' think ye would care! We had grown so close these past days!"

"Close?" he was baffled. "Nay, we are no' close, Beatrice. We shall *never be close.* We shall *never* even be friends!" He tossed her back into her chair. "Pack her things, *now!*" he barked out his command, tossing it over his shoulder to Frederick and Daniel.

Beatrice jumped to her feet. "Pack my things? Fer what purpose?"

"Ye will be out of this room this night, this hour."

"Why? I do no' understand? Why are ye so angry? I thought we had become friends, more than friends!" There was a panic to her voice that matched the look he saw in her eyes.

"Nay, ye are wrong. Ye have overstepped yer boundaries and over-stayed yer welcome here. I want ye out of this room now."

"And go where?" she asked as she tried to regain some of her composure. "Do ye wish me to go to yer room?"

The thought repulsed him. "Nay. Ye shall never step one foot into me room. I want ye out of this keep before dawn breaks on the morrow. Ye are never allowed back on Graham lands."

He turned to leave her for fear he would lose complete control and strangle the life out of her.

"And where, pray tell, would ye have me stay before dawn breaks?" Her voice dripped with contempt.

He stopped and turned once again to face her. "Why don't ye go stay in the room at the end of the hall on the third floor? Ye apparently thought it sufficient enough to put Lady Arline there fer the past four days."

He saw it in her eyes then, the realization that he knew everything and that not only was her time up, so was the game she had played with him. It was only a flash, gone as quickly as it had come, but he had seen it.

She pretended ignorance again. "What has she told ye?"

"She has told me everything, Beatrice. I ken that ye hid her away in a storage room. I ken every vile, disgusting and cruel thing ye did to her and told her."

"Rowan, I'm sure I do no' know what ye speak of! The woman is tetched! I've been trying to tell ye that fer days!"

He clenched his hands into fists to keep his temptation to cause her great bodily harm at bay. He'd not allow her to bait his temper any longer. He left Frederick and Daniel to pack and escort Beatrice and Joan to their temporary quarters. He heard the sound of a earthen-ware jug hitting the wall and Beatrice cursing like a drunken bar wench.

SIXTEEN

Arline, Rowan and Lily settled into a tidy routine over the next week. Lily would come bounding into his room to wake him each morn by jumping up and down on his bed and giving him kisses. It wasn't the jumping up and down that was unusual, it was the hour in which his daughter woke that was so odd.

With Lady Arline taking the reins of governess, she was able to gain a level of control over Lily that Rowan had failed to master after more than four years. Although he was quite grateful that his daughter's manners had improved, that she was eating her vegetables without much complaining, and that overall, her mood had improved considerably, he was left feeling a touch inadequate as a father. Arline had managed to do in just a few short days, what he had been trying to do for years.

Admittedly there were times when he felt a tad jealous of Arline. Often, Lily would run to Arline with her questions and her fears. As far as Rowan knew, Lily's bad dreams had stopped. She no longer climbed into bed with him in the middle of the night seeking comfort and protection. Though he was glad the dreams no longer haunted her, Rowan missed holding his daughter and chasing away the ghosts of her nightmares.

As the days passed by he began to feel less needed and he did not care for it at all. He could not be angry with either Lily or Arline. Arline was doing exactly what he had asked her to do. She was taking excellent care of his daughter, teaching her how to be a lady. Lily was even learning her letters and could read a few words by sight now.

His daughter was happy, safe, and content. How had Arline been able to accomplish all of that in such a short time? Though grateful, there were times when it gnawed at his fatherly pride.

One of the other positive things to come out of having Lady Arline as Lily's governess was that it did free up good portions of his days. It allowed him more time to spend on clan business and to visit with his clansmen who lived further out on Graham lands.

But mayhap the nicest benefit was that he was able to spend time with both Lily and Lady Arline at the noonin' meal each day and the evening meal each night. Aye, spending time with Lady Arline was worth the bruised father ego.

As promised, Selina had created a beautiful gown of emerald green that fit Arline perfectly. Arline was still far too skinny for her own good, but she was eating good meals now and Rowan hoped that she would be able to put on more weight. The dark circles under her eyes had rapidly faded and her skin no longer held the pallor of someone long hungry and hidden from the sun.

The castle had begun to finally settle in the wake of Beatrice being summarily cast out and Mrs. McGregor being tossed into the dungeon. Rowan would have thought the woman would have given in by now, told him what she knew of Beatrice and why she had listened to her to begin with. He would visit Mrs. McGregor each morn before heading to the training fields. The result of those meetings were always the same. He'd ask her questions, she'd glower hatefully at him and spit every time he mentioned Lady Arline's name.

He had just come in from training this morn, covered in sweat and dirt when Lily came racing up to him in the hallway. "Da!" she smiled sweetly as she ran to him. He knelt down and scooped her up and gave her a big hug. Lady Arline looked radiant as she strolled down the long hallway. Hints of the late morning sun shone in through the small windows and bounced off her auburn hair. She was wearing a new dress this morn, made from a beautiful goldenrod silk.

"And how is me lovely daughter this morn?" he asked as he gave Lily a kiss on her nose.

"I be good! Lady Arline says that since it quit rainin' we can have a picnic outside."

Arline had joined them, tugging Lily's wee foot. "And what *else* did I tell ye?"

Lily's smile faded. "That I hafta write me letters five times before we can have the picnic."

Arline smiled warmly at her and then at Rowan. "And?" Arline prodded.

Lily twisted her lips and looked up at the ceiling thinking hard on it for a moment. Her smile returned when she remembered. "I remember! We have to ask Da if it is all right first."

"Good girl," Arline praised her. She turned to Rowan. "Would ye like to have a picnic with us? We might no' get another opportunity for I fear the weather will be turnin' soon."

Their invitation brought back a memory of a happy afternoon spent with Kate. Lily was only a few weeks old and the Black Death had not yet reached their lands. He hadn't been on a picnic since. He almost declined their offer, but seeing his daughter so happy and thinking of having some time away from the keep with Lady Arline, he surprised himself by accepting their gracious offer.

"Good!" Lady Arline said with a smile. "It will do ye good to spend some time with yer daughter."

"Are ye no' joinin' us?" Rowan asked, feeling more than slightly disappointed.

"Ye've no' had much time alone with Lily this past week, Rowan. I thought ye would want to be alone with her." Arline hadn't considered joining them. She was attempting to give Rowan time alone with his daughter. "I do no' want to intrude."

His lips curved into a wide smile, his dazzling and perfect white teeth sent a shiver of excitement up and down her spine. She cursed inwardly for enjoying the tickling sensation that came to her belly every time he smiled at her.

"'Twould *no'* be an intrusion, me lady. 'Twould make me verra happy," he told her. He turned to Lily, knowing full well that Arline would not be able to tell the child no. "What do ye say, Lily? Would ye like Lady Arline to join us fer our picnic?"

"Aye, I would!"

Rowan felt no guilt for using his daughter to get Arline to change her mind. As he watched the loving smile come to her face when she looked at Lily, he knew she'd be joining them.

"Verra well then!" he said, growing excited about the opportunity to spend more time with Arline and his daughter. He tossed Lily into the air once, his heart filled with an overwhelming sense of joy when she squealed with delight. Carefully, he set her on her feet and patted her head.

"Ye go write yer letters while I go bathe. I be certain ye don't want a sweaty, smelly Highlander on yer picnic!"

I find ye quite handsome all sweaty and I do no' think ye smelly at all. I think ye smell like a strong, virile, beautiful man. Arline shooed the thoughts away. *Will I ever be able to look at this man and not feel all tingly and giddy?* She forced herself to remember that she was *not* a wanton woman. But the more time she spent with this man, the more wanton and sinful she began to feel.

Pulling on every ounce of willpower she could muster, she tried to pretend that nothing about him affected her in any way. Her stomach told her she was a liar.

"It will no' take her verra long, Rowan. She's a verra smart little girl."

"Good. Then I shall hurry. Should I meet ye in me rooms?"

"Nay!" she nearly shouted her answer. Rowan gave her a curious look. "I mean, nay. We shall meet ye in the kitchens."

Nay, nay, nay! Neither of us would be safe together in yer rooms, ye devil!

Rowan cast another brilliant and sinful smile her way. She had to force herself to look away for fear her legs would give out and she would turn into a puddle of jelly at his feet. She supposed that's what most inexperienced women did, turn to jelly when they didn't have a clue how to express themselves when around a gorgeous, handsome man such as Rowan Graham.

Deep down, she did like the way she felt when she was around him, although it was all quite confusing. The tingling sensations were enjoyable, but the shocking thoughts that raced through her mind were maddening if not embarrassing.

Ye've been married more than once and ye still do no' know how to act around a man. Yer an eejit.

T heir picnic had not turned out the way Rowan had envisioned it. Instead of a small, intimate affair with just him, Lady Arline and Lily, half his clan decided it was a perfect day to take the noonin meal out of doors.

He hadn't been able to get one moment of privacy with the woman throughout the meal. They were never alone, constantly surrounded by people, or more specifically, his men.

Frederick and Daniel were especially attentive. Thomas stood nearby, watching Lady Arline closely, as if she were going to steal the silver candlesticks or Rowan's private supply of whisky. It was plainly evident that Thomas still held some reservations about Arline.

Rowan knew it wasn't a romantic kind of attention that the two younger men were displaying, but one forged from the time they had spent together all those years ago.

Lady Arline looked rather uncomfortable as Frederick and Daniel began to regale an audience of some twenty-five men, women and children with the story of how they had met Lady Arline.

They had just finished eating and were now enjoying the sunshine and cool autumn breeze that tickled grass and skin alike. A goodly number of Daniel and Frederick's audience were lazing about on blankets while a few had taken felled trees as their seats.

"Och! Laddies," Frederick said excitedly. "Ye should have seen how brave Lady Arline was the night we were attacked on our way to Stirling! As brave as any Highland warrior she was that night. Ye never heard a peep out of her as the arrows -- on fire mind ye -- went flying through the air. The bastards hit man and horse alike as they tried to kill us."

"Aye, everra word Frederick says is the God's honest truth," Daniel said as he sat on a log chewing the end of a long blade of grass. His blonde hair waved in the afternoon breeze and his big blue eyes sparkled with excitement. "As brave as any warrior I ever met, she was." He looked proudly then at Lady Arline who was sitting on a blanket next to Daniel and Frederick's *stage*. Lily sat beside Arline, eating a crisp red apple.

Rowan paid close attention to Arline. Her skin seemed to grow redder as Daniel and Frederick's tale grew longer and mayhap a bit exaggerated.

"Nary a peep nor complaint from her lips. She'd been keeping up with us as we tore along the valleys and glens to get to Stirling. She has a verra good seat, Lady Arline does."

The women giggled and the men guffawed at his choice of terms. Rowan had his own thoughts as they pertained to Lady Arline's *seat*, but good manners forbade him from sharing those opinions with the rest of the crowd.

Daniel shook his head at them. "Ye ken what I mean! She's as good a rider as anyone here, I tell ye."

Frederick agreed wholeheartedly. "Aye, he's tellin' ye the God's honest truth, lads. And brave she was that night, too, when the flamin' arrows were flyin' through the air."

Apparently the flaming arrows were their favorite part of the story, for they had repeated it more than once.

"And then, when we finally made it to Stirling Castle? Och! I've never seen a braver lassie in me life. Only eight and ten she was at the time," Frederick said.

Daniel added his own opinion. "Aye! Just eight and ten and verra brave. She'd carried that box across Scotland, never lettin' it out a her sight, guardin' it with her life."

"And then when we got to Stirling Castle? That's when things got verra scary," Frederick said.

The crowd fell silent as they listened to Frederick explain how the box had been stolen and it seemed all was lost. "Fer a very long time, we thought Angus and Duncan were goin' to hang, ye ken. The only thing that could keep them from hangin' was *what* was inside that box." He paused then, shaking his head and looking quite forlorn.

One of the men piped up. "Well, what happened? What was in the box?"

Frederick and Daniel smiled at Lady Arline. "Well, ye see," Frederick said, lowering his voice ever so slightly. "In that box were papers, papers that showed who had really betrayed King David, the crown and Scotland."

"Aye, and when it was stolen right from under her nose?" David looked at Arline then. "Did she fall into a heap and cry? Did she rant and rave and curse the world? Nay. She did not."

They were all looking at Lady Arline, as was Rowan. She looked exceedingly ill at ease, as though she wanted to crawl away. But she remained mute, pretending to ignore the stares and whispers.

"Nay, she did not. She went and found the box! And she was able to save Angus and Duncan from hangin' and expose the true traitors."

Arline could take no more. She rolled her eyes and shook her head. "Nay, that is *no'* what happened and ye ken it!"

Frederick and Daniel looked surprised. "'Tis no'? Well," Frederick said quietly, "'tis how I remember it."

"And I as well," Daniel offered, looking a bit smug.

"I was scared out of me wits the night the arrows flew!" Arline said. "'Tis why ye didna hear a peep out of me. I was too scared to say anything fer I was holdin' on fer me life! And the way ye all took off, racing across the land? Every time ye jumped a log or a stream, I nearly lost me supper!"

The crowd laughed, not at her but with her.

"And as fer me findin' the box, that's not exactly true. Robert Stewart pulled all the maids into his private rooms to question them."

A woman from the crowd gasped in awe. "Ye met Robert Stewart, the Steward of Scotland?" she asked, looking amazed and intrigued.

Arline swallowed hard. She would not be able to tell them *everything* that had transpired, but there were some things that she supposed were not private or privileged information.

"Aye, I did. He was a verra nice man, verra well mannered."

"Was he as handsome as they say?" another woman asked. Her husband glanced at her, disapprovingly. His expression along with his wife's question made Arline giggle.

"Handsome?" she pretended to think on it for a time. "Nay, I didna think him *handsome*. But he was a verra nice man."

Frederick and Daniel chimed in, evidently not liking the bland manner in which Arline told the story.

"Handsome or nay," Frederick said, "the truth of it is that the box and the letters were found. And Lady Arline stood in a room filled with hundreds of people and told the truth. She named the true traitors and Angus and Duncan were spared."

"It wasn't *hundreds*, Frederick. More like a few dozen."

"It was a *lot* of people, me lady. Ye may no' have notice fer ye were busy keepin' the nooses from goin' around Angus and Duncan's necks."

Arline gave him a warm smile, much like a mother would to a child when she knew that child was exaggerating. "Be that as it may."

Frederick leapt to his feet, "Be that as it may, ye saved two innocent men from hangin' that day."

Arline looked up at him, shielded the sun from her eyes with a hand. "We *all* saved two innocent men from hangin' that day. I didna do it alone. Were it no' fer ye and Frederick, and yer brother and all the other men who made sure I got to Stirling alive, well, the outcome would have been quite different."

"What happened to the traitors?" another of the men asked. "Who were they?"

This was the part of the story that Arline did not like to think or speak about. Her smile faded away and she looked sad. "They hanged them the next day."

"Who were they?" the man repeated his question.

Arline took a deep breath and looked away from the people. "The son and grandson of me husband."

Several gasps cut through the silence. Rowan studied the crowd then. The women looked genuinely concerned for Arline, as if they understood the pain she must have gone through. The men looked at her with admiration. Even Thomas' expression showed he was rather impressed with her.

Lady Arline had shown her fealty and loyalty to Scotland by telling the truth, even when it cost the lives of her husband's son and grandson.

"Did ye ken they were the traitors? Yer stepson and grandson I mean?" one of the men asked in a low tone.

"Aye, I did," Arline answered.

"What did their da think of ye then?"

"'Twas their da who confided the truth in me. 'Twas he who asked me to go to Stirling and seek out Robert Stewart and tell him the truth." Arline turned to face the onlookers. "I had no choice in the matter. I could no' let two innocent men hang for the crimes of others, even if the traitors were me family. 'Twas the right thing to do."

The breeze picked up for a moment, caressing the skin of all those in attendance. As the zypher brushed over the tall brown grass, it made a soft, gentle, swooshing sound. For a moment, Rowan could have sworn it was the sound of a hundred people saying *aye*.

SEVENTEEN

W hen Garrick Blackthorn had learned that three of his men were dead and his former wife was not, he had turned violent with rage. With his dagger, he had sliced away three fingers from the hand of the man who had delivered the news. Tables and chairs in the gathering room had been upturned and destroyed. By his order, everything in Arline's room had been taken outside and burned, from her belongings she left behind to the bed she had slept in. Nothing had been spared.

He took his displeasure out on anyone who was stupid enough to get near him, from kitchen maid to trusted advisor, no one was safe from his fury.

Save for his Ona.

Ona. Ona was the only source of light in his otherwise dark and disturbed world. There was nothing he would or could deny her. She had a good heart, his Ona. He knew it was *her* fault that his former wife still lived, for it had been Ona who had convinced him to spare her life. Ona believed that it was not Arline's fault that she and Garrick been kept from marrying for more than a year. Nay, that was his father's fault.

Ona never begged, never pleaded, never gave ultimatums, never batted her eyelashes or used seduction to get what she wanted from Garrick. She only needed to ask.

Ona was his only addiction. He craved her, needed her as much as he needed air. She was the only reason Arline still lived.

Had he killed the foolish woman first, *before* telling Ona his plan, then Arline would now be rotting in the ground where she belonged. Instead, she was now under the protection of Rowan Graham, the man he had once considered his only true friend. But that was decades ago, when they were children. Too much had happened since those carefree days.

Garrick had learned two weeks after Lily Graham disappeared along with his former wife, exactly what had happened that fateful night. Rowan and three of his men had been able to breech Garrick's defenses, enter *his* home and take the brat. Garrick's men who were on duty that night were summarily tortured before being disemboweled for allowing the breech.

With every fiber of his being, Garrick despised Rowan Graham. Hated him. Wished nothing but ill will toward the fool.

He wanted Rowan to suffer, to die a slow, horrible, agonizing death, just as Garrick's mother had died trying to bring Andrew Graham's bastard son into the world.

Garrick had made a promise to his dead mother those many years ago. Her death had nearly been the end of him. He had adored her and she him. She doted on him, denied him nothing. He had been the perfect son. She had told him so every day of his life.

In Garrick's eyes, she was the perfect mother. Even after he learned the whole sordid truth. He could not blame his mother for her indiscretion. That fault lay at the feet of others.

Doreen Blackthorn had loved Garrick's father. She had all but worshipped the ground under Phillip Blackthorn's feet. Naively, she had believed he returned those cherished feelings. That was until the day she found him in bed with a whore, a girl really, barely old enough to know what she was doing. Seeing them together, in *their* marital bed, had crushed Doreen's spirit, had broken her heart, and had nearly killed her.

Doreen quit smiling and singing that day. Worst of all, she had quit living.

He'd been a boy then, just two and ten when he learned the truth, that Andrew Graham had seduced his sweet, beautiful mother. His father had told him the whole, sordid, painful truth, sparing few details.

His father took none of the blame of course. It was a man's right to have a mistress he explained. His God given right to do as he pleased, when he pleased, and with whom he pleased.

But Garrick knew that had his mother *not* found Phillip in bed with another woman, she would never have sought comfort in the arms of another man, his seed would not have grown in her womb only to kill her in the end.

So Garrick promised to avenge her death. Even as a boy he knew it might take some time before he could put any kind of plan in action. The hope of exacting his revenge was the only thing that kept him going.

Until he met his sweet Ona. 'Twas then that he found another purpose for living. With her long, raven tresses, her soft, blue eyes, and all those glorious curves, he had fallen for her the moment he first laid eyes upon her. In so many ways, Ona reminded him of his sweet, beautiful mother. Soft spoken, beguiling and kind. She even sang like his mother.

But since Ona was Scots and Garrick English, his father refused to allow them to marry. Aye, they lived on Scottish soil, in a grand Scottish castle not far from the English border, but Phillip Blackthorn refused to allow Blackthorn blood to be tainted with even a drop of Scots blood.

With his father dead, Garrick could apply his father's own words to his life. He would do as he pleased, when he pleased and with whom he pleased. And Ona *pleased* him very much.

Even after all these years, Garrick felt honor bound to never forget what Andrew Graham had done to his mother. He would seek revenge in her name, to right the injustice the bastard had served on his mother and, ultimately, upon Garrick. Unfortunately, the Black Death took Andrew Graham's life before Garrick had the chance.

Garrick felt cheated out of the opportunity to watch the life drain from Andrew Graham's body. He looked at that as another injustice, a slap in the face and it angered him.

The idea to make all of Clan Graham suffer came to him in a dream one night months ago. He would seek retribution by making all of Andrew Graham's clan suffer. He would begin by tormenting Rowan, making him suffer knowing his wee daughter was killed by Garrick's own hand.

Somehow Ona had gotten wind of his plan and put an immediate stop to it. She'd not allow him to take the life of a little girl, especially now that their own child grew in her womb. Wanting nothing more than to make Ona happy, he relented and agreed not to kill the child. But she hadn't said a word about *taking* her and holding her for ransom.

Rowan Graham did not know that he owed his daughter's life to Ona. Arline was just as ignorant.

So Lily Graham's life, as well as Arline's, had been spared because Ona had asked it of him. Garrick would make damn certain that Ona did not learn what he had planned for Rowan, for he knew, deep in his heart, that would she ask him to spare Rowan's life, it would be the one time he could not grant her wish.

He had made his decision, quietly and without consulting Ona. Garrick would make certain the son suffered for the sins of the father.

EIGHTEEN

Winter did not come gradually nor softly in the night. Nay, it came roaring in just before dawn, with gale force winds that battered against the stone walls with a fury that sounded like a thousand Trojan warriors with battering rams trying to gain entry. The winds were so loud and strong, that the many inhabitants of *Áit na Síochána* woke wondering if the walls could withstand it.

For three long days, the wind beat against the walls and roof of the keep. The snow whirled in through the fur-covered windows, leaving the floors beneath them covered in the heavy, cold substance. The children, of course, loved the excitement. The adults cleaning up the mess and looking for better ways to keep the snow out did not hold the same level of excitement as the children.

Some of the older clansmen could remember a blizzard of similar force and destruction from their childhood. These older people did worry that the effects of this storm would be similar to the storm they had survived in '23. At least a dozen people had died from exposure and lack of food back then.

Rowan did his best to assure them that no one would lose their lives this time, as long as they stayed within the keep and near the fires.

Their larders were full with dried fruits, cheeses and meat. He reckoned they could survive for three months without having to go in search of meat. Had this blizzard happened last year, or worse yet, the year before? They would not have made it past the first week.

Arline and Selina helped keep the children occupied with games and stories and activities that could be done in the gathering room. He was glad to see that a good number of his people had begun to change their opinions of Arline. Over the past weeks, they had come to see that she was a fine woman, intelligent, kind, and above all else, giving and honorable.

There remained just a handful of people, however, who still believed Mrs. McGregor's lies. They still held on to the opinion that Arline was a spy sent to ferret out whatever information she could to benefit Garrick Blackthorn. They kept their children away from Arline. Though she would not openly admit to it, Rowan knew their actions hurt her deeply. She also pretended not to hear the vulgar whispers that were said behind her back.

While Rowan could order them to treat her with nothing but respect, he knew he could not change their hearts. Only Arline could do that.

Rowan could only hope that eventually they, too, would come to the same conclusion as the rest of the clan -- that Lady Arline was in fact a beautiful and good woman.

Christmastime was not far away and Lady Arline's birthday was even closer. He had learned through his most favorite spy -- his daughter Lily -- that Lady Arline's birthday was just three days before the winter solstice.

Though he had tried on numerous occasions to get Arline to discuss more of herself with him, she usually ended up changing the subject. Why she was more comfortable giving Lily more personal information than she did him, he did not know.

Rowan did feel a connection with Lady Arline, a connection he had never felt with anyone before, not even his beloved Kate. They had come together over Lily and as time went on their friendship grew.

He felt he could talk to Arline about nearly any topic, save for what he was feeling in his heart as it pertained to her. Those feelings and thoughts he kept closely guarded, safely hidden away in the deepest recesses of his heart.

It was more than just a simple friendship, at least that is how he felt about it. He had no idea what Arline thought for she was not one to share her feelings, unless they pertained to Lily, the keep, and general everyday life.

Rowan wanted to do something special for Arline for all that she had done for him and for Lily. He had begun planning a very special gift for her the day after they had returned from Blackthorn lands. He hadn't planned for it to be a birthday gift but things were working out in such a manner that it would arrive in time for her birthday.

Knowing his daughter's inability to keep a secret, he hadn't shared the surprise with anyone but Frederick, Daniel and Thomas. They had all agreed that it was, in fact, the most appropriate gift and one that would show Arline the depths of his gratitude.

As time had passed, Rowan grew more and more fond of his daughter's governess. Fond to the point of distraction. So fond in fact, that her image began to invade his dreams, making sleep nearly impossible.

Before the blizzard had hit, he was able to work off his physical desires by training with his men. In practice he would not have time to think of Arline and it also gave him the opportunity to work out his frustrations. If he could get to the point of exhaustion then mayhap he could sleep at night. It wasn't working.

Matters were made worse by the blizzard. Unable to leave the keep, unable to work off the pent up frustrations was beginning to wreak havoc on his otherwise happy disposition.

He was beginning to feel less and less guilty over having these strong feelings and desires toward Arline. It wasn't just Arline who visited him in his dreams. Kate was often there, chastising him for being a foolish man and telling him to move on with his life.

Last night's dream had been the most vivid and terrifying of his life. In it, Kate was holding Arline's hand. They were standing in a field of spring grass and bluebells. They were both smiling at him, adoringly. Kate was telling him he had to move on, to love again, and that she believed he had made a fine choice in Arline.

I couldna have picked a better woman to be a mum to our daughter than Arline. Rowan, ye must no' keep yer heart to me and me alone. Ye be too lonely. I ken it and it breaks me heart. Ye promised me, Rowan Graham, on me deathbed that ye would give yer heart to another some day. Please, Rowan, give it to Arline.

And then they were both gone. Blackness had filled the space where the two beautiful women had floated in the air. The happiness and joy he had felt with seeing Kate and hearing her speak Arline's praises were replaced with something ugly, dark, ominous. They were both gone, and he had the sense that Lily was with them. The three women that he loved and adored most in his life were gone.

His hands were filled with dust, little particles of memories, hopes, dreams. He was left with the impression that these three beautiful lasses had been taken somewhere far away where they would never be found. In his dream, he knew they were being tortured and there was nothing he could do to save them.

Then Kate was back, telling him it was not too late, he could change the tide, he could save Lily and Arline, if only he would open his heart. *The only way ye can save them both is to love Arline with all of yer heart.*

He woke then, long before dawn, shooting upright in his empty bed. He was covered in sweat, his heart feeling as though it were about to explode and gulping for air.

He tossed back the covers and sat on the edge of his bed, willing his mind and heart to settle. He took in deep, slow breaths and tried to shake the images from his mind and the sense of impending doom from his heart.

He failed at both.

Something niggled at the back of his mind and made the hair on his neck stand up. He had to check on Lily. Quickly, he grabbed his tunic from the back of the chair by his fireplace. He tugged it on over his head, punching his arms through the sleeves. He grabbed his plaid and wrapped it around his shoulder and waist before snatching his dagger from the table by his bed.

Lily's room was connected to his. With his dagger in hand, he silently opened the door and stepped inside. He noticed first that there was no lit candle. The last he had known, she could not sleep without one for she was terrified that the *bad men* would come for her again.

The embers from the fireplace however, cast enough light into the dark room that he could make out her bed. He took a few quiet steps forward.

His pounding heart stilled at the sight before him.

Lily was, as always, curled into a ball, thumb in her mouth and hair twisted around her finger. But it was not her own hair twined around her finger. Nay. The long auburn locks belonged to Arline.

They were lying under the furs, with Lily nestled into Arline's chest. Arline had one hand resting on Lily's stomach and they looked so content and at peace that it stole his breath away.

No wonder Lily did not come to him with her nightmares anymore. Arline was there to chase the demons away.

He felt the dread and despair leave him, taking with them the guilt and fear he had been dueling with for weeks. He was tempted to climb into the bed with them and wrap them both in his arms. He wanted to promise them that he would never allow either of them to be hurt or taken away. In his arms, in his heart, they could always find comfort and protection.

He stood for a time listening to the soft crackle of the embers in the fireplace and watching these two beautiful women sleeping. Occasionally, Lily would sigh and suck on her thumb for a few moments. Arline barely moved save for an occasional soft, contented sigh.

A sense of peace fell over him, like a warm length of plaid or an old familiar blanket. He found that he liked the way he felt, but he wanted more. He wanted to know that this beautiful, smart, witty and strong auburn-haired woman would be with him for the rest of his life.

Soon, very soon, he would tell her how he felt. He could only pray that she had the same feelings toward him.

He left them then, as quietly as he had entered. He went back to his room, but not back to his bed.

For the first time in many years, he knelt beside his bed and prayed. He prayed for guidance, strength and courage. He prayed for the ability to protect his people, his daughter and Arline.

But his most fervent prayer would be that Arline would say yes when he asked her to become his wife.

Arline suffered with delightfully disturbing dreams of her own. The dreams left her feeling like two separate people stuck inside one body. There was the good, decent, righteous Arline who hated how the dreams left her feeling. The good Arline wanted nothing more than to live a clean, wholesome life. A life that would have made Minnie quite proud.

Then there was the less than wholesome, less than godly Arline. The one who thoroughly enjoyed the dreams, relished them. The Arline with the fluttering, swooning, happy insides. The Arline who wanted nothing more than to sneak into Rowan's room in the middle of the night and strip him bare just to see if her dreams had been accurate. In them, he was as perfect. There was also the strong desire to see if all the things she had dreamt were in fact physically possible. She desperately wanted to know if she would feel the same delightful, wicked, excited sensations while awake as she did when she was asleep.

It was becoming more and more difficult to look at him. She was certain he must think her an absent-minded fool, she was certain of it. There were many times when he had to repeat questions for she simply wasn't paying any attention to what was coming out of his mouth, though she was fully aware of his mouth. It could not escape notice for those lips were full and his teeth perfectly straight and white. Had God designed that mouth to test a woman's virtue? Or had the devil, for the same purpose? Either way, it seemed wholly unfair to have such a temptation staring her in the face.

NINETEEN

The blizzard finally subsided and dawn broke over the horizon, casting the lands in vibrant shades of pinks, oranges, and purples. As the sun rose over the horizon, it turned the snow a brilliant shade of gold.

Rowan felt it was a most magnificent morning, a perfect day to ask a beautiful young woman to be his wife.

He pulled Frederick, Daniel and Thomas into his library just after they broke their fast. There were several items they needed to discuss, the best one he would save for last.

Thomas reported that Mrs. McGregor was getting along nicely in her new quarters. She had been removed from the dungeon -- per Arline's incessant requests -- more than a week ago. They had her locked away in a small room on the third floor. Still, she refused to apologize or tell anyone anything.

"I dunna think I ever met a more stubborn woman in all me days," Thomas said, clearly exasperated by the situation. "Not even yer mum was that stubborn!"

Rowan laughed heartily at Thomas' comparison of Mrs. McGregor to his mother, Enndolynn Graham. "Mayhap my mum was no' as stubborn, but clearly she would have been much smarter about things.

Mum had a way of letting everyone ken just how angry she be without utterin' a word."

They spoke for a time, reminiscing about days past before finally getting on with matters at hand.

"Daniel," Rowan said as he gave the man a pat on the back. "I want ye to send a group of men to relieve our lads on the perimeters," Rowan said as he made his way to his seat. They had men located around the outer regions of Graham lands, though not nearly as many as he would have liked. He knew his men were smart enough to take refuge in the tiny huts placed along their borders. Hopefully they had been able to do so before the snow had become too difficult to traverse.

"And take a few men out to check on the crofters. Make sure they be well-stocked. If their supplies are low, ye can offer them to stay in the keep. We may get more blizzards and I do no' want to lose anyone."

Daniel happily agreed. "'Twill be good to get out of the keep fer the day. I was goin' daft with nothin' to do."

"Aye, and 'tis been four days since ye've seen that bonny little MacKenzie girl!" Frederick teased him.

Daniel's face burned with embarrassment. "Yer daft," he grumbled.

Frederick pretended to be confused. "Are ye sure? I mean, if ye are no' interested in Anna MacKenzie, I wouldn't mind askin' her to take a walk in the moonlight."

Daniel's eyes flew open. "Ye stay away from Anna MacKenzie! She's too good a lass fer the likes of ye."

Frederick laughed and slapped Daniel on the back. "'Tis just as I thought. Ye've takin' a likin' to the lass. I can't say that I blame ye, fer she is a bonny thing. But, I wonder," he let his words trail off.

Daniel raised an eyebrow. "Wonder? Wonder over what?"

"If her da will let her marry a man like ye!" he answered playfully.

Daniel rolled his eyes and sighed with indifference. "Who says I want to marry the girl?"

Frederick gave a wink to Rowan before he answered the question. "Ye do. Ye talk in yer sleep, ye eejit!"

Daniel had had enough of Frederick's needling. In one swift motion, he had Frederick in a headlock, threatening to part him from his manhood if he did not cease his teasing.

Frederick was laughing so hard at Daniel's distress that he could not answer at first. "Aye, aye, aye," he said between fits of laughter.

Thomas smacked them both on the tops of their heads. "Settle down, ye heathens. There's work to be done."

Daniel and Frederick finally regained their composure and settled down to listen to their chief. Rowan took his seat behind his desk and tried to settle the wave of excitement that had plagued him since the early morning hours.

"I wanted to let the three of ye know that I have made a decision." He paused for a moment, looking to make certain he had their full attention. "I'm going to ask Lady Arline to marry me."

Three stunned men looked back at him. Thomas tried to speak, stopped and tried again. "Ye canna be serious?" there was no denying the fact that he was astonished.

"I am. I plan on askin' her after the evenin' meal this night. I've made up me mind."

"Then *un*make it!" Thomas said. "Ye canna marry a woman known to be barren, Rowan. The clan council will no' allow it."

Rowan tilted his head sideways and raised an eyebrow. "I wasna aware I had to ask the council permission to marry, Thomas."

"Ye dunna have to ask permission, but ye need their approval!"

"Och! Now yer tryin' to separate the fly shite from the pepper!" He had hoped, after all these weeks, that Thomas would have changed his mind about Arline. "Mayhap it be yer opinion of Lady Arline that skews yer opinion of me marryin' her."

Thomas ran a hand through his unruly ginger hair. "I do no' hold the same opinion of her that I did when she first arrived, Rowan. She is a fine woman and aye, she'd make almost any man a fine wife. But she's no' fer ye! Ye need sons, sons who can become chief of this clan someday. Lady Arline canna give ye that."

It mattered not to Rowan if Arline was barren or as fertile as a rabbit. He loved her, plain and simple. With or without the council's permission, he would marry her. While he did not relish the argument or fighting his decision might cause, it was a fight he would not back away from.

"I'll no' change me mind, Thomas," Rowan said as he clenched his jaw. "She's good fer Lily and fer me."

"Aye, she's a good governess, I'll grant ye that. And there is nothin' that says she canna remain her governess. If it's a wife ye be wantin', there be women here who'd give their right arm to be yer wife."

Rowan let out a long, heavy sigh of frustration. "But I do no' want those women to be me wife, Thomas. I'll no' marry a woman I do no' love."

"Did ye love Kate when ye married her?" Thomas growled.

Rowan shot to his feet. "That was different! That was an arranged marriage. I may no' have loved Kate the day we took our vows, but I grew to love her shortly after."

Thomas shook his head in befuddlement. "What if the council does no' give their blessin'? What will ye do then? Give up yer chief-dom? Give up yer clan, yer family's legacy? Give up all the hard work of yer father, and his father, and his? Does none of that mean anythin' to ye?"

It meant a great deal more to him than Thomas realized. Rowan was dedicated to his people, to the clan. But must he sacrifice his own happiness in order to remain chief and continue the Graham legacy?

"Please, Rowan, just think on it fer a spell. Think what marryin' Arline would mean, in the end, after all 'tis said and done."

"Does the clan council ken that there is a *possibility* that Arline is barren?"

Thomas shook his head as if he understood where Rowan was heading. "I do no' ken and I do no' care. If ye decide to go through with this, ye will have to bring it before us. I'll no' lie fer ye, Rowan, no matter how much I love ye like a son."

Rowan knew that he could not, in good conscience ask Thomas to lie or withhold information. Thomas was more than just his friend and advisor, he was also a member of the council. He would do what he felt was for the good of the clan and its future.

Last night's dream, where he lost Arline for eternity, came crashing to the forefront of his mind. Had the dream been an omen foretelling the future or was it simply telling him what he already knew -- that he could not have Arline as his wife?

His palms began to feel clammy and his stomach uneasy. He could not imagine going through the rest of his life without Arline as his wife. But neither could he imagine living it as anything other than chief of Clan Graham.

He was damned if he did and damned if he didn't.

A fter much back and forth between himself and Thomas, Rowan finally agreed to think on the matter further. The last thing he wanted was to think. He wanted to *feel*. Feel something other than alone and lonely. He wanted a bit of happiness in his life, a bit of contentment and harmony. Was that too much to ask for?

He wanted to feel Arline's hair as he ran his fingers through it. He wanted to know what it would feel like to have her skin pressed against his, her lips on his lips. He wanted to feel her lying next to him as he drifted off to sleep each night and again, when he woke in the morning.

It wasn't just an intense physical attraction he felt toward Arline. Nay, it went much deeper than that. He loved her as a person, as a woman. She was kind and generous, funny and smart. She was strong and honorable. She was all the things he needed and wanted in a woman, and much more.

He did not know how he would go on with the rest of his life if the clan council did not give their blessing and allow the two of them to marry. Aye, he could marry Arline without their permission, but that could lead to so many troubles. The clan council could call for a vote to have him stripped of his chiefdom.

Everyone in the clan would be allowed to vote on whether or not he could remain as their chief. Although many of his people had come to accept Lady Arline as part of the clan, he could not guarantee they would accept her as his wife.

What then? What would he do if he were stripped of his position? His pride would not allow him to stay here while someone else led his clan. He couldn't bear it.

Although being chief of Clan Graham was his birthright, there were still certain protocols that had to be maintained and met. Even though he had inherited his position, his people could take it all away if they deemed him unfit to lead.

And what of Lily? Although she could not be the actual chief of the clan, any potential husband could take on that role. It would strip her of her future by default if the clan voted against him.

He could not remember ever having to make a decision as difficult as the one that now lay before him.

Just this morning he had felt as though he were floating on air. Happier than he had been in more than four years. Now, he had the sensation that he was adrift at sea, holding on to nothing more substantial than a piece of driftwood.

Damn.

TWENTY

Rowan stayed to his library in self-imposed seclusion for the remainder of the morning. He had not realized how much time had passed until his stomach began to grumble. With his mind still considering his choices and his heart in utter turmoil, he left his den of isolation to search for food.

Mrs. Fitz, a comely brown-haired woman of mayhap forty years, was doing a remarkable job in her new position as head cook. She had been working under Mrs. McGregor for the past two years, knew the kitchens and the clans people as well as anyone, so it had been an easy decision for him to make. Besides, Lady Arline had recommended her for the position.

Lady Arline. Every thought looped back around to her. As he walked the length of the hallway toward the kitchens, he shook his head and muttered a curse under his breath. The beautiful redhead was always at the forefront of his thoughts. He could not banish the images of her from his mind. Nor could he stop the thrumming of his heart those thoughts brought.

And he could not escape the fact that she was having a positive effect on most of his clan. Lily adored her, Daniel and Frederick nearly worshipped at her feet, and even Thomas had grown to admire the woman.

There remained only a handful of people who held to the belief that she was a spy, sent by Garrick Blackburn for mysterious and nefarious reasons. Och! How he wished he could change their minds and their hearts toward her. If he was ever to be allowed to marry Arline, he would need the approval and blessing of each member of his clan.

Just as the course of a stream could be altered by one tiny pebble, so too could a man's mind, heart, even his destiny, be affected by one small, simple opinion.

He was paying very little attention to where he was going as he rounded the corner in a huff and walking far too quickly to stop what next happened.

Lily was suddenly in front of him, carrying a tray and Lady Arline was right behind her. He was able to avoid knocking Lily down by spreading his legs far apart to allow his very surprised little girl to sweep through them. However, he could not, no matter how he tried, stop his forward momentum. The only thing he could do to keep from landing on top of Lady Arline as they fell was to wrap his arms around her, spin, and allow his back to take the brunt of the fall.

He hadn't realized that Lady Arline was carrying a tray until he felt it slam against his chest during their less-than-elegant fall to the floor. He also had not realized the strength of his own skull until it bounced off the stone floor.

It had all happened so quickly, the blink of an eye really, that both he and Lady Arline were left stunned, with eyes wide and mouths agape. The pitcher of ale and the earthenware mug were smashed into his chest. He could very well have been bleeding and not known for his shirt was soaked, his brains rattled from the blow to his head and his heart left pounding in his throat.

He closed his eyes tightly and shook away the pain in his head as he tried to catch the breath that had been knocked from his lungs. He pulled Arline closer, using her as a brace against the pain in his thick, Scottish noggin.

When he finally opened his eyes, she was looking back at him. At first, he thought she was frozen with fear. But then, he noticed she was not looking at his eyes, but was staring at his lips.

He was close enough to press his lips against hers and he was sorely tempted. Even with a pounding skull, ale leaking all over him and bits of crockery digging into his chest. Aye, this is where he wanted her. In his arms, on top of him, under him, it mattered not. Remove the spilt ale, the jagged shards digging into his flesh, his throbbing head and their clothes, and he reckoned it would be a most perfect union.

"Rowan," Arline finally spoke, sounding breathless and damned appealing. His groin began to ache and at the same time, sing with delight. He imagined he could have seven arrows piercing his body at the moment and his maleness would still respond to this beautiful green-eyed auburn-haired woman. He also reckoned that she wouldn't even need to be sprawled across him. Just the thought of her would bring him to full attention. His male member was going to be the death of him someday, he just knew it.

"Da!" Lily squealed from very near his feet. He heard her set her tray down on the cold stones. He also heard her little feet rushing to his side. "Lady Arline!" Lily exclaimed as she stood next to them.

The sound of his daughter's voice had two effects on him. It immediately cleared the wicked images of a naked Lady Arline from his mind and acted like a bucket of frozen water thrown on his lower extremities. *Thank God fer Lily or I'd be carrying Lady Arline up the stairs to me chamber right now. Blow to the head and cut skin be damned.*

Rowan closed his eyes again, hoping to settle his nerves and regain the use of his lungs. "Woman, ye'll be the death of me," he whispered without thinking.

Arline scurried away and he did not like the emptiness she left behind. "I be terribly sorry, Rowan," she murmured softly.

He sensed by the tone of her voice that he had hurt her feelings. Of course she could not know by his statement that he was not angry or upset with her.

He took a deep breath and opened his eyes. She was sitting but a few steps away from him, holding on to Lily as if she were a rope meant to keep her from drowning.

He could not help but notice that the bodice of her green dress was also soaked with ale. He could just make out the shapes of delightful, perky breasts. At least in the recesses of his wicked mind they were delightful.

"Are ye well, da?" Lily asked. Her eyes and voice were filled with worry and concern.

Rowan took a deep breath and nodded his head, an act which immediately filled him with regret. "Aye, I will be well."

He took a moment before rolling over to his side. Arline remained frozen, her eyes were as wide as trenchers and moist, as if she were fighting back tears.

"I be verra sorry, lassies. I was no' watchin' where I was going. 'Tis all me own fault, no' yers. Please, fergive me." His words were meant for both Arline and Lily, though his eyes were glued to Arline's.

"We were bringin' ye a meat pie, da," Lily said as she knelt down to look at him. "I helped Mrs. Fitz to make them."

His daughter still looked quite worried over him. Forcing a smile he took a moment before pushing himself to sit. He took Lily in his arms and gave her a grand hug.

Ye almost kissed him! Arline thought before chastising the wanton, harlot of a woman that had invaded her dreams and was rapidly taking over her waking hours. *Ye be a fool, an eejit of a woman,* she told herself as she stared at the object of her torment.

Her nerves were frayed, her emotions all jumbled and making her stomach feel once again as if it housed a school of large salmon. She cursed herself for thinking of kissing him and for regretting not following that urge.

Taking a deep breath, she gave a mental shake of her head and tried to push the thoughts from her mind. *The man was most assuredly injured, and the only thing ye could think of was to kiss him!*

After he had declared she would be the death of him, she felt relieved that she hadn't. Certain she was that he would toss her out into the cold winter if she *had* taken that bold step and done what she wanted most to do. She vexed him, she had no doubt for he had just told her so.

She didn't want to vex him, she wanted to kiss him. Repeatedly. Both her heart and her lips desperately wanted to know what it would feel like. How often had she wondered and daydreamt on that very subject? Too many times to count.

She had often wondered if he would respond positively to such a bold move. Would he take her in his arms and kiss her thoroughly and soundly with those horribly magnificent lips of his? Would he smile fondly and welcome her lips against his?

Nay. She knew that now for he had just told her. She would be the death of him.

Her eyes filled with tears that she would not shed in front of him. She'd die first before she would shed another tear in his presence. It was, of course, to be expected. She was cursed with some affliction she could not identify that kept men -- whether it be her father, her husbands, or any other man -- from loving her.

She was doomed to spend the rest of her life alone. No matter how she tried to convince herself that *that* was exactly what she wanted, to live a life of solitude, her blasted heart refused to give up. Her heart wanted to be loved, to be adored and respected.

Her heart wanted all those things it could not have. It betrayed her, left her feeling abandoned, unlovable, unwanted.

Rowan's deep voice, soft and filled with something she could not recognize, broke her quiet reverie.

"Are ye well, lass?" he asked as he pulled himself to his feet.

Was it genuine concern she saw in his eyes? Mayhap, but it wasn't necessarily for her as a person. He was most likely worried over his daughter's governess, not her as a woman.

She swallowed back the tears and mumbled that she was well. She noticed then his torn and soaked tunic that was plastered against his broad, muscular chest. Taking a deep breath, she swore she would not swoon nor would she cry over that which she could never have.

Instead, she did the grown up, mature and intelligent thing. She could not blame him, for the curse was hers.

"Yer bleedin'!" she cried out in surprise. It wasn't just the ale that soaked his tunic, it was blood.

She shot to her feet and reached out to tend to his injuries. She could not panic in front of Lily so she willed her hands and voice to remain calm. "Lily," she said calmly, "help me get yer da to his room."

She placed her hands on his tunic and began to examine the tears. She opened one of them and peered inside. Rowan gently grabbed her hands with his, and pressed them against his chest.

"I will be well, Arline. 'Tis just a few scratches."

He could feel her hands tremble inside his and he found himself unable to let them go. He felt something then, something warm and loving though it was hidden under a current of fear. She cared for him, he could feel it in her touch and see it in her eyes.

"Och! Ye stubborn Scot! Just let me see to the wounds. Ye do no' want them to get infected!" she tried to free her hands from his grasp. He held on tighter.

That would solve all me problems, he thought. *I could let the wounds fester and die from it. 'Twould be far more desirable to die from that than from me aching heart.*

She was looking into his eyes, her forehead creasing and he could tell that she was about to argue with him.

"I'll have Thomas tend to them. He's our healer on the battlefields. I promise ye needn't worry over a few scratches."

The look she gave him said she did not believe him and for some reason, it made him smile. "Lily, run and get Thomas. Have him meet me in me bedchamber."

He raised a brow as if to say *now do ye believe me?* "I'll help ye to clean up this mess," he told her as he finally let go of her hands.

"Ye will do no such thing!" she said sternly. "Ye go to yer room now. I'll take care of the mess."

He had the sense that she wanted to say more, something along the lines that he was a stubborn fool. His smile grew as he reached out and touched the tip of her nose. "Yer a good woman, Lady Arline. A verra good woman."

And with that, he left her to seek out the solitude his room offered.

Arline followed him with her eyes as he made his way down the corridor. Her breath did not return until he rounded the corner and was out of her sight.

TWENTY-ONE

Unfortunately for Rowan, his wounds were nothing more than a few deep scratches. He could not hope for a raging infection that would end his sorry life thereby negating the need for him to make a decision.

Selina and Lily brought a tray of food to his room after Thomas had declared he was fine and that it would take more than a stone floor and a pitcher of ale to do the man in.

Rowan stayed to his room the rest of the day, pacing back and forth as he mulled over what to do about Lady Arline. He sent word to Arline and the rest of the clan that he would not be joining them for the evening meal under the guise of the knock he took to his skull. 'Twas a full out lie. His head had stopped pounding hours ago. It was his heart that ached.

He wanted her to be his wife. He wanted to remain chief of his clan. How could he have both?

After the evening meal, Selina returned with Lily so that she could bid him good night. He remained in his seat by the fire and tried to at least appear as though he had a headache.

He found it quite odd that Selina had brought her instead of Lady Arline. He found he would not have to inquire as to the location of

Lady Arline, for Lily offered her information up with all the innocence of a four-year-old girl.

"Lady Arline has a headache too, da," Lily told him as she climbed
onto his lap.

His heart immediately filled with worry. Had he somehow injured
her during their tumble earlier? Had the tray that lodged between
them injured her somehow?

He looked up to Selina for some kind of confirmation or
expansion.

Selina smiled warmly at him. "She'll be fine, Rowan. She thinks
she's been cooped up in this keep for far too many days. If the weather
is nice on the morrow, we'll take the children outside to play."

He found little reassurance in Selina's words. He tamped down the
urge to see Arline with his own eyes. Mayhap the less he saw of her
the quicker he'd be able to make up his mind.

Many hours later, he awoke to the sound of Lily crying. His heart
lurched at the sight of his babe standing in the open doorway to his
room, tears streaming down her little cheeks.

He reached her in but a few fast steps and picked her up. Holding
her to his chest, he whispered softly. "Wheesht, babe. Da is here."

Between sobs, Lily explained her plight. "Lady Arline did not come
to sleep with me tonight," she hiccuped and lifted her head to look at
him. "I had a bad dream again," she said. Her little eyes and nose were
red. Her tears left salty trails down her cheeks.

"Wheesht, little one," he whispered as he bounced her up and
down gently.

"Lady Arline has the bad dreams too, da," Lily said as she thrust her
thumb between her lips.

Rowan's heart skipped beating for a moment and he felt very
much an intolerable oaf. Not once had he thought to ask Arline how
she was faring. His only concern over the last weeks had been for his
daughter.

He had thoughtlessly assumed that since Lily did not come to him
in the middle of the night, that she was recovering nicely from her
ordeal. She rarely talked with him about what happened at Blackthorn

Keep. He had assumed that meant that her time there was not as bad as he had originally imagined.

Realizing he had made a terrible error in assessing the harm done to both Lily and Arline, tears stung his eyes. How could he have been so ignorant? So unaware?

"Tell me, sweeting, what was yer bad dream?"

Lily hiccupped as she removed her thumb from her mouth. "The bad men came and took Lady Arline and me. They took us back to their keep. The mean man spanked me again with the strap and he spanked Lady Arline too."

Rowan knew, from what Caelen had told him that first day, that Garrick Blackthorn had taken a strap to Lily, so there was some truth to her dream. She was forced to relive those awful moments and he felt there was naught he could do except hold her.

"I'll no let the bad men get ye again, Lily. I promise." He'd die before he would ever allow Garrick Blackthorn, or anyone else for that matter, to bring any harm to his daughter.

"Ye won't let him take Lady Arline either?" Lily asked as she slipped her thumb back into her little mouth.

"Nay," Rowan whispered softly. "I'll no' let any harm come to Lady Arline. I do so promise."

Lily sighed and gave a little nod of her head as if to say she believed him. She slipped her free hand up his neck and grabbed a length of his brown hair and began twisting it around her finger.

He returned to the chair by the fireplace and sat in the quiet of the night, his insides roiling with anger and guilt.

"Lily," he spoke in a low, soft voice. "Do ye think, on the morrow, we could spend some time together? Just the two of us?"

"What about Lady Arline?" she asked sleepily. "She gets lonely and afraid too."

Rowan tilted his head a bit so that he could get a better look at his daughter. "She does?"

Lily nodded her head. "That is why she sleeps with me everra night. She has bad dreams sometimes too. She is afraid the bad man will come fer her too."

Knowing Garrick Blackthorn haunted the dreams of his daughter and the woman he had fallen in love with made him furious. It felt like a snake had coiled around his heart and stomach and each time Blackthorn's name was mentioned, the snake drew tighter.

"Da," Lily said as she twirled his hair around her finger. "Please don't make Lady Arline leave. I love her."

Her request puzzled him. "Why would I make Lady Arline leave?"

"If her da finds out that she be here, he'll make her go back to Ireland. She doesna ever want to leave us. But she does miss her sisters."

Rowan took a deep breath and thought long and hard before answering his daughter. "I promise I'll no' let *anyone* take Lady Arline," he said as he kissed the top of Lily's head.

I'll kill any man who tries to take her away from us.

R owan had waited until Lily had fallen back to sleep before he placed her in his bed and tucked her in under his furs. Knowing he'd not be able to sleep until he saw that Arline was well, he lit a candle and left his room to seek out hers.

Her room was not far from his, just around the corner and down a few doors. Since their return from Blackthorn Keep, Rowan had set guards to patrol the floors throughout the night. He met one of them now as he padded down the hallway.

"Richard," Rowan spoke quietly. "I take it all is well?"

Richard gave him a curious look. "Aye, all is well, Rowan," the young man answered as he cast a look over his shoulder in the direction of Lady Arline's room.

Rowan chuckled, realizing the young man assumed Rowan was lurking in the halls in the middle of the night, presumably to meet with Lady Arline for a tryst.

"'Tis no' what ye think, Richard. Lily had a bad dream and asked that I check on Lady Arline to make certain she is well."

Richard smiled and nodded his head as if clarity had dawned. "She usually sleeps in Lily's room, Rowan. But this night, she kept to her own."

Was everyone in this castle aware of where Arline slept each night but him? The thought aggravated his already guilty conscience.

"I've no' heard a thing from her room, this night, Rowan," Richard offered. "Is Lily well?"

Rowan ran a hand across his face. "Aye, fer now she is. But I promised I would check on Lady Arline fer her. She'll no' sleep until she kens she is well."

He knew it was a bald-faced lie, but Richard didn't need to know the particulars. "And if Lily doesna sleep, then I'll get none either."

"Go see fer yerself," Richard said before leaving his chief to continue his patrol.

Rowan padded softly and stood outside Arline's door for several moments. He could hear his heart beating rapidly as he took a deep breath and slowly opened the door.

The light of the candle cast a sliver of yellow light into her room. There was Arline, fast asleep in her bed. Wavy auburn locks were tucked behind one ear and fell wildly over one pillow. She held another pillow against her chest and resembled a child holding onto a favorite doll whilst she slept.

He stood in the doorway and watched the gentle rise and fall of her shoulders as she slept. Her face showed no sign of worry or distressful sleep, in fact, she looked quite content. He breathed a sigh of relief and sent a silent prayer upward that she would be able to sleep the remainder of the night in peace.

For a moment, he was tempted to go to her, climb into her bed and whisper the same promise to her as he made to Lily. He'd not let anything bad ever happen to her. Even if he could not marry her, he would always protect her.

Gently he closed the door and went back to his daughter before he made a complete fool of himself.

TWENTY-TWO

ily woke Rowan not long after sunrise. He helped her with
her morning ablutions before tending to his own. He helped
her into a little blue dress, did his best to comb out the
tangled locks without making her scream in protest, and felt more
like his old self than he had in weeks.

He realized as he slipped on his black trews and a white tunic that
he really did not care to resemble his old self ever again. His old self
was a lonely man who spoiled his daughter far too much out of love
and the never-ending guilt he possessed over the fact that her mum
had died.

Lily had no fond memories or recollections of her mother. There
was nothing for Lily to hold on to, nothing that kept her from moving
forward with her life. She had no past to do battle with. There had
been times when he wished that he could live in the same state of
blissful oblivion, where memories did not haunt him by day or
by night.

This morn however, he was not overwhelmed with guilt for
moving forward with his life. Instead, guilt plagued him for far
different reasons.

At some time in the dark of the night, as he had lain in his bed listening to the sweet sound of his daughter slumbering peacefully beside him, he had made a decision.

He could not ask for Lady Arline's hand.

There were a thousand reasons why he wanted to marry Arline. But only one that would keep him from doing that. Lily's birthright.

Rowan did not have the courage nor did he feel he possessed the right to take Lily's future away from her so that he might have one with Arline. Truthfully, he didn't give a damn about his position as chief. He'd gladly relinquish it without regret. But he could not take away from Lily that which was rightfully hers.

Arline would have made such a wonderful mother to Lily. He wanted to give her that. But to give her a mother meant to give up her birthright, her future. Just as he could not remain chief and have Arline as his wife, Lily could not hold on to her birthright and have Arline has her mother.

The whole situation seemed inherently unfair. In a perfect world -- one that currently did not exist, at least not for him -- he could have Arline as his wife and life partner and Lily could have the mother she wanted and needed.

He would do whatever he could to see that Arline remained among his clan. For now, as Lily's governess and mayhap, later, she could find a man who could marry her without reserve and help her have a wonderful life.

He did not enjoy the thought of Arline making a life with another man. It made his heart ache to think of her with another man. Yet, he knew he could not keep from her that which she deserved. No matter which way he looked at it, someone would have to sacrifice for his happiness. He could not do that.

Rowan took Lily's hand in his and led her from his room. Lily was hungry and looking forward to breaking her fast. Rowan found he had no appetite.

They had not walked far when Arline called out for them. She met the two of them in the hallway. She was shocked to see Rowan up at such an early hour and with his daughter. After quietly inquiring as to the wellness of the other, together they escorted Lily below stairs.

It felt *right* to Rowan, this simple act of himself and Arline taking his daughter to gather with his people for the morning meal. They were meant to do this, to be together, as a family. But at what cost?

Lily chattered on about Red John's pups and begged Rowan to allow her to go to the stables today to check on them. It mattered not to Lily that Red John had reassured her that the pups were fine, she insisted on seeing them for herself.

They made their way to the gathering room and took their seats at the high table. Rowan took note that Arline was unusually quiet and, like him, ate very little.

"I'm ready to play in the snow," Lily informed them both as she took the last bite of her eggs.

Arline smiled down at the excited child and patted the top of her head. "Why don't ye go and find yer friends, Lily? I'll go above stairs and grab our cloaks and scarves."

Lily scrambled happily from her seat in search of her friends. Arline stood to leave without saying a word to Rowan.

"Lady Arline, I'll escort ye above stairs," he offered.

Arline remained mute, gave a slight nod of acquiescence and took his offered arm.

"How is yer headache this morn?" he asked as they made their way to the stairs.

She very nearly slipped and asked what headache when she remembered that had been her excuse to remain hidden in her rooms. "It lingers," she lied, just in case she might need to use that excuse again.

A look of genuine concern came to Rowan's face. It made her feel all the more guilty for lying to him. But how could she tell him the truth? That every moment for her was both a delight and an agony? That his image was pervasive, always there, in her dreams, in her waking moments?

Nay, she could not tell him those things knowing full well that she vexed him to the point of frustration. She had seen it in his eyes the previous morn and he had even admitted to the same.

"I am certain the fresh air will help. Ye needn't worry," she said as they climbed the winding staircase to the second floor. She glanced at him from the corner of her eye.

"And ye, Rowan? How are yer wounds?"

Rowan shrugged his shoulders. He knew she spoke of the scrapes and scratches on his chest and not his wounded soul. "I'd hardly call them wounds. Just a few scratches."

Not a word was said between them again as they walked side by side in the quiet hallways. Lost in their own thoughts, there were a thousand things their hearts wanted to say but neither of them possessed the courage to say them.

Rowan lifted the latch on the door to Arline's room and pushed it open. He held it open as she glided through. To help stave off any temptation to either speak his heart or act on his feelings, he left the door open and waited patiently just inside the doorway.

Arline quietly slipped into the small dressing room. Once inside, she leaned against the wall and took slow steady breaths. It was becoming increasingly difficult to be anywhere near the man without her legs turning to mush, her mouth going dry, her palms sweating or having the urge to throw herself at him!

It was quite apparent that her body would not listen to reason. It ignored the fact that he was irritated with her. It ignored the fact that he had not shown one tiny drop of interest in her other than as his daughter's governess.

Nay, her body continued to betray her heart and her good sense! What on earth was she to do? One of these days she would slip up and say something stupid, something along the lines of *Please, take me! Kiss me! Hold me!* She would die from the mortification, embarrassment and humiliation of it.

And if her tongue didn't get her into trouble, her body would. Only moments ago, as they passed through the doorway, she had an overwhelming urge to push him onto her bed and tear his tunic off with her teeth. The only thing that saved her from doing just that was the image of him laughing at her immature attempts at seduction.

She was tempted to disregard donning woolens, boots, and cloak in favor of rolling around in the frozen snow in hopes of catching her death. Death seemed to be the only solution to the tormented thoughts and feelings she had toward Rowan.

As Arline mulled over the temptation of suicide by freezing to death, Lily came rushing into Arline's bedchamber. Arline recognized the little girl's squeals as nothing more than excitement. She let out a frustrated sigh before stepping out of the dressing room.

"Lady Arline! Lady Arline!" Lily exclaimed as she raced into Arline's arms.

"Wheesht, Lily!" Arline said as she patted the excited child on the back. "Do we scream like that when we are indoors?"

Lily blew loose tendrils of hair out of her eyes. "Only if we be under attack or the keep is on fire," Lily replied quickly.

Lily had paid no attention to her father until he chuckled at her quick response. "Ye need to leave, Da. I have womanly stuff to talk to Lady Arline about."

Rowan had to bite the inside of his cheek to keep from bursting out with laughter. Instead, he chose the most serious expression he could manage, crossed his arms over his chest and leaned against the wall. "Womanly stuff, ye say?" He glanced at Arline and could see that she too was trying not to laugh at his excited little girl. Rowan resisted asking what kind of *womanly* things a four-year-old would need to discuss with her governess and why it should warrant secrecy.

Lily nodded her head and brushed the irritating curls from her forehead. "Aye. 'Tis about kissin' and we dunna talk about kissin' in front of men."

Rowan watched Arline's face burn with a blend of surprise and embarrassment. His fatherly instincts took control of his good senses. "Kissin'?" Why would his four-year-old daughter need to discuss such a topic?

Arline rolled her eyes and turned Lily around to look at her. "Lily, we do no' discuss things like that with other men," Arline tried to explain.

Lily looked confused. "Other men? What kind of men are there?" she asked innocently.

That particular question could have taken hours to answer, hours that Arline was not quite ready to spend. "Never mind. Ye can talk in front of yer da, child. Go ahead, what is it ye want to say?"

Lily hesitated a moment before she spoke. "I hit Robert," she said solemnly. "He kissed me!"

Monumental efforts not to laugh out loud were made by both adults in the room. Lily waited quietly, not at all certain if she were going to be in trouble for hitting her friend.

Rowan cleared his throat as he came to kneel before his daughter. "Robert kissed ye?" he asked, feigning insult. "I should slay the impudent and brazen lad!"

Lily's eyes grew wide with horror. "Nay, da! Ye canna do that!"

Rowan tilted his head, looking quite serious. "I canna slay the young man that stole a kiss from me daughter? Pray tell, why no'?"

"Because I like him!" Lily answered as if her father were mayhap one of the most daft individuals to ever grace the earth. She rolled her eyes and turned back to Arline. "I kent he wouldna understand."

"If ye like him, then why'd ye hit him when he kissed ye?" Rowan asked, puzzled by his four-year-old daughter's behavior.

Another eye roll nearly sent Rowan fleeing from the room to look for a quiet place in which to die from laughter. Knowing she'd never trust him again if he laughed at her, he willed his face to retain the frown he had painted there. He was too old and his daughter far too young for conversations such as these.

Arline decided mayhap now was the time to explain. "Don't ye see? She *likes* the young Robert."

Now it made perfectly good sense. If one were a four-year-old girl. Or a full-grown female. As a man, he couldn't wrap his head around the logic. His ignorance must have been plainly evident by the bewildered expression on his face, for Arline gave a roll of her own eyes. That explained where Lily had picked up the habit.

"She likes the lad, Rowan. Lily and I have discussed this recent realization on her part. She's far too young fer kisses and Robert is an older lad, at six, ye ken. And she doesna want the lads to think they can steal kisses whenever they wish."

That he understood completely. While Rowan taught his

daughter how to protect herself and the keep from enemy inva-sions, Arline was teaching her how to protect herself from some-thing far worse than invaders from the north, the Huns, or even the English. She was teaching Lily to protect herself from the opposite sex.

"That's right," Lily interjected. "They must ask ye first, fer permis-sion and he has to understand that if I say no and he still tries to kiss me, I get to hit him."

Were his daughter a few years older, this current conversation would be far less adorable. Arline could never leave him. He needed her to have these uncomfortable conversation with his daughter. His advice would have been far less eloquent and more along the lines of warning Lily that he'd kill any lad that tried to steal even the most innocent of kisses. He would have to permanently erase from his mind the memories of being a young lad if he were to survive his daughter growing older.

Arline stood and gave a nod of approval to Lily. "Now run and get yer cloak and things and wait fer me below stairs. I'll be along shortly."

Lily smiled and left the room in a hurry, leaving her bewildered father and proud governess behind.

Rowan watched his daughter leave the room before turning to face Arline. "Me daughter's first kiss," he said with a smile. "I dunnae if I should be proud of how well she handled herself or worried that the kisses are startin' so young."

Arline returned his smile, feeling much the same way as he did. "I think both feelin's are appropriate."

Rowan chuckled slightly and ran a hand across his face. "She's a wee young, don' ye think? Fer kisses?"

"I'm sure it was an innocent kiss, Rowan. I do no' think young Robert will be askin' fer her hand anytime soon." Her heart melted over Rowan's concern for his daughter.

"I remember me first kiss," he said with a smile. "I was a bit older, ye ken. I was nine and she was eight. Her name was Ella McElroy." Arline could see the memory was a fond one for his smile said more than words could. There was a devilish twinkle in his eyes as he spoke of it.

"I told her I had somethin' to show her, hidden behind the stables. It had taken me a week to work up the courage to kiss her. Och! 'Twas an innocent kiss, to be certain. I pecked her lips and then ran like the devil was chasin' me!"

Arline could not resist laughing at the image he painted. She almost asked if he still ran after stealing kisses from unsuspecting young women, but thought better of it.

"When was yers?" he asked innocently.

"When was my what?" she answered, uncertain as to what he meant.

"Yer first kiss?"

She froze for a very long moment, her smile leaving rapidly. This was very uncomfortable and humiliating territory. Looking away, she answered in short, clipped words. "I'm sure I do no' remember."

Not knowing her circumstances or much of her life, he neither believed her nor realized it was an uncomfortable topic. "Och! Everyone remembers their first kiss, lass!"

She ignored him, left him standing in the middle of her bedchamber as she returned to her dressing room. Her face was hot, burning with mortification and she did not want to explain anything to him.

Rowan came to stand in the doorway between her sleeping chamber and dressing room. "Lass, there be nothin' to be embarrassed over. Not everyone's first kiss was as romantic as mine." He was smiling, trying his best to add some levity to the moment. He hadn't meant to embarrass her, but his curiosity had been piqued.

She was a woman full grown, married twice, and yet she had blushed like a young maiden when he asked the question. Lady Arline was a bold, brave woman, yet this topic seemed to unsettle her.

Arline stood with her back to him, pretending to sort through her trunk in search of something. Her chest hurt, her eyes stung as an empty feeling draped over her.

Rowan began to wonder why she refused to discuss something as simple as a first kiss. He studied her closely, saw her shoulders fall as if weighted down by some unseen force. Although he could not see her face, he sensed she was despondent, but why?

Mayhap her first kiss was not a kind one? Mayhap it had been a horrible experience, one that had scarred her, left her feeling sad and ashamed. Suddenly he felt like an oaf, an uncaring idiot for having pushed the subject and causing her pain. "Arline," he said softly. "I be terribly sorry if I hurt yer feelin's. I didna realize that mayhap yer first kiss is not one ye wish to remember. I be sorry, lass."

She could have left it alone then, let him believe whatever he wished. But the pity in his voice irritated her, like sand caught between her toes. It ground and aggravated and sent her over the edge of reason.

Arline spun around to look at him. "Me first kiss? Do ye truly want to ken the truth, Rowan?"

He started to speak, but was at a loss. Her eyes burned with more than anger. They were filled with hurt, pain, and something he could not quite identify. He decided it best to remain silent for now.

"The truth of the matter is this Rowan. Standing before ye is a woman full-grown, a woman of almost five and twenty and she's *never* been kissed." She threw the words at him like rocks, for the sole purpose of hurting him, even though in truth, the last thing she ever wanted to do was hurt him. But threw them she did for she was tired of being alone with her pain and sorrow and longing.

He looked at her as though she had just sprouted an extra set of arms. "But ye've been married, lass! Twice! How can ye be married twice and no' be kissed?" He couldn't imagine being married to her and not kissing her at least a hundred times a day.

"Twice?" Her voice became louder and more venomous. "I've been married *three* times! Three bloody times and no' one kiss! No one stole a kiss from me as a wee lass! No one stole a kiss from me as a maiden fer I was married at five and ten!" She waved her arms in the air. "So there ye have it, Rowan! I have no' fond memories of kisses to tell ye!"

Rowan shook his head slowly, his mouth open but he had no words. He couldn't fathom it, none of it. Her ire, the fury flashing in her eyes, her gritted teeth, told him she was in fact telling him the truth. Still, it was hard to believe. A woman as bonny, nay as *beautiful*, as the one standing before him had never been kissed?

"Arline, I be sorry, but I truly canna understand it. I had no idea," he paused trying to find the words to express his regret as well as his shock. "I did no' ken ye'd been married three times and I just assumed ye'd been kissed a thousand times." It's what *he* would have done were he her husband.

She pursed her lips together to keep from cursing. She drew in a short breath and tried to shake the anger out through her fingertips. "A thousand times?" Was the man daft? Had the stone floor his skull hit just yester morn shaken all his good sense loose?

He took a moment to gather his thoughts before speaking again. "I ken ye do no' like to speak of personal things, but, please, can ye explain it to me?"

Arline looked into his eyes. She saw nothing but concern blended with curiosity and confusion. He hadn't asked her to explain it in order to torment her or to hurt her. His question was born of genuine concern. She took a deep breath to calm her nerves before answering.

"I was five and ten when I married Carlich Lindsay. He was old enough to be my great-grandsire," she cleared away the walnut sized lump in her throat that always came with his memory. "He was a verra good man. He treated me more like a favorite granddaughter than a wife. We became verra dear friends. He kissed me hand at our weddin'." She felt her face growing warm for it was extremely difficult to explain to anyone, least of all to the man standing before her.

"He couldna," she stumbled briefly over the word and had to try twice before it would leave her mouth. "He couldna consummate the marriage because of his age and he didna have any romantic feelin's fer me. But I loved him and he loved me just the same. He was a verra good man."

She began to feel tired. She closed the lid to the trunk and sat on it. Fidgeting with the sleeve of her dress she went on with the rest of the sordid details of her marriages.

"I returned to Ireland after Carlich's death. Me da gave me a year of mournin', and aye, I did mourn his loss." He had been the only man in her life to show her what unconditional love was, even if it were paternal and not romantic or marital. "Me da arranged me second marriage a few months after I came out of mournin'. He was a Frenchman, Lombard de Sotuhans, from Gascony. We were married by proxy, and me da didna even tell me until three days before I left for France. The only thing I knew of him was that he was no' nearly as old as Carlich. We traveled for over a month to reach his home only to learn that he had died the week before. He had drowned. I met him at his funeral."

Marriage by proxy was not unheard of and although Rowan had never had the displeasure of meeting Orthanach Fitzgerald in person, he would not put such a tactic past him. From what little he was able to glean from Arline, her father was neither an amiable sort nor a giving one.

"I was no' quite one and twenty then. I ken me da wanted me to marry right away, but I held me ground. And rumors had begun to spread that I was an unlucky wife. It mattered no' what me circumstances were." Strangely enough, she began to feel better with telling the true story of her life to someone. Telling it aloud made it seem less daunting, less unreal.

"And what of yer marriage to Garrick?" Rowan asked. He remained near the doorway, leaning against the wall with his arms crossed over his chest. The story of how she became married to Garrick and how that marriage subsequently became annulled was, in Rowan's mind, the most important.

She drew a deep breath in through her nostrils and finally looked up at Rowan. "'Twas yet another arranged marriage." The marriage that, for at least a few days, had held the most promise and hope. Garrick had ground her dreams into a fine powder that blew away on winds of despair.

"Lily mentioned yer sisters," Rowan said. "That ye only married Garrick because of them."

"I only told her the story to gain her trust. If she kent that I hadn't married him willingly, then she'd feel safer with me," she explained.

"But aye, 'tis true. Me da tried everythin' to get me to agree to marry Garrick. I had developed a verra sour taste toward marriage, ye ken. I wanted only to leave Ireland, to take me sisters far away, somewhere safe. Me da knew too well how I love me sisters. He threatened to take them away from me, hide them someplace where I could never find them or see them again. I couldna let that happen."

The tears she'd been holding back began to escape. Frustrated, she wiped them away and took deep breaths. "I love me sisters, more than anythin'. I ken what me da is capable of. 'Tisn't like ye and Lily. He has no fond feelin's fer me, he doesna care if I am in a happy marriage or a miserable one. I'm nothin' more than chattel, to be bartered with, used. So I married Garrick to keep me sisters safe."

Though she didn't say it out loud, he could hear her speak the words he'd heard her say on more than one occasion. *Because it was the right thing to do.* She would sacrifice her own happiness so that her two sisters could be safe.

"And how did it come to be annulled, Arline?" He'd been wanting to know the answer to that question for weeks.

She pushed herself to her feet and turned away from him. She spoke to him over her shoulder. "Garrick had no desire to marry me. He was pushed into it by his father. Ye see, Garrick was in love with a woman named Ona but his da *hated* her because she was Scots. I think his da thought if he married me, Garrick would come to love me. But that was no' the case."

She continued. "Garrick had a clause put into the marriage contract. It said if I didn't give birth or conceive a child with him after one year, a month and a day, then he could have the marriage annulled."

There it was, like a kick in the gut. She *was* as Thomas had feared, barren. He felt like crawling away now, to hide his pain and anguish. He started to speak but Arline went on.

"Garrick made *certain* there'd be no bairns."

Rowan's brow knitted, and he came away from the wall. "What do ye mean, he made *certain* there'd be no bairns."

"Our marriage was never..." she paused, embarrassed and humiliated. "'Twas never made official. On our weddin' day, he gave me a verra chaste kiss on me cheek. And other than the beatings he gave me, he never touched me. He never shared me bed."

Good lord, she was a virgin! As pure as the day she was born! He wanted to shout, to dance about the room, to shout with glee! She wasn't barren, she was *pure! Untouched!*

He stood mute all the while his insides were dancing with joy at this revelation. He could ask for her hand. They could build a life together.

He could not hide his glee as a grand smile formed on his lips. He was just about to go to her, take her in his arms and kiss her, when she turned to look at him.

There it was. His dashing smile and perfectly white teeth. She'd been wrong. He found amusement in her pain, in her humiliation. Her voice, along with that tiny last morsel of hope that she'd clung to all these weeks, left her.

She felt hollow, unworthy, stupid and foolish. She grabbed her cloak from the peg and swept by him before he could respond.

"Arline," he called after her. "Wait!"

She stopped in the doorway and whirled around to face him. She'd be damned if she'd let him torment her further. "Go to hell, Rowan Graham."

Had he been closer, she would have slapped the smile from his face. Instead, she turned and ran from the room.

TWENTY-THREE

Arline pulled on her cloak as she raced down the stairs. The children were playing at the bottom, waiting patiently for her. Robert, Jenny, Lily, and seven other little ones, all happy and unaware of her distress.

They squealed with delight as she swept past them in a hurry, thinking mayhap it was a game. Arline flung open the door, her gaggle of children following happily on her heels. She paid them no mind as she raced down the stairs and into the courtyard.

The cold air pricked at her wet cheeks and made her lungs ache when she breathed in. Her feet sank into the frozen snow, hitting her somewhere mid calf, but she did not care.

Her only thought was to get away. Away from this keep and away from Rowan Graham and his blasted perfect smile. She could barely hear the children as they called out, begging for her to slow down. Her heart beat wildly against her chest as the blood ran cold through her veins.

The closer she drew to the inner wall of the keep, the deeper the snow became. Soon, she was trudging through icy cold snow up to her knees. Her anger and humiliation pushed her forward.

"Open the gate!" she called up to the men standing guard on the wall. "Open the bloody gate!"

The two men looked befuddled by her order as they peered down over the ledge at her. A quick glance in their direction told her they would not heed her request. *Damned bloody men!*

She could now hear Rowan's voice shouting over the din of the children. Arline glanced over her shoulder to see that he was chasing after her, his movements slowed by the clamoring children and the snow.

Certain there had to be a door somewhere along the wall, she veered left, determined to find a way out of this place. The further east she went, the deeper the snow. The wind had carried it in, over the tall walls where it built up inch by inch until it almost reached the top of the wall. If she couldn't find a door, she'd climb the mountain of snow and scale the wall. Reason and good sense had fled the moment she saw Rowan smiling at her in her dressing room. She didn't care if she froze to death. She was determined to get as far away from here as she could. Her heart could simply stand no more.

As she struggled through and up the large bank of snow, she knew she was being stupid by running away. Mayhap she truly didn't want to run far away, mayhap just away from Rowan for a time, to gather her wits and pride.

The more she struggled the more she realized the recklessness of her folly. Her hands began to ache, along with her feet and legs. The snow clung to the hems of her skirts and to her cloak. Mayhap, this wasn't the best of ideas.

She stopped at the peak of the snowbank, her head just an inch or two from the top of the wall. Freedom lay on the other side. But freedom from what?

She turned around and saw the group of children. They had stopped following and now stood huddled together watching her. One by one they began to question if this was a grand game or if Lady Arline had lost her mind.

Arline caught sight of Lily standing in the middle of the group. Her heart paused a beat or two when she saw the look of fear on the precious child's face. She could not leave Lily, not like this, in such a mad and immature fashion. What would the child learn from this? That when things got to be too much to bear, you went running out, improperly dressed, crying like a fool and risking your life?

Then she saw Rowan, trudging through the snow and he looked furious. All sense of reason left her mind then. Quickly, she turned around and reached up to the top of the wall, her fingers slipping once, then twice.

"Arline!" Rowan called out, his voice echoing in the still morning air, bouncing off the walls. "Stop!"

She decided it would serve him right for laughing if she made it to the top of the wall then slipped and broke her neck. He could blame no one but himself if she suffered some horrible injury. Would he laugh then? Or would he live the rest of his life, riddled with guilt?

She let loose with a deep growl, tried once again to grab the top of the wall. Success! It nearly made her wet herself!

She pulled up, with all her might, flung her tired, heavy legs over the cold stone wall, her bare thighs screaming in protest at the frigid air that whirled under her skirts and then again when her bare skin touched the icy cold stones.

Moments later, she was on top of the wall, laying flat, and looking down. Blessed be the saints! More snow was packed into a large, deep drift on the opposite side. She had fallen farther than this down the embankment all those many weeks ago.

Taking a deep breath she sat upright and jumped.

Fell was a more apt description. And as she floated through the air, she heard Rowan and all of his men calling out after her, begging her to stop.

She landed on her feet, fell to her knees, then ended up planting her face in the snow. Muttering curses under her breath, damning Rowan Graham to an eternity in hell, she pushed herself up, slowly. Never, in all her days had she been so cold!

She wiped as much of the snow as she could from her face and ran. She ran as fast as her numbingly cold legs and feet would carry her. Ignoring the men who called out for her as well as the pounding in her head, she half fell and half ran, like a crazed woman, to the outer curtain wall.

The edges of the wall tapered the closer it got to the loch. The snow had drifted over the top of it, nearest the shortest ends. It was, she knew, a ludicrous decision she had made, but she was too overcome with anger to give a damn.

She fell again not far from the outer wall. The men continued to shout, but her heart was pounding too loudly to hear them clearly. She was tiring, far too quickly. Her arms and legs felt as though they were chained to large boulders. And the more she struggled against the snow the heavier they became.

There seemed to be a direct correlation between her weighted limbs and the heaviness of her heart. She had nowhere to run to, no place to seek refuge, nowhere to hide. With those glaring facts staring her in the face, she did the only thing she could think of. She plopped down on her rump, hung her head in shame and cried.

If she froze to death, she'd have no one to blame but herself. 'Twasn't Rowan's fault she was sitting in the cold snow. 'Twasn't Rowan's fault she was nearly five and twenty and never kissed.

Many times over the years, she had been complimented on her good sense. Her good sense seemed to fly out the window each time she was near Rowan Graham. He could not help it if he was a perfect specimen of God's good work. He could not help the fact that he had been blessed with a magnificent form, perfect teeth, or a gorgeous smile that always made her stomach flutter whenever he cast one her way.

Large tears left icy trails down her red cheeks. Her shoulders shook as she sobbed without restraint. She was freezing cold, and filled with anguish and there was nothing to blame but her own ridiculous pride.

The men behind her continued to shout, indecipherable words that were lost in the winter air. She could hear Rowan's deep voice shouting something, but her pride kept her from looking back just yet. He could wait a few moments more.

Her fingers and toes began to sting from all the snow. Recognizing it would serve no purpose to remain seated in the snow for she could cry just as easily within the warm confines of the castle, she took a deep breath and made the decision to quit acting like an inglorious fool and head back to the keep. Rowan would undoubtedly be furious with her and she couldn't rightly blame him. Governesses were probably hard to come by.

She started to roll sideways when she heard something as it flew past her ear. "I'm no' dead yet ye blasted buzzards," she muttered. They were probably circling her thinking she'd soon be dead. The thought of buzzards feasting away on her dead corpse gave her a burst of energy. She rolled to her hands and knees and pushed herself up.

"That's odd," she said out loud as she looked at the curtain wall. It seemed Rowan had called every one of his men to the wall. They were waving their arms and shouting. "What in the world?" she whispered.

It took only another short moment for it to become clear that something was wrong. Whatever it was, instinct told her not to tarry, to run as fast as she could back to the keep.

As she raced back to the keep, she noticed archers taking positions along the wall. Were they going to shoot her? Seriously doubting that Rowan would order her shot for deserting her position as a governess, she tried to pick up speed. They weren't aiming at her, but something behind her.

Her first thought was mayhap they had seen a pack of wolves encircling her to make a meal out of her. Not wanting to be any animal's dinner, she ignored the stinging sensation in her feet and legs and did her best to pick up speed. Mayhap the wolves were going to take the same route in as she had planned on taking out. Little did it matter! She had to get back inside the walls of the keep.

She bunched her heavy wet skirts and cloak in her fists, not caring if the men on the wall could see her bare legs. She would have torn off every stitch of clothing she wore if it meant she could run faster and get away from the wolves!

The image of wolves and buzzards fighting over her dead body propelled her forward. Thinking she'd climb the small mountain of snow and re-enter the keep the same way she had left it, she headed in that direction.

Someone on top of the wall called out for her to head to the gate. *Thank God!* She thought as she ran through the deep snow. She'd not have to try to scale the wall with a pack of wolves on her heels.

She veered left and could hear Rowan's men shouting words of encouragement and barking out orders. Chastising her ignorance and ill-conceived notion of running away, she did her best to keep moving toward the gate. She had not realized how far away from the keep she had been able to get until she had to race back to it.

The gate soon appeared in her line of vision and relief began to build in her belly. Whatever punishment Rowan planned to inflict, she'd gladly accept it if she could make it through the large wooden gate without wolves tearing at her skin.

Just as the gate began to swing open, she felt another bird whoosh past her ear. It caught her off guard, which in turn caused her to lose her balance and stumble again. Taking no time to try and figure out why birds were flying around her, she picked herself up and moved forward.

The gate had not opened completely, just enough for her to slip through, *if* she made it that far unscathed. It wasn't until the third *bird* flew past her ear that she finally realized it was in fact not a bird, but an arrow.

Her heart leapt into her throat when she felt the arrow pierce her cloak from behind, tearing through the thick wool, before landing a foot in front of her. The sudden awareness that it was not a pack of wolves chasing her but someone hell-bent on piercing her skin with an arrow made her blood run cold. The sound of arrows as they flew overhead was both terrifying and a relief. Hopefully Rowan's archers were much better with their aim than the fool behind her.

She was almost to the open gate, mayhap only twenty or thirty feet left before she could squeeze through to safety. She peered through the opening and saw Rowan coming toward her. He was mounted on a large grey horse, his broadsword drawn, a look of utter fury and bloodlust painted on his face.

She knew, beyond a shadow of a doubt, that his fury was not directed toward her, but at whomever it was that was shooting arrows at her.

Rowan was racing across the snow-covered courtyard to save her! Why she had that particular thought at that particular moment proved the depths of her insanity. *I am an eejit!* She thought as she gave her shoulders a mental shake. She had to make it through the gate.

Rowan headed toward her, the grey struggling through the heavy snow. He let out a blood-curdling yell as he kicked at the grey's sides, urging the horse forward.

She was almost to the gate when the last arrow from the bastard behind her found its mark. Tearing through her cloak, then through skin, it pierced her upper left shoulder. Stunned, she gasped, unable to cry out. The pain was so immense, so unbearable that she could not utter a word or a sound.

The world began to spin as her vision blurred and dimmed. She fell to her knees and looked down. The arrow had pierced clean through. She could see its tip quite clearly, dripping with blood and bits of flesh.

The last thing she remembered before the world went dark was thinking what a bloody fool she was.

TWENTY-FOUR

There were only three times in Rowan Graham's life that he could recall feeling this afraid and this furious at once. The first was when Kate had succumbed to the Black Death and then again when he had learned Lily had been taken.

The third occurrence happened when he saw the attacker's arrow had pierced Arline's back.

Had he not been chasing the angry redhead through the deep snow, he would have heard his men shout the warning cry the first time. As it was, he had not heard it until Arline began to climb over the first wall. Had he continued to chase after her, to climb over the wall, chances were great that the arrows that came flying in from the south would have felled him too.

There was no time to contemplate a plan of action. Rowan called out for someone to bring him a horse -- and to forget saddling it -- and for the children to get back inside the keep.

His men on the wall had seen the riders as they approached. Later, Rowan had learned that his men at first had thought that it was either Daniel or Frederick returning from the mission they had left on yester morn. Once they saw that the riders did not carry Clan

Graham colors draped from their saddles, they instinctively called out that riders were approaching. Still, they thought it possible the five mounted men might be travelers only seeking shelter from the harsh winter weather.

Rowan had missed that first call for he'd been trudging through the blasted snow, pursuing a tetched redheaded woman who had gradually taken possession of his heart. The possession of his heart turned into all out control of his good and common sense.

When the men on the wall saw one of the men retrieve a bow from his back, they gave the warning cry of attack. That call brought Rowan's pursuit of the object of his ire to a complete halt and sent him flying into defensive action.

As his men tried to gain Arline's attention by waving their arms and shouting their warnings of possible impending attack, Rowan scrambled back down the large mound of snow, calling out his orders as he made his way toward the stables.

The snow had made things quite difficult and had slowed him down considerably. If he were slowed by the damned white stuff, then the attackers would be having trouble as well. God willing he would be able to get to Arline before the bastards outside could.

Men poured out of the keep to answer the battle cry. Many had not even bothered to don cloaks or gloves. Women were ushering the terrified children indoors.

Red John came running as fast as he could, holding the reins to a grey gelding. Rowan did not wait for the horse to stop or even settle down from the excitement of having been removed from his warm stall. Grabbing a handful of its mane, Rowan pulled himself up and flung a leg over the grey's back. He grabbed the reins from Red John and headed toward the gate. Someone tossed him a broadsword as he kicked the horse and pushed forward.

His feeling of relief when the gate opened and he saw how close Arline was to safety was short lived. He was just beginning to pass through the gate when one of the dozen or so arrows the attackers had sent flying finally hit its mark.

The arrow had pierced somewhere in her back. Time came to an abrupt halt, as did the beating of his heart when he saw the tip of the arrow come through the front of her cloak.

Time started up again, wretchedly surreal and horrifying. Rowan could remember little else after that point. He could not recall moving forward and only knew that he had when he reached her, slid down from his horse and crawled to her.

Arline lay on her side, motionless, but still breathing, as the snow darkened to a hideous shade of blood red. Chaos had erupted all around him as men came flooding out of the gate and arrows from his archers flew overhead. Battle cries were muffled by the pounding of his heart.

Thomas had come to his aid and was shouting at Rowan over the din of the attack. Long moments passed before Rowan could make any sense out of what Thomas was saying.

"I'll take her back to the keep, Rowan!" Thomas shouted. "Ye go get the bloody bastards!"

He did not possess the ability to think at the moment, he could only feel. Anguish, loss, fury, pain. He wanted to direct it all at Thomas, for had the man not repeatedly insisted that Rowan could not ask for Arline's hand, she'd not have an arrow jutting through her shoulder. The snow would not have turned red with her blood this day. Instead, it would be stained with the blood of the attackers.

Rowan blinked away the anger and frustration. He'd deal with Thomas later. Now he had to get Arline to the keep. He could not allow the man in whose fault this all lay touch the woman he loved.

"Get yer hands off her!" Rowan seethed through gritted teeth as he pushed Thomas away. "Stay the bloody hell away from her!"

Thomas was by no means stupid or feeble minded. He understood all too clearly that Rowan blamed him for Arline's injuries. He also understood how Rowan would come to that conclusion for he had thought the very same. This however, was not the time to lay or take blame. It was time to act.

"Damn it, Rowan!" Thomas shouted back. "Go after them! Ye'll never fergive yerself if ye don' go after the men who did this!"

Rowan regretted the fact that Thomas knew him all too well. As they had argued, several of his men passed by on horses in fast pursuit of the attackers. Rowan bent and tenderly kissed Arline's cheek and whispered a promise in her ear.

I shall avenge ye, lass, I swear it. Please, do no' leave me.

A moment later, he was scrambling onto the back of the grey gelding and heading off to kill every last one of the bastards who had done this.

O ra and Thomas had successfully removed the arrow from Arline's shoulder before Rowan returned to the keep. Her clothes had been cut away and she lay semi-conscious on a trestle table in the gathering room, covered up to her breasts with a linen sheet. She mumbled incoherently as Ora went about cleaning the blood from the still bleeding wound.

He had arrived just in time to help with cauterizing her wounds.

"I think the snow helped slow the bleedin'," Ora told Rowan as she tended to Arline. "But it be too soon to ken how she'll fare."

Ora had been the clan's healer for more than ten years. She had tended to every conceivable illness and battle wound. Rowan trusted her implicitly. He could not speak just yet, his worry over Arline paralyzing his voice. Helpless to do anything but offer her comfort, Rowan stepped to the table and held Arline's hand.

Ora had given Arline a potion to drink to help knock her out so that she would not be awake during the process. Unfortunately it hadn't taken full effect when Thomas placed the red-hot iron to her wound. Her scream would forever remain branded in Rowan's memory as one of the most horrific wails he had ever heard. He prayed she would soon wake and speak to him. He did not want the sound of her scream and subsequent curses and cries to be his last memory of her.

Thankfully, she had lost consciousness and remained that way during the rest of the procedure. Once the wound was cauterized and Ora agreed that Arline could be moved, Rowan carried the sleeping lass to his room. With great care and devotion, he placed her in his bed, covered her with furs and stayed by her side.

It would be some time before anyone could answer the question of who in his right mind would attack a keep in the middle of winter with only five men. The men who had attacked were of no use to anyone. Their frozen corpses waited burial in the dungeon below the keep.

It had taken little time for Rowan and his men to catch up to them and even less time to slay all five. His only regret was not being able to glean any information from them. They had foolishly chosen to attempt to defend themselves against fifty of Rowan's men.

Two long, distressing days passed by slowly. Rowan would not leave Arline's side but for a few moments at a time and only to take care of the most pressing business -- finding out who was behind the attack. Besides Arline, the most urgent matter at hand was the missing Frederick and the seven men who were with him. They had not been seen nor heard from since the day Rowan had sent them to check on the men at the borders.

Dawn arrived peacefully on the morning of the third day. Arline was kept heavily sedated to keep her from harming her injury or from feeling any amount of pain. Arline rarely moved and at times it was difficult to tell if she still breathed.

Lily was beside herself with grief. The nightmares had intensified, making it difficult for her to sleep for more than an hour or two at a time. No one was able to comfort the child. Worried that Lily might become exhausted and overwrought with worry, Rowan had a pallet brought to his room and placed between the fire and his bed. He and Lily slept side by side, under several thick furs. She slept fitfully throughout the night at first, but thankfully had finally been able to sleep for longer stretches.

Rowan had not shaved and had barely eaten over the course of his bedside vigil. On the morn of the fourth day, he dozed in a chair he had pulled next to the bed. He held Arline's hand, though he doubted she was aware he was even in the room, let alone holding her hand.

He was roused awake by the sound of many heavy boots and excited utterances taking place outside his room. Moments later, Frederick rushed in with Daniel, Thomas, and several other men fast on his heels.

Frederick halted just inside the doorway, his eyes immediately going to the sleeping form on the bed.

"Christ," he muttered as he rushed to stand beside Arline. Daniel and the others followed suit. The room seemed to grow much smaller when it was filled with so many big Highlanders.

Rowan rose to his feet, relieved to see his missing men. They looked like hell, with wind-burned faces and disheveled clothes. "Thank God!" Rowan said as he came around the side of the bed to shake Frederick's hand. "What the hell happened?"

Frederick drew Rowan in and slapped his back. "I could ask ye the same question," he said as he withdrew and turned back to look at Lady Arline.

Rowan sighed heavily and ran a hand across his several days' growth of beard. "Ye look like hell, Frederick." He had noticed what looked like dried blood on Frederick's green tunic.

"Och!" Frederick smiled as he looked down at his chest. "I look better than the bastard I gutted. And ye do no' look too well yerself, Rowan."

Rowan ignored the comment. He took Frederick by the arm and led him away from the bed. The group of men followed and huddled together. Speaking in hushed tones so as not to disturb Lady Arline, Frederick began his tale.

"When we left we went first to our borders on the east. All was well there. The men were able to seek shelter in the hut. They received a good amount of snow and were glad to see us. We spent the night there and headed back the next morn. I left their replacements and brought Aaron, Sam, and Brown Thomas back with us. All was well until we reached the southern borders." He paused for a moment, shook his head and ran a hand through his hair. Rowan bade him to continue.

"Rowan, it was a massacre. A damned bloody massacre!" he said angrily. He caught himself and lowered his voice. "Derrick, young Phillip, and Red Daniel were dead. The bastards had left their heads on spikes. Flung their innards in the trees. God only kens where the rest of them be."

Rowan swallowed back the bile and anger that rose in his throat. They had been good men, young men. Red Daniel was married and had two wee bairns. Phillip was barely old enough to shave and Derrick was not much older. Rowan hung his head, dreading the thought that he would have to inform the families of these good men that they were not coming home.

"We buried what we could, Rowan," Frederick offered solemnly.

Rowan placed a hand on Frederick's shoulder. "Thank ye, Frederick. I'll speak to their families soon."

Frederick cleared his throat before going on. "Derrick's auldest brother, Patrick, was with me, Rowan. He's agreed no' to tell his mum and da the whole truth. We," his voice cracked as tears welled in his eyes. "We didna think they needed to ken the entirety of it."

Rowan agreed that it was probably best. 'Twas bad enough to know they were gone. To know their bodies had been so violated, slaughtered, would serve no good purpose.

"We left there as soon as we could, Rowan. About two days ago, we came across a group of six men, hiding out in the caves near Loch Breen." Frederick cast a glance at Domnal who was standing to his right. Domnal had been there and was visibly shaken. It had been his first experience in hand-to-hand combat.

"They put up one hell of a fight, Rowan."

Rowan raised an eyebrow. "How good a fight?"

"Good enough that we had to believe they were no' Garrick's men. They fought far too well."

For days, Rowan had been convinced that Garrick Blackthorn was behind the attack, for several reasons. The main reason being that Garrick was the only man he knew who was foolish enough to attack in this weather and to send just five men. "I was certain it was Blackthorn men who had attacked. They wore no colors to prove it either way. We didna find anything in their belongings to identify them or who they may have fought for."

"They were no' Blackthorn's men," Domnal said quietly.

"Domnal is right," Frederick added. "They were no' Blackthorn men."

Rowan waited patiently for someone to tell him who the hell it was that had killed his men and had tried to attack the keep. "Well?" he demanded, growing impatient.

"They were hired mercenaries. We were able to get information from one of the bastards before he died." Frederick smiled wanly. "There are many more men coming, Rowan."

Confusion grew on Rowan's face. "What the hell do ye mean?"

"Someone hired these men. Supposedly, the six we came across were to remain at the border to wait fer reinforcements. They were instructed to kill any Graham man, woman or child they came across. They were to show no mercy. We learned that five men were sent ahead, to watch the keep. I can only assume that they attacked Lady Arline because she was out in the open."

"That doesna make a damned bit of sense!" Rowan growled. "Did they no' think we'd retaliate? Did they no' think we'd fight back?"

"Nay, they did no'," Frederick answered. "Fer they were told there were but a handful of auld men and women at the keep. They were told our men would no' be here, ye'd all be drawn away and fightin' to the west."

The more Rowan learned, the less he knew. He shook his head in dismay. "None of this makes a damned bit o' sense," Rowan muttered. "How could anyone ken we'd no' be here?"

"Because we were to have been attacked a sennight ago," Frederick answered.

The storm had hit a sennight ago. Clarity dawned and Rowan's eyes grew wide. "The storm."

"Aye," Frederick said. "The storm."

"It stopped them from attackin'."

"Aye, it did."

They stood facing one another as the same thought that had occurred to Frederick suddenly occurred to Rowan. "If they were delayed by four days, that means,"

Frederick finished his line of thinking. "We could be attacked at any moment."

"Bloody hell!" Rowan shouted.

"Aye," Frederick said as he followed Rowan out of the room. "Bloody hell is right!"

Rowan found Selina in the hallway. "Find Lily now!" he barked. "Take her to my room. Send the healer there! Do no' leave either me daughter's nor Arline's side."

Selina did not take the time to question his order. She spun around to go find Lily.

Rowan shouted out orders as he thundered down the stairs. People were sent in different directions with orders to prepare for an imminent attack. In moments, the keep was a flurry of activity.

Frederick had tried unsuccessfully to gain Rowan's attention as they bounded toward Rowan's library. "Rowan!" Frederick shouted to his chief's back. "There be more!"

Rowan flung open the door to his library. "I want every able-bodied man assembled in the gathering room within a quarter of an hour!" Rowan shot the order to one of his men.

Frederick shook his head and grabbed Rowan by the arm. "Rowan, I need ye to listen!"

"What is it?" Rowan ground out.

"There should be three hundred men, to the west of us. They're waiting fer their orders to attack. They'll no' move an inch until they receive them." Frederick waited impatiently for that information to sink in.

Rowan mulled this bit of news over in his mind. They could not withstand an attack of this magnitude. Whether their unknown enemy was well trained or not did not even factor into the equation. The enemy had sheer numbers on their side. Hope began to wane and he grew increasingly worried.

"Rowan, do no' give up hope just yet," Frederick said hopefully. "All is no' lost, ye ken?"

"No I do *no'* ken! We canna withstand an invasion of three hundred men."

A smile grew on Frederick's face. "Nay, we canna withstand an invasion. But, we can make certain the invasion never takes place."

For a brief moment, Rowan thought mayhap Frederick had lost his mind. Curiosity begged him to ask the question. "What do ye have in mind?"

Frederick threw his head back and laughed heartily, sealing Rowan's previous opinion as it pertained to the man's soundness of mind.

"Och, Rowan," Frederick said. "Pour me a wee dram and I'll tell ye exactly what I be thinkin'."

L ess than an hour later, Rowan, Frederick and the others departed from their meeting in the library. Rowan was not only convinced that Frederick was indeed in complete control of his faculties, but that the man was brilliant.

Two hours later, Frederick, Daniel and nine of Rowan's best fighting men had left the keep and headed west. If Frederick's plan worked -- and there was a very good chance that it would -- then the impending attack on *Áit na Síochána* would never take place. Only time would tell.

On the off chance that Frederick and Daniel failed, Rowan had dispatched messengers to his closest ally, Caelen McDunnah, asking for his help in defending *Áit na Síochána*.

After his men left, Rowan donned a cloak and left the keep, heading directly to the chapel. It was a place he hadn't stepped foot in since Kate's death. He had stopped praying four years ago. This afternoon seemed as good a time as any to start again.

The chapel, a small stone building, stood on the east side of the keep. It was a simple, utilitarian building that could hold some two hundred people.

They had lost so many people four years ago, including their priest. Rowan, having given up on God, had made no attempts to find a replacement. The Black Death had been all the proof that Rowan needed to believe that God had turned His back on Rowan and his clan.

His stable master, Red John, acted as a priest of sorts, though not a celibate nor sober one. Nay, Red John was married and had eight children -- seven sons and a daughter. Still, he was the most qualified in that he had memorized the Bible, could recite any passage from memory, and most people considered him a kind, generous, and godly man. So he stepped in and led services three times a week.

Rowan paused outside the door of the chapel for several long moments. Before he entered, he asked for forgiveness for waiting so long to return and for thinking God had abandoned him.

Stepping inside the quiet chapel hadn't been as difficult as he had imagined. The late afternoon sun shone through the windows, casting a soft, honeyed glow on the room. Little bits of dust floated in the air, dancing in the sunlight like tiny faeries.

He closed the door behind him and reverently walked to the altar. With no warm fires burning, his breath misted and hung in the air. Crossing himself, he knelt before God for the first time in far too many years.

Rowan prayed for many things over the next hour. He prayed repeatedly for having asininely believed that God had abandoned him when he knew it had been the other way around. Rowan had abandoned God.

He prayed for Arline, that she would recover and would agree to become his wife. He prayed for his daughter, that she would grow to be a fine young woman.

He prayed for his people, for his men whom he had sent in two opposite directions. He prayed for Lady Arline's sisters. He even prayed for Mrs. McGregor.

He prayed for strength, patience, and the ability to see all the beauty that God had to offer and vowed never again to take things for granted. Beauty could be found everywhere, if one looked at things with one's heart instead of one's eyes.

Most of all, he prayed for the ability to control his temper, to be a kind and patient man to all. Just as he had begun his prayers with thoughts of Arline, he ended them there as well.

Please, God, let her live so that I might love her all the rest of me days.

TWENTY-FIVE

Rowan returned to his room and Lady Arline's bedside with a wee bit more hope than when he had left it. Ora reported that Arline fared well and thankfully had not gained a fever. A fever meant infection and most likely death.

He hugged Lily, who had been sitting on the bed next to Arline. She looked so forlorn and full of woe that Rowan had to fight back tears. "Da," Lily said as she sat on his lap. "Is Lady Arline goin' to die?"

The question nearly sent him to his knees. He hugged her tighter, rubbed her back and tried to answer her question. "I do no' think so, Lily. I went to the chapel and prayed for her."

"Do ye think God heard ye?" Lily asked as she rested her head against his chest.

"Aye, he heard me." But whether God would choose to grant his prayers remained to be seen. He would not pile his worries on top of hers.

Selina offered to take Lily down to the evening meal for which Rowan was grateful. Ora left with them after checking Arline's wound.

Finally, he was alone with Arline. He brought his chair closer to her bed and took her hand in his. The dark circles under her eyes were such a stark contrast to her pale skin. What he would not give to have her wake so that he could first apologize for whatever he had done that had caused her to flee the castle. He could only pray that whatever wrong thing he had done, she could find it in her heart to forgive him.

He sat in quiet contemplation for some time, guardedly watching each shallow breath that she took. Ora had said she would soon begin to wean her from the potion that made her sleep so deeply. If kept on it too long, she might never recover, but if she woke too soon, she could be in a tremendous amount of pain. It was a dangerously precarious endeavor, trying to balance the two options.

Day finally gave way to night and still, she had not stirred. Rowan lit a candle and placed it on the table next to the bed and returned to his quiet vigil.

"Try talkin' to her, Rowan."

Rowan looked up to see Thomas standing in the doorway. He looked reticent, uncertain if his presence would be welcomed.

"Come in, Thomas," Rowan said quietly. There had been a litany of things Rowan had prayed for earlier. One of those prayers had been that he would quit being an ass and stop blaming Thomas for what had happened to Arline. It was no more Thomas' fault than it was Arline's.

Thomas entered the room and stood across the bed from Rowan. Genuine sorrow could be seen in his eyes and countenance. "I be truly sorry, Rowan," he whispered.

Rowan gave him a wave of his hand. "Nay. None of this is yer fault and I'm sorry fer blamin' ye. As ye've witnessed in me before, auld friend, me anger sometimes makes me do and say foolish things."

Thomas smiled his agreement. "'Tis true," he chuckled. "It becomes more apparent when yer in love."

Rowan could not deny that. "Aye, love makes a man sometimes act like a fool."

"It can also bring out the best in a man," Thomas said. "I never felt as perfect or as imperfect as when I was in love. 'Twas as if all was right with the world and I could handle anythin'." Thomas had lost his sweet wife more than ten years ago. She had fallen down an embankment and crushed her head against a boulder. "Anythin' but fer harm to come to me sweet Elisa."

Rowan understood that feeling all too well. Elisa's life had been cut far too short, as was the babe's that she carried. Rowan doubted that Thomas would ever get over the loss.

"I am sorry, Thomas, fer bein' an ass to ye. I hope ye can find it in yer heart to forgive me."

Thomas shook his head. "I'll forgive ye if ye'll forgive me."

So a silent agreement was made between the two friends. Rowan promised himself that he'd practice being more patient as well as not let his anger run away with his good sense.

"Ye should talk to her, Rowan," Thomas told him again. "Let her ken that yer here."

"I dunna ken if that is a good idea, Thomas. I'm the reason she left the keep to begin with."

Thomas cast him a puzzled look.

"I dunna ken what I did, but I did somethin' that angered her to the point that she fled the keep and climbed the wall to get away from me."

Thomas looked at Arline then back to Rowan. "Ye must have done or said *somethin'.*"

Rowan had been wracking his brain for days trying to figure out what he might have said or done. He came up empty handed at every turn.

He recounted the events, as he remembered them, of what Arline had told him right before she fled.

"Christ," Thomas muttered when Rowan finished. "The lass has had a rough time of it."

Rowan nodded in agreement. "Aye, she has."

"Did ye tell her ye were happy to learn she's no' barren? Did ye ask her to marry ye?" Thomas urged Rowan to continue with what happened after he had learned the truth behind Arline's marriages.

"I didna get a chance! I was so happy, standin' there like an eejit, so surprised I was. Ye couldna have wiped the smile from me face with an anvil."

Thomas slapped his forehead with his palm and shook his head at his friend. "Ye were smilin'?"

"Aye," Rowan answered, unclear why that made any difference. He'd been so happy, truly elated to know he could ask her to marry him without worrying over losing his chiefdom or Lily's birthright.

Thomas let out an exasperated sigh. "Ye fool! The lass just shared the secrets of her life, her marriages, and ye *smiled* at her?"

Rowan couldn't understand the significance for several long moments. When he finally gained clarity, he could feel nothing but relief. He hadn't done anything unforgivable. And once he explained to Arline what he had been thinking, he knew she would forgive him.

"I'm a complete eejit!" he sighed. "An ass and an eejit!"

"Don't forget *loud.*"

Arline's weak and scratchy voice made the heads of both men spin in her direction.

She hadn't heard the entire conversation, only the part where Rowan admitted to being the eejit she knew him to sometimes be. Her mouth was horribly dry, her tongue felt thick, as though it had grown too large for her mouth. She ran her tongue over her teeth and tried to swallow. It felt like she was swallowing a bucketful of sand.

Her brain pounded furiously against her skull and her shoulder felt like it was on fire. She had no idea where she was or what had caused her to feel like she'd been run over by a team of horses and a wagon.

"Water," she scratched out. For the life of her, she could not open her eyes, her lids felt as heavy as lead.

Rowan jumped to his feet, relieved to hear her voice, even if it was weak and scratchy. He poured water from the pitcher into a small bowl. He tried to conceal his utter joy and excitement, lest she open her eyes and see a smile on his face. He did not want to start their argument anew.

His hands trembled as he held the bowl to her lips. She took small sips at first, just enough to wet her mouth and throat. It hurt to swallow or move or think, let alone speak. She decided it best not to do anything but breathe.

She had no memory of how she came to feel so ill or in so much pain. The last thing she remembered was standing in her dressing room and being consumed with anger over something Rowan had either said or done. But what offense he had committed, she had no clear recollection.

After quenching her thirst she relaxed, feeling only slightly better. Her arms and legs felt insufferably heavy and she knew it would be impossible to move them, if she had the desire to make the attempt.

Though she had the sense of being asleep for an exceedingly long time, she did not possess the strength to even make the attempt to open her eyes to wake. The last thing she remembered before drifting off to sleep again was the warm sensation of Rowan's hand wrapped around hers.

H ours passed before she stirred again. She drifted in and out of sleep throughout the evening and well past dawn. Ora continued to decrease the doses and by morn, Arline was ready to bite steel, the pain in her shoulder was so intense.

Ora explained that the pain was good for her; it let her know that she was still alive. Arline was not as thrilled to remain among the living as she could have been. Her shoulder felt like there was a large horse standing on it, grinding his hoof into her wound. Her brain continued its assault against her skull. And the one time she did try to open her eyes, the light from the one candle burning near her bed felt like the light of a thousand. It burned her eyes and caused her head to throb even more.

How she came to be lying abed in so much nauseating pain, she did not know. That fact irritated her to no end. She could not remember what had happened to her. The last memory she had before waking in such an ungodly amount of pain was standing in her dressing room. She vaguely remembered being angry at Rowan, but for what reason, she could not recall.

299

In her rare moments of lucidity, she could feel Rowan's presence. Always beside her, holding her hand, and offering words of encouragement. He refused to tell her what had happened, what was wrong with her. His responses to her questions were always the same: *Wheesht, lass. Ye need yer rest.*

She didn't want to wheesht or rest. She wanted her shoulder to quit burning and her head to quit pounding. And she wanted answers. Resistance was pointless as her body continued to betray her mind. She kept falling asleep

By the following afternoon, she felt less groggy and the pain in her shoulder began to diminish, though it still hurt like the devil. She was able to open her eyes without feeling like they were filled with burning embers.

Rowan sat in a chair next to her bed. She smiled at the sight of the big Highlander with his head lolling forward as he slept. From the looks of him, he hadn't taken the time to shave in many days. His clothes were a rumpled mess as if he had slept in them more than once. Even in his current condition of disarray, he was a beautiful man.

She lay still, quietly watching him and wished she could remember what had happened and why she had been so angry with him and how she came to be in this room. Had something happened in her room? Had she been attacked there?

And why did Rowan refuse to tell her what happened? It made little sense. Was he only trying to protect her? That in and of itself was a very kind thing for him to do. However, she was not a babe, not a woman prone to histrionics. Certainly whatever had happened to cause her to be here could not be *that* terribly awful that he feared she would fall apart. She wished she could remember.

After a time, Rowan shifted in his seat and raised his head up. He rubbed the sleep from his eyes with his palms. It took a moment for him to realize that yes, Arline was awake and yes, she was smiling at him.

"How do ye feel, lass?" he asked. His voice was filled with worry and concern. He leaned toward her and took her hand in his.

"Better," she answered. She wondered if he realized he was holding her hand. She also wondered how on earth, considering her current condition of ill health, could she possibly get such a fluttering in her stomach and why her pulse raced at the touch of his hand?

"Good," he said and his shoulders relaxed ever so slightly.

Arline tilted her head slightly. "What happened? I canna remember anythin' but bein' mad at ye. I canna even recall *why* I was so mad."

"Ye had every right to be mad at me, lass."

She rolled her eyes. His answer explained nothing. "Why will ye no' tell me what happened?" She was growing frustrated with him.

Rowan let out a long, slow breath. "I do no' want ye gettin' upset again, lass. We can talk about everythin' once yer better."

"I am better," she said through gritted teeth.

Rowan chuckled and smiled warmly. "Ye are? Then let's say ye get out of bed and take a walk with me."

"Why must men be so frustrating?" she muttered.

"We canna help it, lass." He gave her hand a gentle squeeze. "We oft turn to fools when we're around beautiful women."

Certainly he was not referring to her. The arch of her eyebrow told him as much.

"Och!" he chuckled again, softly, and gave her hand another squeeze. "Aye, 'tis *ye* that I'm referring to."

Certain that she must be dreaming, she pinched the side of her thigh. It hurt, but she decided it was possible that she was hallucinating. Who knew what was in that horrible potion Ora had given her earlier. And even if she *were* completely lucid, she held no proof that his compliment was nothing more than his kind attempt to make her feel better. Either way, his comment proved nothing and still did not answer her question.

If Rowan wasn't going to tell her the truth behind her injury then Ora certainly would. Arline knew she had to get Rowan out of the room long enough for her to talk to Ora. Even in her current condition, she was not above a bit of duplicity in order to gain the information she sought.

"Ye look as though ye've not slept well, Rowan."

"I haven't." In truth, he had not left her side for more than a few moments in the past days.

"I do no' understand why ye haven't. Ye should go climb into yer bed and rest. Mayhap take a nice hot bath and a blade to yer beard."

"I canna do that," he smiled at her.

He was being silly and she told him exactly that. "I do no' understand why yer here, why ye've no' slept or shaved, and why ye canna bathe or sleep, Rowan." A huge part of her wished his refusal to leave her side was because he had some feelings for her other than those derived from her position as his daughter's governess. 'Twas wishful thinking, she knew that, but still, she could not stop herself from feeling the way she felt.

She took note of the way his eyes twinkled in the candlelight, the way the collar of his tunic moved with each beat of his heart, and the way he held on to her hand. Odd, quite odd.

"I would no' and will no' leave yer side until I ken that ye are on yer way to being fully recovered," he said in a low, soft voice. "I could bathe, shave, and climb into me bed, but I think ye'd beat me over the head with the candlestick if I did."

"What on earth are ye goin' on about? I be quite certain I'd no beat ye over the head with a candlestick just fer bathin' or going to bed!" Mayhap he, too, had been injured and had suffered a grave injury to his brain.

Another chuckle, a wee heartier this time. "Are ye certain of that?"

She let out an exasperated sigh. The man had lost his mind. "Of course I be certain! Yer makin' no sense, Rowan Graham. Did you suffer a head injury? Or did ye by chance drink some of that awful potion of Ora's?"

He could not help but laugh at her. He hoped she would not take his laughter as an insult. Considering what had happened the last time he smiled like an ignorant fool, he quickly explained why he found her statement so humorous. "Lass, ye be in *me* room. Ye be in *me* bed."

Her brows drew inward. His room? His bed? She had only been in his room once when she brought Lily to him. She'd been so focused on *him* at that time that she hadn't paid any particular attention to his room, his furniture or anything else for that matter. Her focus had been solely on the man himself.

"Aye," he said with a nod of his head when he saw the expression on her face. "Me room. Me bed."

"But why am I here?" she asked. *And not in me own room?*

He stopped laughing and the smile left his face. His expression turned serious. She couldn't be certain, but she thought he looked a bit fearful and embarrassed.

"Well?" she asked. "Or is that another question ye'll no' answer until yer damned good and ready, like *what happened to me?*"

Her original thought had been to convince him to leave her be long enough to speak with Ora. Now she had more questions. Somehow she doubted Ora would be able to answer most of them. She was as confused over what he *had* said as what he had not.

Rowan cleared his throat and shifted in his chair. His jaw muscles tensed and Arline could sense that he was mulling over her question.

"Truly, Rowan, ye are a perplexing man! I do no' understand why ye canna tell me the truth. What happened to me? Why am I no' in me own room?" She shook her head and began to grow weary of his silence. She reasoned that he was not going to be forthcoming with the information she sought.

Rowan remained mute, as did Arline. The only sound breaking through their muteness was the soft crackle of embers coming from the fireplace.

Rowan let out a short sigh before leaning in closer to Arline. "Ye became angry with me because I acted like an eejit," he explained in a low tone. "I smiled."

He had gone mad, she no longer held any doubt. "Ye've gone mad," she said with disbelief. "Why would I get angry because ye smiled?" She could not believe him. If anything, his smile always left her feeling happy, confused, and excited.

"I fear I smiled at a most inappropriate time, Arline. I smiled because I was verra happy with something ye had just shared with me. Something that was verra difficult fer ye to share. Ye mistook me joy as me bein' an ass. Ye even told me to go to hell."

303

He looked genuinely miserable. Arline tried to remember what they had discussed that day, of what she had told him, but drew a complete blank. There were countless things she could have told him that would have been difficult for her to discuss.

"I be sorry, Rowan," she told him. "But I canna remember." She grew increasingly uneasy as well as concerned for Rowan. His expression was pained, as if he were dreading telling her any of it.

"Ora says that when someone suffers a severe injury, such as what ye suffered, their mind blocks out all memory of the event. Some people have been known to lose not just hours, but days. She thinks it's the mind's way of protecting a person, that the memory might be too horrible and painful." He patted the back of her hand. "I fear I do no' want to upset ye further, lass. But I also fear that if I am no' completely honest with ye, ye'll resent me all the rest of yer days."

Arline thought long and hard, all the while her fear and unease increased. Though she worried over what he might tell her, she worried more that the black patches of her memory would drive her mad. "I promise ye Rowan, that I'll no' resent ye. Of that, I can swear. I may become upset, but I have to ken what happened."

She wanted to tell him that as long as he was with her she felt she could face any problem or difficulty. She had grown to value and treasure their friendship. Even if she had been angry with him, she knew, deep down, she could forgive him nearly anything.

"We had been talkin' of first kisses. Young Robert had just kissed Lily, do ye remember?"

Her stomach tightened ever so slightly. A faint memory, as faint as a whisper, tickled at the back of her mind. *First kisses.* She vaguely remembered Rowan asking about *her* first kiss. The nonexistent one.

"Ye told me about yer marriages. *All* of yer marriages, and the lack of *intimacy* in them." He spoke in a low, calm tone, giving her little bits of information at a time so as to not upset her too quickly. Her face paled visibly before turning a deep shade of red. Normally, that would have made him smile, but he could find no humor in her discomfit this day.

"Ye see, lass," he paused, searching for the most intelligent way to explain the rest of it to her. There was probably no way of telling her what was in his heart without rambling on like a fool. He took a deep breath and began again. "Ye see, lass, I have grown to care a great deal about ye. But, there was a question as to yer," he searched for any word he could find that didn't sound cold or harsh. "Yer *fertility.*"

"My what?" she asked, her voice filled with confusion and shock.

He took a quick breath in and let it out through his nostrils. "There were some who were concerned that ye were barren. When I learned that ye were still *pure*, well, it filled me heart with joy!"

Mad, mad, mad. The man *had* lost his mind. She lay there in confused and stunned silence. Hopefully Ora would return soon. Arline could somehow send a signal to her that Rowan was completely insane and needed help.

Rowan watched as she sank back into the bed, looking as though she were trying to hide from him. He knew he wasn't making much sense by beating around the bush.

"I wanted to ask fer yer hand but I couldna ask fer it if ye were barren." His words spilled forth in an almost indiscernible manner. "The clan council would no' have blessed our marriage. I would have had to give up Lily's birthright and I couldna do that to her. I was willin' to live the rest of me life alone, without ye, to save me daughter's future -- and yers! I couldna ask ye to marry me and no' be able to provide fer ye. I was a coward, Arline, a complete and utter coward and an eejit."

Arline froze. She could only make out half of what he was saying. And that half scared her witless.

"But when ye told me finally of yer marriages and the fact that there be no way of knowing if ye were barren or no', well, I couldna help meself! I was so overcome with joy, with knowin' then that I *could* marry ye, that I couldna speak, I could barely think. All I could do was smile. Ye took that smile as an insult. I could see it in yer eyes, the hurt and the pain. But ye told me to go to hell and at the time, I didna ken why. Ye ran out of the room, out of the keep, and tried to run away."

Flashes of blurred and fuzzy images popped up in the recesses of her mind. She could remember feeling cold, afraid, angry, and hurt, but it was all a jumbled mess.

"I couldna get to ye in time, ye ken. I tried, Arline, I tried so hard to get to ye. Ye climbed over the wall and before I could stop ye, our men on the wall saw riders approachin'. It all happened so fast. They shot at ye, their arrows flyin' and landin' all around ye. Ye were trying to get back to the keep, when ye realized what was happenin'."

He hung his head in shame. "'Twas me fault, ye ken. I couldna get to ye in time. The last arrow hit ye in the back and went all the way through yer shoulder. I thought ye were dead, Arline, and it nearly killed me."

She didn't know which part of his story shocked her more. The fact that he wanted to marry her or the fact that he would have mourned her loss. Being shot seemed miniscule by comparison.

Someone on this earth wanted to marry her. He wanted to *marry* her. Voluntarily, with no bartering or threats. She was too flabbergasted to cry or speak just yet. She lay as still as a stone, contemplating all that he had just told her.

His guilt was real, she could tell by the way he hung his head, ashamed to look at her. That he should feel guilty when it was her own stubbornness that had gotten her shot said much. It didn't matter to him *how* she came to be in danger. What mattered to him was that he hadn't been there to stop her from being hurt.

It bewildered her that he wanted to marry her. Either she was far more naïve than she ever considered herself to be or she was a fool. Either way, not once had she ever had even an inkling that he cared for her as anything other than Lily's governess. At most, she thought he considered her a friend.

She finally found her voice, trembling and weak. "No one's ever wanted to marry me on purpose before."

Slowly, he raised his head and looked into her eyes. "I do."

"But *why?*" she asked, still unable to grasp the idea of Rowan possessing a desire to marry her. "Me da hasn't bargained for me, I have no dowry to speak of. I canna bring anything important to ye, Rowan."

His lips curved into a warm smile. "Ye bring yerself, lass, and that is all I need. I do no' need money or land or any other inducement. 'Tis ye I want and nothin' more."

How many nights had she lain awake longing to hear someone say those words? How many hours had been given to daydreams of Rowan Graham professing to love and want her? And now, the moment was here, and had she not been grievously injured, she would have fled from the room in fear. Her hands trembled, her mouth went dry, and those damnable fish swimming in her belly had returned once again.

"Ye canna be serious," she said quietly. She found it difficult to look into his eyes, so filled with adoration and desire that her legs trembled. 'Twas a good thing she was lying down for had she been standing, she most certainly would have fallen over.

"I am, Arline. Verra serious."

"But ye've never done anythin' that would lead me to believe ye cared for me like, like *that!*"

He chuckled and leaned in close, so close that she could scarcely breathe. "I *wanted* to, many times."

The way he said *wanted*, brought a tickling sensation to her stomach. It made her heart flutter. She thought it remarkable that the more he spoke, the less her shoulder ached. But what exactly had he *wanted* to do? She grew a spine and asked. "What did ye want to do?"

His smile broadened to the point that he flashed those brilliant white teeth. A twinkle gleamed in his eyes. "I wanted to tell ye how I felt. And I wanted to kiss ye. I still want verra much to kiss ye, Arline."

Her eyes grew as wide and as round as wagon wheels as he leaned in even closer. "Nay!" she exclaimed loudly as she lifted the hand of her good arm and pushed him away.

"Nay?" He was unmistakably taken aback.

She shook her head at him. "Nay! This is no' how I imagined me first kiss to be!" she told him firmly. "Yer supposed to kiss me under the stars or, or, by the loch, or in an alcove! Not now, when I've been abed fer days, and me hair is dirty and no' combed! I'm no' even dressed! And I've a--"

He stopped her from saying anything else with a kiss. A sweet, tender, gentle kiss. Once he had figured out she did no' protest the fact that he wanted to kiss her and that her only complaint was the timing and location, he could not hold back.

The kiss was as he had imagined it would be. Wondrous, exciting, and magnificent. Her lips felt soft against his. He took delight in her sharp intake of air when his lips first touched hers.

He went in again, like a man diving into warm, inviting waters. He felt her trembling fingers clutch his hand. She hadn't moved, hadn't tried to return the kiss at first. But soon, she leaned in, her lips pleading for more as she returned his kiss. Her innocence shone through in how she responded, greedily yet hesitantly.

Were she not injured, he would have climbed into the bed with her to begin a kiss that would last for days. His groin as well as his heart protested when he broke away.

He rested his forehead against hers as he did his best to steady his labored breathing. He caressed her cheek with the backs of his fingers. His lips felt hot and burned for more.

"Yer kisses are corruptible!" she breathed out. Her entire body seemed to be one big trembling puddle of mush. It was everything she had ever dreamed it would be but decidedly different. It was *real.* Not something her heart or her creative imagination had designed. It was sweet, tender and gentle, yet filled with a level of passion she did not think possible. She was too shocked with her own response to his kiss to tell him how it made her feel.

He pulled away to get a better look at her. Her skin was a brilliant shade of red. Those green eyes sparkled in the candlelight. She looked as amazed as she did surprised.

"Corruptible?" he asked, chuckling at her description. "I've kissed many a lass in me day, and no' one of them ever described me kisses as *corruptible.*"

She remained quiet, trying to will away the lustful feelings his kiss had brought surging through her body. His kisses were not going to be easy to resist. In the back of her mind, she saw Minnie shaking her head and clucking her tongue, disgusted at how her former charge had just behaved. Not at all ladylike.

"Did ye no' enjoy the kiss, lass?" he asked in a deep, low, seductive tone.

"That be the problem!" She swallowed hard and took a deep breath. "Ye canna marry me, Rowan. I'd be no good fer ye."

Puzzled, he raised a brow. "No good fer me? I do no' understand." No matter what reasons she might come up with, he'd find a way to refute them all. He *was* going to marry her.

Her eyes began to water as she thought about how the kiss had made her feel. Alive, excited, amazed, lustful; all the things a good, decent lady was *not* supposed to feel. Throwing all caution to the wind, she knew she must be honest with him. "Ye make me feel things a lady isna supposed to feel, Rowan! I'm a wanton! A harlot! Ye need a good, decent woman who'll not become brazen and excited at yer touch! A woman who can keep her wits about her and no' one who wishes fer more of yer kisses!"

He had to bite his cheek to keep from laughing. He had no goodly idea where she got hold of the notion that he'd not want her to be affected by his kiss or his touch. The woman was the furthest thing from a harlot that one would get. She was damned near a nun!

"Ye'll have to explain to me, lass, how ye came to believe I'd no' want ye to enjoy me kisses." He hid his mirth well.

She cleared her throat and wiped away a tear. She could not look him straight on for fear he'd see how badly she wanted another kiss from him. She damned her betraying body to the devil, took a deep breath and tried to explain it as best she could.

"Though I've no' ever experienced fer meself what goes on between a man and a woman, I ken how it's done. I fear I'll no' be able to do me duty to ye when ye kiss me like that."

"Do yer duty?" He was thoroughly intrigued.

"Aye, me duty. Me maid, Minnie, she came to take care of me after me mum died. She explained it all to me when I married Carlich, ye ken. A good wife, she lies still and allows her husband to do what he must or what he wants so that she can get with child. She must allow him to come to her once a week, as is his right. A decent wife, a true lady, she finds no enjoyment in the act. Only harlots, whores and wantons do! And I fear I'm one of them, fer I truly *did* enjoy yer kiss! Do ye no' see? I canna be a good, decent wife to ye if I'm all," she fought hard to find the correct word to describe how he made her feel. "Excited! Lustful! Sinful!"

He almost bit his tongue in half to keep from laughing at her innocence and misguided notions. He rubbed a hand over his forehead, more to hide the amusement he found in her statement than to relieve an achy head.

"I fear yer Ninny--"

"Minnie," she corrected him.

"Yer *Minnie* was wrong," he told her.

She finally raised her head to look at him. "Wrong?"

"Aye," he said with a nod. "Was yer Minnie ever married? Did she have any experience with men?"

"Aye! She was married fer a time when she was young. The poor thing, her husband died only after a year or so of bein' married. He'd left their cottage one morn, to go huntin' and he never returned. She was certain he was set upon and killed by reivers. Minnie searched and searched fer him, fer weeks, but could no' find him. She thought mayhap wolves got him or the reivers took his body away."

Rowan could feel the sadness Arline felt for her maid, Minnie. He trod upon the subject with great care and thoughtfulness. "And 'twas Minnie who said good lasses are no' supposed to like kisses or joinin' with their husbands?"

Arline sniffed and nodded. "So, ye see, ye canna marry me. Ye need a good woman, Rowan. One who can lay still and no' act like a wanton woman whenever ye touch her. Minnie would be horrified if she knew I was like this! All those years we spent together, with her teachin' me how to be a proper lady are but a waste. I'm sorry, Rowan."

He shook his head, smiled and moved to sit on the edge of the bed. He took her hands in his and tried to be as tactful and thoughtful as he could be. "Arline, no' *all* men want their wives to just *do their duty.*" He took her chin and lifted her head gently so that he could look into her eyes. "I fear I would be terribly wounded and hurt if I kissed ye and ye did *no'* enjoy it. A wife *should* find pleasure with her husband, with his kisses and *all* they do together." He wouldn't share with her his opinions on Minnie's missing husband. The man probably left because she'd been a cold and unloving wife.

Disbelief and surprise filled her bright green eyes. "But, Minnie said,"

He stopped her with another soft, tender kiss. "I do no' care what Minnie told ye. I do no' ever want ye to think ye canna say or do whatever ye wish, when it comes to things of a more intimate nature."

"So it's a harlot ye want fer a wife?" she asked.

"Nay," he said, kissing her again. "I want an honest and forthright wife. One who's no' afraid to say what is on her mind."

If she told him everything that was *on her mind* he *would* think her a harlot! She supposed being silently honest would cause no harm, that is, if he truly did want to marry her. He hadn't actually asked her yet, and she was afraid to mention it.

"Ye must think me a cad, to be kissin' ye while yer abed, wounded, and no' fully recovered."

Truly, he could kiss her anytime the mood struck him as far as she was concerned. His kisses did in fact make her feel better. Mayhap if he continued on with them, she'd be able to climb mountains by morning time. "Nay," she murmured. "I do no' think ill of ye."

"I should leave ye to rest," he said as he left the bed and stood to his full height.

"Please, do no' go just yet," she asked him, hoping she did not sound as needy as she felt.

He nodded and took his place in the chair. That was much too far away for her liking, but she kept the thought inside, along with a hundred other questions she wanted desperately to ask.

Rowan studied her for a time. Even in her current state, with her mussed hair, the large bandage on her shoulder, and pale skin, he found her breathtakingly beautiful. She'd make a very fine wife, a good companion, and a wonderful mother, not just to Lily, but to all the children he hoped they'd be blessed with.

He wanted to make her his wife, and soon. There were things that must be done in order for that to happen. He wondered how much time she'd need to heal before she'd be healthy enough for a wedding.

"We should post the banns," he said happily.

"Banns?" she asked. He hadn't officially asked her if she would in fact wish to be his wife.

"Aye," he said. "I want to marry ye proper. Post the banns, have a grand weddin', a feast, all of it!" He crossed a leg over one knee and began to think out loud. "I need first to let the council ken that ye've agreed. Then I must have Mrs. Fitz prepare a grand menu for the weddin' feast. And ye'll need a dress. I'll need to invite the MacDougalls, the McDunnahs, the McKees--"

Arline cleared her throat to gain his attention. When she had it, she lifted her chin and looked him directly in the eye. "I've no' agreed."

She watched as the color drained from his face.

"Because ye haven't asked me! Ye only said ye'd *planned* to ask. But ye haven't."

His color slowly returned as he ran over all they had said to one another. She was correct. He hadn't asked. Hadn't shared with her what was in his heart.

He rose from his chair and knelt beside the bed and took her hands in his. "Arline, will ye do me the honor of becomin' me wife?"

She scrunched her face and looked up at the ceiling as if she were considering the question. After a moment or two, she looked at him and smiled. "Aye, I will," she said softly. "On one condition."

His brows turned inward. "Condition?"

"Aye," she said. "If there is to be a marriage contract, there'll be nothin' in it about annulments!"

He threw his head back and laughed. "Aye, I can agree to that, as long as ye agree ye'll never look at kissin' me or joinin' with me as yer duty."

"Agreed," she said with a smile. "We should shake on it," she said as she offered her hand.

That seductive smile of his returned. He took her face in both hands, caressed her cheeks with his thumbs and sighed. "Let's say we seal it with a kiss instead?"

Arline rubbed her cheek against his palm and closed her eyes. Aye, she may have dreamt of this moment, may even have prayed for it. But now that it was here, really truly happening, her heart seemed to swell and threatened to burst from her chest.

Someone wanted to marry her. Not just *any* someone. Rowan Graham, decidedly the most beautiful man she had ever known, wanted to marry *her*. And apparently, he enjoyed her kisses!

TWENTY-SIX

Rowan and Arline spent the better part of the next hour making plans for their wedding. And in between, they shared kisses that became increasingly more passionate.

"Yer goin' to be the death of me, lass," he scratched out after one particularly intense kiss. His groin ached and screamed for attention. He'd have to bath in the loch before the night was over.

"I vex ye?" she asked in a worried tone.

"Nay! I mean to say that I canna wait fer ye to be me wife." He hoped he would not have to explain to her the physical effect she had on his person.

"Oh," she said quietly.

The way her lips formed when she spoke made his eye twitch. It was downright seductive, but she was entirely unaware.

"Do ye think we could post the banns fer three weeks?" he asked, trying to take his mind off the kisses they'd been sharing.

"Three weeks?" She sounded dismayed. "Nay! I canna plan a weddin' in just three weeks!" She wanted to be fully and completely recovered from her injury so that she could enjoy every moment of their wedding night.

Rowan thought on it for a time. He did not want to wait until morning, let alone any longer than necessary. A memory popped up and he decided to use it to his advantage. "What if yer da has learned of the annulment? He may try to marry ye off again. And what if he marries ye by proxy a second time?"

She turned six different shades of white and gray in a matter of moments. Clearly, the thought of her father arranging another marriage or worse yet, marrying her without her consent via proxy, made her ill. "Nay," she sputtered. "I canna do that again!" Who knew who her father might choose this time. He'd marry her to the devil himself if he thought it would increase his purses.

No matter what happened she would marry Rowan in three weeks. She'd marry him this night if she thought he'd agree to it.

"Three weeks shall work," she told him determinedly as she tossed the blankets away. "Help me to me feet!" She'd walk through fire if she had to.

Rowan laughed at her determination. He replaced the blankets and urged her to lie back. "Ye will no' have to do a thing, Arline. Ye are nowhere near fully recovered. I'll no have ye takin' the risk of getting ill or undoing all of Ora's fine work. Ye shall stay abed and let *me* do this."

He held up his hand when she started to protest. "Nay! I promise, I'll no make a decision without ye, but I'll no allow ye to do anythin'. Please, lass, promise me ye'll stay abed and allow me to do this. I'll ask Selina to help if it will make ye feel better."

She breathed a sigh of relief when he offered to enlist Selina's help. Selina was a sweet young woman and very astute. "Aye, if ye promise ye'll let me help make the decisions and take Selina's help, then aye, I'll agree to stay abed."

"Good," he said. "Now, 'tis gettin' late. Ora should be here soon to tend to ye. I must leave ye now, to go tell the council of our plans."

Arline agreed, though the thought of him leaving left her feeling lonely. "Ye'll return soon?" she asked, stifling a yawn.

Rowan stood, bent over and gave her a chaste kiss on her forehead. "I do so promise. I also promise to shave me beard and take a much needed bath."

Arline rather liked the beard. It gave him an even more seductive and mysterious air. It was soft, too, and she liked the way it tickled when he touched his cheek to hers. "Ye needn't hurry to shave it, Rowan."

He offered her a warm smile as he rubbed his hand along it. "Ye like it, do ye?"

"'Tis *yer* face. Ye must do what ye like. But if yer askin' me opinion, then aye, I do like the beard."

Rowan kissed her again, made another promise to return as soon as he was able. Arline promised to rest and sleep.

Were she able, she would have danced around the room after Rowan closed the door. It seemed her life was beginning to take a marked turn for the better. Very soon, she would be Rowan's wife. They would start a life together, have children and build a legacy.

He hadn't come out directly and professed his love for her. She reasoned that mayhap he was not quite ready to make such a declaration. She knew that it was difficult for some men to speak from the heart, for fear of sounding weak or less than a man. Arline did not care if he said the words, it was enough that he showed her how he felt. Their entire lives lay stretched before them. There would be plenty of time for *I love ye's* later on.

Aside from the sea opening and swallowing Scotland whole, nothing could stop the news of Rowan Graham's impending nuptials from spreading across the country. In some instances, the news reached those invited to attend the wedding before the invitation itself had arrived.

Word reached Lady Beatrice but four short days after the formal announcement had been made. Rowan had declared to the world that he would be marrying Lady Arline.

Beatrice would have heard it much sooner were it not for the blasted snow. She'd never been fond of winter to begin with. Now, having seen how it had delayed her spies, she hated it even more. Her hatred of winter dimmed in comparison to the all consuming hatred she felt toward Lady Arline.

She'd lost precious time to plot. And timing in these cases was everything. Had she received the news sooner she would have had more time to devise a better plan to stop Rowan from marrying Lady Arline.

Beatrice would simply have to make do. With Joan's help and the aid of a few men whose fealty she had purchased, Beatrice put into place a plan that would, without a shadow of a doubt, keep Rowan from marrying Arline. Arline's life would unfortunately be spared, there was no way around that, no matter how she wished she could watch the life drain from the insipid redhead's body.

With the wedding just days away, Beatrice left the comfort of her home in Edinburgh, along with a small contingent of armed men and her maid, Joan. With any luck, they would arrive on Graham lands with plenty of time to spare.

Beatrice would accept nothing less than total success. With controlled rage, she rode west, tweaking and improving her plan along the way.

Nothing, but *nothing* would stand in her way.

Rowan would *not* be marrying Arline.

TWENTY-SEVEN

As promised, Rowan enlisted Selina's advice and help in preparing for his wedding to Arline. Selina was in charge of making a very grand and enchanting dress for his bride and acted as a liaison of sorts between Arline and Mrs. Fitz.

Rowan spent as much time as he could with Arline. Diligently, he made certain she did not leave her bed. He made certain she ate and rested and followed all of Ora's instructions without question or complaint. At least he attempted to get her to follow them without complaint. After days of being abed, Arline began to grow irritable and plead with him to at least allow her to stand.

He found pacifying her with kisses both enjoyable and easy. He began to wonder if she complained merely to receive his kisses. He decided it didn't matter for he looked forward to those stolen moments, filled with promise of what would soon be their wedding night.

Arline was growing more bold in showing her affection. Rowan supposed Ora had helped in that regard, especially after he discussed Arline's reticence and misguided notions as they pertained to a woman's *wifely duty*. He would be forever in Ora's debt.

Lily was beside herself with joy when Rowan and Arline sat her down to share the news with her. She squealed with delight and danced about the room. In singsong fashion, she joyfully exclaimed to anyone who would listen that she was going to have a new mamma. She was also looking forward to having a wee brother or sister and was disappointed to learn that one would *not* be delivered to her on the wedding day. Nine months can seem like an eternity to a four-year-old child.

It had snowed yet again, but thankfully, this time it was not as fierce as the first snowstorm of the season. Large, fluffy white flakes fell majestically to the ground. Per Arline's request, and the offered bribe of a kiss, Rowan took Lily and the other children out to play. The little ones thoroughly enjoyed catching snowflakes on their tongues and throwing snowballs at Rowan.

Arline watched from the bedchamber window after Ora helped her to a chair. With blankets and furs draped around her, the fire blazing to ward off the cold, Arline smiled as she watched Rowan chasing the children, helping them to build a snowman, and feigning grievous injury when they pelted him with snowballs.

Arline could not remember ever feeling so much at peace. All was right in her world and it was only going to get better. She rose each morn, to find Rowan and Lily sleeping on the pallet next to the bed. An overwhelming sense of joy would come over her when she thought on the fact that all of her dreams were coming true.

Rowan brought the children inside, handing all but his own off to their waiting mothers. He helped Lily into dry clothes and warm woolens before taking her back to the gathering room where she could enjoy the hot cider and sweet cakes Mrs. Fitz had waiting for them.

An undercurrent of excitement was beginning to build around the keep. Rowan was doing his best to keep the promises he had made to God by practicing patience and kindness.

Most of his people were excited about the upcoming wedding, especially the womenfolk. They were all abuzz and atwitter over the first wedding to be held inside these walls since Rowan's last.

Life, he thought as he watched his daughter sipping cider and chattering happily to her friends about the fact that she, too, would soon have a mother, was perfect. His heart swelled with pride, with love and adoration, not just for his daughter, his future bride, or his clan, but for everything in his life.

C hristmastide was just four days away and Arline's birthday fell on the morrow. The gift he had arranged for her had not yet arrived and he began to worry over it as it should have arrived days ago. Hopefully all was well and he would be able to present Arline with a token of his love very soon.

They'd be married two days after Hogmanay and that day could not arrive soon enough for either of their liking. Soon, he'd be counting down the hours instead of the days.

Rowan, Lily, and the other children were all huddled around the fire, the excitement of Christmastide taking up the majority of their young conversations. The children were looking forward to the feast and the Yule log, but most of all, they could hardly wait for the games they would play.

Selina entered the room with Arline's wedding dress in her arms. Arline had chosen the color, a soft, pale yellow, as well as the design. Rowan had asked for a lower neckline than Arline felt comfortable wearing. He hoped that Selina had responded to his request and not his future bride's.

"Good day to ye, Rowan!" Selina said as she approached. "I was just headin' up to show Arline the finished dress. I added the silver and gold thread like ye asked," she told him. "But if she doesna like it, *ye* will have to answer to her!"

Rowan laughed in agreement. "Do no' fash yerself. I am certain she'll love what ye've done." And if she didn't he could easily placate her with more kisses.

He left Lily with the children and was heading up the stairs with Selina when Thomas entered from out of doors. "Rowan!" he shouted over the din of the chattering children and rushed excitedly to the stairs.

Rowan directed Selina to go ahead and to tell Arline he'd be along shortly. "What be the problem, Thomas?" Rowan asked as he climbed back down the stairs.

Thomas waited patiently at the bottom before he answered. He leaned in and whispered to Rowan, "The *gift* ye ordered fer Lady Arline?" he began. "'Tis arrived!"

Rowan let out a happy cry and slapped Thomas on the back. If Arline was at all upset with the added embellishments to her dress, the gift he was about to give her would give him at least ten years worth of getting out of any troubles.

"I do no' understand why I must wear the blindfold, Rowan," Arline with clear frustration. She sat blindfolded, in a large comfortable chair next to the fire. Rowan had wrapped not one, but two furs around her, professing his worry over her catching a chill.

"Wheesht, now," Rowan said. "I told ye, 'tis a surprise."

"Well I hope it's more yellow silk to add to me dress, ye devil! The neckline is beyond scandalous!"

As she sat and waited, she pondered the beautiful yellow gown. Afraid to try it on just yet, for fear her healing wound might ooze even the tiniest amount of blood on it, the gown hung on a hook in Rowan's dressing room. It was beautiful, even if the neckline was far too revealing. The gold and silver threads that Selina had added to the neck, sleeves and hem were perfect. Arline loved the way they sparkled in the candlelight and hoped that Rowan would find her to his liking when she wore it.

Moments passed when she heard a rustling of skirts, slippers and boots alike padding across the floor. She also heard a rush of whispers and Lily's giggle. For the life of her, she could not understand what surprise Rowan had for her that would require so many people to attend.

Rowan came and knelt beside her. She only knew it was him for he had whispered in her ear that he hoped she liked her early birthday gift and mayhap it would earn him a kiss. She burned crimson, placed her fingers over her mouth to hide her smile and hoped no one in the room had heard him.

"I ken how much ye like to draw," Rowan said excitedly. "So I had some supplies brought to ye fer yer birthday. I sent fer them weeks ago and they've just arrived by special delivery."

A blindfold and a room full of people to witness him giving her drawing supplies? Would he arrange a three-day feast, bards, jugglers and acrobats if he gave her a broach? As he untied the blindfold, she was convinced he was tetched and was just about to tell him so when she opened her eyes.

She gasped, covered her mouth with her hands, in utter shock and disbelief. The tears flowed as instantly as they formed and for a moment, she could not move or speak.

"Morralyn! Geraldine!" she cried out her sisters' names. They rushed to her, fell to their knees and hugged her.

They were *here!* With her! She cried, bewildered, elated, and confused. They cried right along with her.

They all began talking at once, professing how glad they were to see each other after all this time. "Och! Ye are a sight fer sore eyes!" Morralyn cried as she held Arline's face in her hands. Geraldine was too overcome with tears to speak but nodded her head in agreement.

Selina stepped forward offering the women handkerchiefs. "I'm so verra happy fer ye, Lady Arline! Yer sisters as well!"

Arline thanked her, handed a handkerchief to each sister. Her joy was overwhelming and she could not stop the tears from flowing. She looked around the room for the man responsible. He was standing in the corner, next to Thomas. Thomas was smiling, enjoying the spectacle as it played out before him.

Rowan was smiling too, that beautiful, gleaming smile. He was leaning against the wall with his arms crossed over his green tunic. She could not find the words to express how happy she was at this moment. Were she at all able to jump up, she would run to him and fling her arms around his neck and smother him with kisses. As it was, her two equally happy sisters had her pinned to the chair.

Arline mouthed a "thank ye" to Rowan, along with a warm smile. He simply nodded his head.

"How did ye do this? Why did ye no' tell me?" she asked him.

"I knew how much ye missed yer sisters. So I sent fer them weeks ago." He left out the part of how he had thought to use them as an inducement to getting her to stay here. He rationalized that it no longer mattered. Morralyn and Geraldine were here and his future wife was overcome with joy. That was all that mattered.

"Aye," Morralyn said happily. "He sent fer us weeks ago. Two verra braw young men!" she laughed aloud. "They told us ye were here, and finally away from that awful fool yer da forced ye to marry. Rowan offered us the same safe haven as he offered ye. And now it appears as if he's offered *ye* even more!"

Arline and Geraldine giggled along with Morralyn. "I am so verra happy that ye agreed!"

"Did ye *see* the two handsome men he sent?" Morralyn asked with a smile. "'Twas impossible to tell them no to anythin'!"

Arline's face burned red. "Morralyn!" She knew all too well what Morralyn meant by that statement. Her sister hadn't been raised by a very prim and proper maid, like Arline had. Therefore she hadn't had the guidance on being a lady, even though Arline had tried countless times over the years.

"What?" Morralyn asked, pretending not to have any good idea why Arline would be embarrassed or feel the need to chastise her. "I've been tellin' ye fer years that life be too short, Arline. And all that nonsense that Minnie put in yer head was goin' to lead ye to a verra dull and unhappy life." She glanced over her shoulder to look at Rowan, smiled and wiggled her eyebrows at him before turning back to Arline. "And I swear if ye heed Minnie's advice and no' me own, I'll be forced to use the good sense and feminine wiles God gave me and make *that* man of yers verra, *verra* happy."

Arline burst out laughing. She knew Morralyn's threat held no truth to it. Morralyn would never do anything to hurt Arline, but she was not above speaking her mind or making threats to get her point across.

"Ye needn't worry, Morralyn. I've recently learned that most of Minnie's advice was not exactly true."

Morralyn rolled her eyes. "Most? Not exactly true? Och! The woman was tetched I tell ye, full of shi--"

Geraldine stopped Morralyn before she could embarrass herself or Arline further. "Morralyn!" she scolded in a whisper. "We're no' in a tavern. We be in fine company. Watch yer tongue!"

"I'd rather watch Eldon's tongue!" Morralyn said with a laugh.

"Morralyn!" Arline and Geraldine exclaimed in unison.

Arline leaned in to her sisters. "Who is Eldon?"

"Och! He was one of the verra braw men yer Rowan sent us!"

Arline sat back and place a hand on her chest. She hoped Morralyn hadn't done anything that would make Rowan regret his offer.

"Do no' fash yerself, Arline," Morralyn said. "I've done nothin' to be ashamed of."

"That's because ye have no shame!" Geraldine said, adding a curt nod for emphasis.

"Yer right! I don't!"

It was next to impossible to insult Morralyn. Geraldine however, had softer skin. She wore her heart on her sleeve was generous to a fault, but not completely above jesting or engaging in more tawdry conversation. However, Geraldine knew there was a proper time and place for such things.

Rowan stood quietly observing the three sisters. While they all shared the same father, they each had different mothers. No one could tell by looking at them, however, that they shared any bloodlines.

Morralyn was a very tiny yet buxom woman, with long golden blonde hair and big hazel eyes. Geraldine was more than a head taller than Morralyn, even though she was a good three years younger. Geraldine had dark brown hair and hazel eyes that leaned toward green, and like Arline, she was as thin as a tree sapling.

They chatted away excitedly, reliving the events of the past year. Morralyn and Geraldine had grown increasingly worried for Arline's safety after they stopped receiving letters from her. They had learned of the annulment and were preparing to leave the little

325

cottage where Arline had hidden them, fearful that Orthanach would find them.

Rowan listened intently. The more he learned of the three women's father, the less he liked the man. Arline was nothing more than a bargaining tool, a means for him to amass more wealth. Her younger sisters meant nothing to him other than as a means to control Arline.

Rowan swore to himself that when Orthanach learned of the wedding -- and he had no doubt that he would -- he would do everything within his power to keep the man away from these three women.

The three women were soon lost in stories of their childhood, memories of better days and worse. Rowan saw that the world around them fell away and nothing mattered but each other. He quietly ushered Thomas, Lily, Selina, and Ora out of the room. He would have refreshments sent to the room and allow them time to reacquaint themselves with each other.

Silently, he slipped out of the room, the sounds of giggling women following him out. He could not help but feel a bit triumphant. He'd done *the right thing*.

TWENTY-EIGHT

Christmastide came and went peacefully, without attack or interruption. The clan's children enjoyed their feast, the stories that were told and the games that were played. It was one of the better Christmastides that Rowan could recall.

Arline could not remember ever enjoying a Christmastide like Clan Graham's. Her father had never believed in celebrating much of anything. No Yule logs had ever burned at their keep. Greenery had never been displayed, no feasts, no music, no games. She had enjoyed them later in life, with Carlich. But the Lindsay festivities were smaller, more intimate affairs.

Rowan had carried Arline down the stairs and placed her in a big chair next to the fireplace so that she could enjoy and participate in the festivities. Her sisters were never far away from her side, though Rowan did take note that Morralyn and Thomas had disappeared for more than an hour. When the two had returned, Thomas wore a smile that Rowan could never remember seeing on the man's face. Morralyn looked proud and happy. He pretended not to notice.

Several of his younger men tripped over themselves to spend time with Geraldine. They fought over who would bring her mulled wine or sweet cakes. They nearly came to blows over who would have the first dance with her. Rowan came to her rescue by dancing with her first, much to Arline's delight and gratitude. Geraldine was an exceptionally quiet young lass, quite bonny and sweet. He could well understand the younger men wanting to spend time with her.

There were moments throughout the day and night when Arline would touch his arm and with tear-filled eyes express her gratitude. His heart swelled with pride for having made her so happy.

Arline was healing quite nicely and had been moved into Kate's auld room. At first, she had protested, explaining that it didn't feel quite right to have her move into Kate's room. Rowan explained that Kate would have wanted it this way. Besides, it was only temporary. Once he and Arline were married, she'd not be spending much time in her own room. He fully intended on holding her prisoner in his, at least until they were much, much older. Eighty or ninety sounded appropriate.

Clan Graham was all aflutter with the excitement of Rowan and Arline's upcoming wedding. Guests began to filter in the day before Hogmanay. The first to arrive were his friends, Nial and Bree McKee, along with their four wee ones.

Bree and Arline became instant friends while Lily fell instantly in love with seven-year-old Jamie. When Arline tucked Lily into her bed that night, Lily professed that she would marry Jamie McKee someday for he was not like the other boys. "He gave me his sweet cake!" Lily informed Arline. "Robert *never* gives me *his* sweet cake, even when I ask politely. Jamie gave it to me without me even askin'!"

Arline didn't have the heart to tell her that Jamie had just been getting over a stomach ailment. She'd not crush the dreams of a four-year-old little girl.

More guests filed in on the following day. Nora and Wee William of the Clan MacDougall, along with their six children and Nora's beautiful fifteen-year-old sister, Elise, arrived in the late morn. Elise was positively stunning, with her long strawberry blonde hair and vivid, bright blue eyes and the younger lads immediately took notice.

Her brother-in-law, Wee William, stood nearly seven feet tall. Arline remembered him from her journey to Stirling when she helped to keep his chief and friend from hanging. He hadn't changed much. He was still the biggest man she'd ever laid eyes on. His brown hair was beginning to gray at the temples. He had a few more wrinkles around his eyes. Still, he was a most formidable man. All he need do was cast a stern glance at any young man who happened to come within ten feet of his young sister-in-law.

Part of Arline felt sorry for the young lass. She'd never be allowed to have any fun as long as her large brother-in-law was around. The other part of her envied Elise. Arline wished she had been blessed with someone like that, so protective and caring, when she was that age.

She supposed her life now would be decidedly different had she not experienced all that she had. There was also a very strong possibility that she would not now be just a few short days away from marrying Rowan.

Findley and Maggy McKenna, auld friends of Rowan's, arrived late in the evening with a small army made up entirely of children. Arline could not hide her surprise when Rowan informed her that Findley and Maggy hadn't brought *all* of their children, just the youngest seven. They had three older boys, all married, who had stayed behind to watch after their keep.

Duncan and Aishlinn McEwan arrived the following day, along with their four children -- three boys and a girl. Duncan was now the chief of Clan MacDougall. Angus had retired the past year.

"Angus and Isobel send ye their best wishes," Duncan told Rowan and Arline as they stood before the fire in the grand gathering room.

"They would have loved to have come, but Angus broke his leg a few weeks ago. He was chasin' our wee ones in the courtyard and slipped on the ice. He was mighty angry that he could no' travel here, but Isobel would no' let him out of bed," Duncan told Rowan as they drank tankards of ale.

Rowan laughed aloud. "Och! 'Tis good to ken that Isobel is still in charge of the auld man!"

Duncan agreed. "Aye. Angus may have been the chief of the clan for all these years, but we all ken the truth. Isobel was Angus' chief!"

Before the day was out, *Áit na Síochána* was near to bursting with clan chiefs, their wives and children, as well as the warriors who helped escort them here. Arline had never witnessed so many people under one roof. She fretted over each and every one of them.

Although she was recovering quite nicely, Rowan still fussed over her. He'd not allow her to take the stairs without assistance. He would insist that she take frequent naps so that she'd not wear herself out before their big day. While Arline reveled in his attentiveness, there were moments when his constant hovering annoyed her. She knew his intentions came from his adoration of her and that he only worried because he cared a great deal for her. Still, there were moments when she wished he would give her just a few moments alone.

The eve of Hogmanay arrived and the excitement level inside the keep was palpable. Lily followed Jamie McKee around like a puppy. As the oldest, with two little brothers and a wee sister, Jamie had much experience with smaller children. He was kind and patient and didn't seemed at all annoyed that Lily followed him everywhere.

Arline had not left the keep in weeks. She wanted to attend the bonfire that had been set up in the pasture to the east of the keep. Rowan adamantly refused to allow it.

"Ye are a stubborn man, Rowan Graham!" Arline told him. "I have healed verra well. Ye worry over me like I'm a babe takin' me first steps!"

"I'll no' have ye sufferin' a relapse or getting' a chill," he told her quite sternly. "We be getting' married in two days and I wish no' to spend me weddin' night carin' fer a sick wife."

Arline pursed her lips together, placed her hands on her hips, and stared him directly in the eye. "There'll be no weddin' night if ye keep on like this. Either ye stop and allow me to enjoy the bonfire and the first footer, or ye can marry someone else!"

Back and forth they went until Rowan finally relented. "Fine! Ye can go to the bonfire, but ye must be seated and wrapped in furs."

Arline retorted. "I'll run around the fire naked if I have the desire!"

The image of Arline running around a large bonfire, naked, with her auburn locks flowing behind her, brought his argument to an abrupt halt. The images he conjured up, with the flickering fire casting shadows all over her fine body, made his groin ache. He was beginning to wonder if he'd be able to keep from tossing her in his bed and making passionate love to her before their wedding day.

He gave her a curt nod, spun on his heels and left the room to avoid further temptation. As he stepped outside to cool off, he wondered if she knew the effect she had on him.

Her skill at kissing had improved a great deal over the past weeks. She was also becoming bolder, touching his chest, kissing his neck, rubbing his back as they lost themselves in those stolen moments. It took great effort on his part to break away from those kisses. Sleep became less frequent as he lay in bed each night, knowing she was just a few steps away.

He walked around the courtyard for a long while, trying to get his mind to quit its adamant focus on his upcoming wedding night. When he realized neither his mind nor his manhood were going to give up any time soon, he let loose a heavy sigh, and fell face first into the deep snow. 'Twas either that or turn around, head up the stairs, and lock himself away in his room with Arline.

TWENTY-NINE

R owan and Arline's wedding day arrived bringing with it crisp blue skies painted with an abundance of feathery white clouds. The sun shone brightly and made the snow look as though it had been sprinkled with diamond dust. The brilliance and luster was almost painful to look at for long.

Icicles that hung from the roofs of the keep, the towers and barns, began to melt as well, dripping frigid water on anyone who passed under them. The children were warned to stay clear for several of them had crashed to the ground.

The keep was alive with the laughter of children and people calling out instructions as they prepared the keep and the chapel for the wedding.

Rowan was glad this would be the last day he would ever have to knock on Arline's door. He stood outside her bedchamber, waiting impatiently for someone to give him permission to enter. Morralyn opened the door a crack, peered out and smiled up at him.

"Good morn, Rowan. What can I do fer ye?" she asked playfully.

"I'd like a moment with Arline." He flashed Morralyn a smile.

"She's no' here. I heard she ran off with some young buck from a neighboring clan," Morralyn said with a most serious expression. "I'd be glad to stand in fer her if ye want."

He heard Arline chastise her sister from within the bedchamber. "Morralyn! Stop that now and let him in!"

Rowan chuckled at the tiny Morralyn as she giggled and allowed him entry.

Arline was sitting in front of a dressing table facing him, surrounded by Geraldine, Selina, Maggy and Bree. They were all fussing over her hair and discussing how she should wear it.

"I say wear it up," Maggy said as she stood with her hands on her hips.

"Nay," Rowan said softly. "I'd prefer to see it down."

Maggy and Bree giggled at the sight of him. He looked like a wolf about to pounce on an unsuspecting rabbit. "Och! All ye Highlanders are the same," Bree said cheerfully. "Ye *love* to see yer women with their hair down and spread across the sheets!"

The women all laughed in unison, save for Arline. Her beautiful face turned nearly as red as her hair. Rowan had grown to enjoy her innocence and the way she blushed so easily. He also enjoyed the way she rolled her eyes and stood her ground. He could not think of one thing that he did not adore about this woman who had stolen his heart.

"I'd like a moment with Arline, please." He directed his statement to the women surrounding his bride, but his eyes never left Arline's.

"Och! Alone? In her bedchamber? What would people say?" Selina said, pretending to be offended. "What of yer lady's honor, Rowan?"

"I don't give a damn what people say. And I can assure ye, her honor will be safe."

Arline's attendants all left the room, casting words of advice to Arline. "Do no' let him get ye in the bed until he's said *I do!*" Morralyn called out over her shoulder.

Geraldine giggled at her older sister. "Morralyn be right!"

Moments later, they were finally alone. Rowan closed the door before going to Arline. "Ye look lovely this day," he told her.

She blushed at his compliment. "Thank ye, kindly, good man."

Arline thought her future husband looked rather lovely himself. He wore a white tunic over black trews. His ever-present broadsword strapped at his waist and a knife tucked into each boot. His beard was growing in quite nicely. Mayhap being alone with him was not the best idea, for she knew she'd not be able to resist him, *I do's* or no.

"I wanted to give ye something special," Rowan said as he reached into the pouch he wore on his belt. "'Twas me mother's."

He held out his hand to display a beautiful necklace. Dangling from the gold chain was a large emerald surrounded by tiny diamonds.

"Och!" Arline exclaimed as she jumped to her feet. "Ye mean to give that to me?"

Rowan smiled warmly at her. "Aye, I do. I ken me mum would want fer ye to have it. It belonged to her mum."

Arline ran a gentle finger across the emerald. She'd never before owned such a beautiful piece of jewelry. She thought of her mother then and all the beautiful pieces she had owned before her death. Her father had sold every last bit of it, not saving back even the smallest piece for Arline.

For the first time in a very long time, her heart felt heavy. She was just a child when her mother died. Arline could barely remember what she looked like, only bits and pieces. She knew her mother had auburn hair, darker even than her own. Her mother had been a warm, loving woman. Arline was certain that her mother would have been very proud of how well she had turned out.

"Ye look far away, lass," Rowan whispered as he touched her chin with a gentle finger. "Do ye no' like it?"

"Nay! 'Tis beautiful!" she said as she took the necklace from him and held it to her chest. "I was just thinkin' of me mum."

Rowan could well understand for he missed his own mother. He'd die before he ever admitted it to a soul, but, he did. "Ye wish she was here this day."

"Aye, I do." Arline smiled fondly. "She would have liked ye."

"Och!" he said with a smile. "Everyone likes me!"

Arline rolled her eyes at him. "The *women* like ye well enough. But fer the life of me, I dunnae why!"

He wrapped his arms around her and pulled her in for a long, passionate kiss. Arline wore the same expression of surprise and delight as she did each time he kissed her. "But ye are the only woman that has me heart."

Arline tilted her head slightly and looked up into his dark brown eyes. It was the closest he had come to professing he loved her since his proposal. "I do?" she asked.

His eyes narrowed to slits as his brows furrowed. "Of course ye do! I wouldna have asked fer yer hand if ye hadn't stolen me heart."

"Oh," she said softly. When put that way, it made perfectly good sense. Rowan was best at showing his affection and adoration. The fact that Morralyn and Geraldine were here was evidence enough.

"And ye?" Rowan asked, still frowning. "Have I won *yer* heart?"

Was he daft? "Of course ye have!" she exclaimed. "All of me heart ye foolish man!"

It dawned on her then that she had not expressed to him what was in her own heart. She suddenly felt quite foolish. She sat down on the seat in front of the dressing table and took his hand. "Rowan, I need ye to ken what is in me heart."

Rowan nodded and knelt before her. "I think I ken, but I'd take great delight in hearin' ye say it."

She smiled at him, clutched the necklace to her chest again and gave his hand a gentle squeeze. "Well, I do no' want yer head to swell any more than it already is," she began playfully. "I think it goes without sayin' that ye are a most handsome man."

He gave her chin a slight chuck with his fingers. "Aye, that goes without sayin'." He said it just to see her roll her eyes at him. Why he found that so pleasing and enjoyable, he could not begin to explain to anyone.

"And yer tetched!" she told him firmly.

"That goes without sayin' as well."

She let out an exasperated sigh. "What I be tryin' to tell ye is that aye, I do find ye quite handsome. But my feelin's fer ye go much deeper than that. Yer kind, honorable, sometimes funny, and ye are a most generous man. Ye don't just give *things*," she held up the necklace as evidence. "Ye give yer time, yer friendship, yer counsel. Ye are a good man, Rowan Graham. A good, decent, honorable man. I love how ye are with Lily, with yer people. But most of all, I love how ye are with me. I feel safe with ye. I ken that I am safe with ye as is me heart. I can trust ye and ye are one of the verra few men I can say that about." She took a deep breath before continuing on. "I love ye Rowan Graham, with all me heart. I wanted ye to ken that before we went to the alter."

A warm smile came to Rowan's face. His brown eyes twinkled with delight and mayhap a bit of amusement. "Arline, I find ye a most beautiful woman. Ye too are kind, honorable and generous. I love how ye are with Lily. She adores ye, as do I. Ye are a good mum to her and I ken that ye will make me a good wife. But more than that, we shall be good together. Partners in all things."

He leaned in and gave her a tender kiss. "I canna say when I fell in love with ye, but I did. 'Twas gradual to be certain. I knew it, without a doubt, before ye were even injured and I be sorry that I didna tell ye sooner. So I'll tell ye now. I love ye, with all that I am. I love everythin' about ye. I'll love ye 'til I draw me last breath."

His honest and heartfelt declaration brought instant tears to her eyes. She leaned into him and placed her palm gently against his cheek. "Of course ye do! What's no' to love about me?"

They shared another kiss, longer, more passionate than was respectable. Had they not been interrupted by the women returning to help Arline ready for the wedding, they would not have stopped.

Rowan left the room in search of a snowdrift. He had to douse the raging fire of desire and lust.

THIRTY

Extra men had been stationed around the keep, in the off chance that whomever had attacked weeks ago would make another attempt. Men from the MacDougall, McKee, and McKenna clans had volunteered to assist. Rowan and Thomas felt confident that should anything happen this day, they would have plenty of men to aid them.

Frederick, Daniel and the others still had not returned. That was Rowan's only worry this day. He had shared his concerns with Nial, Duncan, Findley and Wee William that morning. They agreed that he should have received some kind of word from them by now. After the ceremony, Rowan would send a group of his men out to search for the others.

Rowan left Thomas in charge of the wall. No one was to enter unless Thomas knew them. There would be no exceptions to this rule.

The wedding was set to start at noon. Hundreds of people milled about the courtyard taking in the sun while they waited for the festivities to begin. Squeals of laughter rang through the yard as the children chased each other or Red John's puppies.

Wee William did his best to keep Findley McKenna's son, Liam, away from Elise. The boy had apparently taken a liking to the young lass and Wee William did not like it. His wife, Nora, a beautiful woman with long dark hair and gray blue eyes quietly informed her husband that he was making an ass of himself. "Let the girl be!" she told him as she hooked her arm through his. "Elise is a smart girl, William. Ye can trust her to do right."

William glared at Liam who was walking next to Elise. "Aye, I ken I can trust Elise. It's Findley's boy I worry about! If Liam is anythin' like Findley, then *ye* should worry as well, wife!"

Nora laughed at her husband. "Nay, I shan't, William. Now, if Liam was more like *ye?* Then I'd worry!"

"I warn ye, if he so much as lays a hand on Elise," Wee William began, "I'll kill him."

Nora laughed again at her husband's worry over her sister. "Elise can take care of herself. Between ye and John, she's learned to use her mind, her words, a sword and her fists. She can handle herself, William. Stop fashin' and let us find a place where ye can remind me why I married ye to begin with."

William could not pass by the opportunity to spend a few quiet moments alone with his wife. In order that he could tend to his wife without worry, he sent his children to watch over Elise. He'd learned over the years that it was quite difficult for anything romantic to take place when you had six sets of eyes staring at you.

Thomas was called to the gate an hour before the wedding was to begin. "They say they be here to claim the rest of Lady Beatrice's belongin's," one of the younger guards informed Thomas as he stepped up to the battlements.

Thomas leaned over and looked down. There were two men in a wagon. They looked to be in their early thirties. The one holding the reins, had dark hair and a slight build. The other one, the one he thought he recognized, was very large with short cut blonde hair. Taking no chances, he called down to them. "Who be ye?"

The men looked up, shielded their eyes from the blaring son. "I be

Edward, from near Kirkaidy," the large blonde yelled up at Thomas. "Lady Beatrice sent us to retrieve things she left behind."

Thomas thought it odd that they would appear this day of all days.

"I have a letter if ye need to see it," Edward called up. "We'd been here sooner, but we were stopped by snow east of here. Our wagon was buried."

That made some amount of sense. Still, he did not want to take any chances. The wagon was empty, save for a rolled up bit of tarp. He supposed he could allow them entry, but under guard at all times.

Thomas turned to the young man beside him. "Allow them entry. I'll post a guard on them. Make sure ye check the wagon before they leave."

The young guard gave the order for the gate to be opened. Thomas left the wall to find a man who could keep a watchful eye on the two men.

"I've brought ye tea, me lady," Bridgett bustled into the room carrying a tray. "Rowan's orders, ye ken. He says he doesna want ye fallin' over durin' the ceremony, from lack of food or drink."

Arline smiled at the young girl. She was glad Bridgett no longer looked at her with contempt-filled eyes. "Thank ye, kindly Bridgett," Arline said as she stood up and walked through the sea of women.

"Och!" Bridgett declared. "I've only brought three cups!"

"Do no' worry it, Bridgett," Arline said. "Three is plenty."

Bridgett had been fussing over the tea tray and not paying attention to Arline. Her mouth fell open when she turned and saw Arline.

"Ye are beautiful, me lady!"

Arline was stunning in her goldenrod gown. The gold and silver threads scattered along the hemline, bodice, and sleeves glistened in the sun that streamed in through the window. Her hair flowed down her back in long waves. Bree had affixed little pearls throughout Arline's hair. Maggy had draped a beautiful gold belt around Arline's slender waist. Across her shoulder was a length of Graham plaid, fastened with a beautiful broach.

341

Arline smiled happily. "Thank ye, kindly, Bridgett."

Bridgett gave a curtsy and left the room full of women.

"She speaks the truth," Maggy said. "Ye are quite beautiful!"

Arline blushed slightly and gave her a murmured thank you. She looked at her sisters. "I think ye look beautiful as well!"

Morralyn wore a light blue dress, simple in its design, but it looked rather regal on Morralyn. Geraldine wore a burgundy silk skirt with a matching over jacket, a loan from Maggy. Arline was so very proud of both her sisters and extremely glad to have them here to share in her special day.

"Let us go below stairs," Bree suggested. "Give Arline and her sisters a few minutes alone."

Arline thanked Bree, Maggy and Selina, giving each woman a hug as they left the room.

After the door closed behind them, Arline went to her sisters. She took one of their hands in hers and gave a squeeze. "I be so happy that yer here!" Her eyes began to fill with tears.

"I be glad that yer marryin' a fine man like Rowan, and not some eejit Orthanach chose for ye!" Morralyn quipped.

Arline threw her head back and laughed. "I be as well!"

She pulled them to sit around the small table and poured each of them a cup of tea. "This will be the last cup of tea I have as an unmarried woman!" Arline jested.

Morralyn raised her cup for a toast. "To braw Highlanders who like to bare their knees!"

They drank the tea and slammed the cups down as if they'd just toasted with fine whisky.

"Blech!" Morralyn and Geraldine said in unison.

"Do they no' ken how to make a good cup of tea?" Geraldine asked.

Arline had to agree. "Och! I don't usually touch the stuff, fer 'tis awful. But, they seem to fancy it here."

"I'd rather have whisky," Morralyn said as she winced. "Even *Scots* whisky."

"Aye," Geraldine agreed with a smile. She stood, looking quite devious as she pulled a silver flask from her skirt. "I think I can help with that!"

Both Arline and Morralyn were surprised. Geraldine was never one to tipple, at least not that Arline was aware. And for her to have a flask in her skirt? 'Twas most unusual.

"Och! Do no' look at me like that," Geraldine said as she poured generous amounts of whisky in each of their cups. "Ye act like I've never touched the stuff."

"But yer always the *good* girl," Morralyn said as she lifted her cup and inhaled.

Geraldine giggled and sat back down. "That's just what Domnal told me last night!"

Arline nearly choked on her whisky. "Geraldine!"

Geraldine rolled her eyes and smiled at her sisters. "I *am* a good young woman. I do no' flaunt meself about like Morralyn does." She looked over the rim of her cup at the two of them. "Ye probably think I am still a virgin too!"

It was Morralyn's turn to choke. "Geraldine!" she exclaimed. "Tell me 'tisn't so!"

Geraldine simply smiled and sipped on her whisky. "There is much ye dunnae about me, Morralyn. Like I said, I am the quiet one. It makes things much more fun, fer people do no' expect such things from me."

They sipped on their whisky and talked as they waited for time to pass by. Soon, Thomas would come to escort them to the chapel. Selina would wait until the last possible minute to dress Lily for the child had a way of finding dirt and trouble.

Morralyn yawned and gave her head a shake. "I fear I'm growing quite tired. Whisky usually lifts me spirits."

Geraldine agreed with a nod and a yawn. "While I don't drink as much as ye, I've tippled enough whisky in me day. Mayhap 'tis all the excitement of the past days catchin' up with us."

Arline began to grow quite tired as well. As she yawned, something niggled at the back of her mind and she could not quite put her finger to it.

Her head began to feel odd, fuzzy, as if she hadn't slept in days. Moments later, her arms felt heavy and her legs felt as though they were no longer attached to her body.

Her heart began to race as she realized what was happening.

She tried to call out for help, tried to stand, to move toward the door. It seemed so far away, out of reach. She fell forward as she stumbled out of the chair.

"The tea," she sputtered. "The bloody damned tea."

B eatrice and Joan had been lurking in the hallway. Beatrice had disguised herself as a kitchen maid. Her hair was wound in a braid under a white kerchief and she wore a plain, gray woolen gown. Joan wore much the same get up, complete with a white apron.

They had been waiting rather impatiently outside Arline's bedchamber. They had watched carefully from the end of the hallway in hopes that they could get Arline alone. Beatrice nearly squealed with delight when she saw three women leave the bedchamber. They would have to think of something to get Arline's sisters out of the way.

Joan had slunk her way down the hall and listened outside the door. She heard a loud thump, like someone falling to the floor. She held her breath in anticipation of a great commotion to come from within the bedchamber. When nothing happened, she carefully opened the door and peered in.

Arline lay on her side on the floor. Her two sisters were passed out in chairs with their heads slumped forward. Joan waved for Beatrice to hurry inside.

"They all three drank the tea!" Beatrice said excitedly. "Hurry, now. Go get Edward and Tom."

Joan hurried from the room and Beatrice barred the door behind her. She turned around and stared down at Arline. It was quite difficult for Beatrice to not let out a happy squeal. Things were going as she had planned them.

She strolled around Arline's sleeping form, a victorious smile painted on her face. "Ye may be an *honorable* woman, Lady Arline. But yer a damned fool! I'm sorry, *me lady*, but I canna allow ye to marry Rowan. It wasn't in my plans, ye ken."

There was far too much at stake to allow Arline to marry Rowan. Beatrice had no strong affection for the man, but still, he was an integral part to gaining everything that she had ever wanted and desired.

Joan quickly returned with Edward and Tom. Beatrice unbarred the door and quickly ushered them in. The men carried Morralyn and Geraldine to Arline's dressing room and set them in the dark corner. When they returned, they set about rolling Arline into one of the large carpets. Edward hoisted Arline up and over his shoulder while Tom grabbed a trunk from the dressing room.

Beatrice gave a quick perusal to make certain no one could detect what was really inside the rolled up carpet. Once she was satisfied, she gave a nod of her head. "Quickly now, to the wagon. They're all too busy to notice anythin', but be careful! Remember, there be a reward fer ye after ye get to Edinburgh."

Edward and Tom gave a curt nod and left Beatrice and Joan alone in the room.

Beatrice turned to Joan and smiled. "'Tis time fer me to go marry Rowan Graham!"

Thomas thought it only slightly odd that Arline had not waited for him to escort her to the chapel. He supposed she was tired of waiting and much too excited to start the ceremony.

He met her as she came down the stairs, alone. She wore a beautiful, blue gossamer gown that trailed several feet behind her. A heavy veil was draped completely over her head, covering her face in its entirety and he wondered how she could see. Women's fashions were not something he paid much attention to.

"Are ye ready, lass?" Thomas asked as he offered her his arm.

All that he received was an excited nod as she placed her hand on his arm.

Thomas led her out of the keep and to the chapel. "I ken that I wasna too keen on the idea of Rowan marryin' ye, lass. I'm glad I took me time and came to know ye. Yer a fine woman fer him. Ye make him verra happy. And I be verra proud to be escortin' ye to him this day."

He heard a sniffle and watched as a hand lifted to wipe a tear.

"Och!" Thomas smiled down at her and patted her hand. "I didna mean to make ye cry! But I reckon women more easily show their feelin's than men."

They walked the rest of the way in silence. Thomas could feel Arline tremble ever so slightly. He supposed she was nervous as well as excited. Domnal greeted them at the door of the chapel.

"Are ye ready, me lady?" Domnal asked with a smile.

She paused a moment, then gave a nod. Domnal opened the door a slight cracked, poked his head inside. He gave a nod to the priest before opening the door all the way.

Thomas cleared his throat, patted Arline's hand again and guided her inside.

Lily was waiting with Selina just inside the doorway.

Selina knew the moment she saw Arline that something was wrong. She stepped forward, her brow knitted. "Me lady," she whispered. "What happened to yer dress?"

Beatrice had to think quickly for some reasonable explanation and could only pray that Selina would not recognize her voice. "Tea," she whispered her reply.

Selina's face paled. "Och!" she exclaimed. "Ye spilled tea on it?"

Beatrice nodded her reply.

"Ye poor thing!"

Lily stepped forward and pulled on Beatrice's dress. "I kept me dress clean, Arline!" she told her proudly.

It took a great deal of effort not to shoo the child away. Beatrice had never been fond of children and was even less fond of this one. She hated how Rowan constantly fawned over the child, bragged about how smart she was, how beautiful she was. Doing her best not to give herself away, she gave Lily a pat on her head before looking down the aisle.

There he was. The man she'd soon be married to. She was not worried over what he'd do once he found out he had married her instead of the insipid Lady Arline. By the time he realized what had happened it would be far too late for him to undo it.

She stood taller, thrust her shoulders back and raised her chin. Lily was chatting on about something, but Beatrice ignored her. Besides, it was nearly impossible to understand a thing that came out of the child's mouth, what with her lisp and inability to pronounce her r's and l's.

She took a deep breath and urged Thomas forward, quite ready to become Rowan Graham's wife.

T he moment he set eyes on his *bride,* the hair on the back of his neck raised and his skin prickled. His stomach tightened and he knew, beyond a shadow of a doubt, that something was horribly wrong.

He forced a smile and leaned in to speak with Findley. "Do no' give on that something is wrong, Findley. But I tell ye, that is *no'* me bride," he whispered. "Spread the word to the men."

Findley feigned a happy smile as he patted Rowan on the back. "What do ye mean that be no' yer bride?"

"That is *no'* Arline," he whispered.

"How do ye ken?"

"That woman has a bosom. In case ye haven't noticed, Arline is tall and quite slender." Rowan's stomach began to churn with anger. "And where be her sisters? They were to walk in front of her."

Findley looked up, still smiling, and studied the woman. Figuring that Rowan would know better than anyone if the woman was his bride or not, he turned to whisper in Duncan's ear. Within moments, word was spread amongst the men standing next to Findley as well as those stationed around the chapel.

To the untrained eye, Rowan was nothing more than an excited groom. He waited at the altar with a broad smile plastered to his face. His insides however, were one big knot of anger and worry. He

347

scanned the faces of the guests as Thomas began to walk the woman down the aisle. He recognized many of the faces. Not wanting to cause alarm or worse yet an all-out brawl, he remained mute. Who knew if this woman had any accomplices or not? If she did, and Rowan moved too quickly, lives could be at stake.

Thomas detected something wrong in Rowan's countenance. He also took note of the whispers between the men. Something *was* wrong, he just did not know yet what it was. He would wait for a signal from Rowan before he acted.

Playing the part of the beaming groom, Rowan smiled as he took her hand from Thomas. "Thank ye kindly, Thomas, fer bringin' me bride to me."

Thomas nodded and stepped to the side. Rowan took his bride the last few steps toward the altar and stood quietly before the priest.

Rowan leaned in and whispered in the woman's ear.

"If ye so much as move a muscle, I shall thrust me blade into yer side."

She tensed ever so slightly and Rowan could feel her tremble. If the woman made any kind of gesture, instigated any trouble amongst the crowd, he would do as he had promised. If she had the courage to look at him, she would see the sincerity and the fury in his eyes. If anything had happened to Arline, he'd have no problems killing the woman standing beside him.

"Where the bloody hell is Arline, *Beatrice?*"

As soon as she was next to him and he smelled the cloying sent of roses, Rowan knew who was hidden behind the heavy veil. He never cared for the scent of roses. The only woman he ever knew to wear it was Lady Beatrice.

The question of *how* she gained entry could wait for later. For now, he had to find out where Arline was and if Beatrice had men in waiting to attack.

"Do ye have men in the pews?"

She refused to answer, refused to move.

"Beatrice, I swear to ye that I will ring yer bloody neck if ye do no' answer me. Do ye have men here?"

The priest leaned forward with a look of concern on his face. "Be there a problem, Rowan?" he asked.

Rowan looked up and smiled. "Nothin' we canna handle, father."

"Yer a bloody bastard," Beatrice seethed. *Damn him, damn him, damn him!* "Aye, I have fifty men in the pews and five hundred more waitin' beyond the walls to attack."

He smiled and looked over his shoulder. One look at the faces behind him and he knew she lied. Mayhap one or two, but not fifty.

He turned back to the priest. "Me bride and I need a moment alone, father. She doesna feel at all well."

Rowan yanked on Beatrice's arm and led her away from the altar toward the priest's office. Findley followed while Duncan remained behind. Whispers erupted through the crowd, curious as to why the bride and groom suddenly left before the ceremony had even begun.

Wee William left his spot in the front row to come speak with Duncan. "What the bloody hell is wrong?" he asked.

Duncan put a hand on Wee William's shoulder and drew him down so that he could tell him. The rest of the men began to spread out through the crowd, waiting, watching each person for the slightest sign of trouble.

When Duncan finished explaining the situation as he knew it, Wee William rose to his full height. "Damn."

THIRTY-ONE

Within a quarter of an hour, Rowan had the information he needed. He hadn't learned it from Beatrice but from her maid, Joan, who had promised to tell him all that she knew only if Rowan would keep Beatrice from killing her.

He left Wee William behind to help guard the keep. Findley, Duncan, and Thomas along with twenty-five of Rowan's best men, thundered behind him as he led the way out of the keep.

Rowan knew he was in pursuit of a wagon, driven by two paid men. The same wagon that Beatrice and Joan had hidden themselves in, in a false bottom, to gain entry. Beatrice was taken to the dungeon and he did not care one wit if Arline thought it too cruel a punishment. Beatrice was lucky he hadn't ordered her to hang.

He also knew that Joan had slipped the sleeping potion into Arline's tea. He hadn't bothered to ask *why* for it simply did not matter. If he found Arline alive and unharmed, he would ask Beatrice the whys of it later. If she was harmed, Beatrice would not live long enough to answer any questions.

The wagon was easy enough to follow for it left tracks in the snow and mud. Still, the men who had smuggled Arline out of the keep had at least a one hour head start. Rowan prayed that the two men who drove the wagon weren't stupid enough to do anything to harm Arline.

Many heads would roll this day. As soon as he got Arline back.

Fury simmered, just at the edge. If the men in the wagon felt the need to defend themselves, they'd not have long to live. Part of him hoped that the fools would try something stupid, just so he'd have the excuse to gut them.

A rline was having the oddest dream. She was being jostled about, like onions in a bowl. 'Twas an odd dream for a woman to have on her wedding day.

She felt groggy, disoriented, and quite nauseous. Her tongue, thick and dry, stuck to the roof of her mouth. An incessant throbbing in her head made her wonder if she hadn't drunk too much at her wedding feast.

She tried to shake the fog from her head, but felt resistance. She tried lifting her hands to rub her throbbing temples, but something barred their movement. Were her hands tied?

Panic set in. Through the fog, her memory started to come back. She'd been in her room with Morralyn and Geraldine. They had just drunk a toast to something tawdry…then she remembered. She'd been drugged!

Bloody hell! She tried moving but soon realized her hands weren't tied. She was bundled up in something. She wriggled and tried to kick her feet, but met more resistance. She was bound in something, from head to toe. Breathing became more difficult as the panic welled.

Good sense finally took over. It warned that she would smother if she did not remain calm. It was not an easy feat to tamp down the fear.

She was jostled once again and the force of it rolled her to her back. Although sound was muffled, she could very well deduce that she was in a wagon. Drugged and being taken away from the keep, from Rowan and Lily.

Anger and determination soon replaced the fear and panic. Angry that whoever had drugged her was stealing her away to God only knew where. And fully determined not to allow it to happen.

She stopped her struggle to think and to feel what she could with her hands and feet. If she could just get her hands on the seam, hold tightly to it, she might be able to unroll herself from the carpet. She knew it was a thick carpet, not a tapestry, for it felt far too heavy and too smooth to be anything else. More likely than not, it was the same carpet that had covered the floor near her bed.

Carefully, she felt around with fingertips and toes, but came up empty. The wagon hit another bump of some sort. The jolt took her rolling again, onto her stomach. Mustering her strength, she wriggled until she was on her side. That made breathing much easier.

Focused intently on maneuvering her way out of the carpet, the wagon came to an unexpected halt. She wasn't sure if she should feel relieved or more terrified. Either they had reached their destination or Rowan had found her. *Please dear lord, let it be Rowan!*

She lay still and strained her ears to listen. The carpet blocked out nearly all sound. Everything was muffled and disjointed. Her heart pounded against her breast as she tried to think of what to do next.

It felt as though hours had passed before she felt someone tugging on the carpet. She was being pulled along the bottom of the wagon in great tugs. *Please, please, please be Rowan!*

She was lifted out of the wagon and laid on the ground. At least they hadn't tossed her into a loch or a river! A small miracle, but now there was hope of getting out of this alive.

A moment later, the carpet was being tugged again, and she soon felt herself being rolled out of it, all the while praying that it was Rowan, and not her captors. In a flash, she decided to run like the devil the moment she was free of the carpet. She'd only stop if she heard Rowan's voice.

Another tug and roll and she was free! The bright sunshine stung her eyes as she rolled to her stomach, pushed herself to her feet and took to flight!

Or at least she had tried to. She hadn't taken three steps when large arms encircled her waist and pulled her off her feet.

"Wheesht, me lady!"

She recognized that voice. It did not belong to Rowan or any of his men. Fear enveloped her clear to her toes. Why on earth was *he* here and why had he taken her?

R owan and his men pounded across the countryside, following the wagon tracks. He could not help but feel that he would soon find the wagon and the men who had taken his Arline. They'd been riding for nearly an hour, hell-bent for leather, chasing down the whoresons. A wagon could not travel as fast or cover as much ground as a man on horseback, especially a man like Rowan Graham. With unwavering determination to get his bride back, he urged his horse on. Mud and slush kicked up with each thundering step his mount took, splattering his boots and legs, and occasionally, his face.

Sweat blended with mud, fury with agonizing worry over Arline. He had to get her back, he could not lose her, not now, not after all they had gone through.

They continued to follow the road as it wound its way north and west. His dread and fury grew exponentially with each gut wrenching moment that passed by without coming upon the wagon.

Joan had told them that the men were taking Arline to the ruins of an auld kirk that lay near Loch Rannoch. Once they were there, they were to kill her and leave her body for the scavengers and wolves.

The tracks headed in that direction. Rowan prayed that the men would do as they'd been instructed and not decide to kill her sooner. He swore that if he found her alive, he'd never allow her a moment alone. She'd be under constant guard, four men surrounding her at all times when she was not with him. He would spend every waking moment protecting her.

Soon, they came upon a bend in the road. Not far ahead was the wagon they had been searching for. It was stopped in the middle of the road and he could not see anyone. Not the driver, his accomplice nor Arline. His heart plummeted to his feet, his dread crashing around him.

They raced toward the wagon. Rowan slid from his horse before it had even stopped. He rushed forward with his sword drawn. He saw the empty carpet lying on the ground, quickly inspected it for signs of blood. Nothing.

Findley and Duncan had soon approached, with swords at the ready. They walked to the front of the wagon. Fresh blood covered the seat and the floor.

"Rowan!" Duncan called out as he began to scan the forest.

Rowan rushed to the front of the wagon and followed Findley's gaze. "Blood?" he asked.

"Aye, and lots of it," Findley answered.

Rowan ordered the men to fan out and search for Arline and what might be left of the two men. Rowan was encased in dread and fear as he tried to figure out what had happened.

With Beatrice's help, two men had stolen Arline away from the keep. Now the two men were missing and so was Arline. Had she somehow managed to kill the two men, then flee?

A warning niggled at the back of his mind. It was his fervent hope that she had somehow managed to stab the two men. Mayhap she had only wounded them and they were now chasing her through the woods.

"Rowan! Here!" a voice called out not far from where he stood.

He, Findley and Duncan followed the voice. They soon came upon one of Rowan's men. He was looking down at the ground.

Rowan braced himself for the worst and followed the man's gaze.

He'd found the drivers.

Their throats had been cut and they'd been tossed one atop the other on the ground. Rowan knew that Arline did not possess the strength to carry the men this far from the road. He surveyed the ground and found no signs they had been drug. They'd been carried.

He crouched low, looking for some sign, something, anything to guide him on what he should do next. He found a pair of boot prints in the snow. They led to the two men, then away, back toward the wagon.

Rowan led his friends and men back to the wagon where they

immediately began to look for more signs. Duncan found a set of boot prints, similar to those they'd discovered in the woods. He also found a set of hoof prints.

"Looks like one man, one horse," Duncan said as he studied the tracks. "They look verra fresh and run to the east. I do no' think we're far behind them."

Rowan ground his jaws together and wound his hands into fists. He found himself in the same position he was in just a few short hours ago. Someone had taken Arline and he had no bloody idea who or why.

"Mount up!" Rowan barked as he headed to his horse.

He'd get her back, one way or another.

They had not been riding long when she figured out that he had lied to her when he said he was taking her back to *Áit na Síochána*. They were traveling in the opposite direction. He had lied. He wasn't taking her home.

At first, she thought she could trust him, for he was one of the shadow men. He had killed the two men who had taken her and promised that he was there to help her. "I'll take ye home, me lady," he had promised with a smile.

In hindsight, she should have inquired as to which home. They were heading toward Blackthorn lands. Certainly, he could not mean to take her there.

Her arms were wrapped around his waist as she rode behind him. Her wedding dress had not been designed for travel and did little to keep out the cold. The hem was now ruined, wet from all the mud and slush the horse kicked up as they traveled through the woods.

She knew the further they rode away from *Áit na Síochána*, the less chance Rowan had of finding her. In her heart she knew he had figured out she was missing. He loved her and he would come for her, of that, she had no doubt.

In order to survive whatever lay ahead of her, she knew she must feign ignorance and trust. She decided to play along and at the same time, try to gain some information as to why Archie had supposedly come to her rescue only to end up lying to her.

"Archie," she said as she adjust her rump. "How did ye come to find me?"

"I was at *Áit na Síochána*, watchin' over ye as is me sworn duty. When we learned ye'd been taken, I set off before the others to find ye."

She did not believe him. "I see," she murmured. "Where exactly are we goin' now? I do no' think *Áit na Síochána*, is in this direction."

"I didn't say I was takin' ye back to *Áit na Síochána*, me lady."

She sat upright. "But ye said ye were taken me home." Familiar panic began to rise and she hoped he had not detected it.

"Aye, I did."

She was growing frustrated with his elusive answers. "But me home is *Áit na Síochána*."

She felt him grow tense. He hunched his shoulder and cracked his neck. "It was yer home, me lady. I fear I canna take ye back there."

"Why not?" Even she detected the fear in her own voice.

"I canna let ye marry Rowan Graham. I ken that is what ye want, but I canna let ye do that."

"Please, Archie, explain to me why ye canna allow it?"

"I need ye to marry another."

Her mouth opened in surprise. "Marry another? I do no' understand, Archie."

He let out a frustrated breath. "Yer da waits no' far from here. We have another that ye must marry and we need ye to do it fer Scotland."

What the bloody hell did he mean by that? "Marry someone fer the good of Scotland?"

He responded with a nod. "I be sorry, me lady, but we've no' other choice. Ye need to marry the man we've chosen fer yet."

"We?" she asked indignantly. "Who is *we?*"

He remained silent for a time. "How much do ye ken of yer last two marriages?"

She told him she didn't understand his question.

"Yer marriage to Carlich turned out to be quite fortuitous for

357

Robert Stewart. When yer da learned how helpful ye'd been at rootin' out two of the traitors, he came to Robert with an offer. In exchange for a substantial amount of coin, he'd work with Robert to arrange another marriage with another suspected traitor."

Her blood ran cold and the hairs on her neck rose.

"We long suspected Lombard de Sotuhans. We had been workin' a verra long time to prove he was funneling money to the small group of men who want to bring Scotland to her knees and see England rein over her. We believed ye'd be a verra good distraction for de Sotuhans. Ye could keep him busy while we sought the information we needed."

Robert Stewart had betrayed her. He had sworn that he would always protect her, had given her a letter to use if ever she were in trouble and the shadow men could not be found. In the end, he had betrayed her trust. The knowledge left her chilled to the bone.

"But the fool died before we could get ye to him."

Where on earth would she be at this moment if the man had not died?

"We had also long suspected the elder Blackthorn as well. I was the one that suggested to Garrick that he add the stipulation of *no bairns* to the contract. It was the only way to get him to agree. If he hadn't, ye'd been married to his da."

Another small miracle. Though Garrick's father was not as mean and heartless as his son, the thought of being married to him made her ill.

"So I've been nothin' more than an unwitting spy?" she spoke into his back.

He answered with stone silence.

She was nothing more than a pawn to be used by Robert Stewart and her father. She had grown up knowing her father did not care about her happiness. But she had trusted Robert Stewart. His betrayal of her trust left a bitter taste in her mouth.

"Me lady, I ken that ye love Rowan. He's a good man," Archie said as he looked over his shoulder at her. "But the marriage has already been arranged. We've three men left that we suspect of workin' with the English."

"Bah!" Arline cried out. "Do ye expect me to marry all three?"

"Nay, me lady. We hope that ye'll be able to get the information we need from Phillip Randall. If yer successful, ye'll be rewarded with a home of yer own, anywhere ye wish to live. 'Tis fer the good of Scotland that ye must do this. Mayhap, Rowan will wait fer ye and ye can marry him in the future."

She knew he was trying to appeal to her sense of honor and loyalty. He was also dangling a bit of hope in front of her nose. But wait to marry Rowan? She made a decision then and there. Slowly, she let her arms go slack and she slid from the horse.

Wait to marry Rowan? Not bloody likely!

R owan and his men raced across the glen and followed the tracks into another dense thicket of woods. There, they were forced to slow their pace, which sent Rowan's anger to new heights. When doubt as to Arline's safety and well-being crept in, he pushed them away. He could not think of her injured, harmed, or dead. When he did, his heart would sink with the weight of heartache he had not felt since Kate's death.

There was not as much deep snow in this part of the forest for it was protected under the wide canopy of evergreen trees. The trees themselves were blanketed with snow, but the ground was more mud and slush than anything else.

The men walked for a time and eventually picked up the tracks again. They had turned in a northwesterly direction. Looking up at the sun taking its late afternoon descent, Rowan mumbled a curse and started for his horse. He had to find her before nightfall. Without lanterns or torches, 'twould be next to impossible to follow their tracks.

Rowan was just about to mount his horse again when Findley held up his hand. "Listen!" he said in a sharp whisper.

Rowan strained his ears. For a moment, all he could hear was the breeze as it tickled the evergreens. Moments later, he thought he heard a shout coming from up ahead. His heart pounded as he climbed onto his horse and urged he and his men forward.

There was a possibility that it was nothing more than a farmer out searching for an errant cow. His heart raced as they made their way through the evergreens. *Please, God, let it be Arline and let her be well.*

S he ran from Archie as if he were the devil. With the hem of her dress clutched tightly in one hand, she tore through the trees and brush. An overwhelming sense of deja vu fell over her. She'd fled through trees and thick underbrush months ago to get away from Garrick's men. Now she fled to get away from a man sworn to protect her.

Arline did not worry that he'd kill her if he caught her. Nay, she was far too important to the ridiculous scheme her father had concocted.

She didn't necessarily run in hopes of freedom. Nay, it was nothing more than a means to delay what was most likely the inevitable. If she could find a decent place to hide, she could wait until Rowan found her. That was her sole goal at running; to stall, to find Rowan the time he'd need to find her.

She ignored his calls for her to stop. Dipping under low hanging branches, crashing through bare bushes, she ran in zigzag fashion in hopes of confusing him with her tracks.

Not knowing if he remained on his horse or had left it to chase her on foot, she continued to run as fast as her legs would carry her. The cold snow and slush stung her slippered feet, the branches scratched at her dress. Still, she pushed forward.

Not far ahead she saw a large felled tree. She ran around it, stopped long enough to see if it would make a good hiding place. It had fallen over a good sized dip in the land. If she could wriggle her way under it, she could hide from Archie.

His voice was growing nearer as he called out for her to come back. Not very likely!

"Ye'll freeze to death, me lady!" Archie's voice rang through the trees. "I canna allow ye to die! Come back and we'll start a fire!"

She'd rather freeze to death than return to Archie and subsequently her father. She ran around a few evergreens and backtracked to the log. Panting, covered in sweat, she dug her way through the slush. There was not much room, but enough that should anyone walk by they could not see her. She lay on her side with her back pressed against the cold earth and prayed.

R owan did not know who it was that was yelling. He could barely make out what the man was shouting. But it was enough that he could ascertain the man was yelling for Arline.

Rowan and the others dismounted, leaving their horses where they stood. Not one man made a sound as Rowan waved directions for them to fan out. Rowan and Findley carefully made their way through the band of evergreens while the rest of the men spread out.

The man's shouting drew nearer and became clearer.

"Damn it, Arline! I need ye to come back!"

Rowan and Findley gave each other a curious glance as they stilled themselves to listen further. Hope rose with the realization that Arline was alive!

"I swear if ye do no' come back, I'll kill Rowan meself!"

Rowan stiffened. Whoever this stranger was, he knew Arline well enough to call her by her first name and to threaten her with Rowan's life. Rowan sent a silent prayer that Arline would not cower to the man's threats.

Rowan nodded at Findley and pointed him to wind his way around to the east, while Rowan set off for the west. His goal was to surround the man and bring him down before he could find Arline.

As stealthy as cat-o-mountains surrounding unsuspecting prey, Rowan and Findley spread out, careful to listen for Arline as well as the stranger.

A rline heard Archie's footfalls as he approached her hiding place. She watched as his booted feet stomped through the slush as he passed by. Holding her breath, her body stiffening with fear as he continued to call out his threats.

"I swear it, Arline! By God I swear I'll kill him! If ye want to see Rowan live, ye'll come back now!"

Arline was confident that *that* would not happen. Rowan was a warrior who could take care of himself. She'd not let Archie's threats make her fearful.

She closed her eyes and tried to take in slow breaths as she listened to Archie continue his tirade.

"And after I kill Rowan? I will kill his daughter!"

Her heart leapt to her throat. Lily. Lily could not defend herself. She was but a babe! What if Archie grew weary of chasing Arline and returned to the keep? He was supposed to be a protector, not a killer, of innocents!

Archie's first and only allegiance was to Scotland. His sole purpose in life was to ensure Scotland remained free. If that meant killing an innocent child, then so be it. Scotland was bigger than any one person.

Bile rose, she chased it back and swallowed. If anything happened to Lily, she could never forgive herself. Rowan would never be the same.

She was not given the opportunity to weigh her options or devise any further plans of escape or keeping Lily safe. A large hand reached into her tiny hiding spot, grabbed her by her hair and yanked her out.

She did not go without a fight. Kicking, screaming, clawing, she fought against Archie.

"Settle yerself down!" he barked, grabbing her arms and hoisting her to her feet.

She saw it then, plainly, without question or doubt. Sheer, unadulterated anger and determination stared back at her through hazel eyes. In that instant, she knew, Archie would do whatever he must to get her to her father, to secure Scotland's future.

"I swear, I'll kill every last person that ye love, if you do no' listen to me!" Squeezing her arms, he shook her violently.

To her soul, she believed him.

Giving her a good yank, he pulled her along, back to where he'd left his horse. "Do no' even think of runnin' away again, *me lady*. I'll no' look fer ye again. I'll go straight back to *Áit na Síochána*."

She was too angry to cry. Believing that if she could slow down their pace, Rowan would be able to find her and put an end to this mess. "I'm of an age!" she spat at him. "I no longer have to heed me da's bidding!"

Archie stopped, spun her around and grabbed her arms again. "'Tisn't yer da's bidding, but mine! Ye do this because it be *the right thing to do*." His voice was low, menacing. It sent shivers running up and down Arline's spine.

He had tried appealing to her sense of honor and loyalty, had threatened to kill everyone she loved. Now, he flung her own words at her, wielding them like a weapon.

As she struggled against his tight hold, she thought she caught the flicker of movement out of the corner of her eyes. Fervently, she prayed it was not her father's men.

"Have I no' already given enough fer *yer* country?" She growled. "Ye ferget, I am from Ireland, no' Scotland! My first fealty is to my own home country!"

"Ye gave up Ireland when ye married Carlich, ye foolish woman!"

Her struggling only made him angrier, still, she persisted in her attempt to stall him. As she struggled, she saw the flicker again and it was drawing closer. "I'll no agree to it, Archie! I will no' do it!"

"Och!" he threw his head back in frustration and yelled. "Why? Why must ye be so damned foolish?"

Arline could see and feel his fury bubbling to the surface. Spittle formed in the corner of his mouth. She began to fear he'd have no compunction about killing her.

Enraged and furious, he tossed her to the ground and with drew his dirk. Arline's eyes widened in terror. He was no longer her sworn protector, but a man hell bent on a mission.

"I should simply slice yer throat!" His voice echoed through the forest. He grabbed her by the hair and lifted her head as he placed the dirk against her throat.

"Nay!" she scratched out pleadingly. "Archie, do no' do this!"

Something flashed in his eyes. His lips pursed together. He appeared to be mulling over his options when the sound of a twig snapping behind him drew his attention away from her.

Findley and Rowan were standing not ten feet away, with broadswords drawn and expressions of complete determination alight on both their faces.

"Step away from her, and I'll let ye live." Rowan's voice was as cold and firm as the blade of steel he held in his hand.

Arline's relief at seeing Rowan was short lived. She lay between the two men, afraid to utter a sound or move the tiniest of muscles. Archie snatched her hair up again and yanked her to her feet. She groaned and tried to pry her hair from his hands. He yanked harder and pressed the dirk against her throat again. "Rowan, I swear I'll kill her if ye do no' leave us be."

Rowan cocked his head slightly. "Ye'll be dead before she hits the ground."

"If he doesna kill ye, then I will," came a voice from behind. Archie spun around to see Duncan just a few steps away from him, with his sword drawn.

"Let her go, and ye'll live," Rowan repeated. "Harm her, and ye are as good as dead."

Archie pulled Arline closer, using her as a shield, pressing her firmly against his chest. He wrapped one arm around her neck while he pressed the dirk against her throat. Taking careful steps backward, he was dragging Arline along with him. His breathing became jagged and harsh, like an animal caught in a trap.

"Ye dunna understand!" he yelled at Rowan. "This is fer Scotland! Fer her freedom!"

"Ye put too much faith in one person," Rowan said. "What can she do that hundreds of others have no' tried or done before her? Why is she so bloody important?"

Archie paused, still clutching a very terrified Arline to his chest. "He's right, Archie!" she squeaked out. "Ye can find another to help ye."

He cocked his head to get a better look at her. His expression told her he thought she was insane. "Another? Nay! Ye be the only one we can trust. Ye be the only one with a sense of duty and honor!"

He began dragging her away again. "I canna be the only woman in all of Scotland, Archie! I canna be the only one who can do what ye ask!"

"Shut up!" he howled at her. "Shut up!"

He jerked harder, increasing the pressure of his arm. If he did not stop, he'd either end up strangling her or breaking her neck. She looked to Rowan who followed them step for step. His eyes told of steadfast resolve to see her through this alive and unharmed. It bolstered her spirits and gave her hope. She made a split decision, one that she hoped would not cause Rowan's death, or her own.

Pretending to faint, she let her entire body go limp. Archie fought to keep her on her feet, but with one arm holding the dirk and the other around her upper chest, he was hard pressed to manage it.

He howled in frustration and let loose his hold on her. Arline fell to the ground in a heap, while Rowan, Duncan and Findley sprang into action.

Archie continued his retreat. Unsheathing his broadsword, he held it outward with one hand, the dirk in the other. Waving them back and forth and the three men approached.

"If Scotland falls, I'll make sure the whole world kens it to be yer fault, Rowan Graham!"

"If Scotland falls, it will no' be because of me or Arline. It will be because cowards and traitors," Rowan said as he pursued Archie.

Once Arline heard the men walking away, she pushed herself up to her feet. Though she no longer feared for her own safety, she did fear for Rowan's. Of the men surrounding Archie, Rowan was the closest.

"That is what we are tryin' to avoid, ye fool!"

"I be no more a fool than ye, if ye think one slip of a woman can save Scotland."

She didn't take it as a personal affront. Arline knew Rowan was simply trying to get matters under control.

Archie lunged forward, toward Rowan. Rowan saw it coming and jumped sideways. The blade of Archie's sword barely missed Rowan's abdomen. Too stunned and terrified to move, Arline could only stand by and watch, utterly helpless to do anything.

Findley took note of Arline's distress. Uncertain if she would fall to pieces or do something foolish and attempt to intercede on Rowan's behalf, Findley went to her side. With one hand on her shoulder and one on her elbow, he stood beside her and tried to offer her some reassurance.

"Rowan's good with his sword, me lady. Ye needn't worry."

Arline thought his statement one of the most ridiculous that she had heard of late. Do not worry? How could she not?

"Lad, ye do no' want to do this," Rowan told Archie. "Put yer sword away and ye can live."

Incensed, Archie refused to back down. "Nay! I shall no'! Ye dunna understand what yer up against, Rowan. 'Tis something much bigger than either of us. Let me take Arline and ye can go on about yer life!" Rowan met Archie's sword as he swung it sideways, successfully blocking his shot.

There was not much room in the tiny clearing amongst the evergreen trees. Soon, the perimeter was surrounded with Rowan's men. They would not interfere or act on his behalf unless it was absolutely necessary. This was a fight that Rowan had to battle alone.

Rowan made no attempts to swing or thrust. Archie was too angry, too infuriated to battle well. His movements were jerky, choppy, and Rowan knew he would soon wear out and tire. All Rowan need do was take a defensive stance, block the unbalanced and erratic thrusts, jabs, and swings.

Archie grew more frustrated with each swing that missed his intended target. He was coming apart at the seams, losing control; something shadow men never did. He tried channeling his anger, controlling it. He was slipping and he knew it.

Hope was quickly replaced with despair. He was surrounded by

Graham men. Good, decent men who were loyal to Scotland, but they were first loyal to Rowan, which in his mind made them just as dangerous as the traitors he sought. He needed more men to help him fight Rowan and the men of Clan Graham. If he could just get to his horse, he could go to the camp where Arline's father awaited them. In little time, he could have at least fifty men at his disposal, men who would fight tooth and nail to get Arline back.

As he contemplated his next move, turning in circles, thrusting his sword wildly, Rowan stumbled over a large rock and fell backward, landing on his back.

Archie took no time in making his move. He lifted his sword high above his head, ready to plunge it into Rowan's chest. The only way to get Arline to agree to marry anyone was to kill Rowan Graham.

Duncan acted swiftly before Archie could bring his sword down. Flinging his knife through the air, it landed exactly where he had aimed: left of the breastbone, straight into his heart. Archie fell to his knees, still holding his broadsword high above his head.

Rowan rolled away before Archie fell forward, plunging the knife in even further. The sickening sound of blood as it gurgled in his throat and sputtered from his mouth made Arline turn into Findley's chest and cover her ears with her hands.

Duncan immediately came to Rowan's side, extended his arm and helped him to his feet.

Rowan let out a big breath of air, shook his head and thanked his friend. "Thank ye, kindly Duncan," he said as the color finally returned to his face. "I thought fer certain I was dead!"

Duncan gave him a firm slap on his back. "No man should die on his weddin' day!"

Rowan gave him a quick nod before he rushed to Arline. He pulled her away from Findley and held her close, rubbing her back, and offering soothing words of comfort.

"Wheesht, lass, I be well. 'Tis over."

Arline knew it wasn't over. It would never be over until she settled matters with her father once and for all.

Someone offered a cloak to Rowan who carefully wrapped it

around Arline's shoulders. "Come, let us go home," he said as he kissed her cheek.

More than anything, she wanted to return to *Áit na Síochána.* She wanted to marry Rowan and begin a life with him. Fearful that her father or one of the shadow men would eventually interfere with that plan, Arline shook her head.

"Nay, Rowan," she said firmly. "There is one more matter we must deal with before we go home."

THIRTY-TWO

Arline sat on Rowan's lap as they headed to her father's encampment. With his arms protectively folded around her, Arline explained matters as best she could and as she knew them. The more Rowan learned, the more furious he became. Grinding his teeth together, he remained silent as he listened to her tell her tale, beginning with the events that took place more than seven years ago.

She left nothing out. She told him about Robert Stewart, the letter in Carlich's box, the shadow men; everything was laid bare before him.

He was proud of his wife. Aye, they weren't married in the biblical sense just yet -- he hoped to have that issue resolved completely before the sun rose on the morrow -- but still, he thought of her as his wife. Although she'd been through much these past seven years, had been married to two suspected traitors to Scotland, had been beaten, nearly killed by an arrow, drugged and taken from her home, she still held on to her dignity and pride. She hadn't fallen to pieces, hadn't cowered in fear. Nay, she faced it full on, as brave as any warrior he knew.

And she was about to face one of the main sources of her fear. She'd not back down from her father. She'd not cry or plead or beg.

The more she talked, the more indomitable she became. Rowan was quite glad to have her as an ally and soon, as his wife.

Her father's encampment was not far from where Archie lost his life. He was housed in a small clearing, scattered with tents and fires. A quick survey told Rowan that Arline's father had mayhap only twenty men with him. Most of them looked barely old enough to have sprouted chest hair.

Rowan stopped near a group of lads sitting around a fire. "Where is Orthanach Fitzgerald?"

Three sets of fearful and confused eyes stared back at him. Only one lad moved. He raised an arm and pointed toward a group of larger tents. "He's in the big one at the end," the lad answered nervously.

Apparently Orthanach had not felt it necessary to bring men or soldiers instead of inexperienced lads, who didn't even bother to inquire as to who he was or what he was doing here.

That could prove a fatal assumption on his part.

Rowan clicked his tongue and urged his horse forward. They passed a few more young men, all with the same confused looks on their faces as the lad who had directed him toward Orthanach's tent.

Rowan brought his horse to a stop, swung a leg over and lowered himself down. His men followed suit, each of them keeping a watchful eye on their surroundings. Rowan lifted Arline down from the horse and took her hand in his.

He did not stop to ask her if she was certain she wanted to face her father. Her green eyes flickered with purpose. She would do this and he would stand beside her while she did it.

Rowan held the tent flap open while Arline ducked inside. He followed in behind her, but remained back a few steps, with his hand on the hilt of his sword.

The tent was large. A full-sized bed stood off to the right. Finely upholstered chairs sat around a large round table. Carpets adorned the floors while tapestries hung on the walls. Dozens of lit candles, some in silver candlesticks, others in large candelabras, were scattered about the room. Ostentatious was the first word that came to Rowan's mind.

Orthanach Fitzgerald sat behind a long table in an ornately carved chair. His booted feet were propped up on the table as he held a document in his long slender fingers.

He had short-cropped light brown hair that had grayed at his temples. His nose seemed far too large for his hollow-cheeked face. Dull blue-gray eyes looked up, first at Arline then at Rowan.

Orthanach made no effort to stand. He carefully laid the document down, twined his fingers together and rested them on his belly.

"Arline."

There was no warmth in his voice, no sign of fatherly affection.

Arline refused to offer him a curtsy as was due his station and title. She was not going to beat around the bush.

"I've been told ye arranged yet another marriage fer me."

He gave a barely perceptible nod of his.

"I'm here to tell ye that *that* won't be happenin'."

He breathed in deeply through his nostrils and let it out slowly. "What's done is done. We leave on the morrow, fer Edinburgh where ye will marry Phillip Randall."

Arline did not so much as bat an eye. She did not flinch or move or otherwise act afraid or frail. She stood her ground. "Nay, I shan't."

"Arline, do no' give me any grief over this. The arrangements have been made, the bride price paid. Ye shall go to Edinburgh and ye shall marry Phillip Randall."

Arline walked forward, placed her palms on the top of his desk and leaned in. "Nay. I shan't. I will no longer be yer pawn. I will no longer cower and bend to yer will. I am of an age where I can decide who I want or do no' want to marry."

Orthanach was about to speak when a small commotion began just outside the entry to the tent. Rowan lifted the flap and stepped aside.

Findley came in, bearing Archie's lifeless body over his shoulder. "Where do ye want, this Rowan?"

Rowan motioned toward the desk. Orthanach shot to his feet as he watched Findley give a curt nod to Rowan. He walked toward Orthanach and Arline, went to the side of the desk, and with a slight heave, he tossed Archie's body off his shoulder. It landed with a thud in a heap next to the desk.

Findley gave a slight nod and cast a smug grin at Orthanach and quit the tent.

Arline stood with her hands crossed over her chest and glared at her father. "I believe ye ken who that is?" she asked, giving a nod toward the dead body at her father's feet.

Orthanach was speechless. He looked dumbfounded as he stared at Arline.

"I ken him as well. Or did."

Orthanach looked down at Archie. He was visibly shaken and pale when he turned his attention back to Arline.

"Hear me, and hear me now," Arline began. Her tone was serious, firm, unyielding. "Ye will *never* contact me or me sisters. Ever. Ye shall leave the three of us in peace. No more barterin' fer marriages. No more bargains with Robert Stewart. I'll never be yer pawn again." She took a breath as she leaned forward to look him in the eye. "Ye will never threaten me, me sisters, me husband, me daughter, or any future children I may have. Ye shall never send the shadow men fer me or mine. Fer I swear if ye do, I will run me blade through yer heart, just like I did Archie's."

Orthanach didn't need to know who actually plunged the blade through Archie's heart. It was enough to keep him guessing, fearful, and understanding that she meant every word she spoke.

Orthanach leaned over the desk, placing his hands palms down on top of it. "Ye wouldna dare," he challenged her.

In the span of two heartbeats, Arline drew the dirk Rowan had given her and thrust it through her father's right hand until it hit wood.

For several long moments, he was too stunned to speak. He looked disbelievingly at the knife sticking through the top of his hand. Blood trickled from it.

Arline held on to the hilt and leaned in closer, her nose almost touching his. "That will be yer only warnin'. Heed me words or ye'll no' live to regret the day ye didn't."

Using both hands, she removed the knife from his hand, turned and walked away.

Blood spilled out and ran down his arm as he lifted it to his chest. "Ye stabbed me! Yer own father!" he cried out in shock and pain.

Arline stopped and turned back to him. "Remember, *that* was yer only warnin'. Ye'll no' get a second."

She took Rowan's hand and hurried from the tent. She didn't want her father to watch as the blood drained from her face. She didn't want him to see how ill she'd become.

Rowan climbed onto his horse, extended an arm to Arline and lifted her up. He wrapped his arms around her and without speaking, he took her away from the encampment.

Night had fallen but Arline begged Rowan not to make camp for the night. She wanted to go home, back to *Áit na Síochána*. She wanted to wrap Lily in her arms and hold her. She wanted to marry Rowan before dawn, and fall asleep in his arms.

A sense of peace, a kind of comforting peace she was not accustomed to, draped itself around her. Arline knew that her father was neither dumb enough or brave enough to test her promise. She was certain he would never bother her, her sisters or her family ever again.

She rested her head against Rowan's chest and wrapped her arms around his waist. How wonderful it would be to fall asleep like this each night, and wake to him each morn. She could barely wait to return home, to marry him, to start a new life and, hopefully, to bear him a few dozen children.

Much time passed before Rowan spoke. "So when we return to our keep, do ye wish to sleep?"

Arline nuzzled her cheek sleepily against his chest. "Nay, I do no' want to sleep. I want to find the priest, say our I do's, and begin our weddin' night. Or weddin' day, dependin' on how fast ye can get us home."

"Good, good," Rowan said. "And yer fully prepared to do yer wifely duty?" he asked playfully.

Arline sighed contentedly. "Well, here's the thing about that, Rowan. I've been talking to Ora, and a few of the womenfolk, ye ken. I'm told that I canna get with child if I just *do me duty*. Ye have to pleasure me in all sorts of ways, and many, many times. So if it's children ye be wantin', it seems *ye* have a husbandly duty to perform."

He threw his head back and laughed. "A husbandly duty, ye say?"

"Aye," she said with a yawn. "And 'tis a duty, I'm told, that ye must perform several times a day. Do ye think yer up fer that?"

Rowan kissed the top of her head and gave her a hug. "Aye, I suppose, if I'm to be a good husband to ye, I'm willin' to make such a sacrifice."

Arline giggled at his jest.

"Well, 'twould be the *right thing to do*."

THIRTY-THREE

I t had not been the wedding they had planned for the past three weeks. The pews were not filled to bursting with friends and family, the sun was not shining brightly, and Thomas did not walk her down the aisle. Most of *Áit na Síochána* was fast asleep at this late hour.

They didn't take the time to wash away the mud and muck or even change their clothes. Arline did wear her goldenrod yellow dress even though it was tattered, torn, and otherwise ruined.

Findley sought out the priest, rousted him from a deep sleep and brought him to the gathering room.

"'Twas a verra fine weddin' feast we had, Rowan," the priest informed him. "'Twould have been better were the bride and groom able to join us."

Rowan and Arline were glad to learn that a good time was had by so many and that they had been missed. It would have been a shame to have all the food Mrs. Fitz had prepared go to waste.

Findley and Duncan stood up with Rowan, while the rest of the men acted as witnesses. Arline refused to wake her sisters. She would fill them in on all the details later.

Opting for a much shorter ceremony that what had been planned, it took very little time for them to become formally man and wife. When the priest finally gave permission for Rowan to kiss his bride, he scooped her into his arms and rushed her up to his room. He had husbandly duties to perform.

They discovered Lily, fast asleep in the middle of his bed when they stepped into his chamber. A candle burned on the table in the corner. Arline smiled down at the little one, her eyes alight with relief.

After making certain Lily was well and safe -- and Arline had draped an extra blanket over her stepdaughter -- she and Rowan slipped through the door to Arline's chamber.

On all those cold, lonely nights when Rowan imagined how it would be with Arline when they were finally able to consummate their marriage, he had envisioned taking his sweet time, savoring every moment, delighting her with long, languishing kisses and warm, soft caresses. He had planned this moment as they had planned their wedding. Carefully. Meticulously. With great thought and care.

His bride apparently had other ideas. As soon as he closed the door behind them, Arline leapt at him like a cat-o-mountain. All thoughts of slow, artfully crafted and strategically placed kisses were rapidly tossed to the side. Along with his dirty tunic, trews, and mud covered boots.

No fire had been set in the fireplace. He found they didn't need it. Arline's smoldering desire was enough to keep him warm for hours.

Arline had stripped him to complete nakedness in a matter of moments, much like an experienced mum preparing to toss her mud-covered wee one into a tub. But she didn't toss Rowan into a tub. Instead, she pushed him flat on his back, sideways on her bed. His calves dangled over the edge, his arms spread over his head.

"Lass, do ye no' want to slow down a bit and enjoy the moment?" he asked as she smothered his faces with hungry kisses.

She made no effort to stop the kisses or to slow her pace. "I *be'* enjoyin' meself!" she told him excitedly.

He chuckled, then flinched when she pressed a kiss on his sensitive skin, right below his belly button. "As ye wish, me lady," he said with a dutiful air as she worked her way back up to his face. He lay there and took her kisses and ministrations like a man.

She plied him with frenzied, borderline desperate kisses, explored his face, his neck, shoulders and chest with her hands and lips. She worked her way up and down his body for a time as she straddled his abdomen.

He could finally take no more. He pushed her up gently and began to slowly lift her dress over her head. Apparently he hadn't moved fast enough, for she took over, removed her dress and chemise in one fluid motion and tossed them somewhere over her head.

"I love ye, Rowan Graham," she whispered as she pressed another kiss against his chest.

"I love *ye*, me lady wife."

Arline had waited many years, through three previous husbands, to finally have a wedding night. She wasn't about to waste a single moment of it to propriety or misinformed notions. Had things gone as planned yesterday, she might have thought how to take her time and allow Rowan the lead.

Waiting be damned. She was finally married to a man who truly *wanted* to be married to her. She loved him, and he her. They could take their time later. At the moment, she was a desperate woman, sitting atop the most magnificent man she had ever had the pleasure of knowing, and she happened to be married to him.

Later, much later, and by bright candlelight as Ora had suggested, she would take her time to explore every square inch of his gloriously perfect body.

Rowan wrapped his arms around her waist and pulled her down against his chest. His skin was hot, the hair of his chest tickled against her bare breasts. She took great delight in his heavy breathing and found she had no need to ask if she were doing things properly. In one fluid motion, without breaking their passionate kiss, Rowan rolled her over to her back.

The urgent need for *more* swelled and rose in each touch, each kiss, each frantic breath they took. Minnie be damned! This was sumptuous, heavenly, wondrous -- Och! It hurt like bloody hell!

She sucked in a deep breath and held it, closed her eyes tightly, and prayed. Prayed for the pain to pass, prayed that Ora was right and Minnie was wrong, that the pain would be brief and not as bad as some made it out to be.

"Arline," Rowan said, halting, lifting himself up onto his forearms. "I be sorry."

She could not move, did not wish to move, could not speak. Slowly, the pain faded, and she let out the breath she had been holding. Relief washed over her. It had hurt like the devil, but it had subsided.

"We can stop," Rowan began.

Arline stopped him from finishing his sentence. "If ye stop now, I'll kill ye."

He chuckled and began again. Slowly this time, methodically, with restrained passion and lustful purpose.

The wickedly pleasurable feelings Ora had told her of soon made themselves known. Arline felt it grow, gradually at first. Like filling a sack with grain until it reached the point of bursting. She matched him thrust for thrust, breath for breath, kiss for kiss until the sensation overpowered her ability to think, to do anything but feel.

And feel she did. Suspended on the precipice of something unknown, as if she were about to embark on an adventure to find the lost mines of King Solomon, the sack of grain burst and Solomon's mines were found.

Bright, crashing, explosive, wondrous, she found what she had sought. Apparently, her husband had found it too, for he shuddered, said her name repeatedly in a harried yet seductive tone, before he collapsed against her.

For a moment, Rowan felt as thought his ballocks had imploded. It was nearly impossible to get his breathing under control. And his heart? It was currently making a grand attempt to pound its way out of his chest.

He had never experienced a moment in time like the one he'd just shared with Arline. It wasn't so much the sweet joinin' of a man and woman. Nay, 'twas a frenzied, feverish, sweaty thing they'd done.

Dawn came and went as Arline slept in the crook of Rowan's arms. Their first moments together as husband and wife were quite remarkable.

They slept for only a few hours before Rowan woke, ready again to experience all that his wife had to offer. He took wicked delight in pleasing his wife. Repeatedly, just as any good and dutiful husband would do.

EPILOGUE

It was very late in the afternoon when they woke. Rowan was fully prepared to do his husbandly duty again, when Thomas knocked on the door. Rowan cursed and Arline wished the man to the devil.

"Frederick and Daniel have returned, Rowan," Thomas spoke through the closed door.

Arline agreed that the interruption was an important one. They dressed quickly with Rowan promising to return as soon as he could. Arline smiled, kissed him sweetly and informed him she would check on Lily.

Rowan met his men in his library. They not only looked road weary but battle worn as well. He poured Frederick and Daniel each a cup of whisky before sitting on the edge of his desk to listen to their tale.

"Garrick Blackthorn is dead," Frederick said before he downed the entire contents of his cup. He held the empty cup out and Rowan refilled it.

"Our information was correct. There were three hundred men waitin' to attack. They were no' as well trained as ours, but they were ruthless bastards just the same. As we suspected, they were paid mercenaries. It seemed Beatrice has an abundance of coin."

"So it was Beatrice who hired them?" Rowan asked with more than just a hint of surprise. After the fiasco of yesterday, when she had sabotaged his wedding to Arline, nothing should surprise him.

Daniel nodded his head in agreement. "It did no' take much convincin' to get them to change their minds, just as we hoped. They were verra tired of waitin' fer orders." He drank down his whisky in one big gulp. Rowan refilled his cup, sat back and waited for them to go on.

"Och! They'd been caught in that horrible snowstorm. They lost fifteen men before all was said and done," Frederick took a sip of his whisky and took a chair. He was worn out, tired, and bedraggled. It had been a very long few weeks.

"They were frozen, near starved to death," Daniel said as he took his own seat. He looked just as worn out as Frederick.

"So convincin' them *not* to attack *us* was easy," Frederick said. He let out a tired sigh. "So we offered what we could. We stayed with them fer a few days, hunted and brought them fresh meat, fer which they were verra grateful. They're Lowlanders and no' used to all this snow, ye ken. They be tired of fightin' the English and fightin' with each other."

Rowan crossed his arms over his chest. The Lowlands had been decimated by the Black Plague. They were in a constant state of anarchy and chaos. He could well understand why their swords had been so easily purchased.

"So after we got their bellies full and did a wee bit o' negotiatin', we set off fer Blackthorn lands. It took us six days to reach it, what with all the snow," Frederick explained. He took another sip of the warm whisky and began to finally relax. "It took us less than eight hours to fell the Blackthorn Keep. We killed every last one of the bastards. We didna harm the womenfolk though."

Daniel snorted and nodded his head. "Garrick Blackthorn was a coward. He hid behind his woman's skirts. Used her as a shield. We didna mean fer any harm to come to her, Rowan. But 'twas in the heat of battle, ye ken."

"Aye," Frederick added. "Arrows were flyin'. Daniel was hot on Garrick's heels when his woman came runnin' out of his keep, wavin' her arms, screamin'. Garrick grabbed her and held her in front of him, like she was a target. It couldna be helped. The arrow pierced through her heart and into his gut. It took a few hours, but he eventually died. Bled to death. Slowly."

They sat in contemplative silence for a long moment. Rowan had always known Garrick to be a coward, but to use his own woman as a shield? 'Twas unforgiveable. Then he reminded himself that it was English blood that ran through Garrick's veins. Still, 'twas a piss poor excuse for such cowardly behavior.

"'Twas odd though, Rowan," Frederick said. "Before he grabbed his woman, he was screamin' at the top of his lungs that he would avenge his mother's death. He was wavin' his sword but no' usin' it. I dunnae what that was about."

Rowan grimaced. He knew all too well what Garrick referred to. "Garrick Blackthorn blames me father fer his mother's death."

Daniel and Frederick looked up at Rowan with knitted brows.

Rowan took a quick breath in and let it out before explaining himself. "Ye see, his mum died in childbed, along with her bairn."

Frederick quirked a curious brow. "And what exactly did Andrew have to do with that?"

"Nothin'," Rowan answered. "Garrick's father was tetched. A wretched man to begin with. He was neither kind nor loyal to her, ye ken. He bed many a woman before and after he married. She caught him in bed with one of his women one day. It broke her heart."

"And how do ye ken this?" Daniel asked.

"Doreen Blackthorn and me mum were verra good friends. When Doreen found her husband in bed with another woman, she and Garrick came to stay here fer a time. After a few months, she returned to her husband. She carried another man's babe."

Frederick and Daniel stared at Rowan in utter disbelief. "Ye canna mean yer da--"

Rowan shook his head. "Nay, 'twasn't me da's babe she carried. 'Twas Thomas'."

Frederick whistled while Daniel just stared at Rowan, completely surprised by this bit of news.

"Doreen refused to tell who the babe belonged to. Garrick's da blamed mine. From that point on, Garrick blamed me da fer his mum's death when he should have blamed his own father."

It was a tragedy any way one chose to look at it. Rowan poured himself a cup of whisky and sipped it slowly.

"Did we lose any of our own?" he asked.

"Nay, a few injuries, but nothin' the lads canna survive."

"And the others?"

"We're findin' places fer them in the barracks, the men's solar above stairs. Anywhere we can tuck them into. We're watchin' them closely. But I think they'll work out well among us. They be verra grateful fer a roof over their heads and food in their stomachs."

Rowan nodded and contemplated the situation. In a few short hours, he had married and his clan had doubled in size.

They had a rough road ahead of them. It might not be easy for the newcomers to acclimate themselves to Clan Graham ways, but he was hopeful that over time they would come to appreciate all that his clan had to offer.

"I'll speak with them on the morrow," Rowan told them. "After the noonin' meal, assemble them in the courtyard." He tossed back the rest of his whisky and set the cup down.

They sat in quiet contemplation for a time, each man mulling over the events of the past months. Daniel finally asked what was to come of Lady Beatrice.

"While I would personally like to see her hang, Arline will have none of it. I plan to write the sheriff in Edinburgh and I will press charges against her. Until the sheriff comes fer her, the wench can rot in the dungeon fer all I care."

"Have ye asked why she done it?" Frederick asked, curious to know what would drive a woman to such lengths.

"I dunnae, yet, but I've sent fer Thomas. Mayhap he has the answer to that question."

They enjoyed another cup of whisky and discussed the new men. Daniel and Frederick each was of the opinion that most of the men were of good character. A few however, would require being watched very closely.

Thomas appeared some time later, looking rather stunned.

"Beatrice was of no help at all," Thomas said as Rowan handed him a cup of whisky. "But Joan was full of verra useful information." He took a long drink before turning one of the chairs that sat in front of Rowan's desk around to face the other men.

"Beatrice is -- or was -- Garrick Blackthorn's sister, born on the other side of the blanket, ye ken. No' a *real* lady by birth." He paused to take a glance at the three surprised faces staring back at him. "Aye, I about fell off me stool when I learned it! Apparently, Garrick promised that if she could get *ye*," he pointed to Rowan with a nod and his cup, "to marry her, Garrick would formally recognize her as his sister. The plan was fer her to marry ye, then kill ye off. Once ye were dead, then Beatrice would hand everything over to Garrick, take the title she's apparently wanted fer years, along with a good deal of coin. Takin' Lily was a way fer them to find out if ye had as much in gold as they hoped ye did."

Thomas sat back and watched the men absorbing the news. It was, indeed, a stunning bit of information.

"Apparently, Beatrice is just as ruthless as her brother. Joan was afeared fer her life, ye ken. I saw the bruises and marks Beatrice inflicted," he took another drink in hopes it would wash away the bitter taste left in his mouth from what he had witnessed.

"Well," Rowan said, sounding both perturbed and relieved as he stood to his feet. "I hope the sheriff can come up with a punishment befitting *all* Beatrice's crimes."

Rowan had had his fill of intrigue, mysteries, and bad news. He wanted to go back to his room, climb into his bed, and make love to his wife again.

He tossed back the last of his whisky and placed the cup on his desk. He turned to look at Frederick and Daniel.

"The two of ye go and bathe, get some rest. I have a feelin' the next few months willna be easy."

Frederick and Daniel stood, stretched their long arms and worked the kinks out of their backs.

"I hear congratulations be in order," Frederick said with a smile. "I hear the lass said aye and that ye were married last eve."

"Aye, she did and we were. In fact, ye be interruptin me husbandly duties. I must hurry back to me wife, now."

Frederick and Daniel chuckled. "Has she got ye by the shorthairs already?"

Rowan flashed them a smile. "Nay, lads. By me heart."

It was well after the midnight hour when Rowan left his contented and satisfied wife asleep in their bed. Quietly, he donned his tunic, trews, and boots, wrapped his cloak about his shoulders and left their room. He made his way quietly down the stairs. Silently, he passed by Thomas who had fallen asleep by the fire in the gathering room. He grabbed a candle from the mantle before opening the large wooden door that led outside.

A rush of cold air swept in, bringing with it a bit of snow. The cold night air bit at his bare face and tickled the flame of the candle. Carefully, he closed the door behind him. He held one hand in front of the flame so that the night air would not extinguish it.

Stars twinkled against the midnight sky as he crossed the courtyard and made his way to the empty kirk. His pace was quick, purposeful. He did not want to be away from Arline for too long, but there was something he needed to do.

He quickly stepped inside the dark and empty kirk and made his way to the altar. He set his candle down and knelt before God. His heart was a blended mixture of joy and sorrow, contentment and the remnants of guilt. Much time passed as he thanked God for keeping Arline, his men, and his people safe. He thanked Him for bringing

Arline into his life and asked that God guide him and help him to be a good husband to her.

Slowly, he raised his head and looked upward, toward Heaven. "I've come to say goodbye to ye, Kate. I loved ye, with all me heart and I do miss ye. I am keepin' the promise I made to ye. I ken it was a long time comin', fer I was too much a coward to let ye memories go. I kept me heart to ye as long as I could, Kate. I ken ye didna want me to do that, but it was so hard lettin' ye go." He tried to choke back the tears, but 'twas impossible. They fell down his cheeks, leaving trails along his neck and dripping onto the collar of his cloak.

"Lily is a good girl, Kate, much like ye," he wiped his face on his arm and tried to regain some composure. "She loves Arline. 'Tisn't how I pictured our lives bein', livin' without ye in it." He took a deep, cleansing breath. "I ken in me heart that 'twas ye that sent Arline to Lily and to me. Arline is like ye in many ways. She's kind, she's fierce, and she's verra good to us. I love her, Kate, verra much. She's good fer me."

He wiped away more tears as he sat quietly, breathing in deeply. He did not want to return to Arline with tears running down his face. He doubted he would be able to explain it to her in any way that would make sense.

"So, I've come to say goodbye, Kate." He hung his head, not knowing what else he could say. He hoped Kate was looking down at him now, listening to him. Mayhap she could look into his heart and understand all that he was feeling, better than he could say it.

"Ye needn't say goodbye to her."

The voice came from behind him, startling him out of his quiet reverie. His heart lodged in his throat when he spun around to see Arline standing there. She shivered in the cold, wearing only her chemise and her cloak.

"Arline," he exclaimed as he searched for something intelligent to say to her.

Arline walked to him, opened her arms wide and wrapped them around his torso. "Rowan, please, do no' say goodbye to Kate. She be

Lily's mum. Lily needs to ken that she was important to ye. Ye canna ferget her."

Rowan rested his chin on the top of Arline's head. The love he felt for her grew by leaps and bounds as one moment passed to the next. Until a few months ago, he would not have believed such a love could exist.

"I do no' intend to ferget her, or let Lily ferget her." He pressed a kiss to the top of her head. "It was just me way of lettin' Kate ken that I've fulfilled the promises I made to her. I promised her I'd no' keep me heart to meself, that I'd love another someday. I just wanted a moment to let her know."

Arline hugged him tighter. "She kens, Rowan. She kens."

They stayed in the kirk for a while longer, each of them kneeling in prayer, thankful that God had brought them together. When they were done, Rowan took his wife's hand and led her back into the keep and up to their room.

In the early morning hours before dawn, they expressed their love for one another in a slow, tender and gentle joining of their bodies, their hearts and souls. Arline fell asleep in the crook of her husband's arm, knowing for the first time in her life what it felt like to love and be loved unconditionally.

FREDERICK'S QUEEN

SCOTLAND, SUMMER 1355

Aggie McLaren had known for years her father was insane. That they were now on their way to see Rowan Graham to ask for his help in finding her a husband was all the proof anyone needed.

Mermadak McLaren was dying. Aggie had known for weeks. He had a disease of the lungs and not much time left—mayhap a year at best. Aggie hadn't needed a healer to tell her what she had long suspected. His coughing fits had increased in frequency and duration. He wheezed whenever he took a breath and he was beginning to lose weight. Death seemed inevitable.

If her father would simply die and not worry over finding her a husband, she might begin to see a glimmer of hope for her future. But the arrogant, selfish man refused to go without leaving someone at the helm of his clan.

'Twas why they were on this hopeless trek. Aggie was his only child and according to their clan's rules, as a female she could not take over as chief of Clan McLaren. Aggie was not ignorant of the ways of other clans. Plenty of women stood quite successfully as chief. But Clan McLaren was not so advanced in their thinking about a woman's capabilities. According to her father and his men, there were but three things a woman was good for: sating a man's lust, bearing his children and keeping a hearth.

She knew it wasn't kindness of heart or worry over his only child's future that motivated Mermadak McLaren. It was a combination of greed and a very twisted mind.

Her father's selfishness, his mean streak, would not allow him to simply appoint a successor. Nay, he wanted a young man he could mold into his own image. He wanted someone ruthless and unhindered by common standards of morality or decency to take over the reins. He wanted someone who could be just as brutal as himself.

And since he did not trust anyone within his own clan to carry on his legacy, somewhere in the twisted regions of his mind he concluded that a husband for Aggie was the only course to take.

As they rode across the glen, she sat behind Donnel, her father's first lieutenant, forced to hold on to the smelly man. A tremor of revulsion trickled down her back. Donnel was of the same ilk as her father—just as vulgar and just as mean.

Aggie'd learned long ago not to ask if her life could possibly get any worse, for when she did, "worse" would inevitably appear.

A husband, she mused.

By anyone's standards, she was an old maid, long in the tooth at three and twenty. No one in his right mind would want to take her as a wife.

Any man who would agree to such a union would have to be as tetched as her da. And just as old, mayhap older. With her luck, he'd be just as mean and vicious. Aggie knew there was no hope for finding a decent man. Decent men simply did not exist.

There had been a time, long ago, when she had been considered pretty. She used to laugh and sing, when her father was not around of course. She had possessed a free spirit then, a fondness for amusement, a zest for living. That innocent, carefree little girl no longer existed. She'd died ten years ago.

Now Aggie was flawed, damaged. With her scarred face she could no longer be considered pretty. She no longer laughed or sang. She didn't even speak.

It wasn't that she *couldn't* speak. Nay, she was fully capable. But her father detested the sound of her voice. "Yer voice makes me ears bleed!" He'd only needed to tell her that once. Self-preservation had forced her into her false state of muteness.

They'd be at Rowan Graham's keep very soon. If there was a God —for years now she had questioned His existence—He would open up the earth and allow it to swallow her whole. Any attempts to reason with Mermadak would be ignored.

To speak, to voice her opinion, to share her thoughts would mean a beating. And Mermadak McLaren had never shown any mercy when inflicting punishments. She had the scars to prove it. Nay, it was best to remain quiet. Aye, the beating would come later when he realized no man would be able to look past her defects or her scars.

The last man her father had tried to betroth her to had backed out when he saw her for the first time. History oft repeats itself, and Aggie had no doubt this time would be no exception. No man would want her.

Mayhap she could try running away again. She was older and wiser now. She would make certain Mermadak was truly passed out from too much drink. She would take little Ailrig with her. Her heart felt heavy when she thought of the sweet child. Through no fault of his own the boy had been born a bastard. Aggie's mother, God rest her soul, had brought him to live amongst their clan. Her mother could not formally adopt the babe. Mermadak would never have allowed it. Still, she gave him a home, and, together with Aggie, lots of love.

When Ailrig was three, Lila McLaren had died. 'Twas then that everything began to fall apart. Mermadak grew meaner by the day and not because he missed his wife. Truth be told, he had never really cared much for Lila. But she was the only person who seemed to be able to rein in that temper of his. With no voice of reason, with no one there to temper his anger, Mermadak did as he pleased and became the man he was today: vicious, cruel, hateful and greedy.

Aggie had long ago resigned herself to the fact that she would never marry. She possessed too many scars. Many of them ran much deeper than those left on her skin. A sane man wouldn't want someone like her, what with all her defects and imperfections.

Still, her father was hell-bent on trying to find her a husband.

ABOUT THE AUTHOR

USA Today Bestselling Author, storyteller and cheeky wench, SUZAN TISDALE lives in the Midwest with her verra handsome carpenter husband. All but one of her children have left the nest. Her pets consist of dust bunnies and a dozen poodle-sized, backyard-dwelling groundhogs – all of which run as free and unrestrained as the voices in her head. And she doesn't own a single pair of yoga pants, much to the shock and horror of her fellow authors. She prefers to write in her pajamas.

Suzan writes Scottish historical romance/fiction, with honorable and perfectly imperfect heroes and strong, feisty heroines. And bad guys she kills off in delightfully wicked ways.

She published her first novel, Laiden's Daughter, in December, 2011, as a gift for her mother. That one book started a journey which has led to fifteen published titles, with two more being released in the spring of 2017. To date, she has sold more than 350,000 copies of her books around the world. They have been translated into four foreign languages (Italian, French, German, and Spanish.)

You will find her books in digital, paperback, and audiobook formats.

Tap Here to download Suzan's FREE app for readers!

ALSO BY SUZAN TISDALE

The Clan MacDougall Series

Laiden's Daughter

Findley's Lass

Wee William's Woman

McKenna's Honor

The Clan Graham Series

Rowan's Lady

Frederick's Queen

The Mackintoshes and McLarens Series

Ian's Rose

The Bowie Bride

Rodrick the Bold

Brogan's Promise

The Clan McDunnah Series

A Murmur of Providence

A Whisper of Fate

A Breath of Promise

Moirra's Heart Series

Stealing Moirra's Heart

Saving Moirra's Heart

Stand Alone Novels

Isle of the Blessed

Forever Her Champion

The Edge of Forever

Arriving in 2018:

Black Richard's Heart

<u>The Brides of the Clan MacDougall</u>

(A Sweet Series)

Aishlinn

Maggy (arriving 2018)

Nora (arriving 2018)

Coming Soon:

The MacAllens and Randalls

Made in the USA
Middletown, DE
18 July 2018